NIGHT ON THE SHORES OF ATLAN

Cija sat up under the big Atlan stars, fingering nervously the snake-necklet at her throat. "Let me see," Juzd said. He always meant what he said. Cija showed him the cold maps she kept in a leather pouch under her rags.

"These are maps of Atlan's insides," he said.

He was very interested in her cold maps. He took them and examined them, and she said, "Keep them, my friend. I do not want them back again, any more. They trouble me."

"They shall trouble us all." Juzd sat and closed his eyes.

Books by Jane Gaskell

THE ATLAN SAGA
  The Serpent
  The Dragon
  Atlan
  The City
  Some Summer Lands

Published by POCKET BOOKS

Jane Gaskell

SOME SUMMER LANDS

PUBLISHED BY POCKET BOOKS NEW YORK

POCKET BOOKS, a Simon & Schuster division of
GULF & WESTERN CORPORATION
1230 Avenue of the Americas, New York, N.Y. 10020

For Dwee Counihan
(whose SAGA is such a joy)
and Barbara

CONTENTS

PART ONE

◆

1

My Grandmother's
Hygienic Palace

THIS PALE YOUNG woman, looking romantically out of windows, is my earliest memory.

My mother lived a lot of her life at windows. As she was cautious and sensible, a natural observer of life unless forced to be a protagonist, and a coward too, windows were absolutely her element. I remember her at the windows of the castle where I was born. They were high-beamed, bleak windows, empty of all but sky with gales in it. "Watch here, Seka," she would say to me. "Watch and see if your father arrives over the hill." She said it as though it would be an interesting treat for me if he did, something to make my day exciting before supper-time. Those were the very early days, before I lost my voice without hope of finding it again. But even then, when I could have spoken to her, I didn't say to her: "He won't come. He doesn't arrive. He never does arrive."

She knew that. She didn't say it.

I knew it. Why should I say it?

When we reached my grandmother's safe little palace, the comfort lapped us round like warm bath-waters, warm wines. Suddenly, after the long chilly greasy travels, we were part of a long gold summer. We ate such nice things. We wore clean soft clothes. Instead of those gentlemen with greedy busy faces and bodies who used always to be pulling and pushing us around, here loving sentimental women with their heads sweetly to one side smiled at me and clucked at me as they rolled us into the food and the comforts. And there were quiet languorous decorative easy scenes for my mother to watch unfolding beneath her window.

And then she stopped watching. One day she was as usual sitting for hours looking at it all out there. The next day she wouldn't go near the window. She made detours round our furniture so she could keep well away from her golden windows (with their pierced screens made to deflect assassin-arrows, and with luck the pterodactyla which still sometimes scavenged around the high turrets of my grandmother's kingdom, hawking and honking like filthy old men flapping at private windows.) (But most of all the screens were to deflect eyes.)

Say she was near a window. Then in the dark shadowed apertures of honeycomb walls of the barracks opposite, across the square, a flash of red cloak or of weaponry was seen; as some officer talking with fellow commanders over there turned before some window, caught one moment in the omnivorous sun—then, then she would dart away from our own window.

She would put a hand over each breast in a typical personal gesture, as though eyes could bruise her tenderest nicest places. Holding her little breasts—she had a soprano bosom, high and sweet—she would hurry away as if to be seen herself could be some ultimate terror. I knew what had happened. He had arrived.

He had ridden at last over the hill.

He was here in my grandmother's barracks. And my mother, she was terrified.

Even at that early age, I found it pretty clear that my cautious, sensible mother was an extremely silly lady. She was always either very happy or very unhappy. She was very brave about being unhappy, desperately hiding the fact, even from herself, which involved effort and some drastic chronic resignation. She was unhappy only about situations which did not exist. As, for instance, this man she didn't love had not appeared in the window. Or, on the other hand, for instance, this man she didn't love had now appeared after all in our kingdom.

She thought she had herself almost under control, but the give-away, even to one of my tender age, came when she insisted that from now on she would not be leaving her apartments at all.

"Not coming down to dine?" my grandmother asks.

"You can say," my mother explained in what she

thought a cool voice, "that I have taken a Vow of Silence, a religious thing, with which no one dare argue."

"You can eat without speaking a word. If only he could _see_ you."

My little mother looked down at her vulnerable lap. "How should his _seeing_ me do you any good, Mother? His consort is with him."

"How can she be his consort when you were crowned his Empress?" snorted my grandmother whose grasp of State law is always based on what she for the moment considers moral. This is all right in her own dictatorship, where the law of the land and the justice of the realm are ever on the wing, and are never anything but what she wants. But other emperies, other ethics.

"That lady is providing him with her own personal army," my mother replied, and she picked me up and nested me on her lap, which she these days often did as though I were therapeutic to hold against her stomach.

I'd noticed her stomach was a bit more interesting these days in fact. It had got peachy, and was always warm; even her breasts seemed more of a handful for her to manage now: they were peaches too, instead of those thin hard little pears.

"So you see," my mother went on reasonably, "of course _she_ is his consort. Any woman who can provide Zerd with anything at all is to be heaped by him with honor. That's the law of _his_ realm." I slid off her and walked back into the fountain where I had seen a superb cockroach.

I wondered whether to go and play with the door. But I'd already done that twice this morning and the second time a woman had seen me and stopped me. "Bad girl, you know you are _not_ to do that. Get off that door at once." And I hadn't even finished, and it left you in a funny state for a while to be stopped from playing on the door, holding both its handles tight and rubbing yourself against the edge of the door with a leg either side of it, if you weren't allowed to get to the bit where you worked up to feeling "the bumps" coming banging between your bottom. I thought I wouldn't bother to start in case I was stopped _again_ before the bumps; it wasn't worth it. Perhaps later, when my mother didn't need protecting from my grandmother, when my grandmother had gone I would sneak up on the roof and watch the parade.

"Besides, the crux of the matter is," my mother ended fretfully, "that she was his first love."

"Nonsense," my grandmother regally spat. "Did I not engineer it," she demanded, "that he should love you to the exclusion of all other women?"

"You engineered, Mother, if you remember, a little matter of my attempting his assassination."

"*Ah*," my grandmother triumphantly said. "Exactly. And he was so taken with your sweet little attempts to kill him that he married you."

"I refuse to meet him, now of all times," my mother said drily, "now he in his own land has proclaimed me witch and whore."

She stood, to dismiss my grandmother. I could see that the movement swam her head. A nearby slave, and I, both looked up alert. The slave came nearer.

My grandmother rudely shoved the slave aside and smoothed Cija's forehead with maternal murmurings. "Now he's here," she hissed, "right in my dictatorship, on our soil yours and mine, and will you lift a finger to keep his power and friendship mine! For our little land that has seen such bloodshed and erosion! For our little nation! Oh, that a daughter of mine . . . Besides, if you're going to see him at all, which you know you will sooner or later, you'd better do it before your belly betrays you."

My mother shuddered. She signed frantically to my grandmother, who didn't understand. "The slaves," Cija muttered. "I don't trust your slaves."

The slaves who always stand at the end of my grandmother's train keeping its serpentine yards off the ground stood with impassive faces, but I know they have ears like lynx'. My grandmother won't use mutes because they're no good to her as spies (just as she never realized *I* might be trained into something discreet and useful, with my two ears and no voice) but today she said impatiently, "For Gods' sakes, Cija, I can have their tongues cut."

"Don't be so wasteful."

My grandmother did dismiss them. They backed into the black inner apartment, superciliously passing Cija unimpressed by her intervention, and went off with the train to comb the sleek monkey-heads with which it is fringed.

"Why do you think I may be pregnant of all things?" my mother inquired.

"A mother's heart can tell from little signs," the Dictatress syrupily said, "little things like the way you vomit at breakfast-time."

"Well, then, you must see my meeting *him* would do no good at all. If he sees I am pregnant—"

"How far are you gone? A month or two? Why shouldn't he. be brought to believe it's his? Go to him and conceive it this very evening."

"Mother, listen for once. This won't be a human baby at all."

The Dictatress looked at Cija with surprise, crossly. "Then I'll send one of my doctors along to you. You are amazingly lackadaisical, you know, Cija, really. This should all have been seen to long since."

"I want this baby."

The slight emphasis when my mother said *"this* baby," went into my consciousness too. Hadn't she been glad with me?

She added, painfully, "It is the one thing that is left to me of Ung-g. It is a blossoming of the clean love I knew in the jungle, the only clean love I've ever been allowed."

She was now fingering, as often, the necklace like a snake twining her collarbone. My grandmother the Dictatress has an instinct about jewelry, a subject she herself finds sentimental; her eyes narrowed: "What's that?" she said.

"Ung-g gave it to me."

"*Given* by an ape? Dug by a scavenging creature from some grave or barrow—it might as well have been hyena as ape. And you fondling it as carnal proof of your bestiality? Bestiality can be fun, but let's not romanticize it, dear."

My mother again took me on her lap where I made a series of hideous faces at my grandmother who smiled approvingly. "I've done with it all," my mother said quietly. But I could feel the pulses in her beating. "I've done with the lies, the third-bests, the impersonations, conjuror-tricks and politics—"

"Done with politics?" my grandmother violently echoed, politics to her meaning life itself, the two concepts indivisible.

My grandmother walked to the balcony, and pointed with a stabbing finger through that screen erected to shield the balcony from intruders, arrows, eyes.

"Our land," she said, her voice expressionless and all

on one level. "Not *my* land, Cija; our gallant little nation's land, and yours too."

I stared at the gallant cockroach still struggling past water-jets on the curved marble basin. This was my grandmother's "our little land" speech. I knew it off by heart, I thought of it as some rhythmic nursery-verse such as the ladies sang to me, and God knows how many times my mother must have heard it.

"Our nation is like a sore," my mother remarked. "Always growing, always weeping."

"I've salved it, I've stitched it in fact," the Dictatress answered, and—"Have I pulled it together to see it laid waste again, infants slaughtered and cattle-graze diseased again, because a girl won't go to bed with her lord?"

"*He won't bed me, Mother.* He won't save me from Sedili. She just is his top wife at the moment. Please admit it. And she will contrive, as soon as she finds me available, to finish her work of dishonoring and destroying me."

"I hope she'll try," the Dictatress said. "The people, the army will rise in riot and Sedili will find her gracious self in trouble."

"Zerd will still back her. He needs her regiments more than he needs our City."

"Not when he's *in* our City, Cija."

The sunlight beat through the pierced screen to play jaguar on the floor.

My mother's hand hovered over fruits a slave had earlier piled high.

"Weigh each in your hand and imagine it on your tongue," the Dictatress said, watching her. "How to judge a fruit—if it's full of ready juice and heavy, just like choosing a good cock really."

My mother did not even shrug.

But her eyes did in fact in a moment slide to the window, to the place where maybe there strode the best cock in the universe.

"I don't know what you have against him," the Dictatress snorted hopelessly. "Wasn't he a good husband? Did he ever neglect, after a major infidelity, to bring you a little present? Did you ever see much of him, always away fighting as he was? Didn't he even have a statue of you reared in Atlan's capital, so I hear tell, a statue of you in rock-crystal? There were jokes that no bride ever was honored with a bigger erection. Come along. Up from your hammock. I'll send my slyest woman to you within the hour. She's so sly, she can even paint my breastworks when I choose allure for my armory—but you're not too much in need. Early pregnancy gives you bloom like a magnolia exploding with pollen."

I saw my mother wince.

"I'll send her in. She's gentle as a dream." My grandmother, knowing nothing about our dreams, clapped for her slaves who fell into place behind her with her exiting train.

My mother was able to smile, as my grandmother left her.

But when she walked back beyond the cages of fluttering pretty crop-happy birds, she obviously had difficulty sitting again. Were her legs trembling too much to bend?

I kept my mother as happy as one can. I jumped on her lap, stuck feathers from the bird-cages in her dress to tickle her. But her eyes constantly went to the dark apertures in the honey-colored hot stone wall (all lounging lizards and deep windows) we saw from our main terrace. She was waiting for the flash of a red cloak in one of those windows, or even the distant reverberation of a dark laugh, which would have entered her not through her ears but between her thighs.

I guess, from times in her tent while a lover was on her too busy to notice I was there, I guess from how she moved and how she didn't, when she seemed urgent and when she seemed just polite, I guess she was a clitorally-interested young woman, my mother. But I know she was very sexual. I know that even when she was alone and yearning she'd have a fast reaction—wet and fast. I knew when with an amused, almost greedy quirk of her mouth she stood up and quickly brushed her cloak across the leather stool she'd been sitting on, wiping the tell-tale evidence that she'd been thinking intensely again about Zerd —(I knew when she thought about him: her whole face became guarded, greedy; defensive, offensive.) She was amused and sensual. But it was a shy, lonely sexuality to be saddled with. She had never, I think now, been long enough with a lover she could admire and trust—never long enough to be taught and understood.

Of course I didn't know words then like "subjective" or "romantic," words for the trouble women like my mother have between their legs.

But already I knew how sounds can affect different parts of your body. And I think I understood my mother. In our travels, I saw her so often under stress.

My mother lay back in her hammock and looked ill again as it started to swing under her slight weight.

My grandmother saw in her the ripeness of fresh pregnancy. But under her eyes were the shadows of the night-hours that had stolen sleep. Her skin was healthy—but under it her bones were sharp as a haunted cat's.

So she was to see Zerd tonight. Her eyes fixed at a polished metal mirror (my grandmother kept few glass-blowers) and forward with the hammock she approached her reflection.

The noon sunlight stealthily entered the big black rooms, and the General Zerd, my father, had arrived too in my grandmother's palace. The sunlight entered by stealth. The General had entered openly, as mostly (I was to find) was his way, attended as he was by army enough for his needs, however he obtained such armies.

These were hot black rooms.

Never one to do anything by halves, my grandmother had decided all these apartments, the dignified ladylike living apartments, should be colored black. Nevertheless the sunlight coiled in like serpents. The sunlight zoomed in through the intricate patterned fretted window screens, it slid in cycles, it spat in sparks. It lay zithering in corners. It darted up the black ceiling. It hung hidden in the dark wall-curtains, and when you moved them or shook them it sped out again in flashing little aureoles and twitters. It hurt your eyes often, the dizzy sun, even though it was outside and you were in. It was a relief to turn to the black of the rooms' darknesses, and rest your eyes on them, and sink into them.

Even the trumpets played in the courtyard outside were *hot*. The women in their striped shirts and scarfs, trousers rolled loosely up almost to their brown knees, women like striped jewels, with their laundry in the palace ponds amongst the expensive rare ducks, discreetly withdrew for a time, to make way for the two brigades which paraded under the lines of snowy washing.

I thought now I would climb up my secret way and watch the parade. I was not allowed to leave our rooms *at all*. But the sunlight crept like a cat up to the roof; so did I.

I clambered up the back of the linen-closet, careful with the ventilation grille I'd long ago loosened. I emerged on my hot hidden golden gutter.

I encountered a dead roof-guard lying there, his uniform partly pilfered—in much disarray, his tunic gone.

Shrugging—he hadn't been a nice guard, not like the one who always smiled and at times offered me candies when he saw me slip up through the grille; this less lovable guard had always pissed near my grille, then "neatly" shaken his thing so the drops annoyingly spattered far and wide, and after all if I roused an alarm my sneak-place would be discovered and forbidden to me—I lay on my tummy and inched along the baking stone.

Then I heard steps nearing me along the gutter. Quiet supple steps. Leather boots came into my view.

I looked up. I saw a person I knew must (like myself) be up here nefariously, since he was not in uniform. A man with skin made of scars, as though he'd had smallpox and then been scarred in fights and had already been scarred by a weapon or two before the pox. He wore plain, un-interesting clothes, all leather with metal patchings like the way mothers darn. He bent a blue dark gaze on me.

"Which way," he asked me in a light busy voice, "did the assassin go? The man who killed this guard lying here beside you?"

Getting no reply from me, only my long stare then a shake of my head, he said in irritation: "Dumb insolence."

He kicked the dead plundered roof-guard, he booted me aside out of his way. He continued on along the gutter.

I wasn't bruised. I am always in control of my limbs and go floppy when I need to. Only my wrist was grazed. I heard somebody scrabbling at the grille under me. I inched into the shadow, saw the grille move and up came what seemed to be an old woman, carrying something under an enveloping hooded cloak.

A blast of linseed and poppy smell came up into the hot air too, and I assumed this to be the lady admitted to oil, massage and paint my mother. My grandmother has a penchant for the employing of bent old crones who cringe to her and bully everybody else.

As the figure scrambled up with bizarre agility, I could see (from where my face lay on the hot grit) right past the figure and into the passage below. Past the linen-closet and into my mother's private fountain-room. The steam from the central gush coiled green-ish in the thin spoke of sun that could penetrate from the high ceiling-aperture in the green marble cell. My mother's sandals lay there alone, spreading the rivulets across the floor.

I looked again at what the cloaked figure held. Of course it was my mother the cloaked person was carrying.

My mother was wearing only the shift in which she would have allowed the ordered massage. Her shift clung to her knobby little hip-bones fragrant with the oil still on the figure's hands. Already the scent almost deafened me —it started to ring in my ears, magnifying the trumpets whining.

And I knew. There was a poison, a drug in the massage oil.

Now from the shadow I saw my mother's face. Her eyes were half-open, but there was no one in.

"You are drowsy, Goddess?" the cloaked figure crooned, handling her in an accustomed manner. "My clever salve, Goddess. It will make the fine General's nostrils widen."

I followed, down the roof-slope of the back gutter, dry and sparkling with lizards crusting it. The roof-tiles began to burn my naked toes. It is always the toes that pain before the soles. We were going in the opposite direction from the man dressed in scars who had discovered the murdered guard; I wanted to go back and bring the nasty efficient scarred man to stop this, as I was sure he would. But then I might lose my mother altogether in the meantime.

My mother was passed like so much laundry to another man waiting—in sentry uniform—on a small terrace.

The dry high open heat must have cleared my mother's head a little. I heard her say to the sentry she now saw, "Kill him."

But the "sentry" saluted her abductor.

I suddenly launched myself against the backs of the pretend-sentry's knees. He picked me up and tossed me to the person in Major's uniform, now removing his disguising-cloak. He laughed. "Your loyal half-wit child, Madam. I suppose we'll need her—or she'll *tell* on us. Bring her to be your soul for you, Madam. And you can be the rest of yourself for me, all yourself."

My mother's face changed and she reached for me.

The Major, hardly taller than the bent tirewoman he had impersonated, sprang down yet another roof-level;

here two cavalry-birds restively waited saddled. He mounted, my mother was passed to him.

The soldier with him looked questioningly at me. *"It* won't call for help, it's incapable of speech," I was described by the Major; my uncle Smahil, yes, I remembered him from the visits he paid my mother when we lived precariously in the suburbs. So I was included on the soldier's saddle.

"Like all consciences, *it* is silent," Smahil shoved a finger in my mouth and nodded as, though my tongue beat against it, I made no sound whatsoever. He took his hand away. A saddle-cloth was dumped over me.

My mother, weak, put an effort into the one thing she could do—she kept her eyes on me to make sure I wasn't out of her sight. I kept watch on her through that saddle-cloth. Smahil wrapped the cloak across her, muffling her mouth, though she was obviously too drugged to manage speaking again. "I shan't tell you not to be afraid, Cija," he said, a smile in his self-enclosed voice.

"I am quite content, quite *happy* to see you a little afraid. But really there's no cause for panic. You will be quite safe. And even comfortable. I have exorcised my desire of the autumn. It is spring now, and I no longer ache to revenge myself on you. I have come to rescue you."

I suppose she stirred. With his old closeness to her, which had always been apparent, he seemed to know what she meant.

"Nothing to rescue you from but myself, you would say? Try not to sneer, my dear, reserve your strength. I am rescuing you of course from the threat of your reconciliation with your husband. Since he has arrived, your 'reconciliation' presumably is on the schedule."

Smahil had no more trouble, of course, if there had so far been the slightest trouble for him. He was saluted, in his Major's-gold of Sedili's army, and passed through by every sentry of my grandmother's. Couldn't they look under the shako-peak? If they did, surely his would not pass as just another officer's face. For some months my grandmother had had a warrant out for his arrest, but in her City's alleys and warrens it is easy to hide out. Too many new strange officers in Northern uniform here suddenly this spring. The palace passed away around us, the marble and the coolth, and the hard clash and din of the City took over. The din and the colors must be hitting in my mother's poor head. I wished I could touch her. What a view we had from the saddle of the black and pied bird, seven feet of vicious disciplined fowl; the soldier and I following Smahil and my mother through smells, of beggars, of cook-shops. I could see enough through the loosely-woven saddle-cloth which had been wound tightly round me. I knew it all, the hordes of slum-dwellers long since crippled by historic Northern depredations, the flapping of vultures in the middens, the storks' nests in the rafters of the market-arcades and the storks bowing and nodding civilly to the huge cavalry-birds who lifted their great heads and barked up at the parent storks. The storks clattering with their beaks; untidy colonies in broken roof-drains, males standing lugubriously on one patient leg, waiting (on a botched-up nest lazily filched from a smaller bird) for a female who might never arrive, killed or snared as she might easily have been on her journey from the loving South; for her husband who had arrived before her to prepare the home, a sad wait, since storks are ridiculously monogamous. I knew about the storks, from my days in the streets, playing under the great nests like rafts sometimes eight feet across and repaired year by year with anything at all. (I had once seen my own sandal-strap woven into a rag-bag of a nest.) But what I didn't know about was human fathers.

What sort of nests did they patch together?

Why was my father always on a migration away from the direction of my mother's migration? If Cija was so reluctant to be with my father, perhaps we might be better off altogether with this Smahil.

Up an alley seemingly tied together with lines of washing (would the alley fall to pieces if all the washing were taken down at once?). Down another alley with slope-hump pavings people live under—the alley-pavement is their wall, a hole in it serves as entrance/window.

The winding alleys twisting full of the clack of cavalry and the tramp of foot regiments. The soldiers passing jingling like money in the pocket, which to my grandmother they were. She had quickly nationalized all brothels; now they were earning for the State. The soldiers, bored and violent with boredom, in every tavern, every inn, door, and whore-window. How could they hear the bells the prostitutes wore swinging just inside their vaginas? This fashion made a walk even on their own a pleasant experience, tuning the overplayed muscles ambling themselves ready to enjoy whatever fresh customer next alerted by the sweet muffled alarm. I had liked the little joy-bells-sounds when pretty ladies passed, when I lived with my mother in the City ways, but I doubted if anyone could hear these days. Sergeants' roars interrupting the City's civilian hubbub in four currencies—the Dictatress's native barracks-boors; Zerd's seasoned campaigners; then the smart simmer of the Northern King's regiments here, under that King's favorite Prince Progdin; then Princess Sedili's "rebel" troops, split off from the same King's main army and needing now most terrible disciplines to keep them from the throats of the taunting "loyal" troops, who take every opportunity to cry *Traitor!*—every tavern, every brothel, every civilian kitchen in town had to be put out of bounds for both sets of Northern troops. i.e. Progdin's loyalists, and Sedili's rebels. They'd been given her by her father the Northern King to lead in his Northern name, but now she had brought them as dower-gift to my father, the Dragon-general Zerd. A sweet treachery of hers for which he recognized her once more in his bed and on that Throne to which he once begged my mother.

- (The early history of my father and my mother, and by "early" I mean before I was born, I finally understood only when my mother's rambling Dairies rambled years later into my hands.) How my father held together those armies I still don't understand. No matter how my mother deplored his wars, what would that General have been if not a General? A fairground bouncer? What a waste of the great leaders if there were no human misery for them to manipulate.

Traitor! cried Progdin's lily-white unsullied troops at Sedili's whenever they met.

Senior officers at aristocrats' elegant supper-parties had been known to clash to the death, or what passed for the death, their blood in the wine and their heads under the ladies' skirts, at a word amidst the formally impolite conversation. Though officially all were allies met here in this hot-bed of a town, my grandmother's tiny kingdom was boiling like a rice-bag left in the sun, ready to explode. Savage arrests every hour, executions every week, and what my grandmother called "the tinkle of broken curfew."

It was our approach to the first of the network of canals which now waked my mother.

This was the brothel-quarter where, I was later to learn, my mother as an un-spectacular incompetent prostitute had gone on strike.

The stench of the water pierced the haze of the drug. And the neighborhood, I suppose, always roused her to a sense of nightmare. Being a romantic, she hadn't understood the way her colleagues here had refused to take a pride in their squalor, I suppose.

"Smahil—" I heard her say.

"Hush, little sister."

"Smahil, tell me where you are taking me? Not to your barracks?"

"My insanity, my dear child, has unfortunately for you reached no such excess."

Suddenly I felt about to fall. The man with me had stopped and was hauling toward him, by the curl of his whip-thong, one of the pretty ladies. No longer ambling, she was dragged heavily but surely across the road to his stirrup. She was smiling fixedly in surprise, the whip ever tighter licking up under bunched skirts with their edges of bells, a harmonious package, and biting into the innerside of one thigh with its blue tattoo edged by a blur of green. Smahil's whip-handle smashed savagely across the man's gloved hand, already at his trousers. Smahil's face remained without expression. The man gave a whimper. He let his whip slacken. The pretty lady dropped. We rode on.

The cavalry-bird's great claws, sheathed in steel, rang on a rough road. There were the intolerable smells of agriculture on the outskirts of a cheap City—no fresh hedges—simply manure laid again on rotted manure, bones, excrement, some cat corpses. Animal manure locally smelt as bad as the human variety, for the animals were never healthy. Some poor kine we saw wandering with terrible rumps where occasionally the peasants slice off meat to eat—yet not enough to kill the useful animal. Here they had taken to using the human corpse as a scarecrow. The human scarecrow, our peasants' status symbol.

Humus of hay.

The sky and the straw-land tilted. The bird was bearing us, Smahil's man and I, up a slatted grooved gang-plank, on which his claws clockered striking off hot seasoned seed-scattered weed-sprouting wood. We were riding up the side of a crazy old building with many gables and dilapidated turrets in which, through black orifices, I could see hens pecking and clucking away as though they were safely on the ground sixty feet below. An old vine, a gigantic thing, languorously encircled the structure. Our bird's harness struck the leaves and set them asway.

"Is Seka all right? Take that thing off her head," my mother shouted, and this made her double up.

He seized her from the saddle as both birds at last entered a covered-in level. Dismounting in one quick movement he pulled her to a pile of straw and he held her hands and her head while she retched. He nodded curtly across her at the man, who pulled the cloth off me.

My mother held out her arms weakly and he regarded us as I went to her and stroked her hair and her poor forehead.

The birds wandered off into the humid gloom. One laid its claws in a quick cage over a rat which ran out from the straw. This it poked to death, through its caging claw, with the curved point of its beak and thence tossed it down to its ruminant crop.

Smahil spoke to the man while Cija hoarsely murmured a string of words to me—"My pearl, my joy, my dusk," *dusk* being something she often called me because I am that blue-ish color, like my Dragon father.

The man saluted. He was pulling off his gauntlet. But the thumb remained in the glove where Smahil's contemptuous whip-butt had smashed it. Pale, pulling his gauntlet on again to keep the hand of a piece, the big man went away.

"This is a granary?" Cija asked.

"It is safety," he said.

"You are deluding yourself, Smahil, but not me. I do not need safety," she said boldly. "But you will never be safe again if this kidnap is discovered. Take me back while you still can, and I shall never speak against you."

"You won't speak against me wherever we are found together," he asserted lazily.

She lay back, with me in her arms, against the scratching smelling straw and let her eyelids droop as she considered him.

Was the very deadliness of his punishment, were she to testify against him, his protection from her?

2

The Neighborhood
Abortionist's Barn

SOMEONE HAD ALREADY pulled away the ramp up which we'd arrived.

Far below now I saw the straw-littered baked-clay courtyard, the strutting cock with his comb up, the dun pecking hens, but no human figure. It was a large courtyard, and it was boundaried at quite a distance by a very high creepered fence, dense with lavish purple blossom like huge blisters, and beyond that were high fern-trees sparkling under a relentless sun, and only then could be glimpsed, yet farther away, the scummed coil of green water which meant Canal and populace. Not that my mother should want to be found with any of that Populace; she was better off with Smahil, who at least cared about her, whether to harbor or harm her.

I would be able to climb that fence. But she wouldn't be able.

She talked to him a bit sulkily, as girls I'd played with talked to their brothers. "You won't weaken my resolve."

He replied quickly, "You don't imagine I'm to beg you to sleep with me, when another man's embryo lives in you?"

That caught her up short. That he *knew* was commonplace enough—not only from whatever spies he employed, but also from his sixth sense where she was concerned. But I am sure it had never occurred to her that Smahil could find her repulsive.

"I could hardly bear to touch you," he went on, "when I had you there barely clothed in your wet room."

He said this carelessly, not even watching her for reaction. It was not a trick to wound her.

It is from this moment that I can trace the genuine hardening of my mother's heart against Smahil. Till now, her blood-closeness and their old friendship had always sustained her, and even when she hated or loathed him most, it had been a glowing hatred. But now her vanity congealed.

"Then why am I here?" she asked, bewildered. "You do not mean to love me. Nor to kill me—or so you said—"

"No need to remind me," he gestured gently. "You aren't going to be hurt, rest assured."

She said desperately: "Smahil. Stop talking to me as if I am a stranger."

His glance deepened. He liked her saying that. He crawled toward her over the straw, pulled her breast out of the cloak, and rubbed the nipple briefly, as good masters pull a dog's ears. Instantly he let her be again, and I saw that he really would rather not touch my mother.

"It is you who have put the large distance between us," he orated at her. "I have never wanted much more than to live with you in perfect amity. I have ambition where the army is concerned, that's true, but whatever honors and rewards my military career has gained me I have wanted only to pour into your silly little lap, to have you for my nearest and my dearest and almost my very self, to make a home and keep you in it for my friend and my sister and mine. Bred with our foul blood, you and I both orphans tossed out separate and alone on a monstrous world in which by a miracle we found a way toward each other. Why have you always run away and spat on my loving kindness when all I've wanted is to cherish you?"

"And to consume me . . ."

"I only consume because you fight against me," he said darkly. His eyes narrowed in the seed-shimmer, and he snapped the hank of straw with which he'd been toying.

"Let me go, Smahil."

"To go back to the Dragon?"

"I fear him but he is my husband. All my duties lie there—to my mother, to my country—"

"Ah . . . lady."

This was addressed to a bent crone, obviously the owner of the cloak my mother now wore, who had shuffled up some back stair.

She came and peered at me.

I thought I could kick her usefully in her ancient shins, if I had to.

Her eyes were filmy. She had cataracts.

"This is the one." Smahil led her to my mother.

She reached a dirty hand and pulled aside the cloak. "Easy," she mouthed, prodding my mother's stomach.

"Smahil," my mother said very levelly, "I am not going to suffer an abortion, least of all by this creature. The baby I carry is precious. It is the little one of Ung-g, my one sweet lover, who saved my life, and later gave his large life for me—and, Smahil, try to understand, I lived with him in the only happiness I've actually unofficially found happy, in a clean place, away from streets and back stairs and even from vocabularies, from—"

"She is the one I could find who most surely will be discreet," Smahil thought he answered just her first remark. "Don't worry, she is very practiced, and I'll make her wash her hands."

I noticed it was my presence distressed my mother maybe most of all. So I tried to keep out of her sight. I am very glad I was there though.

I was really young. I think I wasn't distressed, and I can't remember feeling anger. (I found, almost in baby-hood, that if you can't yell anger is lonely and boring.) But I remember knowing that in spite of my mother's apparent horror, nothing really had gone terribly wrong —the woman was just doing things I'd always been told not to—I mean she boiled water in a pot with dregs of something in it—in our old house near the marshes I used to be allowed to boil water on the hearth, but only if the pot was clean first. Now medicine-water for my mother's obviously ill bottom was not being kept as clean as water we used to pour on the scullery-ants.

This old woman was another of the Stupid grown-ups from whom we never were safe. Things might go Wrong any time now.

"Keep—Seka away—" my mother said through the sweat pouring off her upper lip, but her eyes were shut so I stayed. That rag, none of the women I knew would have allowed it within yards of a wound. My mother was bleeding. I yanked off my undershirt and handed the woman that instead. I don't think she knew any difference. Smahil was no good. My mother at this point despised Smahil too much to care how he humiliated her, thus she was not humiliated by his presence and that was one distress removed. But though he gripped her hands and soothed her brow, for most of the operation he was staring glassily into middle distance with a fixed little smile, presumably of poetic triumph, on his mouth. The old woman was standing back finished, mucky, proud. My mother lay with her legs still spread, moaning. Smahil started, pulled her shift down, patting her. I took his flask and swabbed her with the alcohol on a new strip torn off my dress where it ripped easily at the cleanest place: as my mother used to swab me when I was itchy there. "What are you—?" Smahil was shocked. With an appalled oath, he roughly pulled my mother's shift down again to cover her, and shoved me so hard I fell sprawling.

The woman went out with the wrappings of bloodied straw. My mother reached for me, took my face in her hands which wouldn't stop their tremble, and looked a very deep question into my eyes. Had I myself been horribly wounded by her experience here, my mother most of all wished to know. She had a habit of communicating sometimes as silently to me as I to her.

I smiled at her in a motherly way and pulled her hair off her face.

Smahil put me to one side and took my mother into his arms, his hands now more inclined to wander over her since presumably she was de-contaminated of whatever he had resented being in her. "It's all over, it's all over," Smahil informed her soupily. "It's all over and really you're glad, now the happy time begins."

As though she were a happy sleeper, he hunkered beside her while she lay in a waxy semi-coma, his eyes tenderly caressing her features, his hands drifting over the neck of her shift, its hem, as though she were his parcel soon for the un-wrapping.

But as at one of these more intimate touchings she started and trembled and turned away, a dark disapproving rebuking look descended over his face.

"Has your child eaten?" Smahil frowned at her, when she woke.

She stared differently at him. *"You* know," she managed to whisper, "whether she's eaten since you took us!"

"You haven't thought of her, have you," Smahil said. "Now stop feeling sorry for yourself, wouldn't that be a good idea," he suggested, "and be a mother to what you've already spawned."

"Can you provide food for her?" my mother asked Smahil. She remained oddly unsurprised by almost anything Smahil did. He brought some cold stew, which was quite nice. She couldn't have any, but she made sure that I would. My mouth still hurt from his contemptuous finger. Smahil sat with his fine strong hands hanging across his updrawn knees and looked at her somberly.

"Cija," he said, "if you get pregnant or have children without my permission, it's like children being forced out of me without my will. After all, I am part of you and you of me."

I could see that she was not shocked enough by this remark.

In a terrible kind of way, she was still surprised and grateful that he felt so "intense" about her. She did say: "If you allowed me freedom, since I am part of you, then my freedom would mean your freedom too." She thought she felt nothing for him, but she was still conciliating him.

He leaned forward.

"Freedom," he said at her, "is another word for cowardice. I am involved with you, Cija. Don't you know that involvement is something real, something splendid in your dim, escapist little world? I shall be committed to you until we die. I am involved with you as any man with the woman who is part of him, just as the first man was involved when he committed himself to the first incest—with his daughter, since First Woman was created *from* First Man's very body." He almost hissed, spitting love at her. "And what have *you* done with that body Man gave you? Where do I fuck you now? In your wound?"

The setting sun reached in and the straw again was crimson, all crimson, and the big bleak clouds wrapped the sky in cloud-shrouds, and not a cricket harped its legs.

I cuddled up to sleep against my mother's pained side, having tried to make her as comfortable as possible ("Yes, comfort your mother, Tongueless. Lullaby her, Tongue-gone," said Smahil, and he left us then, like iron his righteous steps descended the gangway, out he went with his conscience clear into the erubescent world, having dropped coins into the old woman's hand to indicate she watch us, looking forward to tomorrow when he'd return to greet his cleansed sister, emptied and purified like a sacred vessel, and no doubt after her sleep properly grateful to him and quite herself again) and I dreamed an ugly dream. I was wandering in City streets like the streets we'd been through—though I did find that in some way I was exhilarated to discover the ugliness didn't *matter,* it wasn't part of life itself, only lying on the visible surface around me as scum does; or rather, having only a borrowed body, a non-physical body borrowed for the dream, I didn't matter to the streets. The roofs began to meet overhead, the filthy claustrophobic streets were pulling so close together. I found a bookshop, and turned in to it. It was a very dark shop indeed. Unlike the one shop in our City which sold paper and ink, and some books, and where my mother used often to take me before she undertook her solitary confinement. Long corridors now in the night, lined with musty books stretching high over my head to a spotted brown ceiling which sagged. The books smelt so damp I almost thought that at some time they had all been drowned. They were dead books, that had been killed, otherwise I shouldn't be allowed to be among them unchecked like this; alive books are a different matter, too perilous for the sort of world in which I'd got trapped. There was a small strange bookseller wandering around coughing in adjacent corridors, keeping an eye on me in case I took down a book and browsed through it without paying. I took down a rheumy-looking binding and opened it. I flicked through the pages and an illustration caught my eye—another corridor rather like the one I was standing in, as though even artists around here couldn't or daren't think of anything but the official surroundings. But standing in the distance, at the end of the pictured mildewy corridor, was a tiny almost illuminated figure of a man, I mean almost luminous, as when paint has a fine base maybe of gold leaf shining under it. Even at that distance, I could find clearly his keen glance (I had been going to turn the page over but was caught by the glance). When I looked, he started coming to life and toward me. His eyes were fixed on mine. Although he was still a picture, he was more real than anything in that dingy large officially "real" place around me. My heart started thumping. I was sure he wouldn't step *out* of the page. That would be too good to be true. And *he did*. He held my gaze and in all his beauty and strength he came real and stepped right out of the book and stood right there with me. Oh, the generosity of his stepping *out*. Not promising a miracle but performing a miracle. I woke. Oh, you man, you still cheated. You performed the miracle and then didn't after all; because I woke.

I looked anxiously at my mother in the grayish darkness coming through the barn door. She was wide awake, and obviously had been so for a long time, staring up into the rafters.

I thought, now we could both escape. The old woman was in the corner, but she was hawking and snoring. The two birds, tethered at the far end of the barn, were silent, almost as though roosting I thought. But my mother must be far too weak to manage. She looked a lot like I felt the time I had fever and couldn't even roll to the side of my mattress.

There'd be time. Tomorrow, or soon, I'd get us away.

Crunch, crunch came boots of a sort, up the straw-y, slatted planking.

Smahil's heels and spurs would make quite a different sound. So this wasn't Smahil coming to tell us how things were all for the best, all for one's own good.

It was a man who peddled soaps-and-salves, and I felt better at the sight of that handy, well-sewn sack he carried. The woman brought him a bowl of welcoming morning vinegar, recently tinted by best grapeskin. Then she brought one to my mother, who made me sip it ("A little wine will put heart in you, sweetpie") till she saw me make faces.

"Now," the old creature triumphantly addressed my mother, "you see, you lady. Don't apologize, I could tell you thought yourself in the hands of some amateur. But all the officers bring their dear ones to me and the reason is hygiene."

The man boasted about his sales to the Empress Sedili. "What a bather that one is." He wriggled. "A woman that her Complexion *matters* to her," he approved. "And she cares about pleasing her man with the little purchases

that *taste* when his mouth is applied. A Dragon's bride.
No ordinary man could handle her. She'd drown most.
They'd be sucked inside and never seen again. She relies
on me. For my discretion. What couldn't I reveal about
the dear Empress's intimate freshness?"

The woman saw how my mother seemed too weak to
feed herself, and she started spooning a gruel into my
mother's mouth. She ignored me, and so did the soaps-
and-salves man, both giving me uneasy looks when they
couldn't *avoid* seeing me, as though I were some sort of
aborted thing. An un-skilled abortion that had gone wrong
—and ended in a *child*.

Stupid grown-ups were one thing; stupid grown-ups
were the enemy, the people into whose power one could
get so easily, just because one never expected them to
turn out to be quite so stupid. The old woman was one
of those, and so was Smahil. Either he was crazy, or he
was nasty. Perhaps he was one because he was the other.

But silly grown-ups were a different matter. Sometimes
they could be very useful indeed. The soaps-and-salves
man was silly.

When I fingered his "bottles" he paid no attention—
he assumed I was admiring them.

I guessed which was the sleepysalve: he'd nodded
proudly at it as he mentioned it. So I un-did the twine
round its neck without anyone seeing.

I picked up the opened sleepysalve (I could smell it
at once) and threw it in the two stupid grown-up faces.
The old woman spluttered and her eyes were outraged.
The soaps-and-salves man said, "Hey, what is this, what
are you at," and I threw the rest as though I were tossing
a pancake. Of course it wasn't very effective. But while
they were dazed, Cija had lurched herself to her feet and
she picked up the sack and pulled it over the old woman's unappetizing head and tied it in a good knot with
its string. The man laid hands on her to stop her, but his
eyes were swollen and bleary with the stuff splashed in
them, and I ran at him very hard and butted my head
in his horrible stomach and Cija had time to pick up a
knife.

"If you stay where you are . . . I shan't hurt you . . ."
she told him unsteadily.

He stayed, dithering from one foot to the other till I
thought his knees would fall off. My mother ruffled my

hair with her other hand. "Well done, clever sensible darling," she said. She was trying to saddle one of the big birds tethered in the back of the barn. He wasn't a nice bird (they rarely are) but he was well-trained, one of Progdin's cavalry birds, and as soon as he felt that her hands were accustomed, he let her and was even helpful, lifting his llama-like neck out of the way when necessary.

My mother un-did his rope and put me up on the saddle.

Then she was able to get herself up rather untidily behind me. She held me tight, and we clockered down the ramp. The morning met us. The man made a bit of a rush at us, then thought better of it. But he yelled in a squeaky voice, "A whole pint of salve you owe me for," and he added on, *"Bitch,"* as though he'd be letting himself down if he didn't call a terrible name like that at someone who'd stolen wares of his.

Hens rushed round like the soaps-and-salves man, ostensibly getting out of our way and in fact racing in circles up to the huge claws they thought they were avoiding. One by one they dropped over the edge of the ramp, squawking and flopping out their wings in a pessimistic way. I felt happy and pleased and morning-y. But I knew my mother must still be wretched and in pain. There was blood on my dress where I was cuddled against her. What if she fell off?

"Fresh blood is antiseptic anyway," my mother faintly said. "That's what I was frightened of. Sepsis. Even though Smahil used bear-dung as an antiseptic ointment." She seemed fairly cheerful now we were away and together.

"I know we're in the right direction," she said in a pleased voice. "The canals get dirtier nearing the industrial quarter in which your grandmother and her forbears have so democratically dwelt."

Alone with me, she generally tried to keep an almost constant flow of "conversation" going—as though I might worry that I couldn't entertain her. She tried to work out what I found most interesting, so that she perhaps could almost voice it for me.

A lot of noise around now. A vicious rioting sound. "As long as Progdin's army is leaving town as scheduled today through the main streets," my mother said, "the back streets will be fairly quiet." She added, "Not that all streets in your grandmother's City aren't in fact back-streets."

At one point we did get caught up in the rout, and my mother said to one man on foot, as in the general mass we were pressed to a wall to let past the Progs in their solid tramping columns, "Was it not agreed Progs shouldn't be harmed till beyond boundaries?"

"Stoning," he shouted back to her in a thoroughly civic way, "does not constitute *attack*." And he hurled his stone, as all citizens in the street were hurling theirs.

To march under stoning is about the nastiest method of travel I can think of. I have often left (and entered) cities in this way since. It is horrendous. The Progs hardly broke step. They mostly kept their eyes straight ahead, but from time to time they dug a handy scabbard accidentally into a citizen.

Please, I said in my head to our little Cousin, our family god, just don't let any of those soldiers get hit in the face. Then it happened right in front of me, and I was scared to look in case the soldier had no face left. I did look. His eye was filling with blood, but only from the gash on the brow over it, and he apparently found it a relief to be able to put an expression legitimately on his face instead of remaining impassive; the man beside him held his arm to keep him in the line. I tried to see the message for me in the immediately blocked prayer, then decided that was greedy of me, it was the soldier's business and not mine.

Our bird was very good, he had probably left a City under stone-shower himself now and again.

I felt my mother stiffen behind me. I looked. A man, not in uniform, was riding past. He was wearing a plain dark tunic with dandruff on the shoulders but I could tell he was important by the way he slouched at ease with the reins looped on his pommel, not straight like the other officers. He looked across, obviously saw my mother, and gave a short bow. My mother after a pause bowed back to him. Then she kicked the bird's sides and we gradually pushed our way into an emptier street.

She was breathing hard.

"That was the Prince, Progdin," she informed me in a fast low hurrying voice as our bird stalked along. "I think perhaps he *won't* tell Smahil he saw me. He always lets well alone, as far as I can tell of him. I've wondered, often, how does Progdin feel about the failure of his backing the Priests last year against the Dictatress. She was lucky, the Priests got the worst of that. But Progdin himself was far too strong for your grandmother to dispose of. So others, like Smahil, she made the official scapegoats. And she pretended not to know of Progdin's part in all that. That suited Progdin too, close-mouthed as he is. He has gathered control of the battalions Smahil originally brought from the North. Progdin has long been a favorite of the North. Well," she said in a soft very thoughtful voice, "things are under way. The Dragon-General wouldn't be letting Progdin and his four War-strength companies out of here unless he means to be out after them to get them for himself pretty soon now. Soon he'll be gone too, Seka my love, the Dragon will be gone, and we'll have the place to ourselves again."

She was quiet then as we traversed the old trade-docks, which were always quiet too these days—almost everyone seemed to have put a blockade on everyone else, and the walls were greased by the spines of idlers.

There were crowds of people around the great paved semicircular courtyard before the main Palace entrance; mostly because someone had set fire to a building near-by. There were flakes of black stuff floating, and a lot of milling around.

"It's milling for us, too," my mother remarked. "I'll wait till noon when it's all gone quiet. Then we can slip in, scandalizing perhaps only one guard." She added that if Sedili's creatures found us, she might be tortured while Sedili, who hated to waste a moment of her day, dictated a letter and had a manicure. My mother sounded both frightened and sarcastic.

Her voice was getting faint. I did feel anger now, though for an instant I wondered what this tight physical feeling could be, like a knife wandering into my chest. It's not familiar to me, anger, but if I were far bigger than Smahil I could make his stupid little teeth rattle.

I wanted to get a message to someone big to do this to Smahil. It came to my mind that the Dragon-General would be the person to "tell." I believed my mother that he was dangerous. But then perhaps he would be dangerous to Smahil too.

It all seemed so unbearable, even to someone my age, that my mother couldn't just walk into her home. Besides giving rise to endless scandal, all these murderous

lodgers seemed now more at home than she in the place
—pretending to be good guests till they could catch you
sneaking in, disguised and vulnerable; no one need ever
inquire about a sick woman in an old cloak, disappeared
before noon on a day of general City riot.

My mother with a sobbing sigh leant forward on the
bird's great neck.

I slipped down from the saddle, down off the big
bucket-shaped stirrup which I have since found can be
so dangerous to its owner in battle, but helps control
tricky bird-back harness. I went over to a fruit-seller.

He had a barrow of spiny fruit he handled with gloves
on; there was a big block of hill-ice standing amongst the
fruit, in the barrow-middle, and he'd cornered a place
under a magnolia tree. He'd kicked aside the leper whose
begging-place in the shade this usually was. The leper
lay panting and noon approached.

I held out my hand mutely.

The barrow-man laughed at me.

"An overripe yam she'd buy for a brass-coin. A rotting one she'll do you the favor of taking from you," said
the leper from the sunlight.

We were so bedraggled to be treating him like this that
the barrow-man laughed, spun the yam in the dust and
watched me grovel for it. I ran back to my mother, a sore
burning on my wrist where one of the dogs yapping at me
for the yam had pushed his almost pig-like bristling head.
But I had the yam. I offered it to my mother, but she took
it and threw it away again into the yellow dust. "You're
not to touch that, Seka," she said sharply.

I was hungry and I watched disconsolately. It rolled and
the dogs rolled after it.

I sat down in the Palace-yard dust, since there was nowhere else to sit, and clasped my arms round my knees.
Yellow, sticky dust sprayed in my eyes as a carriage
passed with its huge wheels thrumming.

I tried to glimpse inside the window, in case it were my
grandmother or any lady we knew. A crest glittered on the
carriage-panel. It hurt my eyes.

The carriage left, but the light of it stayed, the glitter of
it lit my eyeballs. There were boots beside my face, new
boots, with gold twiddles on them. I stood up politely, as
little girls should when adults are bang in front of them. A
fair-haired lady had got out of the carriage.

And she said to me: "What a dear little blue-y girl! Now, haven't I met you somewhere before, sweetheart?"

I was always being told I'd met people before. I couldn't really remember her face, but she was pretty and I nodded.

"Is your Mummy with you, love?" the lady asked.

Cija came up beside me and took my hand. Although it was near noon her hand was icy. She was doing everything slowly so she shouldn't limp.

"You remember my daughter Seka, Sedili," my mother said.

"Why, so I do."

Sedili tapped her woman's arm. "My dear. Let's run a bath."

Her woman curtsied hesitantly, squeamishly, to this pale young woman in the bloodstained hooded cloak.

Sedili's handsome mouth curved humorously. To make her way through the dust she had picked up her skirts, and under the drawn-thread-lace and broidery of her trousers her long gilt-strapped boots twined up her legs. She smelt of some tremendous scent, but mainly of health and strength. Her knees and lustrous thighs, nearest my eye-level, were dusted with gold sparkle-dust over their muscles and dimples.

"Come, little blue Princess." Sedili reached down a hand for me and I slipped my dusty paw into it. Even her lovely fat golden knees have muscles, I thought admiringly.

We went up the high marble veiny steps. The barrow-man stared as though at a universe turned upside down.

Sedili's apartments were a blaze of grace.

Sedili pulled down her trousers and sat on a saddle-stool. Her legs spread. Her big skirt billowed and a page-boy, small handy compact size, crept up inside it and began to rouge the insides of her thighs.

My mother stood, aching I knew, pretending not to shiver. Slaves toted around baskets of fruit and civilized scrubbed vegetables—Sedili believes in a healthy mind in a healthy weight-lifter. She now was elegantly flexing a little coil on a gilded spring, which keeps her sword-wrist supple.

My interest waned again as it became apparent that I was to be given not poison but a *bath*. A kindly treat for Cija's daughter.

Two burly female slaves laid hands on me. I was lowered into a pool too deep for me. I found I wanted to cry.

My mother looked at my face and suddenly laughed. She came over to me and knelt on the pool-side, still hugging about herself her ghastly borrowed cloak. "All right, little pearl," she said softly. "Just to get you nice and clean."

Sedili from her stool regarded me. "Soap," she ordered. "Come, little blue girl, my nice ladies will make you all lovely again just as you should be."

My head was doused. I had a dizzy glimpse of the slaves holding me, young blue women, more pure-blue than me, lithe and jolly as panthers, their eyes rolling with the jollity of it all, the steam condensing into navy globules rolling down their bobbly breasts to the curly purple nipples to be shaken off almost as soon as they hung there, and Sedili sitting watching, her eyes alert and happy too. A look as at wrongs being righted. A housewifely satisfaction.

"Ah, now, Empress," she was saying. "You may perhaps agree what you are wearing to be hardly suitable for supper tonight. You are to attend tonight's banquet? Let us find you a gown, Empress, which if you will accept from me it will be my privilege to give . . ."

"The Empress has taken a Vow of Silence," observed a gruff voice.

I turned in my bath. There had come in a big man, to whom Sedili's slaves were bowing. He wore high-commander's uniform, Northern of course.

"Clor! Our conference—" Sedili swiftly stood, upsetting the boy who rolled out from under her skirt with his rouge-pot, and there was a glimpse of the cellulite thighs still pitted with heavy pink, as with real guilty haste Sedili hurried to this man. He bowed to Sedili curtly. And he strode to my mother. "Madam." He went very properly down on one knee before my mother.

"Clor," my mother said . . . and "Clor."

"Clor, you may with impunity, dear Commander, interrogate the Empress, may he not?" Sedili lightly crooned. "The Empress's Vow of Silence, I think, has been mislaid by dint of necessity."

"That is what has been taking place here, interrogation?" Clor deduced heavily. "Empress," to my mother, "you have been wounded." He thought she should note these things. Being the Dragon's man, was that why *he* addressed my mother as Empress? He beckoned his adjutant. "Let us escort you, Empress, to your worthy and illustrious Mother," Clor saluted.

"Empress, can you—walk?" the adjutant inquired, looking with distress at my mother.

"Empress, I am carrying you," Clor said in the most unexceptionable way. As though he were not touching her at all, he lifted my mother and to Sedili he remarked that perhaps conference must be postponed, and Sedili waved her dyed-plumage fan airily and then (I saw as she turned back to the bath and spread her thighs for the rouge-pot again) flicked her fan so irritably against herself that its handle for a moment partly disappeared inside, and I leaped from the water and pattered wetly after up the stairway to the Dictatress's own halls. The adjutant gravely removed his gold-frogged thingobob, sort of truncated nominal stiff cloak of great beauty, and placed it around me. Forbidden this stairway since the army's arrival, now how liberated I felt to be padding up it, up that thick stair pulling one like a fly on web-thread higher and winding up to the Dictatress—the lift of the army commander Clor's big flat knees, the tread of his boots of extremely experienced leather, aged on battlefields across a continent; my mother's peaky little face already more relaxed and tinged with contentment lying across his shoulder, looking down from time to time at me with the sweetest smile.

Thick warm honey rock. My grandmother lives as her appalling ancestors always have lived, perched atop and yet just within the old old-palace. There is not a right-angle in the old-palace. A carpenter here would throw away his set-square, an alien instrument. As we climbed we might see farther below us the intricate other web, the web of my grandmother's City. The tawny sunlight softly slathered itself over the City.

We'd glimpse a roof. Palace women sunning themselves within view of sentries who stood spear-handed against the heat. Or grouped throwing dice on a crenellated look-out perch. Or saluting and stamping at guard-change yet higher.

Trumpet calls in the Dictatress's army seem more languid, heavy with heat, than in other armies I've known. A "distant" languor, sounds spiral up from a parade ground so far below layer on layer of the hot air in which this country really does specialize.

Women, soldiers; little birds hopping and flirting from

shadow to sunlight, lizards, shafts of sun, spiralling just like trumpet calls in the hot dark. I saw my mother's eyes again as we turned a rough bulging rock unworthy of the name *corner*, and I reached a hand up and touched one of her feet swung below Clor's arm. It was crusted by City-dust. I very clearly and distinctly thought: *"Will she always need looking after? Will she grow up?"*

As we climb the honey-rock stairs, Sedili's servant-boy climbs rapidly past up to the slaves' lavatories, carrying a chamber-pot over which he bends his head with eyelids half-heavy and nostrils aflare, the pot's undoubted aroma proclaiming the passing of a drug a bladder hadn't been able to accept—the servant's only way of sharing the mistress's drug.

Zinging heat and singing shadow and tension right through the palace—the tension even in the lizards crusting (like City-crust) the steps we climb. Never was languor so tense. Something is going to happen. My mother thinks it is the imminent departure of the army.

The Dictatress was in her whipping-room. We didn't have to go right the way up to her halls. She came out of the small room to one side of us. We had heard the thin sound of the whip. The adjutant toed a lizard off the step in front of us. It fell, separating—it had been two lizards copulating in apathy. "Your daughter, madam," Clor congratulated the Dictatress, "has been found."

The Dictatress had been trying to look interested in the whipping, on other things as her mind nevertheless must be, and now she trod out to us across the rusty floor which is difficult to walk over because of the gutters in it to drain off the blood. Her slaves, divested of their official audience, carried on in the background. Also with less attention to duty.

"My daughter!" the Dictatress uttered.

There was a moment while Clor remained expressionless and Cija looked at the Dictatress in a distinctly amused manner. Then Cija played the proper game. She reached out of Clor's arms to her mother, and he let her gently down on to the step, and she was enfolded in the Dictatress's embrace. "And Seka, too, Mother," Cija said. "You can see how Seka in her regimental pelisse is pleased to see you."

"How do I know," my grandmother said, "what Seka feels?"

This to her is a reasonable remark. I had no voice, so my grandmother reasoned "the child cannot communicate."

"She was found where? You, Commander, found her?" queried my grandmother from the depths of official loving embrace.

Now was the time my mother should tell tales on Smahil.

But she said nothing. Her eyes were rather self-conscious, she knew she was "shielding her brother" and there was a vague lift of her chin.

Clor bowed, he is not good at bowing. "She appears, Dictatress, to have suffered some kind of medical attention." I gave the adjutant his garment. He clicked his heels as he received it. It swirled across the hot golden stairway as they turned and left us. Thoroughly rescued.

And yet not rescued at all. For as soon as my mother struggled out of one muddle, she would drift into another.

3

The Lynx in the
Withy Cage

I LOOK BACK now on that time as one of utter determination on my part. I didn't put it then into words in my own head; but I had every intention of getting my mother off my hands and into the care of someone who could look after her correctly.

My grandmother was not in the running. I didn't once consider her. I had been most favorably impressed by Clor. I thought how somebody like Clor would be exactly what was needed.

"Don't think me unfeeling of your welfare, Cija. But you are well enough to eat in my room here. Therefore you are well enough to eat downstairs at a big table like a grown-up girl."

The Dictatress swooped on my mother, rocked her waist in her hands, and all Cija's ladies winced in sympathy, and she let Cija go again and whirled to the window embrasure.

As some people take a cup of something warm throughout the day, so the Dictatress would refresh herself with a quick sip of life at the window.

There wasn't really too much of a panorama, but she could somehow or other ingest the mood of the land. Blazing heat over it now but also *wind*: rubbish being blown. Great balls of rubbish rushing along like those hoops of gathered weed in a desert, also little porcupines being blown along in rolled-up balls too, for there are always little porcupines nosing around investigating the rubbish dumps in the City. Still, the Dictatress was sanitating like mad. Building drains, sewers. It was hard to congratulate her on this, as the work was never done, the tunnels were always falling through (only at the very last minute, as this meant the diggers could be employed all over again for a longer time) and the City-stench was worse than it might otherwise have been.

Sedili herself came to my mother in early evening. With two women and a severe attack of wardrobe. "Do choose one, Empress. I'd sooner you weren't shy. They are my dresses for Court days in the North" (*therefore I'd have nothing so elaborate, eh?* Cija's face inquired sniffily) "and I don't wear them these days. It would be truly my pleasure if you'd choose and accept one. Here is silk spun by free-range worms and traded from beyond Rutas-Mu. How low a neckline are you happy in?"

Sedili wasn't a very tall woman really, in spite of this impression she gave people who were constantly reporting her as a sort of six-footer walking vagina, but she always stood taller when Cija was around. Sedili became extra-dominant, extra-splendid. And Cija refused to compete. She generally diminished herself, became small and unobtrusive and expressionless. But I later realized that this was aggressive conceit on my mother's part too. She wasn't herself when Sedili was around, and she was determined to show Sedili up as vulgar and overpowering; so she became a contrast, *innocent* and *honest*.

I myself never discovered an aversion to Sedili. I knew she had once tried to kill my mother, and had also dishonored her in Atlan-across-the-ocean, where my father ruled. I know Cija blamed her for the loss of my brother Nal, who had been a strange little thing anyway by all accounts, and sure to be lost sooner or later. I knew that Sedili was my father's first wife, for which Cija would never forgive her. But at that age I just liked to look at Sedili. Cija told me once a good way to like someone was to imagine them as a child. I tried imagining Sedili a little older than myself. She might have been vulnerable without being nice. I didn't imagine the small Sedili playing with toys, interesting though toys were to me. Her toys must always have been other people's venal heads and silly hearts.

Sedili frowned at one of her women, and I noticed the woman flinched.

My mother never managed to get women like that. Either they liked her, which was all right, or they did what they liked. "Why did you bring this for the Empress?"

Sedili drawled at her woman. "This, so plain, why, it's the kind of dress for catching your husband with his mistress and drawing yourself upright in." A sidelong glance at Cija. "When what anyone wants to wear is the dress in which to be caught with your lover by his wife."

Sedili now treated Cija to a little lecture. (Sedili's insight into the all-absorbing battle of the sexes was her great gift to humankind. Constantly.) She explained to Cija how one should always be one's husband's *mistress*. "Feminine," she said several times, as though it were a magic password. "And those little touches," she said, and it turned out what she meant wasn't what Cija thought little touches meant, but things like fresh flowers in your tent even when on campaign. "Men notice these little touches. It can be difficult, particularly of course on forced marches. Such a shame you won't be on campaign with us —after all, one presumes you feel still some residue of affection for the Dragon . . . in spite of your more recent loves."

Who are my more recent loves supposed to be? I could watch Cija working it out. It all depends on who Sedili's thinking of, whether I compose my face to that of a pure soul thinking of her ape-man and idyll, or to a slightly mocking look befitting someone who did nearly go off on the long road with an Atlantean bandit but who knows Sedili had her uses for the bandit.

"Of course," Sedili lit a small cheroot, "I personally find it very important to be *faithful* a lifetime—if your love is worth having then it's worth having." Sedili never drops messy ash when she smokes.

As it became obvious that Sedili had no intention whatsoever of actually parting with any of her dresses, someone else arrived, one of the Northern noblemen, who now had dedicated his own small personal household in Sedili's service. She did introduce him to my mother but neither of us caught his name—a very glottal name, composed of sounds like stuffy sinus. He paid no attention to my mother, even turning his back on her throughout their brief interview; it was obvious he would never forgive *her* for being the Dragon's subsequent wife. There was simply one glance of contempt at me from wide-set smoky violet-gray eyes surrounded by long lashes like soot-smatter. They all went down the marble steps to eat.

The ladies had forgotten to come and put me to bed,

they were so absorbed in dressing. So in the comparative darkness of a lower landing, I hung over the balustrade and watched until my eyes were sore with torch-smoke and general fatigue.

Near the main banqueting bit, a terrible growling. People in their evening clothes, mainly female, were clamoring round a big gilded withy cage wheeled in. Hunters surrounded it. They had brought back the prize of their day's catch, a large jungle lynx, giving an effect twice its own size as it hurled itself upon the bars at one side and then at another. It seemed entirely to fill its cage because it was in each part of the cage at least twice every minute. This lynx was pure auburn, and would be worth a lot of money for some lord's collection.

I could see my mother from above, as she reached the banquet. She paused and looked back at the lynx. Ladies were up by the bars now, teasing the prisoner and demonstrating their courage by pushing into the cage necklaces and pins they withdrew at the last instant with tinkling laughter at their own sauciness inciting such balked fury.

Flutes and tamborines accompanied my mother and Sedili to their seats. The hunters drew the withy cage away so it shouldn't disturb conversation. Sedili sat by an empty chair, which presumably should have been Zerd's. I was sorry he was not there. I was quite interested to see my father. He must be doing army things, and probably rarely feasted. Sedili's was a lower chair than his, for though she is his legal wife (he has this policy of never divorcing) she is not his Empress (though a lot of the Commons, like that soap man, seemed to have the idea that she is) and this lower chair made her look feminine and wifely. Cija picked up her first oyster, and everyone else was able to begin—inside Cija's shell a little round thing lay.

"A pearl begun but far from completion," I heard the Marshal say.

For some reason the lump, which might have been a good omen, looked shivery I thought.

As far as I could hear, as I hung over the baluster, getting chilly in my nightie in the marble darks, the smoky-eyed young noble was discussing river-verse at the top of his voice. I gathered it must be a branch of folk-art, and that in his part of the Northland since time immemorial the peasants have chanted to the river-gods incantations which take riverine forms, i.e. they wind and ripple with different "currents" moving simultaneously. Presumably he himself was a Riverliver, or Riverine. His cloak was dagged and shirred and pulled over his arms and wide muscly shoulders in strips like the most immaculate rags (ripples?) and amongst the decoration on his codpiece coiled a glass thread inside which water continuously bubbled.

"We have found some fine poetry in Atlan," Sedili said.

"All about unicorns," someone else said. "The unicorn motif."

That was the first I knew of the Atlantean arts—this talk of the unicorn. Dearest Gods. Atlan had had the seeds of knowledge in her mouth since the beginning, and even when she started to spit out those by then terrible bitter seeds it was as poetry only. Sweet Atlan isolated across the ocean, singing through ages of the unicorn— that beast which is Atlan's symbol, gentle in the thickets, already in half-extinction, for since we of the rude mainland entered Atlan we had taken the unicorns for our riding and the beast does not breed in captivity. The unicorn, the white soul, integrity which trusts, and for trusting is betrayed.

My mother picked with her skewers among the rare beef on her plate, and I hung staring above her. No one had given me any supper.

"Do peasants invent verse about unicorns?" someone asked. "I thought only poetesses liked the sickly beast— its noble snowiness and proud prettiness."

"The real verse about unicorns," cried Beautiful, his smoky eyes aflash, "are of course by peasants. From whom but the peasant, and the roots of mud and life through that peasant, can come the true poems—the bitter poems, for the true poems are the bitter poems—of trust, and betrayal by a virgin?"

"The greatest fiction for which man is responsible is the virgin," an indulgent derisory voice added its mite to the aesthetics.

People looked. In rode a latecomer. He literally rode, for he was mounted on an unattractive skewbald pony. The way a good working hand can be spatulate—well, this pony was spatulate all over. Perhaps it was a great working pony.

I'd been reluctantly thinking about getting off to bed,

because if this was the way banquets were then they were not the exotic delights I had been led to believe, and on the whole it was very sensible of children to be asleep while grown-ups dragged off to banquets.

But I peered through the torch-smoke at the newcomer. I could make him out to be, yes, the man who had kicked me when I couldn't answer his question, on the roof the day before. He looked a patchwork of scars and leather, knives like a butcher's threading his belt.

Beautiful rose to his feet.

"You arrive at table this way?" he said with disgust. "Are you battle-commander or un-tutored savage? Is this your Southern etiquette? Have you no respect for the ladies here, for the Lady Sedili?"

"This," the scarred man replied imperturbably, "is a most civilized and urbane animal, fit to arrive at any table." A dozen hands reached wine to him. He selected a brimming ale-tumbler. "Now you note," he said, "how my gentle beast will see to it that no drop be split."

He held the brimming ale aloft and suddenly the pony at a ghastly gallop on the marble hall approached the table. Ladies screamed. Only Sedili continued to lounge back in her chair, smoking and almost smiling. As suddenly as the animal had begun its gallop, it stopped, an inch or so from the table. The ale did indeed remain intact. The demonstration would seem to have defeated its purpose, for the table was in an uproar and women had run everywhere. But Beautiful as well as Ael (for this was Ael, the chief of the Southern bandits, now these days scarred in service as Zerd's ally) seemed satisfied completely by the pony's excellent manners and obedience. Ael stepped grandly on the table and raised to his lips the tumbler of which not a drop had spilt—until he drank, for now he splashed it all down himself.

Ael then fastidiously held up his sticky fingers.

A couple of bandits eagerly leaned forward presenting their beards for him to wipe his hands on. He beneficently selected one.

"I drank then to the Empress," he said.

"Shall I drink to you, Ael?" Cija said and she drank. The bandits shouted.

Ael sat down cross-legged on the table, among the flagons and center-dishes, and accepted a leg of roast.

"I would give you my chair," Beautiful told him in a loud voice, "but that I should be shamed to offer you a place below the center of the table, where I find myself although I am Riverine of a thousand generations—to your hundreds," he leaned forward to add gratuitously in the direction of the younger officer who had spoken first about sickly poems. The young officer curled his lip and remained seated while Beautiful, by now insulted, waved his sword around the rare beef and salad.

Ael glanced up. I thought he saw me, and I drew back in the gloom above him.

"Not my honor," Beautiful said, dancing about and looking athletic, "but the honor of my ancestors whom I represent here in this barbarous land for the sake of our lady Sedili, is at question."

He pointed his sword on the officer's dress-breastplate. My mother and Ael went on talking, but I couldn't catch much of it now because of the noise of the fight going on in the adjacent area. "A punctiliously correct fight," Ael shrugged. "A *taught* fighter . . . young man who was given an army by his grandfather on his birthday." And, as Ael finished off the spicy bone: "Now . . . after spice, I always eat a small child." I thought milk was a much better idea. I thought he looked toward me again. I shivered. Then I realized someone was standing beside me. I turned and there in the darkness I just saw a few little gleams at the level of an adult's head. The person spoke and was limned by the light of the nearest torch now guttering. "What are you doing here? Spying on your mother? Why aren't you in bed? Don't you need sleep at your age? Of course you do. Do you think you're different from other little girls?" She paused, a woman rapidly stroking the little diamante moustache she'd worn for the evening.

"Well," she said, "let me tell you (as a friend, and I hope you'll think of me as a friend even if I am a grown-up) that the fact you can't talk makes no difference. What makes a difference is the life your mother leads you. It's not right that you should be up at this time of night, barefoot, no one to make sure you are tucked up in bed, and very likely no supper either. Were they too busy to feed you before their own dressing-up for the feast?"

I shook my head and nodded my head.

I began to feel very sorry for myself. Yes, my feet

were cold on the nasty chilly marble. So were my shoulders and hands and arms.

The empty gap in my tummy was exactly the shape of a pudding with cream and nuts and a nice little glass of watered mulled wine. But no one had bothered to make sure I had this, though it had been left at my bedside with some chicken and mushrooms. Even if I went and ate this now, it would be as nasty and as cold as the marble.

The woman laid a hand on my shoulder, a courteous touch I suppose, very light and dry and rather leaf-like. But I knew that she didn't really want to touch me at all. I thought of my uncle Smahil not wishing to touch his precious flesh on my mother's unless she was considerably free to be his, or to be imagined his.

"Come, I'll see you along to your door," the woman said.

My mother came in and passed the lady leaving our doorway. The sentry clicked his heels and saluted and said the lady had just brought me off the stairs.

My mother thanked him warmly but didn't go out to thank the lady. She tucked me into my bed, pulling the sides of my mattress right up round me with the rugs, goatskin on to which huge pointy edges of coarse white linen lace had been sewn. This was what she called my little boat, sailing off on the sea to lovely adventures. I accepted her word for it, because I sometimes enjoyed my dreams, and I sometimes enjoyed *bits* of adventures. But as a connoisseur of the adventure in general, I really couldn't say much for it as an experience.

"You ignored your nice little hot supper," she said. "Aren't you a silly naughty little girl? Well, you were terribly good and brave when we had our horrible day, so I won't scold you. Did you clean your teeth?"

She looked to be in her dreamy anti-climactic mood.

But then, how constantly she expected anti-climax. She wouldn't have known a culmination if it jumped on her.

She shrugged out of her dress, and I leaned out of my boat to help un-clip her broaches. She pulled her shift over her head, her fingers wandering over her breasts and nipples as though she wasn't quite sure what this feeling was. She sat, making no move to undress further, staring into the embers of the torch left as a night-light near my bed.

"That woman," she presently said, who brought you

back here, I am almost sure I recognize that woman. The woman who brought up Smahil as her own son, the pale viperous little waif," and Cija half-laughed in spite of herself at the thought of an infant Smahil, "she found in a basket with swaddle-clothes, milk, embroidered coverlets (and a Priest's ransom in Temple coin) under a shady rhubarb in her garden. Being a good church-goer, she took the hint, so Smahil has told me, that this was not a baby to be thrown out with bath-water. And sure enough regular contributions of Temple coin, anonymously delivered, followed with extras on the brat's feast-days and when he became a man.

"Seka, rinse your tooth-rag *properly*." (I'd been slow and fumbling and child-like in the hope she'd say that and stay longer. Half she was talking to herself to clarify fate by hearing how it sounded; half, I knew, she was all the time telling me *everything*. Always telling me everything she could think of in case some of it, even one stray thread of ramified information might sink in for me and emerge as useful to me who knew when, or where, perhaps some day when I was in trouble and Cija herself not by to help me.)

"It occurs to me, Seka, and pull up the coverlets, darling, that when the witch-nurse Ooldra and the High Priest sent out into the world their little harbingers of ill, they really did know what they were up to. We helpless agents of ill-luck to the world, babies with the bad blood of forbidden union, are already making our mark.

"Smahil and I, for instance, what have we done? Tossed out upon our separate currents, we each nosed out the mainstream which would whirl us to Atlan. It was as though in-built antennae, put into us when we were first blue-printed, showed us where the world was the best, the perfect, the pure.

"Smahil in his essentially straightforward way (for he sees not himself but the world as the aggressor) and I with a lot of prim mouthing as to integrity, we insinuated ourselves into the last pure Garden of the world. We wriggled our little ways past the barricades. And we got going busily the minute we met each other on the formation of another busy squalid sin, another blasphemy ready in its turn to get busy."

She bent over me. I was nearly asleep. She laid her

head wearily on my coverlet. Almost dreaming, I heard her sad voice continuing like a lullaby of resigned woe.

"I am tired of my own voice in my head. Mine is essentially a tiresome and puerile internal voice and anyway I get enough of it as I reel out pages of my diaries.

"Anyway, again of course through Ooldra-Highpriest-Smahil, I have lost my little friend.

"My little friend in there, whom we were presently to meet and get to see and get to know properly, my little apeling who would have had eyes like raisins and fresh raw courage like Ung-g, is butchered and gone. I lost my first sick blossom in Atlan, I don't think he would have been a good big brother to you, Seka. In other words, Seka, sweet pearl, your brother Nal should never have been born and is now gone.

"But Ung-g's baby—how I miss that friend we are never now to know."

I woke because the fountain in the corner was gurgling. It had gone wrong again. There was always trouble with the fountains in these higher-up rooms, because it was difficult for plumbing to be piped so high.

It made a sound like an ill-tempered pig in the room. I lay and listened. I thought of the lynx in the cage in the great hall. I sat up carefully.

My mother had fallen asleep, still in her gauzy trousers, her hand on her subjective bosom, her possibly orgasmic little bosom, her head on my bed. She didn't look comfortable, but I thought it better she get her sleep.

I eased out of the bed. I was lovely and warm now, like toast. I went out past the sleeping sentry, his head on the door-post and his poor neck ricked, he'd wake in the morning more uncomfortable than my mother.

I padded down the stairs, past the torches mostly now no more than fume and glow. I could hear growling in the dark over there, so I knew the lynx was still awake too. I heard the creak and give of its flexible woven cage as now and then the beast with a bound, still grimly, hurled itself against it.

The lynx was un-attended. Its guards must have gone to a far corner, near one of the banked fires, to play dice. It was crouched in one corner when I went to it. It ignored me, gazing out through me, tired of people's tricks. Its endless eyes glared. I came up close and stood on tiptoe to look at its pixie-ears and great controlled paws which lately its mate had known, now still rippling but alone, the lynx lustrous in the lateness. I saw the catch on its cage-door. It was only fastened with withy too. It was an ordinary all-purpose cage, bought from local peasants after the hunt had gone so well. I thought, I could un-do that badly gilded catch.

My mother was quite right. I was a very silly little girl.

The lynx did not at first realize that the cage door had changed its nature. It had been a closed cage. Now it was an opened cage. But the lynx presently caught some thought from me as I stared breathlessly. (I had run a tiny bit away, as you do after you have lit the beginning of an explosion. But I still kept my eyes and my beckoning concentration on the lynx. Come on, lynx, come on, lynx.)

With a catlike cautious movement the lynx nosed the door open.

Its glorious muscles humped at its shoulders as it prepared to slink through the smallest possible space it now guessed might be available. It had no need to snake itself. The space was everything it needed, and in one moment when my heart lurched with terror and pride out bounded the beautiful animal, rather awkwardly, as a cat moves when it is unsure. It circled, the light of its eye momentarily passing across me as I stood still and breathless in my nightie in the shadow. It heard a sound of the men by the fires, as they raised voices in a dispute over their dice. It didn't want to go anywhere near men-sound. It started to slink away, its movements sure again now, across the shadow and the window-glass-reflections like glorious colored sores reflected on to its strong clear no-color fur, across the veined marble, arteried marble, varicose marble, marble like old blue cheese, places of man it should get fast away from altogether.

Some men were coming in from outside, from the direction of the barracks. They were energetically spitting, to clear their heads in the warmth.

The lynx swerved to avoid them, lowering its belly to the floor.

But the men caught the glimpse of movement. "Hey, what's this? Over there. Puss is out."

A man ran forward with a stave held shortened for grappling in his hand. He dodged around in front of the lynx and blocked its way to the outdoors. The lynx' patience was tried too far. It sprang.

The man staggered and slipped on the cold marble. The lynx was on him. It raised its head from his throat, which yawned not red but black in the no-light, and it snarled threateningly.

The men paused watchfully. One of them was Beautiful, the young Riverine noble. He saw me standing a yard or two behind the lynx by the open cage. "Was it you?" he asked me. "You let him out?"

I wondered what to do.

Beautiful went white around his mouth. "You see?" he said across the lynx to me. "You see what he's done. One of my men. He's killed one of my men."

But you get men for your birthdays, I thought, remembering what I'd heard.

It's not me who should be blamed if your birthday presents get themselves killed.

"Now what do we do?" asked another man. "It's not in a good mood."

The lynx, having tasted freedom and tasting frustration, had begun an ugly sound in its throat. It moved its head as the men moved, keeping all three of them under effortless surveillance as they circled it. Its great eyes stood out almost oblong scratched by tiny stars of malicious pupil.

Suddenly it sprang again. It aimed for the man now beside Beautiful. For one instant, as he attempted to stand his ground, he and the lynx were stretched chest to gold breast like dancing partners. Then somebody else had come in and now strode to us and had seized the lynx by its throat as it drew back its snarling mask to claim this man too. No time to reach for a dagger. The lynx went berserk. It was several hundredweight (if I have my weights right) of fury. It twisted, each turn enough to knock a man flying. But the newcomer had both hands around the throat, holding that mask of fury at arms' length, and imperceptibly the snarling turned hoarse, became a sob of balked hate, and still the feral muscles bunched and contracted and the man swayed with the beast and never relaxed his grip, only tightened it, tightened. And with a final glare of hate, the beast collapsed, the life ebbed from it, its golden glory slumped. The blue scaled hands at last un-clenched from the fur throat. I stared at my father. His face was calm. It had stayed calm, matter-of-fact as he throttled the lynx.

My father looked at me.

Beautiful pointed at me. "Responsible," he said. "Responsible for the death of my man."

Beautiful, his lip between his teeth, came over to lift me roughly by my armpits and yoik me over to my father. But I brought my heel back against his shin, the edge of my heel, and though it can't have hurt him he was so offended that he let me go.

I was already pulling up a gob of saliva into my mouth, ready to spit in the elegant way I saw the soldiers do it—one day I'd be as good at it.

"What is going on here? May I ask, General, what has occurred?" My grandmother's voice. "Has there been trouble here?" With her train and her slaves and her usual nucleus of entourage, my grandmother briskly returned from whatever business she had had at dawn on the brink of another army's departure. Stripping off her leather gloves, she tapped me with one. "Seka, why are you down here?"

"Seka?" my father repeated. "Is this Seka?"

He hesitated, as no lynx-throttler is expected to hesitate. The little bubbles were still fizzing in Beautiful's codpiece. They could even be heard, so quiet it was before the blue dark General repeated, "My daughter Seka?"

I spat at the floor before him.

He stared at me thoughtfully.

"Your dear little daughter Seka, General, yes." My grandmother stood beaming a moment. "Unfortunately I can't introduce you properly, she has no voice. An intelligent child of course, make no mistake of that. A sweet-natured child." To a guard: "Get those bodies out of here." Adding thoughtfully to Beautiful: "Oh dear me, one of these bodies is yours, isn't it? I recognize your delightful uniform. Would you like him for burial yourself?"

Beautiful bowed. Yes, that would be procedure.

"Come, General, let us be seated here, there's a bench over here. So, what do you think of your daughter? Seka, stand here in front of your father. This is your father, dear. He is a mighty soldier." A choker of animals, I thought.

I took my opportunity, and very seriously indeed stared into the General's face. I was amazed and heartened to

meet just as serious and quite as questioning a gaze. Very
few grown-ups ever looked carefully at my face. His skin
was blue, more definitely blue than mine, the color of the
underside of storm-cloud. It was patterned all over with
tiny scales like a snake's. My skin is not like that. He is
not human. He is descended from the big ab-human tribes
of the far North. What a godsend, what propaganda for
the war-artists of the powers opposing.

"How fortuitous to meet you, Seka, like this," the General said. "This is most unexpected." He had a voice with
a timbre to it, a distinctive dark voice, at times like suede,
other times with a harsh edge. "So you are to some extent
zoologically inclined?" The quirk at the corner of his
mouth deepened. I wanted to correct him and say anti-
zoological. (When I wanted to speak, it was usually to
say something people would probably have called impertinent.) "How is your mother?" he asked me.

In that man's eyes, always *consideration*. Always an
un-hurried, waiting, considering, un-moved summing-up.

I sat down un-invited, the way I had seen other small
girls do. As soon as I had plumped myself down on the
bench between them, I felt myself lifted again, by very
firm courteous hands with much strength behind them,
but I could tell they were not used to children, he hadn't
expected me to be quite so small or so light, and I was
held against him just a moment as he placed the spare
folds of his big scarlet campaigning cloak to make the
bench more comfortable for me. Then I sat on that, and
soon I leaned back on the bench as though I were drowsy.
I had expected my grandmother to start talking about his
imminent departure with his armies, but instead she
started off with: "The plumbing in the palace is terrible
at the moment. It has all gone wrong again."

When I woke, it was late morning. I had fallen asleep
to the talk of drains and hydraulics my grandmother
seemed to think more important than the military/political
secrets I had really hoped to glean. I was still on the
bench. The servants and sentries and slaves were moving
round preparing the hot water and breakfasts to take up
to the apartments. I must get up to my mother. I had not
been disturbed after falling asleep; I found that I was still
half-wrapped in a piece of red cloak with an edge severed
by sharp blade; rather than move me, he had cut off the
corner of his cloak. There was sunlight sneaking here and

there and around into its accustomed pools. A cook passed me on his way to and from the kitchens, and smiled because I was awake, and gave me a big handful of groundnuts off the salver he was carrying.

The palace very soon smelt. Cija hated blocked fountain-rooms and walked around trying not to breathe. "Come, Cija," the Dictatress said. "I think we might venture out for a little air. I'll order a plain carriage brought to a side-exit and we can take Seka out for a quiet airing."

"This is as motherly as I've known you," Cija said.

"So it isn't maternal of me to want to see you reunited with your wedded lord?"

"It would be kinder to want me divorced."

"We need venture out only a half-mile or so, a nice route in the afternoon."

But it was a two-mile tangle in itself to leave the City, through the mandala of streets and · canals. "It is all so run-down," Cija unnecessarily pointed out. "It really isn't the great trading capital you think it. It's shabby and nearly at a standstill."

"You know nothing about economics, Cija."

It was hot, but there was a gray foggy cloud over everything. The City wives passed in their tinsel, their threadbare cheap shawls sewn with bits of broken bottle, their heads and necks laden with glitter, necklaces of farthings with holes punched through them one after the other and string threaded through, worn proudly— "money going completely spare."

Without all that tarnish and glitter and tinsel, most of our street-people's clothes would have looked very dismal indeed under our strong sun. But this afternoon, in this gray light, everyone's tinsel looked tawdry and squalid. You can't win. Poverty, misery and above all shoddiness look sad in either light.

Our driver cracked his whip at our carriage-mules, and up they kicked their iron heels. He was heavily armed under his plain tunic, and so were the footmen, one beside him, one at our running-board to clear beggars from our path.

The Dictatress, mindful of her love of her commons, threw them copper, and some silver coins. Soldiers came up, laughing, shoving aside a crippled child carrying a baby with rickets.

"Alms? A hand-out? Alms! Alms for our hands!"

The footman tried to keep them at a distance. One jabbed the footman's stomach up under his belt with a vicious threatening spear-butt. The footman, conscious of the good horn-handled dagger under his tunic, looked inquiry at us. My grandmother tossed them coins. "These louts should be rolling under my beggars' bunions," she growled.

"Bunions," Cija murmured, "are a rich man's disability. Your beggars have no shoes to cause bunions. Most hardly seem to wear feet."

"This City is a bloody barracks." The Dictatress was irritated.

". . . what a busy Canal. Is this a tidal Canal?"

"The tides are getting so strong. The astronomers say in their picturesque way that the tides are tugging like mules with bits between their teeth. It's not natural for solar tides," my grandmother said, frowning at the unnatural water. "Even out in the sea, there are monstrous tidal waves, rearing and going about in circles."

"I've seen them from the tower."

"It's more like the old eons of lunar rule."

"Is there truth in the old tales of a circle called the Moon in the sky?"

The Dictatress snorted. "Is there truth in the 'vague rumor' that you and I, Cija, and our grandmothers are cousins of the Gods? The Moon was a fat round star which used to accompany us, warming herself at our light and our speed and our general emotional flashpoints."

"Was she with us all the time?"

"She joined us every night, just about supper-time, as the lonely night closed down over the wastes of the universe. She always stayed right till dawn. But she was too eager altogether. She came closer and closer. We were too brilliant for her. Like a shy silver moth, she dashed herself to death in our flame, silly moon, caught in our orbit. Of course, she was not really a moth. She was millions of boulders of metal, sizzling after their fall upwards through space. The holocaust of that cataclysm, which sank Mu the mother continent at the umbilicus of the world, would be equalled only by the cataclysm with which we would greet the capture of another Moon."

"A new Moon is coyly tip-toeing perilously into our orbit?"

"That's an astronomer's guess, not mine, Cija. Our Cousins have said nothing to me of it."

Cija said she'd heard something about the moon was the sky's shield. But the cataclysm-dragon fought the sky and the shield was lost.

The Dictatress grunted.

This was moving into the realm of fantasy. She didn't approve of that.

I climbed out of the carriage, since it had come to rest while my mother and grandmother admired the view over canal to nearer-mountains.

"Watch where you walk, child," the Dictatress called to me. "Don't walk where that gentleman just spat."

So I didn't wander far, and looked at the stalls under awning in the little market but soon returned. I sat on the warm carriage-step. It was gritty and I knew the back of my dress would get grubby. The footman smiled at me.

"*All* the theories, doubtless, are correct," the Dictatress was saying broad-mindedly.

"Even Zerd's incredulity and skepticism?"

"Of course."

The footman reached and ruffled my hair. His fingers were heavy, not like ladies' fingers when they do that. He drew his hand back when the Dictatress glanced our way.

Cija said: "You know, Mother, I've often thought of that birth-prophecy."

"Birth-prophecy?" The Dictatress seemed never to have heard of such nonsense.

"You know, how you were all so worried that I would bring disaster to my land by my love," said my mother. "The prophecy made at my birth. And so you kept me locked up in the tower so I wouldn't meet a man. And then I did meet Zerd. And he was the first man I'd ever met. So I'd never been, you know, immunized against the dangers of love. And suddenly I was exposed to the infection of Zerd. And I married him. And I brought my land under stranger-rule."

"Not so bad, really," said the Dictatress. "Though of course you mustn't be surprised when married men do not make the best husbands."

I found the footman's voice was rumbling into my ears. "What balls it is," he said, "superstition and personali-

ties. It seems you and your mother make up almost
a whole person between you. She so emotional· and impulsive, you the watchful judging but not very influential
observer. She's emotion. You're spirit. I seen your eyes. I
seen your face."

When I looked up at him, he was staring ahead into the
sun-death. But his voice continued to reach me, a grumbling monotone.

"Who's the third part, then?" he asked the side light
ahead of us. "The *body?* Who's that?"

"But in fact Atlan is my real land," Cija was saying to
my grandmother. "Atlan is *my* land, Mother, whether you
believe me or not, the land I care about. And the Dragon
may not in fact, as it has turned out, have harmed your
land. But he is harming Atlan."

"Because he's threatening to change it a little? Con-
querors always change." The Dictatress was very tolerant
about Zerd as conqueror today.

"Let's take a walk along here by the Grand Canal," the
Dictatress added.

"Is it safe?" Cija inquired.

For answer, with a reassuring gesture, the Dictatress
threw off her carriage rug, and stood there revealed—not
in her usual gold, scarlet and purple, military decorations
and slave-borne train—but incognito in green, orange
and pink stripes.

"We can melt into the crowd," she murmured.

We followed her from stall to stall, where with the best
will in the world nothing was buyable. My mother bought
some cotton that had already been un-picked from the
dress it must have been used in, then wound back on a
piece of old bone. This was slightly more useless and
pathetic than tunics and slippers which really were hateful
with hanging threads and bad embroidery, but she said
she felt they less deserved buying. The Dictatress regarded
with satisfaction a shouting vendor, selling news-sheets
with big headlines lampooning the Dictatress's government: he sold these for giant sums to furtive customers.
The Dictatress actually financed the paper, and the editor
belonged to her. "Whatever propaganda I wish to put
out," she said, "is all the better disguised as rebellious
anti-establishment, to trick those energetic beings already
rebelliously disposed."

And she presently announced: "We'll cross the Canal to the Delightful Side."

The Delightful Side was the other side, the side with shrubby secondary-growth trees. So we waited for the slow ferry-barge. The Dictatress didn't allow boats to speed on her canals—the strong wake after a while can break down the banks.

But when we trooped down with the rest of the queue, and the man told us the fare, the Dictatress, although incognito, stared angrily. "Come on, Mother," Cija said, reaching in her purse. The Dictatress made my mother put her purse away. She whispered loudly: "I won't pay it. What a large sum. Of course I won't pay to cross the Canal. I *own* the Canal."

As our carriages thrummed homewards through dusk, we rounded a bend to find boat after boat being loaded by Zerd's Northerners. "They're moving off tonight!" my mother cried in a quick voice. And her look changed as she saw two officers stride toward her.

"Your dear husband."

From the pleasure in my grandmother's voice, I guessed at once that my grandmother had known he would be here at this hour.

Zerd and his chief commander Clor looked up in such a gentle and courteous way as our carriage rolled to a halt by the stone lading-bay.

A footman came to take my mother's elbow, to assist her alight. She got in a flurry. She had tried to leave the carriage by the other door, farthest from the Dragon; Zerd, strolling forward and bowing very deep indeed to my mother, had already reached for me and lifted me down. I went willingly into his arms, leaving her. I saw the swing of his great cloak in the dusk. One corner had been shorn, sliced cleanly across the corner.

I think Cija had realized Zerd was here just that little tiny minute before she quite saw him. Her eyes were hardly focused. She looked like new-born kittens I have seen, finding the sight of the world too much a strain. Her fists started clenching tight in her skirt.

"Madam." Another bow from my father. "Do you join us?" He carried me up by his shoulder.

Ushered by the Dictatress, Cija followed willy-nilly. She looked dazed, she looked ill. She also looked more alive than she had looked for weeks.

The busy soldiery were quieter and more efficient than the stiff shrieking chains of my grandmother's laders. There were little gates in the walls reaching up and again up by the Canal, and ladders bolted on the walls, and platforms, on which heavy-boned men in grease and leather aprons hauled and yelled generally as they loaded and un-laded great hooks swinging goods by rope or chain. But tonight this Canal area was given over to the massed Northern exit.

"I am leaving tonight, Cija," Zerd said.

"I am touched if you wished to bid me goodbye," she said, and so she thought she was.

"You are coming with me."

This man had not seen my mother since before she took ship from Atlan for this mainland and this Dictatress's City, since before he had issued a warrant for her arrest on charges—any charges, I think, so that she could be brought to him again. But charges that had turned out to be those of witchcraft, an idea of Sedili's.

His face as he looked a little to one side of her, and above her, not directly at her, was very closed. He looked alert and alive certainly, and though he was always so, with all the presence of a warrior, I seem to remember that at this immovable moment, the evening air itself around Zerd was alive—with menace? With a relentless intensity, with waiting, with control held in abeyance, with all his usual sense of his not being part of this effete, deteriorated, specialized human race which he must watch and study at every new turn, in order to maintain his mastery of its pathetic resources. Only Cija, I was to note later, aroused this particular intensity of watchfulness from Zerd. He would never quite understand her. She did not work by the clockwork of the humans he had stripped of their pretensions. He did not know which way Cija would jump, nor if she would jump at all.

She stared into his face and Zerd's face stared back past hers. The dying light glowed at the edge of each of his scales.

"Madness," she said. "On what trail? On what trail do you propose to position me? I have no clothes, nothing packed as baggage. Even you, my lord, must remember a woman and child must travel with some household."

The starlight touched the dull gleam of Zerd's armlet as he gestured briefly to a cordon of coaches even now ar-

riving beyond the lader-bay. The armlet gleamed duller
than the scales on those muscles. Starlight lay lively in one
half of the sky where the sun pulsed to death. I saw roofs
strapped high with baggage, and at the coach windows the
peering faces of my mother's most trusted ladies—they
looked quite bewildered too, and pretty relieved when they
saw us.

"We follow Progdin north," Zerd stated. "Progdin is
making a way roughly, through your mother's lands and
her border-allies', and he goes north to the King who remains my potent enemy and masses his forces even now
against me."

"Thank the Gods. A potent enemy left to you."

My grandmother made an embarrassed movement.
Zerd lifted a brow. But I could see he enjoyed Cija saying
this or anything. He too looked more alert than when I'd
seen him that other time, and since people look quite involved anyway when throttling large animals, that's saying
something.

"Would you thrive, my lord," Cija murmured, "where
you had no enemies to tilt?"

"He must be removed before I can rule in peace."

My mother paused. But where she would have concili-
ated Smahil, she was her full self to Zerd. She invited
him to laugh at the fact he carefully explained to her a
reason for setting out to manufacture war. Cija said:
"Rule in peace. Peace is hateful to you. You march to lay
waste another countryside, under the guise of preventing
Progdin from doing so; you will burn the homesteads
Progdin does not burn, loot another culture and slaughter
other children. I wish you fair weathers and a good campaign. Un-harness my coaches."

"Our daughter cannot speak," he said. "How is this?" I
felt his electric energy as he held me. But my mother said,
"Come to me, Seka," and I left him for her arms.

When she walked up the Palace stairs to our apartments, she still carried me, holding me close.

He strode up from the great hall at this moment, having
arrived by swift bird before us. He mounted the steps beside us, just as though he always escorted us upstairs.

My mother, not knowing what expression to wear, wore
none whatsoever.

But my mother looked very thoughtfully at the Dictatress as we passed her. Not as though she looked at treachery—for she expected these Zerd-aiding tactics from her mother. And the Dictatress looked back equally thoughtful; she knew better than to appeal to Cija emotionally or maternally.

Presently, as we moved up the stairs, we noticed how there was water dripping off each. Water was moving substantially *down* the steps toward us from above.

On the first landing, where Sedili's apartments were now being emptied of the last furbelows, people were working wearing their trousers tucked high. Cija found her slippers water-logged. She bent to take them off and had to put me down a moment. Zerd picked me up in a helpful way.

More stairs, and now the water hurried toward us like rills, like scenic waterfalls. We were splashing. A spout from between the balustrades of a higher landing wet Cija's hair. Tendrils sprang around her frown. She said nothing. Zerd, attentive and absolutely unexceptionable, accompanied us respecting her silence. He said nothing too.

I could see him looking around, his eyes pausing with some wonder on the amount of sheer clutter in our rooms. I think he could never get used to the number of *objects* presented to royalty by people and nations, the toys which are all that rich acquaintances can think of to give the monarch who has everything. Since nothing can ever be chucked out for fear of giving offense, all must remain on view and it is this that prevents royal apartments from ever looking well-designed.

We traversed eddying drain-holes. My mother's trailing sodden hem was tugged into one. "Allow me," Zerd said, after he'd observed her struggle with it. He unplugged her hem and knotted it a bit for her. "How kind," she said.

The Marshal who had proposed a toast to my mother at the feast came past. He was carried on the back of a burly slave. "How are you, how are you, my dear," he greeted my mother affectionately. He was carried off along a corridor like a swirling tributary of the main hall.

We reached our apartments. The sentry, standing ankle-deep in water, saluted smartly. Our apartments were denuded, for most of our things had been packed into the baggage-carriages while we were out of the way in the town.

The Dictatress, wearing large boots, tramped in from another archway. She was followed by two slaves carrying our well-splashed bedding. "I suppose you want everything unpacked for you placed back just exactly where it was before?" she said cheerfully to my mother.

"There seems to be rather a lot of water to set it in," my mother remarked. We could all see how wretched the flooding had made her. The rooms were her refuge, she must to herself have been calling them *home*. The Dictatress could see, I could see, and Zerd with a steady measuring glance could see, that my mother was irritated beyond endurance by this metamorphosis of hearth and home. She was about to make a dash for it, anywhere dry, even the open air of war.

"You're right, yes," the Dictatress agreed. "Fountains on this floor seem blocked a bit. They'll be fine in a matter of weeks. I've brought in a very able contractor to see to them—he *should* be here the day after tomorrow. But you know plumbers."

My mother walked very quickly, small quick steps, to our coach. My grandmother said to Zerd, as he quickly followed my mother: "*I'll* give Seka to her, General. If you, General, say anything at all to her, she will cling to the steps, she will fly back to her rooms, in spite of our so handily blocked plumbing."

The Dictatress added as he handed me over: "But she knows that she is homeless and placeless *here* from this day if she stay. She has always been an obedient daughter."

Clor was there to help my mother up into our coach. He said gruffly: "It should be a fair journey, Empress. You will see the Spring over the marches."

Behind, I heard Zerd laugh at my grandmother and her pride in the way Cija had been made obedient. "Obedient daughter she essayed to be," he said, "when you sent her to kill me."

PART TWO

1

The Norther Hills

I THOUGHT EARLIER that there is not a right angle in the old palace. Of course, in fact, there is not a right angle in my grandmother's entire land.

The only Northward exit from the outer rim-wall of our City seemed to be this really bad tunnel, Progdin's poor battalions having negotiated this. Now us with our entire army.

The Dictatress had never bothered to keep the tunnel in repair. "All right," my mother peered at it in wonder, "not repairing it makes it theoretically difficult of enemy approach. And saves on sentry posts along it. Which I am sure," she added, "is false economy."

But in the last ten years, new melting snows had formed a huge new waterfall. Pouring down the side of the steep mountain through which the tunnel is bored, the new waterfall had split the tunnel. And cracked it. The army thus found itself in the position of having to ford this ghastly slanting cliff, half in and half out of the unsteadily poised basalt tunnel, right through a powerful fall and at a precipitous angle. "More water," my mother sighed. "Is this fate?" Carriages, baggage animals, and cursing foot-soldiers with weapons jogging against the rocks, the water, each other. Actually, mounted men seemed better off. Those birds really must be a branch of the mountain-goat family. Would that be possible? So neat and sure of claw, their rudimentary wings up and their heads forward barking as though the gouts of heavy spouting water were enemies to be got out of the way once and for all. But at night time! The torch flares and the swift flashing water created delusions of each other, and that was really a disgusting drop below us.

"Couldn't we have gone another route?" my mother inquired.

"Would have taken a month or two," one of our ladies was able to reply, having asked an officer in the 6th Blues some geographical questions already.

I don't know our losses, some anyway.

The Dictatress had indeed known the fall was there.

At the very last instant, she'd said something about it, as we rejoined our trundling coaches by boat; by then you could have walked along the Canal itself—treading from boat to boat, all loaded with soldiers as the water-side barracks disgorged. I was too small, we found, to reach ashore so someone made me step on to a shield and I was raised to shore standing up on that shield. I'd heard my grandmother say to Zerd: "By the way, I probably forgot to inform you, a new fall at the end of the tunnel—I'm sure you will negotiate it," she gave him a mother-in-lawish pat on his shoulder.

He thanked her for her timely information, already brought to him in previous weeks by scouts who, being Ael's mountain banditry, had patched up the tunnel there as usefully as possible in the time at their disposal.

My mother had sworn once she would never ride another Northlands bird. But obviously the thought of being in a carriage, with our poor ladies, in that black tunnel was just too claustrophobic.

My mother got the captain to find her a bird—he was the captain from my grandmother's household who was accompanying us personally with twenty men as our own bodyguard.

He came back with one he later told us he'd bought from a leader in the Blues who breeds them. It was a nice bird, a pinkish color, eager and nervy but responsive and with beautiful manners, a young bird with constant darting head movements as it explored its surroundings.

Clor's batman came up to us with a sack of wine and a man carrying good glasses.

"To Spring on the marches," everyone said, and I was allowed to have some wine too.

"And may there be disaffection in the Other's ranks," the Dictatress added, squinting at the glass Clor traveled with, which was better than hers at the palace. A fine rain came down and diluted the wine.

There was a heady cheer from behind us. A boat had moored from which Sedili, in her elegant uniform as commander of her own troops, stepped to join the great lines moving off. A long-tailed pet-bird teetered on her plumed cap, bending now and then to peck grain which she lovingly placed between her lips. She saluted her enthusiastic men, she waved.

The Dictatress embraced my mother. Not a hug, a proper dictatressly embrace.

"Anyway," she said bracingly into her ear. "Husbands are very useful. No wife should be without one."

"No dictatress, it seems, should be without a daughter."

"On your sexual triumphs, Cija, may depend your country's stability."

She gave me a goodbye present, a bracelet with bells on it, and a very nice doll with bells on it too. "Now," she said, "your mother shouldn't ever lose you. If she calls you, answer with your bells."

"There is a beggar, Mother, in your entrance courtyard," my mother said. "He has no hands and likes to crouch under the magnolia in the west corner. I have been having him fed. Perhaps you could carry on feeding him, daily?"

"Perhaps you'd like me to get some *hands* made for him too?"

"And, Mother, that red lynx the hunters brought in. What about letting it go? You could charge me."

"Your daughter has already seen to that," the Dictatress said. My mother looked inquiring. "I think that you do owe someone a debt—you owe a new man to the young Riverine." Then my grandmother added practically, "Anything of yours which I might sell to raise the price, I gave you in the first place. Cija, you are so muddle-headed."

They coldly kissed. My mother kneed her bird. It turned for the tunnel and the ragged flare-lights. "I must suck your conscience some time," someone suggested a dark murmur, a lazy caress. "Your conscience must be how sweet, how fresh?"

In all the to-and-fro, one sidelong glance was enough for her to acknowledge the pleasantry. She rode off toward

her carriages making for the tunnel, and the red cloak to
a corner of cavalry. But when she reached for me, and I
was passed on to her saddle through the nearby carriage
window, scraping my tummy, I noticed her hands—scored
and swollen. I touched one. "Oh, yes," she said, absent-
mindedly. "They're all right, Seka, I've just been digging
my nails in them all evening."

"Surely her little highness will be safer and happier in
the carriage where she can sleep now, Goddess?" our captain remarked. He was young, with an un-married look
about him. But it was from now on his duty to think do-
mestically, as is the fate of military men who get promoted
in some noble household.

"I prefer her with me through this tunnel," my mother
said. "I don't trust a carriage by those loose stones. Why
are we performing this remarkable trick at night, anyway?"

"Because Progdin won't be expecting us to do anything
half so reckless. He must by now be on a height com-
manding both the norther marches and the exit of this
tunnel. We have orders to douse all torches as we emerge,
and keep on marching swiftly, so that by morning when
he sights us we should be much nearer than might have
seemed likely."

And off, and through the tunnel, and fording that monster waterfall on the slant above the night halfway up a
mountain and half-in half-out of a black basalt death-trap
for which the architect and engineers originally responsible were, one hopes, suitably rapped by whichever strong-
minded lady was dictating at the time.

Foliage clustered along the roof-rims and inner walls.
From this the small birds we had roused dashed at the
marching troops. Daft gallant cheeping beaks, like
darning-needles with which to defend their territory, their
nests, against the strange new winding tramping human
serpent which tramped and wound throughout the tunnel.
The little wings whizzed everywhere in our columns, and
the little birds were falling then to be squashed, having
stunned themselves in flight against a shield or breastplate.
I think they *couldn't* get out of a soldier's way. Not if it
meant they'd have to fly into a neighbor-bird's territory;
their invisible barriers were too strong for the litte victims.

My mother must have returned with me to the carriage,
for it was in the carriage that I woke. Sun poured through

the blinds. My mother and our favorite lady, who was to
share our own carriage on the journey, were asleep on the
broad mounds of pillows. Their hands had wandered
protectively into their petticoats in the night, and a sudden
knee glowed like a pearl lit by white lace and whiter sun.

We were still travelling at a real pace. Beasts and men
must have been all well rested the previous day. This was
a light carriage, as carriages go, and nicely slung, good suspension. It wasn't one of the Dictatress's monsters, built
like four-poster beds. This was one of Zerd's long-distance
models. I was much too warm now. I pushed off the fur
travelling-rug, embroidered with ribbons, which had been
tucked around me. I crawled across my mother's spread
legs to the window.

Lifting a corner of blind, I saw that in spite of the sun
to which we were exposed up on this height, dew was still
in evidence. Down there, the jungle in the valley, simmer-
ing in the valley, still in shadow but already parboiling in
its own humidity, and in the piss of many large animals,
like a cauldron constantly on the bubble as stock was always added. Blues, greens and almost purples of giant tree
crowns to which sloths must be hanging. Up here, boots,
claws, axles. But also boulders, ferns, grassblades, the
coarse cobbled webs of the rapacious mountain spiders.

It did occur to me that if we were going to live in tents
and carriages now, there would be no more doors for me
to swing with myself on. Carriage doors are not thick
enough, I thought, sizing them judiciously, to be satisfying
between one's gripping legs. I would have to find something else to do.

My mother woke, pushing something off her face, which
may have been the humid scents.

She smiled at me and at the lady, and they stretched
and yawned and tucked away their glowing thighs and
asked each other (and me) how had we all slept. I
crawled to my mother's shoulder and cuddled into her nice
neck. She drew up the blind and asked if our lady
minded the window open, and she smiled again. At the
sunlight shafting into our carriage, at the insects which
zithered in too. She smiled at the little rains of the jungle.
It rained pretty constantly here through the sun, but only
for a moment or two at a time, and then the big orchids'
rain-pushed heads sprang up once more, as purple as
pain. It did just occur to me that my mother was giving a

very mediocre imitation of someone who loathed with all her fine soul the very thought of being on campaign.

Our bodyguard captain rode up beside our window and said how had we slept and would we like a piece of honeycomb one of the men had found for the little princess?

"Are we to eat on the hoof?" the lady inquired. "Shall I get out and go to ask—?"

"If I know anything of this General's travelling methods," my mother said, "we'll eat, sleep and bathe while moving."

"We don't mean to engage with Progdin as soon as we catch him up, do we?" the lady faltered.

"We won't," Cija yawned again, "catch him up."

We were told to bivouac in fact, though a bit farther on where the mountain folded into itself like just a big hill. There was more air, since we were temporarily above the jungle again, and yet we were mainly behind cover, not yet visible I would suppose to the marches beyond, and surrounded by good vantage for our own scouts. My grandmother didn't know a good cook from a bad, but accidentally had provided us with a good one. Even the breakfast eggs had little flowers painted on the shells. Isn't that one sure way to define a good cook?

It was while everyone was packing to start off again that a baggage-cart slid down the hill above us. It was charging down on a narrow twist of mountainy road where the foot-regiment found itself with nowhere much else to make for except over the precipice. Involuntarily we waited for the bang.

"Oh, stop, you idiot cart," Cija muttered, interrupted in her conversation.

She was audible, as at that precise moment the runaway cart locked itself on a root of twisted bent hill-tree. Men rushed to get it clear, which before would have been impossible unless they fancied getting hurled before it.

We climbed higher throughout the day. It was thinner, crisp sun now. At evening, some men came up and helped our guard setting up our tents (no fires was the order.) My mother went to thank the men. I think she half-expected them to be men she knew from a previous campaign, and was surprised to find they were Sedili's. She looked a bit suspicious. But one of our bodyguard showed her a stout tent-pole we had been given as a present. It was better than our own rather decorative things.

"That's the gratitude in the case, madam," said one of the men, drawing a line with his spear in the earth and stepping over it with his fellows to look across it at us. "All on our side. After all, madam, it's all over camp by now how you halted that cart. Your men have told us how it's a Goddess you are in your own land. It's to you we owe the fact we're not lying broken down that gully."

Cija's eyes changed, and she looked over and exchanged glances with our own captain.

"For all I know, my Cousin really did stop the cart. It's the kind of thing he'd think a good idea. It certainly wasn't me," she disclaimed later to the guard captain. "I am not even psychic. And my little bits of schoolgirl magic—well, I honestly can't even remember the stuff my nurse Ooldra used to drum into me—the kindergarten abracadabra, basic mantras and so on."

"Still, that's good for us too," he smiled, meaning his own men. They were very keen on their image of guarding an undisputed national goddess, being as they were such a little pocket of my grandmother's men among all these Northerners.

By the end of the following breakfast a small deputation had arrived asking Cija to fix up a corporal's broken thumb.

Cija explained in a precise, modest kind of way how this was not possible.

"How do you think," she said, "the medical men would like that? By the time I'd expended my nervous energy (it takes plenty of energy to do these bits and pieces) I'd have none left with which to protect myself against the doctors. I mustn't seem to set myself up in competition to anyone else. I am only a hostage, really, you know."

They laughed uncertainly at the bit about what it was worth expending energy on or not.

"Not a hostage, madam," one of Sedili's men looked around at the others and then took the liberty of correcting my mother, "so much as a figurehead."

"How do you mean?" Cija asked. "No, please go on, we are the last people to know this about ourselves."

He explained how she was a visible guarantee of good faith to the lands of the Dictatress and her allies through which we must travel. Cija was the Dictatress's daughter, she was a member of the local divine family, and if Zerd's army carried her with honor, if she was as it were

giving Zerd's campaign her blessing, then all should be
well. I slipped away up on the hill where a little man in
uniform was perched drawing.

I came up beside him gradually, to give him plenty of
warning of my approach in case he was doing something
very private or in case I put him off his stroke. He smiled
at me most kindly and held his sketching-board at an
angle so I could see it. It was a mass of small lines and big
loops, with rhomboids of shading here and there.

"The dear General," he said, "noted as we left the
City that the maps of this area have never been, apparently, topographically correct. I am rectifying that error.
But stippling does make one's wrist ache, until I feel the
sound of all those little dots falling on the paper will be
heard by the fierce hill-tribes for miles around. Would
you like a cold hen-liver? It's been cooked, I just didn't
have time to finish my plateful."

I took it with proper gratitude.

He smiled at me again as I sat down by him to eat.

"Luckily this is just a topographical map. Thanks be
to the gods, I don't have to put in all the bits I call political. I shall have to do that on another map, but not yet.
Fill in where we think all the enemies are, and though it's
only a question of us thinking where they may be, I
mustn't get it wrong. We shall soon be moving into very
unexpurgated farm-land around here, you see. The farmers around here, who ship their agricultural produce in
hollowed-out tree trunks down the streams and rivers and
into the City's canals, they perch in villages like eagle-
eyries on the nearer crags. They are loyal to the Dictatress
of the City: but," he stippled very hard and with great
satisfaction, "antipathetic toward the dear General. What
a shame our presence must be broadcast."

He took my hand gently and the bells on my bracelet
tinkled.

"You are the Dictatress's little grand-daughter, aren't
you, dear. I have heard that you don't do much talking!"
He twinkled at me. "So I am sure that to make up for it
you do almost too much listening. I am talking on at you,
and I mustn't bore you."

I shook my head to show him I liked hearing him.

"I tell you what," he said. "Now I shall take you back
to your Mummy, because she must be a bit worried about
where you've got to. You show me where her tent is."

I never got used to people calling Cija "Mummy" on my behalf: I couldn't call her that.

I took him to where our tent was being packed up and loaded and Cija indeed looking around for me because she was about to mount.

"Seka, into the carriage!" she cried. She was riding today. "Where on earth have you been?" She saw the cartographer. "Thank you for bringing her back, sir." She recognized his uniform now as that of Zerd's own household.

"I have been giving your enchanting daughter," he bowed, "something of a geography lesson. I hope I did not cause anxiety."

"A geography lesson!" Cija echoed eagerly. "Then you know the layout of this area. You wouldn't have time to show it to me, I suppose?"

He arrived at our supper-fire that evening, with his untidy portfolio slipping from under his arm and nearly as big as himself. He let me mix some of his paints up for him, very thoroughly and carefully, while he told Cija about the farmer-tribes. "You saw those plants we passed this afternoon?" he said. "Like giant ditchweed, with a thick fluff all over its leaf on the underside? The peasants up here have to wear their cloaks lined with the fluff off the leaves. It can get very cold. They have to be fierce," he said, "just in order to keep warm."

Cija was in love with listening. Anyone could tell her anything, and she would sit enthralled. Perhaps she had never been able to pull enough stories out of her nurses.

She let me stay up late so that I could listen to Scridol too. We would sit there hunkered by the embers, maybe on our rug or, as the weather became colder, on neat low folding camp-stools, and I would watch the little can of birch-bark boiling over our fire for Scridol—this was what would turn into yellow dye for him. He got a more or less satisfactory "golden" from boiled onion peel too. While I watched the dye, our batman watched the other pot bubbling away with the hot milk or rum in it. "We mustn't get those two cans mixed up," he'd say. And Scridol would cry out in alarm: "No, I'd never be able to paint with rum."

He told me the things he could use for dye, and I'd keep an eye out on the day's march for the moss he could turn to crimson, or the berries and roots he'd char for ink. Then I'd hook one leg over the window-opening of our carriage as it jolted along, and hang on the running-board to pull leaves off a passing thicket, or I'd jump down and collect my goodies for Scridol and then follow along behind the carriage till there was an opportunity to catch it again. Our driver grew used to seeing my face appear from below his perch and sometimes up between his very boots.

"Mind you, the dear General is very generous," Scridol said. "If I need something precious just for paint, he'll offer it before I like to ask. Gold leaf he's given me to incorporate in paint simply because I expressed a fancy for a sunset one night and he said that was one thing I couldn't puzzle over getting wrong, doing sums with a set-square and rule. He commissioned the sunset from me, he said, instead of an engineering diagram I was due to do, and real gold paint helped there."

When I was too tired to "help" Scridol any more, but refusing to admit my eyes would like to close, I'd sit by my mother with my fingers hooked in her travelling cloak to keep myself upright as we listened to him. My mother had this special cloak into which not one stitch had been laid. It was completely plaited all of thick silk ribbons woven one above, one across, and one below the other, interspersed with thick bands of fur. There were two layers of this (so it was very insulating) so that one side was the lining of the other side. It was all pink with bands of blue one side, all blue with bands of purple on the other.

Presently, conversation would become desultory. It was always the stars that stopped play. One or other of my companions would look up at the sky, and fall into something of a reverie, talking slower and with longer pauses. The other would follow that gaze and falter on an adverb or a noun, and soon Scridol might say quietly: "The stars are swarming tonight," as though they were wasps.

I would be bundled into our tent, by Cija or our lady, and soon I was in my cool fresh linen nightie, washed that morning in a hill-stream and bleached dry throughout the day, spread out on a jogging saddle to catch the heat. I'd hear the dew fall on the tent. Through the flap I could smell the airs, from mountain and cooking-fires. I'd pull the rugs up round my face. I'd dream of things I thought would be useful, like being able to paint pictures that moved, or being able to stop a cart by telling it to. We'd be woken at dawn by the camp-noises all around, and in would peer the sky, blue as a little bird's first egg. My mother invariably crawled to the tent-flap to look out at the hills to be traversed that day with a strange gleeful sleep-walking expression. There might be a cheerful morning volcano belching jolly pink fire to greet us among the pastel mountains on the horizon. Scridol might turn up for breakfast, with a present for me, a stick of pointed charcoal for drawing, or a set of hinges for sticking collected things in collections, or some colored pins. I was getting a little store now of Army stationery.

One day my mother let Scridol see the maps she had taken from Atlan. "I've always kept them," she said, "because they're so old. But I can't understand them." Scridol looked at them with silent attention. "They're cold," he said in a moment. "They make my hands and face feel quite cold."

"Yes, I know," said my mother. "I think there's some kind of radiation in them. Is it in the parchment or in the inks? I don't like putting them next to clothes in my trunk in case they're dangerous in some way. But of course I couldn't be so wicked as to throw them away."

"It's an extremely complicated vast dyke-system on several levels," said Scridol, turning it this way and that. "It's a remarkably sophisticated method of presenting water-engineering. But this is definitely cold energy. For Gods' sakes don't throw them away. I tell you what, these are going to be immensely valuable to you or somebody else one day. Keep them close and one day you'll be able to bargain for anything you want with these."

He didn't suggest that he take charge of them, or hand them over to the present ruling interest of Atlan. "Well," my mother said, "they ought to be *for* something. They're not really beautiful antiques."

Scridol by now of course had gathered that there was no contact between the General and my mother. And he never behaved as though there might be. He never said— "But, of course, you'd know better than I" when he spoke of the General. And he never insinuated almost-questions into the conversation.

At the time obviously I accepted this as normal. Mothers on a campaign stayed near their tent and carriage and daughter. Surely they didn't expect more company than their daughter? And fathers ran the army from headquarters somewhere else.

Cija generally accepted as normal whatever happened, just the way I did. If it was happening, then it must be normal, was her non-philosophy. But she took to writing in the carriage in her fat diary, in her tiny spindly writing with its twiddly abbreviations and initials running riot.

Had she expected Zerd to invite her to the long tables in his own tents? (She'd have been eating with Sedili there.) Should he have acquainted her of the present policy of the campaign, since she was to be a figurehead on it? I am sure she was glad not to be at the long tables. She was not too happy with all that competition and the demanding mixture of balanced protocol and horseplay which went on at HQ, or at least she found that kind of atmosphere a strain unless she was winning hands down. She couldn't be expected to win with Sedili around, Sedili who thought you a coward if you weren't full of aggressive competition, and pressed home her advantage almost as a righteous duty to punish your "softness." Sedili was one of the commanders of the army, and it seemed at times that every man she commanded worshipped her. Cija was only a local goddess with twenty men as bodyguard. Obviously she was happier being domestic in fresh air, just riding along sight-seeing like a tourist with the march. But had Zerd thought any of this out, and if so, which bit? He was busy with the thousand rather time-consuming duties of a General on the move, but that meant nothing; he could always make time when he decided to, he could spin time out of the most appalling schedule. Sedili, her colonels, even her adoring foot-soldiers must be kept comfortable, self-satisfied and partisan. Whatever my father's motives, they would always be thought out practically. I read his palm once, years later, and it was days and nights before I could get his head-line out of my mind. It calmly, matter-of-factly dominated the heart, the mounts, the life . . .

When we glimpsed shaggy creatures in twilight on the move, Scridol squinted at them and remarked: "Look, over there, what are those?"

"Kine," my mother said. "Obviously wild—they are like fast-moving bramble-hedges, and look at those horns."

Not long after, we heard "Hai! Hai!" and several of

Ael's bandits, who were meant to be several companies away, came swerving and bounding through our lines, almost standing in the stirrups as they urged their chunky little horses, scattering our more placid beasts. "I saw a fat mother cow," shouted a lyrical country-loving bandit, "in the grasses with her little *veal* running beside her."

And as we settled to our evening meal that night, if you glanced over to the rise on which the bandits encamped, you could see them lighting camp fires with all the glee of pyromania—and it was veal you could smell.

The daily kine-hunt became a noisy feature, the cattle roaring and bellowing as they swept the air with their awful horns, and not every bandit escaped unscathed. Some were very scathed indeed. No one but the bandits were reckless enough to go near those horns and hoofs, but the bandits' hill-ponies with their traditional harness, bits in three pieces for better control as they swerved on the slopes, could dart in and retreat and dart in again like scorpions on the attack.

"When I saw those shaggy shapes among the grass at first in the dusk," said Scridol, "I thought they were apes."

"*Apes?*" my mother said, looking scornful, for she considered apes her own subject and no one else's.

"Why not?" Scridol said. "There must be some around, there were by the tunnel. Didn't you see them?"

"No, not at all."

"There were signs of them in the tunnel," Scridol said, "but they left it to make way for our passage, and could be seen in the dark sitting crouched in caves along the way outside and gazing on us."

"Poor, dispossessed beings," Cija said sadly. "No place for them, the left-over apes."

Before the week was out, we were left in no doubt as to whether the kine were considered left-overs or not.

I was down at the river just after dawn, gathering reeds and lichens for Scridol. There was definite dawn wind these mornings, and it came scudding and racing hard before the sun, driven over the ridges before the relentless sun and flattening the grass of the broad hills like silvering sea or smoke. The reeds bent and sighed this way or that, pushing in each other's way, and hissing like a whole marshful of snakes. I saw the deputation from the hill-farmers coming over the hill with the wind. Their best weapons, newly polished for their visit, shone in the new day's sun. They looked very, very dignified indeed as they stalked to us in measured strides, and such dignity speaks of danger.

"You, small cunt-type-child, lead us to the Dragon's tent," one said through his moustaches. So I nodded obediently.

The long dark-blue weather-washed tent was pitched on the slope of a low hill on whose ridges perched Ael's bandits on the look-out. As soon as they saw the farmers they started going "Hai! Hai!" and gathering together and running into and around the tent.

The farmers were ushered in, not just under the big outside awning but into the main tent, because that made them beholden for hospitality under the Dragon's roof. I'd brought my lichens and my egg and toast along with me, and they wobbled with emotion as I sneaked in with the farmers, past the guards, slaves, ghirza-players, strutting staff-officers and such assorted HQ rabble. The farmers looked for the General and his commanders with blank expressions, before they lowered their gaze and saw that the floor was covered with out-spread crackling detailed-scale maps, on which their hosts were kneeling. Clor, who had been perusing a rift valley as though it were dispatches, crawled over a mountain range on his knees, scrambled to his feet and invited the newcomers in. Zerd and his officers one by one rose politely to their feet.

There were ceremonious greetings and introductions and expressions of much mutual respect.

The General's conference table stretched the length of his inner tent, but the chairs and stools had all been removed. The table was used for wine flagons, ale flagons, and Scridol's inks. Scridol was squatted on his heels beside Zerd's two secretaries. There was a camp-stool for him, but this he used as a shelf on which to sort and set out unsteady sheaves of paper that looked as though a crazy pigeon with inky feet had tottered over them.

Scridol started when he saw me, and made his eyebrows go up and down in a sort of frantic code. I went over and sat on a cushion beside him and he mouthed at me: "It seems that the breakfast-break may be protracted today."

Cup-boys came running to pour drinks for the farmers.

"Are these your bandits?" one of the farmer-lords indicated Clor and Isad and Eng, Zerd's chiefs of staff.

"Would you ask Ael if he might come in?" Zerd politely asked a nearby captain.

Ael instantly appeared, almost before the words were out of Zerd's mouth. Ael sauntered very casually and insolently and placidly into the tent, closely surrounded by a group of his men, flicking the corners of their cloaks, pointing their toes and looking down their noses.

"Your bandits have been stealing our cattle," the farmer-lord informed Zerd.

Ael now looked at the lord. "I have better things to do, my friend, than to scratch fleas with you," he remarked to the lord. "Are you or are you not our allies? Do we starve as we traverse your land, pursuing an enemy as much yours as ours? Do we see you stirring from your agricultural activities to deal with the enemy, or do we have to do all, on your behalf as on our own? Do we waste time talking here over a few sides of beef, like market-girls, or do we use time to pursue Progdin? Did Progdin live off your land as he passed through, or did he not?"

"He stole and slaughtered many cattle," the farmer-lord said. "But he is our enemy."

"Do you give less to your friend than to your enemy?" Ael countered.

The farmer-lord looked at Zerd. "We ask indemnity," he said, un-moved by Ael's rhetoric.

Beautiful at this moment hurtled into the tent.

"Six of my men have just been killed down at the river," he said, "by these scum."

The farmer-lords put their hands on their weapons at once. "Your men attacked first," they said. This was a matter of form, before they knew any more about the incident at all.

Since, it emerged, six of their men also had been killed (no one had done any proper counting yet, but six was a useful specific-sounding unit meaning "several") they demanded recompense.

Beautiful looked around, now resigning himself to involved parley, lifted his chin and said:

"My chair, my lords, is nowhere to be seen."

Clor and Isad looked at Zerd, and Zerd looked bored and reminded the Riverine how at a previous conference the minutes had consisted mostly of a debate as to the precedence of seating at conference.

"We demand indemnity from your bandits for our cattle," said the farmer-lord, addressing Zerd, Clor, Isad and Eng. "And for our men from your riverers."

The Riverine lord, his beautiful face twisted, vaulted the table, adding with his trailing dagger to its interestng surface texture.

"Are the Northern Rivers," he bitterly inquired, "being asked to flow up-hill?"

"The Northern Rivers," Zerd drawled, "are entirely out of course. Would these Rivers pay us the signal courtesy of taking part in our present war?"

Beautiful bowed very stiffly.

A big black-bearded lord now arrived at the tent-entrance and began explaining his business with the General in a louder than necessary voice. As it was obviously intended that he should, Zerd noted this arrival of the most pig-like (in my opinion) of the allies marching with him. The Black Pig had brought to the Dragon's strength a force of more than four thousand men under arms. While committed totally to the war against the Northern King, and with nowhere else to turn if he failed Zerd too unless he wished for virtual exile, still he made it obvious that he might remove his presence if circumstances demanded. "Admit him," Zerd signalled, since the Pig always felt it was a loss of face if he had to wait for an appointment.

The message was relayed to the entrance, where the Pig strode in bristling. He hung around uncertainly once in, not sure whether to approach Zerd or wait as current business was settled. His shoulders were hulking and his neck went straight up the back of his head. In order to take in the gist of any situation he had to turn his head and shoulders from side to side and back again, and this gave him an uneasy awkward and looming presence. Zerd saluted him and so the Pig came over and shuffled from foot to foot beside Zerd.

Zerd rather flatteringly introduced him to the farmer-tribes, who in their turn seemed somewhat impressed.

"A trifling matter," the Pig said now that he'd got his way in. "But if it could be settled before we move off today. My coffers are at present still in the City. They are to follow shortly, when the Dictatress has converted them to the grain and goods I have personally purchased for the good of the Army."

Zerd motioned to his secretary to sign a chit for the

Pig, and didn't wait to hear how much the Pig wanted, and what it was for, and why it was so desperately needed now.

The assembled lords bowed to each other, each neck stiffer than the others. A strange coagulation now resulted in the company as not one lord would continue his supplication in front of the others, or stride out first, each hanging back to show the General a superior modesty.

Scridol beside me bent his head and regarded the stippling I'd been helping with. "Oh, well done," he said softly. "Spot on."

Zerd looked across at me. I wondered whether to tremble. He spoke to someone who spoke to a cup-boy who brought a slightly alcoholic honey drink across to me. I looked with delight across at my father to thank him, but he was now speaking patiently and obviously mendaciously to the farmer-lords.

I looked around at the assembled lords, only a sample of those with which Zerd had to march in the palm of his hand. Each invaluable in terms of men and arms, and altogether such a collection of high glances, darkling brows, bull necks and even club thumbs.

I was to learn later that Zerd was in fact the only member ever to benefit from these early conferences. Not much was ever decided except what was, after all, to be of paramount importance—which voice spoke loudest or heaviest, which blustered and which carried weight. Under the guise of administrational and topographical policies, the points of precedence were hammered into shape by mailed gloves. Zerd calmly watched the demeanor infighting of each lord, saying to his commanders, "He guards his back," or *"He* lets his men do the work."

"Aren't you the lord of Fourthcrag?" Beautiful asked one of the farmers, who acknowledged the fact.

"Well, now that I come to think of it," said Beautiful, "when I was on my way down here to offer my poor assets to the lady Sedili, should she be good enough to accept such an offer, it was Fourthcrag which swooped upon me and slaughtered and pillaged to the tune of—" and he named the sum to the last farthing. "In view," he added, "of our present priorities, I could consider waiving my right to blood but if I did claim it," he continued more darkly, "each of my men would be worth, at the accurate average, 1 3/4 tribesmen."

The Pig cleared his throat.

"Since we are on the subject," he said humbly, "I had been meaning to bring this up when it seemed most convenient, but I must insist that the Riverine lord make me a present of three hundred men to compensate for injuries received on my part in street brawls in the City."

The farmers were not to be blinded with science. They had come to talk cattle-mathematics, and these they had at the tips of their fingers and indeed their spears.

There was another disturbance at the tent-entrance, and a pale young woman came hurrying in. She saw Scridol before she saw Zerd, and hastened to me. "Oh, Scridol," she said, in a hushed voice because she knew there was a conference going on, "thank the dear Gods. I was told you were here and the absolute brat with you." She took my hand. Perhaps the back of her neck felt as though it were being stared at. She turned to see the General was looking at her. She bowed deeply to him and to the assembled company.

"My lords, my lords," she gracefully winningly said. "Many and deep apologies. I have been searching for my small daughter, and she has made her way here when you are all at important business."

The farmer-lords had by now recognized the uniform of our household captain who had accompanied her.

They looked from the captain to my mother to me, and back to Zerd, and then as one they fell upon their right knees. "Goddess," they said, a low multiple hum, "Goddess," as they touched their foreheads to the maps on the ground.

The scene in the tent had stilled. A small bird strayed in. Its thin squealing chatter and the bass, baritone hum "Goddess" were the only sounds. I saw Zerd look at my mother, who looks beautiful when she is worshipped: she is conditioned to respond to acts of worship, and when worshipped she stands taller and becomes vivid, becoming a current I suppose to pass the worship on and up to the proper world-channels, to her heavenly counterparts, as all earthly divinities are taught to do. It was an awe-inspiring and ludicrous moment. The farmer-lords, their wild dangerous clamor still echoing, as they bent each before her, very unpremeditated and savage and graceful. The shock and pique on the faces of Sedili's faction, a rueful dead-end—knowing that this was one honor Sedili would never find accorded to her: not many young women ever receive such a demonstration as of ancient, awesome highly useful right.

The lord of Forthcrag then went over to my mother and took her hem and kissed it reverently, and he spoke not to her but the captain with her. "Would the Goddess accept from me," he inquired, "a small and unworthy tribute, a little herd of kine, just a little personal herd of my own and my dear wife's, in token of our joy at the recent birth of our son? A small celebration with the Goddess in our territory."

He turned to the assembled company. "Let all debts be forgiven," he said, "in recognition of the gracious presence of the Goddess."

While everyone was drinking with fitting forgiving grace, Zerd wandered over to myself and Scridol. "That's very good mapping going on here," he told me. "But do you write yet? It would seem that your letters might be of value to you. Scridol, would you take her on as a pupil? She would need several hours a day, I am sure, while your assistant could of course take over some of your other arduous duties."

"Sire," Scridol addressed him by the Atlantean title, "it would be my treasured joy and my privilege to do all. I have no assistant."

"Well, you shall have now," Zerd said, and signed to a secretary to see to it.

What to do with all this steak?

The little herd of Fourthcrag was a milling lowing horned mass of beef. Cija of course turned it over to the quartermaster, but he insisted that she should be properly paid, and so she had money in hand which she said would come in useful for the paying of our bodyguard when that got into arrears. Since any bodyguard is prepared to count their pay as permanently in arrears, this resolution made her very popular in our corner of camp.

The Dictatress, otherwise, was not particularly kindly thought of in the Army. Before the outset of campaign, there had been a new issue of arms, and a lot of grumbling from men not used to the new designs—"it had only put money," they said, "in the pockets of the Dictatress's ironsmiths."

The newer designs were all based on the idea of lightness and flexibility, for speed and ease of carrying on long marches; an innovation for Northern weaponry. They had always laughed at the heavy body armor of, for instance, the troops of the far South. But they were unhappy with these new spears, so light that cast once or twice their points were twisted, and so incidentally of no use to the enemy in whose ranks they ended up. Our Northerners had the feeling they must cosset their spears now like babies, for fear of spoiling them before their time, and it made them nervy.

Their sulkiness extended to the new jerkins, lined with light quilting, into which they swore the seamstresses of the Dictatress's City had stitched poisonous fleas. But soon, with the chill of the hills increasing, the jerkins were found to be an improvement and were forgiven.

I was more often at conferences now, because Scridol would be in the middle of a lesson with me when suddenly he remembered there was something on at HQ which he really wasn't supposed to miss. He would haul me along with him, my legs aching, and sit me down by him to finish writing out my alphabet or, quite soon, my exercise—while he listened to the discussions of a change of route, and made notes. I often felt that poor Scridol was struggling on his own against quite literally the rest of the world—against the mountains, their foot-hills, the rivers, their sources and tributaries, the plains and peninsulas. Not only that, Eng would turn to him and say: "Scridol told us this was friendly territory," and I would pray that enemy tribes hadn't moved in meantime; I was sure Scridol would be blamed for their mobility. I often thought he would be wiser to pretend everything was enemy territory, so he couldn't be blamed if it was. I realized too that though I couldn't say so to Scridol when I got important ideas like that, that one day I would be able to write messages to people I wanted to tell particular things to, so I hurried on very carefully with my lessons.

Neither Scridol nor my mother had any real idea of time, so often I would still be copying out my letters by candle-light, or scurrying through the camp after Scridol on his way to a late call at the big tent, while he sorted through his mapping notes and at the same time muttered to me, "Now don't forget, I don't want to see those fat undisciplined loops on your glutinants, they climb all over each other like lizards on a stone if you have more than one in the same word."

Almost invariably, the conference went on for longer than we expected, and half-way through Scridol might send me home with a captain or a cup-boy, whoever was handy, or he would find time to take me himself; he always carried a screwdriver for adjustments to box-lids and frames, and this he would take out and heft meaningfully when walking through the camp at night with me. He didn't trust soldiers at all.

I liked to look at the lords' faces, on the whole, more than the faces of Sedili's ladies when they were around.

There were lords and officers with marvelous encrusted waistcoats, all precious buttons. Short cloaks, slung from one shoulder. I liked Zerd's big red cloak too. I found it a sort of landmark, to show me where he was even in a crowd or in the distance, and I liked its shorn corner from when he had let me sleep on it and not wanted to disturb me.

I used vaguely to gaze at one of Sedili's women, idly trying to work out why sometimes the socket of her eye was edged with blue and yellow. I realize now, of course, this was the woman currently spending time with Ael.

Sedili's women were giggly and elocutionary, most of them, chosen for their sheer femininity. They were supposed to set the mood of her entourage, just as her potted plants and her pink dagger were remarking: "All right, I'm a career woman, and shall be distressed if you don't treat me like any of the officers—unless you *actually* treat me like one of the officers." Her women were picked for a quality of cozy cunning, a way of presenting a united front to the enemy—the men and officers of our entire Army—no matter how divided among themselves.

In spite of their style—they felt themselves to be on a stage constantly—Sedili's women were hard put to it to maintain decorative standards. Most housewives in most towns or homesteads could present a better appearance without thinking about it. Sedili's ladies had in common a fetching feverish eye, but bits were always falling off them. They were slaves, not exactly to their lovers but to the pace which they all set each other. One woman, I remember, lost a nipple—bitten off one night by her bandit of the week. Ravage-repairing was more grim a fight for the ladies than an entire campaign might be for our soldiers.

Still, the war was already grim for Scridol. He had got three maps mixed up with each other and he would

have to check with Sedili herself the whereabouts of a
city we were making for sooner or later, which would
welcome and replenish us because it actually belonged
to Sedili. It was Ilxtrith, her dower city, which under
the terms of an old will had become hers on the date of
her marriage, and which remained hers because her father
had told Zerd, newly married to the Princess, that he was
not to claim it.

But she had not visited Ilxtrith for years, and she
found it nearly impossible to place it.

When Scidol again and again said: "No, that can't
be right," Sedili became unamused. She injected her
bored face with another candied orchid (unlike her reg-
ularly distraught ladies, she never ran to fat) and simultaneously yawned cheroot smoke into Scridol's intent
concentrating eyes: "Then since I am obviously misinformed as to the locality of my own city, perhaps you
had better sort out your own problems. Are you paid
for map-making, or are you not?"

This wasn't really fair, since I knew Scridol hadn't
actually been *paid* for a long time.

Scridol struggled on with the Ilxtrith thing, talking to
a brigade-major of Sedili's who tried to be helpful but
knew less than she did, and I got bored copying out my
lessons and stared at the candle-flame on the dish on the
camp-stool beside me. The candle, which had begun to
sweat, now trembled, now died. Now had I killed it? I
had indeed thought: "That candle ought to *gutter* now"
in a vehement spiteful kind of voice inside my own
head. I tried the opposite. I tried to relight the candle
by order. It wouldn't light. I lit it with the flame from
another, and then told it to go out. It did, at once. I was
very pleased with my new game, although I had discovered it is easier to be destructive than creative. I
worked out what at the time I thought must be the explanation. I thought, "My mind has kept my speech
bottled up for so long, with such clarity and yet so form-
less and frustrated, that my thoughts and demands have
got to come out *somehow*." Now I am not so sure. That
would be simply elementalism, I know, the frustrated
pops and bangs of strong emotionalism. Too self-indulgent
to be disciplined, that kind of intensity has to reveal itself
in small savagely motivated tricks.

Or perhaps I began like that, and within years learned

how to direct and hone and with-hold and send it far, and at what strength; it became, at any rate, my present measured skill and not simply a blind phenomenon.

"With two more days' steady march, we should arrive," Scridol said, "on the borders of this—this desert—" and he placed his finger tentatively, as though afraid of burning his finger in scalding sands and winds, on a large blank area on his map.

"How about two days' erratic unstable march?" Zerd inquired.

Something firmly descended on my shoulder, a hand with quite a weight and a grip to it. I twisted round and looked up into a pale bland face, seemingly more scars than actual features, except for the two dark blue eyes running as fast and deep and cold as Northern tides.

"Here, Seka, and plait my hair," commanded the bandit Ael.

I stared at him a moment, as I always inclined to stare when someone ordered me to do something and I was surprised; I couldn't ask for confirmation, I couldn't ask had my ears tricked me, so I left a pause in which he and I could hear the echo of his request. He didn't say "Oh, well, never mind after all, I realize it's an odd command;" so then I clambered up on to the small dais behind us, and crouched by his shoulder, and took in my hands his mane of soft light hair which flew up at me and stayed on my fingers, for it was alive with electricity.

Without changing the flow of his conversation with Zerd and Scridol, he passed up over his shoulder to me a broad bone comb with wide spaced hook-ended teeth.

I divided Ael's fair mane into strands of three, and started to plait them awfully neat. The smoothed strands smelt of smoke and leather and something else—rather like dog-fur. I'm a cat-person myself.

Zerd glanced at the tableau we made, his bandit and, unexpectedly, his child. When he saw that I had caught his brief glance, he smiled.

"And now," Zerd said, "it is time my daughter was taken back to her mother."

He stood and held down a hand for me. I was amazed when I realized that he was going to take me himself back to our tent.

Sedili put down her embroidery and stubbed out her cheroot.

Ael asked might Zerd wish for company on a fresh fine night. Zerd's mouth quirked. Ael beckoned one of his bandits, and as we left he was speaking to this warrior sweetly: "My love, my syphilitic sweetheart, do thus and thus—"

Zerd swung me up on to his saddle outside the huge tent, and mounted behind me.

Between the regimental fires, sentries, tents, pallets. Men still grilling and charcoaling meat which had been soaked on march in the ale and onions in their canteens —to be eaten accompanied by high-caliber sunsets. Sun had left by now. Up there, nebula spawning its new stars. I always thought of the constellation of the Dragon as my father. I knew that Dragons and great war-leaders were born under the sign of Capricorn, the hooves which climb and climb again only to stay on their allotted undeviate course, all four hooves on the cardinal earth, but bound for the heights of it. The stars stang the sky up there, and I was uneasy on the General's saddle. I had seen the faces around us as we mounted. Scridol's startled eyes; Ael's watchful impassivity, which showed that something was afoot; Sedili's terrible face.

Past the 9th's pickets, and so to the baggage lines. Down a hollow of silky smoky grass. My mother at the tent opening.

Her hand flew to her breast, as she saw us, as though to protect it.

Zerd rode to her and he looked at her, down at her from the saddle.

This big ab-human had wanted my mother with a steady, patient, determined cold fever (which to her seemed intrusion) ever since he first saw her. He still wanted her, I by now could see it and she uneasily fascinated as she was could not, with every hourly twitch of his testicles. But he is a waiter. He is a placer of priorities. He could still not believe that a small madwoman was of abiding priority to him.

She hesitated, her eyes almost completely blank, so great was her effort to hide her agitation. Then she reached up to take me from the giant mount. Zerd took her hand before she touched me. He gravely held it and he bent low so that he could place it to his mouth and he licked her hand, gazing at her under his straight brows.

I thought my mother had stopped breathing.

She stood, sensuously paralyzed, a full moment and then snatched away her raped hand and covered it with the other as though wiping it cleaner or hiding its shame.

In this way, she made it impossible to take me after all.

Zerd dismounted, swinging me down in the crook of his arm—my head seemed about to pass the stars, to descend to the grass, till I was righted and set down on my feet. Zerd brushed me down a bit, as though delivering quality goods door to door. He said of me, "She is useful in my tent, she can groom Ael's head, but she must sleep or she will be unable to shave him in the morning." I nodded to him, he nodded to me, I kissed my mother and she suddenly clung to me and as suddenly, as though she were afraid she might contaminate me, she let me go and kissed me very delicately and said: "Sleep, little pearl." I crawled into my sleeping-rugs in the dark inner tent and I gazed through the canvas-slit and in our outer tent the stars were blacked out a moment as they entered and then her face was limned again. My mother and Zerd stood, stared at each other. I could hear the bird moving outside. I saw the gray silk on my mother's breast moving to the volcanic silence of her heart. Cija's ladylike dressing-gown was knotted too tight for him to undo. Cija looked sadly at him, divided from him by her careful garments. Zerd didn't laugh. He gazed somberly at her. He bent his dark head to the knot, and tore it apart with his teeth. It hung ripped and shredded.

Later in the night there were sounds outside which, since no one else paid them any apparent attention, I too ignored, feeling secure. There were grunts on the slope of our hollow, and the controlled stamping of feet, the sort of stamping men make when locked one with another. There was heavy panting. And a long gurgling. Then the bitter parting curse, already familiar to me for I had heard many men murdered, of the winner as he wends his way still hating.

Still later, Cija came to bed.

I woke to glimpse her as she crawled across me to her own rugs. The whites of her eyes could have been washed in silver. The arches of her feet were nowhere near the ground. She entered her holy bed as though its sheets, too, had been washed in silver. I had no need to pretend to be asleep—needn't fear she'd have suspected or investigated me.

In the morning two men were lying knifed to death on the slope of grass by our tent. They wore Sedili's uniform. There was a lot of blood mucky on the grass around them.

Someone from their company arrived later with a cart to take responsibility for them.

Cija ate an abstracted breakfast. Presently she rode in search of Zerd. I was with Scridol by now in the big tent and I heard her talking with Zerd, amongst the usual morning bustle as HQ made ready for marching. "Zerd," she said very urgently, and I heard her words, "it is impolitic . . ."

"It would be less politic," Zerd said lazily, "if—" and something about "still in your Mother's lands and her allies' lands."

"There will be reprisals," she said. "Ael's bandits will be 'punished.' Anyone could see Sedili's men were lying there—anyone could see those were bandit slashes and stabs. Those were vicious deaths."

"More vicious," and Zerd laughed, "if they had not died."

She paused then. "Ael sent his men beside you last night," she said in a thoughtful frightened way, "because he knew Sedili would also send men, spies to watch if you stayed with me."

Zerd shrugged, and fed her with meat from his duckling bone. "Ael merely seized his excuse to amuse his men at Sedili's expense. He knows there is no need to kill Sedili's spies. He simply *likes* to kill her spies."

"No need?" Cija cried, though still in her urgent hushed voice. "They might have assassinated me, on Sedili's orders, after you had left me. They may do so tonight, or on the march today."

"They might have done so yesterday, or last week," Zerd reassured her, kissing the meat into her mouth, "if I had not had a cordon of my guards around you since the first five minutes of our march."

She sat and chewed while her eyes narrowed. "So," she said, swallowing. "You have chosen the right time for us? When it has become obvious to Sedili's armies that I am necessary to our safe conduct through these lands?"

"You are more or less useful," he agreed, picking over the bone.

"Then what is it you are telling Sedili by your public acknowledgement of me? That she must be careful? That she must not feel too necessary?"

"Come, Cija," he said mildly, amused, "can a night of affection, very precious to me and I hope not regretted by you, maybe occur for its own sake?"

She rode stiffly that day. For Ael's sake; for Sedili's sake, she was obviously quite sure the night of affection had been. Her eyes throughout any conversation followed involuntarily any flash of red. She stared during conversation in directions which I noted always revealed, in some vista, some red-cloaked back, until generally it turned around and wasn't him. That night he came again to us and stayed till morning. As Scridol arrived at our breakfast fire, his eyes widened on the General emerging from our tent, his black shirt open and the scales on the wide bas-relief chest shining dully. Ael and a half-dozen bandits arrived too on their ponies. "Shall we breakfast in the bright air?" Ael greeted Zerd. Ael bowed to Cija, and smiled very cheerfully. He held out a hand to me. "Good morning, little one. Are there boiled eggs and hot biscuits?"

Our cook bustled, feeling very important. He was very glad to be away with us, he assured Scridol who asked quietly if it didn't seem like too many guests this morning. "The only use the great dear Dictatress really found for a cook," he told Scridol, "was to nip down to the kitchen on the death of a favorite adviser (political of course) and order the cooks to prepare strong household brine in which to pickle him awhile so he'd be around for speech day to ensure votes." He looked at my mother, pretty sure she'd laugh; she had shown herself very understanding and domestic on our household campaign. Now she was talking with her hand held intellectually to her chin. I knew as her nostrils dilated that she kept her hand there as a comfort during this overwhelming social breakfast, so that she could smell her fingers (they still smelt of him.)

Clor arrived from an unexpected direction. He imparted a distinct impression of having not been to bed all night. Somehow, though, he had known where to find Zerd. Wine had been split all down his uniform, but it was a good vintage.

Isad arrived. He bowed very low to Cija.

"I brought my cook," he said to her in an aside. "I thought there might be rather many for breakfast. He has a boy with plates and knives."

The Pig appeared with several lieutenants over the brow of the slope. "I heard this was where morning conference was to be held," he said uncertainly.

And Beautiful erupted into the gathering, by now, of lords each in love with the sound of his own shout.

Beautiful stared around, showing the whites of his eyes as though at a scene of terrifying and savage licentiousness. He took his place, very much on the far edge of the lords' assembly, so far from the center of conference as to be a separate conference to himself.

Of Sedili there was no sign.

But there was a jostling among the soldiers on the hill. One of Sedili's ladies, a tall pale lady of proud and haughty mien, was making her way disdainfully through the ranks, accompanied only by a sergeant in Sedili's colors. She had chosen too thick and unaccustomed a crowd. She was grasped, pinched, and couldn't resist crying out "Ooh" through the clenched teeth of sheer delight.

Beautiful sprang to assist her, his hand on his Riverine dagger.

Now what happened? Oh, a very bad fight between Beautiful and one of the Pig's men. Isad sighed, and slouched over and pulled them apart from each other, and got smeared with their blood.

"Do we not perhaps need our own men?" Isad limpidly inquired of Beautiful as Beautiful glared at him.

The sky began to palpitate—like an adolescent heart.

"Rain," Isad remarked. "A storm, refreshing marching weather."

"You save your army, counting your second-rate souls, at the expense of Riverine honor," Beautiful panted at Isad.

Isad knelt expressionlessly on the ground and with his own personal dagger drew the sign of the river— wavy lines, a most naïf sign. On this he laid the blade and swore to offer one of his prisoners, next time he took any, to Beautiful's river-god if Beautiful would just leave our own men alone. Rain had begun bucketing upon us in dollops. Beautiful obviously thought this a

most proper omen. The little river-sign on which Isad
had generously sworn was now gurgling away from the
breakfast-ground, and Beautiful with a nod accepted
the vow.

We started packing up. Zerd helped Cija mount—she
wanted to ride her bird, she said it was warm pleasant
rain like a long dip in a valley pool. The rain stayed in
round drops upon the feathers before her. These birds'
plumage is watertight, full of oil, each giant fowl is a
giant loping umbrella for the smaller creatures of the
baggage-train, who fall back during heavy rain in order
to scurry along in shelter under the wings, the forward-
arching necks, the balancing harnessed tails. Kids, geese,
and the young of our giant hens themselves.

Yet being so big, and so much on their legs, they are
prone to arthritis. Wet weather doesn't help. "Are we
into a rainy region?" Cija asked Scridol as we fell into
our accustomed place on the march. She had taken me
on her lap and kept a fold of cloak over my head and
cuddling round my shoulders.

"No, indeed," said Isad passing us. "Tomorrow we
reach the desert. It will be a hot hard dry time, from then
on, across desert."

By next noon we sighted a great glimmering away off
beyond the cliffs. "Deserts shimmer like that, in the heat,"
everyone was telling everyone else knowledgeably. "It's
called mirage. It's most exotic."

Finally we arrived at the mirage and dipped our feet
in it unbelievingly.

"Well, well," the General said.

Scridol was called for and splashed miserably in the
desert.

"I think it's flooded," he said wretchedly. "It ought to
be a desert. I think it floods once every decade. This is
the time it floods."

People all kept looking at Scridol and Sedili tapped
her cheroot with a most savage superior glance.

Scridol neatly wrote WET SEASON and the year, over
the desert on his maps. We stayed here awhile, laying
siege as we seemed to be to the desert, and I got to know
the rats who presently swarmed in a friendly squeaking
fashion through our trenches. I didn't know where they'd

come from. I supposed they'd been waiting a long time for an army to arrive here.

My writing and reading lessons were coming on. Scridol took my education very seriously, mainly I think because his General now wished me to be educated. Most of my anatomy lessons had to be seized as and when a fight occurred. Scridol would rush me over, point out the dorsals and the adaptabilities of the solar plexus and so on as the men stripped to their ragged breeches, leather kilts, or whatever chic their regiment favored.

"See how that man," he indicated Ael's bandit, "girds his biceps before the fight? That's to keep them huge throughout the fight, he might as well paint something frightening on his forehead too," Scridol sniffed.

I had noted on my own account how men's nipples went stiff with excitement before a hard fight. Each man solemnly presented the other with a few coins. These were to be taken, in the event of either man's death, to be given to his widow in our baggage train. Then the grunting and stamping began and Scridol sighed. He did get terribly bored by all this education.

I still had some of my lunch with me and I started breaking it in rat-meal pieces and throwing it to one gratified animal. The lunch was then removed from my hand.

"Don't *feed* them," Ael said. In a really fed-up, well-this-is-the-end type of voice.

He had arrived to see how the fight went. He is always very possessive about his men, and sulks if they get killed.

He hunkered down on the trench-edge beside me. I glanced at him and he caught my eye and suddenly bared his teeth. I wondered was he snarling or smiling. Or, to him, were the two much the same gesture anyway . . . He doesn't deal in emotion. It's not Ael's currency.

And neither did I deal in emotion. If I, a speechless doll, expressed emotion it might lead to reaction from anyone around me, with which I wouldn't be able to deal.

Under the hubbub Ael's voice sounded beside me. A light blank tenor voice, which I realized spoke to me.

"My hair is tangled," it remarked; "un-plait it. As you put out the candle-flame the other night."

A pause before I realized what he meant. Then a

cold shiver went through me. He had noted me destroying the candle-flame by my act of will.

I felt all sorts of things—exposed and vulnerable, cheap and ashamed, as though I had publicly indulged in something remarkably private, and the *worst* possible observer would now connive jeeringly with me, whether I would or no, in "our" secret.

I was even now that much older and wiser than when I used to think it was nobody's business if I got a nice feeling swinging on a door; and now this was as if instead of stopping me, which was normal, one of my mother's women had come and encouraged me and swung with me.

I had one mulish, irritating defense.

I turned to him, looking no longer just blank but *very* blank, childish and uncomprehending.

It was the look that had made him kick me the day on the hot roof when he asked me the way someone had gone.

Having ascertained that his man apparently had the victory (since he had his opponent on the ground and appeared to be biting his nose off) Ael nodded to me. To follow him. He swung to his feet. And he strode off. I looked at Scridol, who nodded to me and could then be discerned, watchfully following us at a discreet distance through the camp.

Ael paused by the bandit picket-lines, where innumerable bandit-ponies were edging around, dancing a little with each other, being groomed by their affectionate grooms, who handled them with endless pride, even masturbating them when they were restless, which could prevent mares falling pregnant on campaign.

Ael whistled un-musically.

So from among the pony-flesh lolloped a very young, sturdy bird—he reached only to Ael's chest, so you could tell he was little more than fledged, even before you saw his fluffy baby feathers he was just starting to lose. He looked very tatty. All feathers, stuck out at angles, and stubs of infant feathers. This little bird shook itself, and off went another cloud of feathers. It looked with interest at me, as more suitable to its eye-level than most things walking around, and then solemnly pecked for my bell-bracelet, which it ate.

"See how gentle," Ael said. "It took that bracelet off your wrist without breaking the skin. Do you want it?"

I did want my bell-bracelet back, and I felt quite up-set. Then I realized he meant the bird, did I want the little bird?

"Try him," said Ael. He lifted me on to the little bird's back, and I tightened my knees because birds without harness are awful to stay on; Ael was so used to seeing bandit brats mounted on unsaddled ponies. "See," Ael announced as the bird twisted its head to peer at me, then barked a bit in distress at seeing me there on its very own back, "he likes you. You like him? He's yours. He's no good with us. He belonged with the fowl of my lieutenant Dlann, killed last week." Ael scowled.

He added, "Bird and horse don't stable together, don't rest in the same field, don't enjoy each other's smell." Like I don't enjoy dogs, I thought. "Both get nervous, and then mean," Ael told me. I realized he was bothering to inform me. "You have him, General's daughter."

Ael rode daily to inspect progress. Rafts, and shallow boats which were half-raft in fact, were about ready. The "desert" would soon be ours. Scridol and scouts had found us a good crossing-place—it started three miles up-country from where we were encamped. There was a town, visible from this spot, some way out on the water. "That town has covered the whole of its island," Ael narrowed his eyes to observe it. "It seems to have no wood or agriculture of its own, barely a vegetable garden. Yet the islanders haven't come out to the shore to gather whatever they need, not since we've been here."

"They've no piers either," said Ael's new lieutenant, riding with us, standing up in his deep shovel-shape stirrups and shading his eyes. "They must fish direct from their banks."

Our scouts had paddled out in coracles, and seen the islanders harvesting nourishing weed from the great floating masses out there in the waters. The islanders poled around it in narrow little craft, but would not let our coracles close enough even to "Halloo-oo" a carry-ing call across the gray currents. Either they poled swiftly away, or raised their boat-hooks threateningly. "Such shy fellows," Ael said. The town did, however, have the Dictatress's signs, pink and green octagons, fading on its towers and walls. We were still within the lands friendly to her.

"Their fields are presumably all under water," guessed the lieutenant. "It would be interesting to know how long the water stays for."

"Could be close on a year at a time," said Ael, "once the wet year arrives." The rain started again. He showed his teeth at it.

The rain drummed on the water, which remained peculiarly unlovable. It was gray and full of grit, being half-desert anyway. The rain also drummed on our hoods as we made our way over to a small bandit fire, smoking under an overhang. Ael, remembering I was on the saddle before him today, because he'd noted how learning to ride had made pure pain of my bottom, lifted me down as he simultaneously dismounted. We put the ponies under the overhang with the fire. We ourselves had to sit out under the rain a bit more—there wasn't enough room for us in the dry too. But when I was handed a shallow helmet, being passed around as a bowl full of wine for us each to drink of, Ael dropped into it a coin he had made red-hot in the fire. It hissed agreeably.

He motioned me to just sip (without saying anything; Ael was very good to be with in that way anyway, he used his brows instead of speaking out a question, or a jut of his chin as command, so that he was a communicator in my own "language").

His eyes demanded, did I find it too hot? When I half-smiled, he made his other people round the fire wait while I drank. It was a comfort in my throat and presently my head and ears and chest felt warmer too.

When I had gulped the wine, Ael picked out the gold coin and opened my mouth with fingers hardly gentler than Smahil's had once been, to place the coin hot and heavy on my tongue. As he continued serenading his men, I took the coin out of my mouth and stared at it. I had never had money before. Money that belongs to you has solid shine, I found. I'd always pitied rich people before, having to carry so much arithmetic around.

Returning to camp, we charged at a gallop at a trench. We reared up in a heart-stopping halt. Ael was utterly shocked; his dark-blue eyes were round like a surprised child's; Beautiful, like me the other day, was crouched by the trench feeding rats.

"Rats only *look* like a few rats," Ael announced. Ael's light tenor voice was squeaky with his sincerity.

"Rats are really always hordes. Rats send out spies. Any single rats you ever see are spies, sent out from the main horde. Rats will report back about good feeding—and they'll descend on us in a plague. You should kill, not feed, rat-spies."

Beautiful whistled, a bubbling whistle through a mouthful of saliva. Chirruping answered his whistle from every side, and more than a dozen large rats arrived to gambol in the trench before him.

"These are *river* rats," the Riverine countered Ael's natural-history lecture. "See their webbed feet," Beautiful added, as though this changed everything. He watched with a smile of admiration, as the rats darted off in a spreading efficient ripple of spines and tails. Waterfowl had been standing fishing in the shore-reeds. Now there was a snappy rattle of disgustingly healthy white rat-teeth. One bird, its delicate reed-like legs attacked, stumbled. Its feathers water-logged now, it couldn't flap away. There was no need in this case for its nearest rat to kill it quickly.

"See the skill and cunning of that foot-work," Beautiful continued to admire the sadistic rat.

Ael automatically remained to watch the kill. His eyes bulged a little, as they did when he focused attention.

He then kneed his pony, contempt returned to his face, he rode past Beautiful without acknowledgment.

"But note," he said to his lieutenant, "all this fish and fowl and rat. There is indeed river around, at the moment feeding this 'desert.' We have found no river joining this side of the water. Once we are across, let us embarrass this river by the closeness of our scrutiny. It is all too probably the hell-hole river."

"The river that flows to us past Ilxtrith?"

"Hell-piss," Ael nodded.

This was the first I knew that not all the army was looking forward to reaching Sedili's dower-city.

Ael, dismissing his lieutenant, undertook to visit another scout post and I was still with the bow, short sword and canteen slung on the back of his apology for a saddle. A saddle of lamb pressed under it slowly casseroled itself hour by hour in the pony's body-heat, and Ael's armory-cum-kitchen hung with good hitches in a leather thong so old, loyal and supple it was like a thinking serpent by now, always ready to take the stress where it was accustomed. Now I too was part of Ael's furniture. We were traversing a wide land of sedge, brown reeds hissing in the wind, big brown buzzing country flies everywhere, I thought I preferred them to town flies. Now and then I was splashed, the pony's hooves took water or marsh. I looked ahead, round Ael's back, and saw the long wavering horizon. I also saw Ael's hand playing about something sticking up in front of him, coming out from his leather-patched trousers which he had loosened as soon as he was alone. Now I'd noticed this, I preferred to watch it rather than the horizon or the birds and water-beetles which whirred up crroooking and whikketying from beneath the hooves. As the pony jogged, this splendid stubby strong warm-looking thing maintained its springy stand, and in fact at times grew, jerking perceptibly higher into the marsh-light as though feeding greedily on the open air. Presently little pearls appeared on it. Ael's fingers scarcely flicked it; he seemed busy, as I peered up at the arch of his jaw and eye, scanning the horizon. I very much wanted to reach to that fleshy inviting pillar, and help pull the little pearls out of its eye, but I kept my hand to myself with an effort because I didn't want Ael to think I was the sort of child who would play with a grown-up's prick: I didn't want him to disapprove of me.

The town on the island in the middle of the water waited till the army was in midstream, then attacked us. Suddenly the islanders whizzed up beside us in their narrow craft, harrying, wasp-like. We were stuck with our not very mobile water-transport. We had of course arranged larger craft in a line along our raft-bridge to mask the columns from currents and enemies. But we had expected neither, and were slow to react. The order was given to retreat, and we pulled our way back in to shore, closing in our hardly-opened mandibles.

The town was nervous, obviously. Well, we could understand that. We had sent signs to say we were only passing. But they had not allowed us near enough to explain, and perhaps they had misunderstood our gestures. We should have to realign even farther from them. We couldn't go too far, on the other hand, since in other places the water seemed sucking and treacherous.

We spent the afternoon burying our dead. Then we marched off ostentatiously. We camped that night out of sight and sound of the islanders, so they should get over their alarm. At dawn we started our crossing. But the town was there again, in front of us.

There it was, looming up in the first light. In the night it had rowed itself downstream keeping pace with our march.

Barely had we put out our first attempt at a pontoon, when once again, faster than ever, the town loosed its swarm of thin boats at us bounding and bouncing over the currents and whirlpools. Mean arrows showered stinging amongst us. Once again Zerd politely retreated.

The guess was that the town, by now seen to be a giant raft itself, was indeed friendly to the Dictatress. But it didn't accept her new alliance with Zerd, clinging to the older enmity against him.

It was still hardly day, and we were checkmated for the moment. My mother and I sat our birds in hushed expectancy. Beside us a dying man was holding his wound like a rose. And the stars dancing at the funeral . . .

But it was Beautiful who dealt with the floating town. He was summoned with his men to Zerd's long tent, and when they emerged he and his men went down into the water's edge and their keening bubbling whistling went out over the water. The town, which had crept nearer to observe us, visibly shuddered and rocked on its own wake.

This was not the welcome-whistle with which Beautiful had called the rats to picnic.

It was a rising falling damp nasty whistling. What it did in the town, apparently, was to madden the islanders' population of rats. It was a rutting call, a territorial-challenge call, a season-of-rats call, an all-the-rats-together call. What it should have done was turn the rats on us, since we were making the call. But we were not handy, and the townspeople were handy. While the townspeople were fending off the hordes, the plagues, to quote Ael, of crazed rippling spines and tails and teeth, we were crossing our desert at last.

* * *

Now we were rising again, into the higher norther hills, and the air was bright and dryer. It rained less, even arrows—although we were still in lands disenchanted by our presence.

My memories of my early childhood are mainly of movement. Jogging, fanning, maneuvering. Scouts spiraling out over a hill or re-appearing across a valley, such delicate dancing, so that a cat's cradle was woven around the valley, the hill, the enemy.

Then fires lighting up at night. Each fire making a cupboard of life in the dark, as during the pleasant evenings Beautiful's riverers sat recounting old genealogy; rubbing bacon-dripping on their nearest wagon-wheels to obviate next day's squeaking. Or the bandits wrestled, their hard soles levelly beating down on the earth at the same rate and rhythm till it too was hard. Peering from my tent-flap I could hear the crickets creaking like comfortable old nursery furniture (our canvas was pitched a little off from the men's pallets) and then still later I might wake to see the men stamp out each fire, the cupboard's walls collapse, the night stretch wide and wider.

And I remember the flavor of any particular night or day by the absence or presence of my mother. Sometimes she was there, noticing me constantly. Often she was gone.

At first my mother would hasten back to be with me when I woke, hurrying breathlessly in at dawn, leaving outside a knot of the bandits Zerd sent to accompany her. But I was *always* awake before she got to me.

Then he stopped her leaving him in the morning. Later on I would be taken to the big tent. Here she would greet me as she lay still in Zerd's bed under the red fur blanket embroidered with rubies. Usually he was up and running the army. But once I walked in and saw him still on her, and so clearly did I see the external spurs which he could manipulate beside his genitals actively caressing her, like the vestigial legs used by snakes to hold a mate during intercourse, that for some time I was convinced all men had these and I just hadn't been paying attention when I hadn't noted them on other men. For Cija, who needed more than penetration unless she were feeling incredibly trusting and passive, those spurs must have helped matters along. But Cija could manipulate Zerd too.

Sedili had officially lodged complaint about the morning conferences at which the commanders now arrived in time to share hot wine with my mother around Zerd's bed. Zerd's answer was plain. It was politic to be seen to be on decent connubial terms with his Empress (Cija) while still in the lands keen on our Dictatress.

"I have given Sedili my oath," he added as he tugged off a boot, "that she can kill you when we are well into the North at last."

"And you will let her?" Cija asked smoothly.

He turned to regard her in astonishment. The hinged panels of the scuffed decorated leather screen swung as I gazed past it.

His hands and tongue were all over favorite parts of her, his narrowed eyes still shocked with the grievousness of the grief he might have inflicted on her. "No," he said, "and no, little Cija. She has no sanction whatsoever to move until I say. Otherwise she will be court-martialled and executed, and that has been made clear to her and of course her men. I have only *promised* her my permission will be given once we are in the North. Only gradually, Cija, need she realize how indefinite, eternally indefinite, will be the date."

My manipulative mother was satisfied. Or she was as satisfied as she ever allowed herself to be.

Yet she knew Zerd too well, and she thought she knew life too well, to trust even the next five moments of life.

Zerd threw me a doll which spun and leaped in the air and somersaulted to a jolly stop beside me. It had articulated chubby head, arms, legs and penis. It was carved wood dressed in straw. I knew he had picked it out of the charred beams and ashes in some village recently fired. He gravely watched me playing with this, listening critically to the necklace of bells he had got the harness-smith to make before I could receive it, then went on pulling off his other boot and said to Cija very softly, as if air around her ear-holes must be protected:

"Look at your breasts. Touch these underneaths. You are very plushy. It has occurred to me you might be pregnant?"

Cija just laughed. But in fact I think she was stabbed to the heart by questions from the camp-followers— "What do you look forward to, boy or little cunt, bless it?" "When is it due, bless it?" According to her diary at this time, she knew the fetus had not been removed properly in the barn, but she knew that when it was finally expelled it would of course be dead, an abortion carried overdue. I remember her pointing out to a woman talking about "the little one, bless it" that her own child's face needed a wipe, and Cija reached out to take it and clean it up with her own petticoat-hem: it was Cija's excuse to hold the other woman's baby.

Cija did these days look luminous. I remember thinking hungrily that if you bit into my mother anywhere, you'd get a mouthful of cream.

There was also a tension. This was a tension she entirely approved in this situation. She had never been with Zerd without this attendant tension, in which she made it clear that she disapproved of his war-makings. Thus, her sense of her own identity, and indeed of her own "integrity," was, also excitingly for her, much heightened by Zerd's presence.

She rode around with that face on her I now know as the face of a buggered twelve-year-old—a look of someone who has been *made* to come, again and again, not by their own volition particularly, not even by choice, a face pared down to youth and basics physically, a nude face with swollen eyelids. I don't mean that all twelve-year-olds particularly like being buggered—I didn't much when it eventually happened, and I was lucky, he was small and thoughtful too; I mean faces of those who have been repeatedly *made* to come become twelve-year-old faces.

Apart from small opals, and washing her hair almost every evening, she played the under-statement game. She wore lots of black, and gray, and cotton not silk; loose spinsterish dresses, without decoration, clothes which said: Just *look* at me. Being *extremely* unobtrusive.

She was delighted to find that she wasn't trying to impress. She had rather obviously opted out. She wouldn't compete, whatever happened or didn't happen. (At the moment, it was happening.) But Sedili couldn't be expected to understand this, and she looked more vulgar every day in contrast to my mother, and obscurely sensed this and then to make sure she couldn't lose out became even more groomed and braided and more than utterly perfect.

Sedili presumably saw my mother as impossibly trivial, scruffy. Sedili was a large-hearted woman, and I don't think very prone to jealousy. But Sedili was bewildered that Zerd's whim for Cija *continued*.

Sedili knew that Zerd's being was all about conquest. She herself, Sedili, the king's amazing daughter, had been Zerd's first big amazing conquest. He had planned Sedili as he planned any campaign. He was still proud of her. Sedili was still tactically gloriously useful.

Cija was a conquest too, I suppose. Zerd had waited years, watched her sulking and almost magically muddling through barriers that only a fool or angel would have gone anywhere near at all. Now he had her, she could still surprise him by her unexpectedness—simply because Zerd, and everyone else he found important, worked on different assumptions about life. He had never worked Cija out. But she seemed the most enchanting chess game. Cija or I could have told him there was nothing to work out—except her simple lack of ambition. It seemed almost a miracle to Zerd.

She still had one bone to pick with the world. She wouldn't really forgive it for not being as wholesome as it was lively.

But she had not, apparently, been bored by something dead in the visible world which had always bored me until I noticed I could make a candle-flame *behave*.

Riding looking at scenery, no matter how joyous and joy-bringing, I usually got irritated by something dead about it.

It gives nothing to you, said Zerd without interest, exhorted once by Cija to admire. *What,* she cries. *It gives scent, movement and life. You really are materialistic if you can't sense the joy and life around us.* He shrugs, and I think she's really lucky to have him discuss her enthusiasm seriously with her:

"It might as well not be here," Zerd says of the inoffensive charming scene. "Or be a desert. It says nothing. The animals are like sapper deployments: quick, bright, intelligent and busy—but they say nothing to you. They are infinitely expendable."

He seemed touched by her disbelief, however. He reached to rip an orchid from a tree (we were in lush

land) and held her foot clear of the stirrup as she rode
by him, and tucked the orchid in between her toes. He
continued, almost pityingly, to show he knew what she
had been trying to "show" him:

"A meadow of flowers can nod under a breeze like a
meadow of joy. A trick again, and all the more cloying
because it wastes one's time, it leads one to imagination
or emotion which are fruitless, Cija, and in fact an exercise of dour will is necessary to remind oneself in advance not to be led astray. Nature is like a picture or
tapestry to a child: the child runs to touch the magic
and be led into it, and behold it is only dye and stitch-
ing. This . . ." Zerd looked at the landscape, "says nothing much to you, Cija, except that you want it to. It is
only wood and only sap under shifting lights."

And again Clor, in amusement as she insisted on telling him about the ant-eater she'd seen licking ants from
its larder in fact its own tail which bushily swarmed with
them, likened my mother to a lady out on a country-
visit with watercolors and sketch-pad.

After I heard Clor say that to her, I noticed how
once you decided to help wounded men if you ever
could, but otherwise not torture yourself more than
would do good to them (since sharing their unimagin-
able pain sentimentally and imaginarily was only useless
impertinence anyway) things all came to you more
immediate and truthful. You saw more. You even saw
trees and ants better. And thus might be more able to
do something helpful should the opportunity after all
arise. It was in those days most of all that I began to
sort the emotion away from the fact.

So I know that my mother meant no harm when for
instance she wrote: "One of those little skirmishes . . .
they're most picturesque of all in the early evening, with
the pink light limning the edges of shield and knife, and
you can't see the wounds much in the mauve glow."
Except that my mother wrote this bitterly. Greedy for
experience of her own as she was, she felt that the
world was still only presenting her with other people's
grievous experience.

Perhaps I might have felt this too, a "blank," unlikely
ever to have a life of my own. But I found that I took
on so many colors in the eyes of those who glanced my
way (wishing still to see only themselves essentially)

that I seemed often to myself to shimmer all day. Children, and cripples, are generally it seems to me a reflection, in any social life they are admitted to. I was both child and cripple . . .

"She is like the young of my kind. They mature fast—so that they need not long be dependent and helpless, as are the more specialized," and here his voice was dry, "races."

The mist was already weeping on the hill, and my mother sat wrapped in their red-fur blanket.

Someone inside the tent was making up the mattress with new hay full of mint. I could smell this good sleep to come. The lamp from inside the tent gave shadows as big as birds to two moths making love, skittering on the outside canvas of our tent-wall. I sat down on a bit of my mother's blanket to watch them. Because of the moths, I remember this conversation—as neatly as the other talk once between my mother and grandmother when they discussed the horrors of husbands, when I fitted words to the rhythm of a cockroach.

I wondered if I could affect the lamp-flame *through* the tent-wall. I used that mental muscle which had given me control before. Yes, I could make the lamp-flame rear and spurt again.

Nowadays I wonder at times if odd parentage (the primitive pre-human, acting on the more evolved awareness from my mother's side) perhaps gave me the powers of long-range candle-torturing I was discovering.

(As though I were somehow double-jointed? With a psyche so loosely-hinged I could turn it around to face either way—toward the ab-human, but with extra sensitivity; or toward the highly evolved, yet with extra aboriginal flair.)

I have since then learned, too, how biologists now feel sure that mammals did in fact evolve from reptiles. That would make my father the missing link? Or his mother, rather, for he—just like myself—had mixed parentage. His father had been a nasty human soldier and his mother was a big dark scaled reptilian lady. I teased the moths outside with the flame inside, till they became unfairly excited. It must all have seemed such a gigantic emotional frisson to the moths.

"It will be baking hot tomorrow, Seka," my mother caressed my hair. "You are to wear your sun-hat."

I sighed. My sun-hat was babyish, itchy, and flapped.

The moths, united, hurled themselves in their delirium
into my hair. I wonder now what a moth's orgasm means
to it. Is the air of summer twilight, when it is full of mating
midges, in reality throbbing as thick as any upstairs brothel
room? The General reached into my hair and idly
squashed the uni-creature, convinced as it was of its grand
passion. Now one silver smear on his dark thumb, they
had lost their world for lust.

I looked up at my mother, thinking of more sun-hat detail to communicate to her. But she was staring at Zerd.
Her eyes were narrow, the fur of her blanket standing up
straight like a cat's in approaching electric storm. The
moths' death made me feel empty. It seemed that intensity
for its own sake, as a would-be Superb Gesture, pushed
events out of their working rhythm—and suddenly one was
left with a gap where there should have been a perfectly
serene insect.

During the next day's battle I ground paints on a nearby hillock with Scridol, somewhat out of the area.

"They won't come over here," he said, gratefully reliev-
ing me of the portfolio I had helped him drag up here, and
setting it out with his other bits of gallery; now his art was
in the right place, he could enjoy the view. "This quag is
the haunt by the look of it, Seka, of some really lively
species of ditch-drinker butterfly. A cartographer and one
small girl can make a way easy enough from tussock to
stone. But no army is going to get its feet wet in that."

My little bird was. Here it came, after us, though I had
left it with several other young birds. That groom took advantage of my inability to tell on him, and often let my
bird escape.

My bird, all frabjous feathers in the sun escorted by
gregarious brownbottles buzzing a sort of victorious fan-
fare, picked his way daintily up the hill to us. He nuzzled
me, pecked at Scridol's nourishing colors, and wandered
down to a quarry-like pit beyond the stream where there
were lizards to annoy.

We could hear the battle. But it was visible only now
and then from our hot hill, with its spattered shade of
blossom-bush.

This was more civilized than the other recent battle,
when all day we'd had to perch up a tree. And you had to

climb carefully to a private bit of foliage and wish it was
lavatory.

Here for company we had a friendly stream trickling
down our hill among bright shiny stones with quartz-
glitter in them. Scridol put our melons in it to stay cool till
luncheon. I lay looking up at the sky through my closed
eyelids—still big it was, and bright.

Last night Zerd had suddenly said to my mother:

"You know, *Atlan* was alive."

I thought how if candle-flames could seem pretty and
predictable to all people over all centuries, and then be
communicated with by *me*, Seka, then maybe just as most
physical landscapes could be summed up quite rightly by
Zerd as illustrations glued on horizons, yet there in Atlan
could be met with much more *real* landscapes of trees
which thought and rocks that recognized, so perhaps there
was hope behind the silly disappointing visible world after
all.

Perhaps most silly disappointing visible things (including ourselves) were only shadows of the *real* things, as
landscapes here were sleeping and landscapes in Atlan
half-awake.

Was I starting to wake myself as I quietly toyed with
fire?

The very hard high wind was blowing the sky over my
face like flames.

"*Get up that tree,* I was told by my first platoon commander," Scridol was telling me. "*Draw the valley. We
want a firing-plan. Map it.* I shinned up the highest tree
around, Seka, with my sketch-box, and my heart swelled
up like pride. It was a valley of eagles and trees already
aflame, with berries and red flowers together, a river winding through. I had to either eat it or fuck it, you'll know
one day what I mean—had to possess it somehow. I was
nearly court-martialled when I came down the tree with
my painting."

I could hear Scridol's story and the regular scratch of
his charcoal on the pad. They were much more real sounds
than those of the fighting.

"If this battle lasts till dusk, I'll get this bit of work to
the editor on time . . ." His voice trailed off into his determined stippling. I realized that by the editor he meant the
Dragon-General. *The editor of the Army.*

"Thank God," Scridol went on, he often mentioned just

one god, "soon we'll reach Ilxtrith. Running hot water and a morning lie-in. One thing to be said for marriage—wives can own places like Ilxtrith."

"For instance," he added, "when I married my wife—" Scridol must have got it wrong, I thought—didn't he know women got married and men didn't?

Then Scridol's head jerked up and he sighed heavily. Much too near, men were charging with a yell trailing off with a ragged whine. "It's the Dragon's confidence in his bandits again," Scridol said wearily, uncertain whether to hurry me out of the area. "The enemy determined to cut the Dragon off on this flank—but has in fact been led into the hills and bogs where no real cavalry can follow, but where these drunken bandits are as active as grasshoppers."

The grasshoppers swept past us like some horde from hell. As the enemy in their Prog/Northern uniforms fell meshed in mire, the bandits were upon them, and so were their howling women too—"like weasels," Scridol noted without particular distaste. "The males kill twice a day, the females once only."

The regular soldiers used to make this same hackneyed remark quite bitterly. But I couldn't see why women shouldn't pay for their Army keep by fighting the enemy. All the camp-followers fought each other anyway—there were always pockets forming in the lines, on march or at rest, often around respectably gray middle-aged mothers in their aprons, each spitting in the other's face as they prowled each other with vegetable-knives at the prod. I suppose the regular soldiers felt it a reflection on them that the bandits' bitches could do as they.

"Look," Scridol sneered, "at those crumpled tatty leather shields. Do they always have to sleep in their shields?"

As they cut down the fleeing enemy, the bandits in the heat of engagement would pause finickingly to remove a man's shirt or jacket before the final blow so that it shouldn't be soiled by blood to the point of being unwearable.

A regiment of river-foot, led by Beautiful, came splashing into the issue. *"Ael* hurls all before him," Beautiful yelled at his men. "Do we stand sucking thumbs?" Beautiful's battle-cry was less fortunate than usual, since he was forgetting the golden rule about ending on a rallying

note—a long-drawn howl of "sucking thumbs" didn't seem
to me very inspiring, but his Riverines pitched in horribly.

More Progs had been swung down upon us here.

The Tenth were brought up and I saw Beautiful on the
knoll below us knock aside Isad's dagger as he was using
it—("Sacrilege! Sacrilege!" he was yelling. Presumably
this was the dagger on which Isad had diplomatically
sworn by the River itself.) There seemed no end to the
Progs. "Progdin has been recruiting from nearby towns
and tribes," Scridol said, hugging his knees, looking at the
carnage below. "I hope to God Ilxtrith is still loyal." There
was a sound in the undergrowth near us. A wounded man
had crawled here somehow—the fighting was close below
now. His face was sliding down his skull. Scridol gently
placed his hand over my eyes and with his other hand on
the nape of my neck turned my head away from the man.
Now I was looking downhill and saw Beautiful fighting
swordless against a dozen Progs, an arrow through both
cheeks and no weapon but his shield. So this was the end
of Beautiful. Before Scridol could grab me, I darted down
to the stream and filled one of our emptier paint-cans with
water. I was carrying it back up to the wounded man on
our hill when he pitched forward and his terrible face was
in the water. Frothy scarlet bubbles made their way downstream and coagulated around our melons. I took his hand
very gently. He jumped at first—he couldn't see me, and
I couldn't make any sound to reassure him. But I put my
other hand round his too, and stroked his hand very
lightly and carefully. He made hideous gargling noises and
grasped on my hand convulsively. After he had died I
found my fingers swollen and bright.

"I've caught your bird. We've got to get away from
here," Scridol said, shoving paints into his leather sack.
"Is there never any peace during these battles?"

Again I found it a disadvantage not to be able to speak.
I simply wanted to say, where could be better than this?
The baggage lines were simply a prime target for the enemy. There was no guarantee of safety there. I took my
chalk and scrawled on the slate: DANGER COACHES. I could
spell Danger because it was the first word my mother insisted I learn. I wanted to put BAGGAGE LINE but COACHES
was easy. Scridol read it with half an eye, then seemed to
hold back, sighed, and let me lead my bird down into the
quarry. As Scridol followed, I was elated and started danc-

ing for joy. How exhilarating to have the power of the pen at my fingertips in this manner. Now I really could read and write. From now on I would wear a small slate around my neck wherever I went.

Scridol sat looking at me. "A dying man's hand one moment," he said, "capering the next. What kind of childhood is this? Where will your proper values be, child?"

He stroked my hair. "Poor little princess."

Later there was a great ululation as the retreat went hammering past. Scridol inched himself on his belly up to the hill-crown to look, so I snaked up beside him. "The butcher's bill will be exorbitant," he muttered, "of course. But it is the Progs who are in retreat. Zerd appears to have told his bandits, *encourage them a little*."

Cautiously we watched the retreating columns who, whenever they let fly with lances or began to beat out with swords, found the bandits merely scattered in a thoroughly craven fashion, only to allow the enemy to get on with the retreat and then harry him again.

In the roughest or boggiest terrain, one even saw the bandits (as now) dismounting to run alongside their ponies for a mile or two to spare them. Speed and mobility were hardly diminished by this, since mount and rider were a pair and would wheel in the same direction, often without a spoken command, even when both on the ground. "I'm sure Ael carries his pony when the going gets rough," Scridol muttered sarcastically.

The plain lay spread out before us, around our vantage mound.

It was covered with the debris of every stale battlefield —the horses or birds galloping riderless, whinnying for a vanished hand; the bronchitic bark of the giant birds; the call of men unable to stagger, to crawl, to move, or finally to breathe.

Then suddenly it all pitched and shifted. Our hill creaked. A line of trees shimmered a moment as though seen through the heat-haze over a brazier, except there was no brazier. Then everything righted itself—but it had been, like standing aboard ship.

"Oh, dear, perhaps I'd better make a clover-count," Scridol began to mutter. As I reached for my little bird's bridle, it all happened again—the hill fell apart, I was sliding down scree, the bird was honking dismally caught with me in a sliding rain of stones. I bounced to my feet and looked for Scridol. He was nowhere. Suppose the stones had knocked him unconscious?

I listened with every pore of my body. I turned my stomach and my forehead into ears—but I could only hear the groans of men newly caught in the odd quake, and the rumblings as the earth seemed to settle again around us.

Oh, Scridol, call me, call me, it's Seka here, please call me. I can't call you.

A silky light hung in the sky quietly.

What had the quake done to our victory? The enemy's retreat, certainly, had become a horror. But even Ael's bandits could not wheel and caracole out of earthquake. What had been an even slope to my right had become a jagged cliff. Two men spun off it, still locked in combat as they had hurled themselves too near the edge, one managing to knife the other as they twisted through space to the rubble of the newly created valley.

I must get back over the battle-plain to my mother. To the baggage-train—or to my father's tent, the General's tent.

I led the bird. Crossing this queasy ground, I didn't want to be high up—if the plain started once more to buck like my old rocking-horse in the Palace nursery, I could topple heavily. And I would be a target too for any javelin-happy soldier roaming the shambles now on the look-out for loot or blood.

My bird was dancing a bit. He didn't like the bodies and the moaning. I gave him the ribbons of my sun-hat to nibble, dangling them around his neck like ornamental reins, and he beaked at them and quieted down. His serrated claws dug daintily through the red bog.

Night was rushing down out of the sky. I didn't want to be left on the battlefield in the dark. I prayed to my little God, who was a cousin of ours according to my mother, that I would find a warm billet that night, wherever or whatever it was, and not be left exposed here. Then I thought of the night to be spent presently by the wounded who made the plain so terrible.

I skirted what, by its clothes, was a bandit. What was left of it still moved a little in the half-light. It lay belly-down, its head disappeared into a trough of earth. If badly wounded, Ael's bandits dig themselves holes in the earth. They bury their faces. They suffocate themselves.

The stars were small and niggardly. I remembered

what I had heard a sentry say of a bad night—"a night as black as the King's heart." I was very sleepy. I made my bird fold his knees and lie down, and I lay against him, creeping somewhat into the straggly warm fluff of him. It was nasty in this King's heart, I thought.

What King, anyway? The bad Northern King who was Progdin's master. Once he had been my father's master.

Sedili was daughter to the bad King. But now she was fighting against him, with his own troops which he had given her. She was fighting her father because she liked Zerd, and she wanted to win with Zerd against the bad Northern King. Then Zerd would be King instead, Zerd would wear the crown of all the Northern lands, and Zerd would share the crown with Sedili, because Sedili had helped him. You shared sweets with people who helped you.

My dreams were interrupted by the roar of falling dew.

We woke, my little bird and I, and stretched and looked around at the ugly dawn.

The nearest human being was waddling as she gazed from side to side, searching not too hard for some recent husband who might be among the dead. Evidently in her petticoats somewhere she was holding a bundle of dough, thus gradually cooking it between her legs so that by night-fall it would be risen ready to eat.

When I planted myself in her path she bore down on me in a frightening flapping manner and for a moment I was engulfed among the rags and dough and thigh-heat. She shook me out and held me up, shouting *"Now here's a pretty. What's this worth? Who will be raffling for this?"*

Men came over, sauntering casually, foot-soldiers of the 16th, wearing new loot and tasteful pink wounds.

"This is valuable enough," one man said, pulling at my fine linen trousers. "Someone with money will be on the look-out for this." And he nodded knowingly at my little bird too.

"I'll tell sergeant," said my woman. "He'll know how much we should charge for its return."

The man glared at her. To make the point that she was not behaving intelligently, he picked up an arm from an open grave recently dug nearby, and swiped her across the face with it.

"Well, what *do* us do," she asked reasonably, "then?"

"You leave it missing, some time," he told her. "Till they're frantic for it, sure it's dead. Meanwhile you feed it cheap enough here with you. Then is when you contact them, say it's been found and they can have it for a consideration." So far they had not asked me my name, nor my guardian's. Presuming that children could hardly speak (I found later that many of theirs couldn't really) they were not surprised when they discovered that I couldn't at all.

But this made it a little difficult for them to know who to contact for my ransom. In the meantime they fed me fairly well, not just because I mustn't sicken, but because children were something with mouths you always had to stuff. They fed my greedy little bird the same way. The men were to be used as grave diggers now after our victory, and our first family meal was taken around one great gaping grave, not yet covered but into which liquor (this was plentiful) was tipped to douse the stink. The flies congregated like crows around the graves.

One soldier reaching in his saddlebag for a pigeon-wing to share with me revealed in there a pair of big watchful eyes in a thin infant head. "My son—I've brought him with me on the march because I like him—and his mother died in sad circumstances," he added carelessly.

We bivouacked that night below the nearer ridge, and I played quiet knuckle-bone games with the little boy in the knapsack. He was nearly as silent as I. The soldier lent us good ivory knuckle-bones with silver marks.

I hoped just as much as the soldiers that my mother was missing me. I hoped she was frantic with worry and was searching and praying and raving for me. It would be nice to reward her by being restored to her loving little bosom. And would one see Scridol safe?

The big woman looking after me did not have to trudge on the march next day. Someone led a nasty mule over to her. "You shouldn't tramp while spoiled brats ride," the NCO said amiably to her, indicating me on my little bird. We were tethered together, my ankle to hers, my reins to her wrist. She was now almost as much a prisoner as I, and glared at the NCO but said nothing. She handled her mule very badly, and I wondered how I'd manage if she fell down a handy precipe. Perhaps I could arrange that. I didn't like her fat smell.

We seemed to ride with the 16th or in their wake. We

followed the river. We were in a ravine. At first there was
foliage and blobs of sun, parrots flashing or perching in
jewel-like lights, and a sound of squawk creak hum chatter fiddle above the marching noise. Then all grew gray
and once there was a sudden poking slenderness of dino-
saur neck slicking out from a cave some way above us,
then as swiftly slicking in again right out of sight.

"Where is Ael? Have you seen him?" a bandit reined
to a half-stop beside us.

"He must have gone ahead to take a look at the approach to Ilxtrith. Like as not the demons in that witch-
town have devoured him and spat out the horn already,"
grumbled the bandit, "or he's deserted us already for their
hell-spells." There seemed a feeling of dread about nearing Sedili's respectable dower-city Ilxtrith. Several times
after during that day and the next, Ael's orphaned bandits
came pathetically inquiring after him.

A chill had fallen long before noon. The Army was
used to cold. It had taken mountains in its grumbling
stride. But this was a miserable malicious black clamminess. My little bird kept ruffling up his spikes and stubs of
feather. But the only air to find its way between them
was the air of misery. That night the fat woman who had
started wishing she'd never kidnapped me was still roped
to me, and every now and then a soldier popped along
to see she hadn't persuaded a friend to part us. This was
all right, because it was by now obvious to me she had no
friends. He stayed once to tumble her, which was good-
hearted of him. They rolled around in her blanket, while
she went on grumbling. I was jerked up and down this
way and that by her ends of the ropes tied to our mutual
wrists and ankles. At one point I was somersaulted on top
of them both—I was too light to withstand such tugs—
and had to scramble off their heaving forms. They hadn't
noticed me, and this gave me an idea. I started picking
away at the rope round my ankle. But it was too stiff and
professional a knot for me. Presently the tips of two of my
fingers were lacerated, like small pin-cushions, and my
thumb-nail was loose.

At dawn the woman yanked on my ropes, barely waited
for me to crawl up off the ground again (she had pulled me
over) and chose to ignore the blood I started showing.
She dragged me over to what was already a swamp built
up not of earth but of excrement. As she squatted she

glared fiercely at me because I was still standing up. I
was about to go sprawling again (thinking my bird would
never let me near him now, I'd not smell of me any more)
when I noticed I was so angry that there was a sort of
vacuum around my limbs. I'd noted this before in moments of anger—a sort of intensity around myself as
though I were burning up extra air as well as adrenaline.
This was a time to take advantage of it. I lifted my feet
off the ooze, so that since they weren't even resting on it
they couldn't slide on it when she pulled me. I just hung
there, a tiny space above the ground but useful, not
astonished by my levitation, which she hadn't noticed,
but by her own weakness. She continued squatting like a
female toad and then waded away again to our animals.
Dragged after her, I still did not actually set foot to ground
and I stayed clean-ish this way. But it was a relief to let
the tension ease and put my foot in the stirrup. I always,
to this day, find it hard to levitate for long.

Through this day I practiced un-doing the knots of the
rope binding us together.

I concentrated on the rope as I had concentrated on
putting out the candle-flame. Ael had challenged me to
un-do his plaits by concentration. Well, perhaps I could
slacken each strand of the rope-knots.

After two or three hours I noticed a corner of my brain
had gone very cold. It felt isolated like a little nugget of
diamond icily burning away in the geography of my skull.
I took care not to glance too often at the rope.

A lot of earnest argument started. It only now, apparently, occurred to them that it was really difficult to
contact whoever I belonged to. I couldn't tell them who
that was. "Dumby," they kept saying and looking at me
uneasily. "Child's a dumby." They kept coming back to
that.

"Empress Sedili will know which lady has lost a much-
beloved tiny," said our friendly neighborhood sergeant.

"Let her think her's got away," was one mutter, "then
see which way she leads us."

While I was wondering how to find something to write
on to tell them contact Zerd or Cija (from our last
family dealings with Sedili, I gathered she was not really
competent at re-uniting loved ones)—the sergeant who'd
been talking fell dead with a shooting-star instead of a
head. I scrambled to one side of the panicking ravine,

with the woman snarling and hauling the rope as though she wished it were round my neck.

Other men were crying out and staggering under strange burdens. These things which lighted on them for a moment and then exploded on them were very pretty—like starry lights or burning rainbows. They hissed a bit as they killed, flared up and went out. I had never really seen explosive, for though the Northern scientists were reputed masters of the chemical explosion, it was all far too tricky and expensive to be used as an army weapon, and anyway wouldn't travel reliably.

The explosive was storming down on us from the heights of the dark cliffs. Ugly smells now wavered around us. A sort of fog was building up from the ravine floor to above the height of a man. It was a remnant of this gassy smell, gone stale, a deathly smell with no moving air in it, which had hung around so clammily when we entered the ravines yesterday. This must be a favorite way of slaughtering strangers around here.

As we looked up we could occasionally see ranks of figures up there on the cliffs. There were plenty of them too, and very high up, up there in the clear air and utter safety. We couldn't survive. We couldn't stop them.

Then a more gruesome rain was falling on us. Men, screaming or already dead, were falling to the pulping rock floor—I watched the twisting descent above me of one figure, growing larger as he neared, who had plunged in the path of the explosion-'star' he still held in his hand. Its electric tentacles whipped back and around him, sucked by the speed of his fall, but he was already a scarecrow with a broken back when his jerkin began to char and flare. Black flakes began beating around our faces and I found pieces of skin and even bone, sticky and melting, in my bird's feathers and my own hair. The intention had obviously been to roast us alive in the ravine as in a good oven. My bird refused to leave me. I thought he might even stand on me or the woman, he was so troubled.

Suddenly soldiers with swords were pelting down on us —on foot, racing along the ravine, it seemed straight at us. That glare of swords.

The woman, still trailing our knotted and now very intertwined ropes, hurled me at them as a sort of mobile shield.

One man caught me. He looked at me, tossed me

aside, gave a howl and raced on the woman, sword up—
sword down, and she was jumping around like a bag of
jelly on the rock. As she died, Ael with his voice lightly
breaking as ever in emotion remarked reproachfully to
her;

"This little girl has dirty grazes all over her."

I was glad the men with swords were ours (Ael's) and
glad to be rescued. But that routine gladness paled into
insignificance beside my utter joy and triumph when I saw
the ropes all hung loose.

Ael mounted me, before him this time, on his piebald
skewiff pony. He held me gripped between his knees, so
that as he directed the beast with his whiplash left knee
or his muscular rather bandy right calf, so he kept control
too of me—I was perched too high and forward to look
after myself on the unfamiliar saddle. Ael doesn't use his
reins really. If they weren't there, he wouldn't miss them.
My little bird lolloped anxiously along beside us.

As we cantered through our battle, Ael pointed out to
me the disgusting old man who was directing our enemy.
High up on the precipice above us, visible now as the
bandit pony spurted and trajectoried along, sat a strange
figure in a sort of carved bone shrine. He was directing
operations with great verve, his teeth glinting in his
snarl; he pointed here or there with his baton, as though
drawing a map of his plan of battle on a table, and drawing up a flank here or pulling round his light horse in a
sweep of pure irritation.

Since his fireworks display had failed, he had to loose
his men on foot and hoof into our midst, right down here
among us. Up there on the clear height beside his can-
opied shining throne, marshals and messengers scurried
to implement his orders.

"The heat of this meat is blunting my knife," Ael fretfully pointed out, "rapidly."

Ael's lieutenant, riding on our right (while my little
silly kept up on our left, eyeing Ael's big broach longingly) leaned his head forward without a word, inclined
his hairy mouth around the blade of Ael's up-held knife,
and licked it clear of blood.

Ael grunted, and proceeded to use it again.

"Where are the warlocks?" Ael demanded. "I went to
enough trouble to get their help."

"They'll not enter this pass by the looks of it," said his

lieutenant and withdrew his own blade from an enemy jerkin. "They'll be waiting in their precious valley."

"Then the sooner we sweep this mattress-fluff before us, the quicker we can dump it in its own incinerator," Ael chirped with his ghastly giggle. He suddenly looked down and said to me, "You've got very dark and dusky. You've let that fellow of yours eat your sun-bonnet, haven't you?"

My bird and I looked suitably guilty as Ael and his lieutenant and a small personal body of bandits with us charged shoulder to shoulder through a shocked line of enemy, who were there massed across the defile before us one moment, and the next had melted away like bloody dew.

Suddenly we had come down into the secret warm green valley of Ilxtrith.

We were on a plateau of green carpet. It was in fact moss, so thick and resilient it muffled even the carnage. I noted foot-soldiers slid a bit on it, but our hooves and claws held well. The air shimmered to the right where a small volcano bubbled like a sullen cook-pot. Here the enemy of the defile and the fireworks, a smallish and obviously mountain people dressed mainly in sheepskin still stinking of mutton, were expeditiously driven by our men into the waiting arms of what must be the Ilxtrivans. These household guards of Sedili's dower city, for there were no more than a regiment of them, were very smart in their burnished breastplates and greaves and plumed shakos.

They did not in fact dispose of the mountain louts in the cooking pot. They smartly took them prisoner and seemed to prefer this to slaughter. The battle was all but over. The Ilxtrivan "force" was already marching off their prisoners in the direction of what seemed to be a thick wood beyond which towers and spires rose like illustrations in a story-scroll. Their commander turned and his drummer raised his long gilded sticks, Ilxtrith pennants flying off each, in turn in salute to us before disappearing into the thick green.

There was only a little mopping-up for Ael left to do on the promontory. Ael's and Zerd's men did indeed lob a few enemy into the small volcano, which fizzed gratefully. To my surprise Ael shook his head as he watched the defile into the wood of the captured mountain men.

"Sooner the pot than the pan," he said. "Eh?" His

lieutenant nodded: "Gods know what those bitches do to their captured prizes."

I had noticed a month ago how the underlying amusement Ael had shown in all his actions when I first saw him in my grandmother's Palace had recently on the march evaporated. On campaign he had been very matter-of-fact. Now nearing Ilxtrith the amusement had reappeared as an undercurrent in Ael and his lieutenant too. Life appeared to them, obviously, to be all irony and, besides, oddly *hilarious*. I realize now that to a bandit the thought of a roof is always *funny*. Ael and Yshur had probably even spent last night right inside Ilxtrith, persuading the witchy-lords of the sense of aiding us against their neighbors the mountain lot, and the heavy daftness of statesmen, aristocrats, females and politicians all sauntering around under an arrangement of rafters as though it were all serious, was once again upon them, as whenever they had to take a place in civilization.

Now we were properly in train, as befitted an army at last entering the territory of its ally. We made our way quite ceremoniously through this humid forest. Great blossoms almost floated between the trees, festooning them in thousands of milky clinging arms. Here on the moss before our claws burned the red daisycup, the color of murder. Such thick moss was on the trees, it seemed to have been grown from the silence. The Army too fell silent, since its tramp anyway made no proper sound— the first time we'd ever failed to hear our own passing. Soon the mosses hung so hugely engorged we could hardly push between the trunks. I looked and saw moss closing the way ahead which when I looked at it from farther away had been open. I realized—the moss was *feeding* off the silence. But let's see. Since silence must always more or less be the state of rule in this portion of forest, the moss was feeding rather off the *human* silence—in other words, off the men's etheric fear. I looked at Ael's lieutenant Yshur jogging stolidly along beside us. I seized the curly horn on its strap over his back, drew it to me and gathered all my breath to blow while he and Ael regarded me, waiting to see what I did, not stopping me. The moss crumpled, a bladder pricked, hanging wizened off its bough as though punctured. The Army with us at a sign from Ael, who gave a crack of delighted laughter, now began a concerted shout.

The moss deflated for yards around.
The Army entered surprised Ilxtrith, chanting.

I always enjoy entering or leaving a new town. Except, as I said earlier, when it's raining stones which unfortunately the weather at the time so often turns out to be.

This was a triumphal entrance, which was a bit of a surprise since even though the town belonged in name to Sedili, it might reasonably have been confused to discover that she was now the enemy of her father the Northern King on whose marches the town of Ilxtrith lies.

The Ilxtrivans had turned out along the way to see us. They showered us with petals and sprinkled scented water on us, which now that it was so humid was not a bad idea. They chattered at us and each other as finches might do, speaking in a chirruping patois, and though there were no great scenes of enthusiasm they seemed decently pleased about us.

Ael cursed on behalf of the animals; he doesn't like petals on roadways, they get so slippy.

The towers and turrets on turrets of Ilxtrith were heavily mossed too, but it seemed perfectly ordinary picturesque moss. Pretty breasty ladies in black flappy lumpy-veiled head-dresses leaned out of the windows in the towers, where beetles (mainly busy scarabs rolling bird-dung) burrowed in the moss around the lintels.

Why were these ladies all in black? (Their head-dresses appeared to be veiled with the wings of small bats.) Why had they pearls pasted under their eyes like teardrops?

Ah, these were stylized tears. There was to be a funeral this evening, one willowy Ilxtrivan inn-girl explained to Yshur as he bent to cross-examine her while graciously accepting the long lily she offered. The Queen died three nights ago. It is on her bier, lying in state in the Thin Tower before going to her narrow grave, that she will alas receive us on the evening of our welcome to Ilxtrith. We see that some ladies wear diamonds beneath their eyes. What good grief.

Our procession trundles on through the heady Ilxtrivan twilight. Ael, his expressionless eyes missing nothing around or behind or above us, has very steadily inched one blunt scarred hand up under my skirt. Now beneath it he tugs the waistband of my trousers. His fingers past my navel made it want to curl up like a tickled anemone.

His fingers *now* stopped as though they had met a small unfamiliar creature, then very slowly, and with what I now understand as totally disciplined deliberation, they very firmly and very amiably caressed it as they might any small and unfamiliar creature.

This was such a gripping ride through town that I had forgotten about my mother. I remembered her again when I saw Scridol.

Scridol was crouched over a small portable gilded desk under an awning. He was surrounded by important people in grand clothes. He looked very agitated and as though the harder he concentrated the worse he felt.

We had arrived in what must be a city Square. There was a great plinth in the middle with a statue on it of a grim scowling stone king, obviously a Northern King and with a great likeness about the jowl to Sedili, who must be a descendant of his. Her jowl would be like that some day soon, a double jowl like aggressive, extra bosoms under her chin. The place was crowded around its edges by citizens, but the people in the middle were obviously too grand to be closely approached—besides, guards stood about alertly.

A lady looking very pure and exquisite looked at us, stiffened with eager surprise and moved toward us. Along came a whole group of her retinue too. Ael and I and Yshur, as we sat there on the sturdy bandy ponies, were suddenly knee-deep in gentle beautiful people. The main lady said very sweetly to me:

"Little one, what do you here with these savage heroes?"

Ael didn't speak for me. The lady refused to be put-off by this silent confrontation. She said, "You obviously need a bath, hot milk and an early night while all the grown-ups are boringly involved in ceremonious greetings."

Ael's knife blade appeared between the lady's hand and myself.

"You shall see where we lodge her," the lady courteously told him, refusing to take offense. "Please join us."

Ael regarded the lady. He pointed his knife on her throat and a red blood-drop appeared. It lay on the milky neck which Ael continued to regard until a bandit stepped forward and staunched it with his silk head-band when Ael had viewed it.

One of the lords in the lady's retinue wrapped his

cloak defensively about her. She looked shaken and shocked and allowed herself to be led away.

More people hurried over to us. Scridol was one, his sheaf of papers under his arm. Sedili and a couple of her big porky, beefy commanders bore down on us also.

"Princess," Scridol cried to me, "little lost Seka. Thank all the Gods in Heaven."

He stood there beside me, patting my boot in the way you pinch yourself to make sure you're awake; while Sedili, rigid with outrage, her teeth grinding on each other as she controlled herself, informed Ael that she was demanding official heavy reparation.

"That Lady is a noble Ilxtrivan," she said several times. "You have dishonored her and us. I have led this Army here to my dower City which for my sake has received you all in good faith. To do before all in the common market-Square . . ."

She repeated herself, unable to stop herself. One of her big commanders stepped in. "I suggest, Madam," he said outright to her, "that the bandit is arrested here and now. He can then await at your leisure a chance to explain himself later."

Sedili shot a trembling, resentful glance at Ael. She did not dare quite do this. Ael's men are not even supposed to be *called* bandits, so official are they in Zerd's army.

She fastened a look on me. "What is the brigand doing with the General's child upon his saddle?"

Many bandits had gathered around Yshur and Ael. My little bird jiggled about, gratified at so much company. Ael kept his deep expressionless stare on us, and it was odd that the very blandness of it seemed to express contempt. He had begun quite idly picking at his teeth with his knife.

"With respect, Madam," Scridol ventured, "I would say that, praise be to the Gods, the little Princess has but now been discovered after the quake and upheaval during the recent battle in which I lost her."

Sedili turned a deadly look on little Scridol.

Scridol looked pale. He had obviously been through a time of strain. His fingers were picking at his portfolio and agitated beyond control he began stuffing bits of blotting-paper in his mouth.

"And how was it, if I may ask," Sedili silkily demanded, "that we led our troops to battle in an earthquake? Was it not yourself in charge of the landscape?"

I longed to say *You can't blame Scridol for the earth-quake!* But this I could not say, and it appeared that it occurred to neither Sedili nor Scridol either that she couldn't hold him responsible.

"The Goddess Cija," Scridol said bravely, "this little one's mother, is beside herself with ill despair and dread for every moment the little one is absent. Give me leave to take her to her."

For here before us towered up the great walls of the Ilxtri-citadel proper: all turrets, spires and domes between which mists and fogs of black cloud fled restlessly here and there.

Ael suddenly spat the knife from his mouth so that it shivered into the saddle-pommel before us:

"I'm not letting her go in there," he said.

A lord of Ilxtrith stepped forward from behind Sedili, and thrust out to Ael a hand in a gauntlet which clanged gold war-insignia.

"We are sensible of the favor your presence brings us," the lord said. "We have helped each other against the ravine-men."

Ael inclined his head, took the proffered gauntlet and clasped it briefly, then silently held his own hand out to a bandit who stepped forward and spat on Ael's palm, which Ael then "washed" with his other hand to cleanse it of the Witch-master's touch.

Never one to let an audience suppose she might let an insult pass, Sedili tapped her riding crop on her boot.

"We are not then entering Ilxtrith tonight, beloved?" Ael's lieutenant respectfully asked of him.

"Bring me a corpse," Ael ordered, "for a pillow, and I shall sleep as sweetly in the wood as you in the City."

Of course this meant that not one of the bandit brigades would enter the Citadel, except for a moustachioed buck who had been restively eyeing a pudgy curly Ilxtrivan subaltern and now muttering "Excuse me, I'm just about to get myself married," he made off in the right direction.

Scridol, with a speaking look at Ael, held up his arms for me. Ael hesitated, then without a word to either of us dumped me with Scridol and turned his pony. In a body the bandits wheeled and moved away through the town, their hooves thundering and then drumming off into distance.

2

Turrets

SCRIDOL HAD TO inquire again and again where my mother had been lodged in the Citadel. (He called her the Empress now that Sedili wasn't in earshot. But this confused people. Most people were firmly convinced that Sedili was Empress.)

At last it transpired that my mother was in a small tower above one of the main halls. "She is being tended there by our own Ilxtri-nursing staff," said our informant, a steward here.

Scridol hurried me along, after stabling my little bird, following directions. He explained to me that my mother was ill, but I must not alarm myself. "She will be so out of her mind with ecstasy to see you, she'll probably go into a feverish relapse," he said encouragingly, "clasp you almost delirious and find she has a blinding migraine and then at last she'll be able to sleep. When we go on with our lessons, Seka, maybe there'll even be time tomorrow, you must try to write out for your mother and me where you've been and what happened to you. And thank the Gods," he stopped and started to pat my shoulder but missed and patted the stair-rail, "you're found, and seem unhurt."

He peered at me. "You are unhurt, Princesskin?" I nodded, he beamed.

I wondered in fact what the throb up between my legs was. Oh yes, it must be from Ael's hand that had done nice things there. Strange how hanging bumping on a door and Ael's fingers could give you the same feeling. I was proud to make scientific breakthrough.

We were ascending a crooked stair now and there were

121

slitty windows in the deep stone of the wall. The moss around them had crept inside and spread along the interior wall too. It had even crept on to the stairs, so that you had to be careful not to slide on a pad of it. It was moss the color of sick emeralds, of elderly copper.

A nurse came down past us carrying sweaty linen and a bowl. We could tell she was a nurse by her expression of soupy virtue and her flat sandals. She pointed us sternly back down the stairs.

"Is the Empress asleep?" Scridol said. "Well, I think even if woken she will sleep again all the better for having seen her daughter restored to her."

The nurse, a brisk elegant woman with her stomach held high, stared down at Scridol, lifting one recently-shaven brow at his assumption. "You can wait downstairs," she said.

Scridol hesitated. I could see him thinking that it was perhaps the over-emotional choice, after all, to wish to force oneself in and wake a woman at last getting a little sleep.

I bumped the nurse's tray and the bowl bumped off down the steps, breaking, and the linen spilled in great swathes. I then contrived to start crying. I can cry effectively, gasping and crowing for breath.

Scridol clasped me protectively (I think he thought the nurse might slap me). "She has been lost," he said, "she has been through a lot. She wants to see her mother."

I hoped the sounds might penetrate the door and my mother come out. If only I could shout, if only I had a voice I could raise, a sound I could effortlessly produce which meant something to people who loved me.

I ran up the stairs and pushed the door. I think now it should have been locked by the nurse when she came out of it, but she had neglected to do this because she felt well in charge isolated up here.

The door opened and I ran in.

The nurse's furious voice, stridently raised, sent a physical shake through me. I heard her bound up to slam me out of the room again, but it was Scridol who got to the door first and stood there with me looking in. Scridol was a little man, but the nurse dare not touch him.

My mother lay restlessly turning in a narrow high bed.

Her eyes were half-open, since even her lower lids seemed too swollen to shut properly, but her bright glazed gaze was that of a sleeper. She was flushed and pretty, and her hair in tossed curls and tendrils clung to her brow and neck and pillow. She had been put into a proper white linen gown with neatly tied neck, and there were flowers and water by the bed. Everything seemed *medical*.

"She has been given something to help her sleep," the nurse said severely, standing behind us. "If you try to wake her, it will make her quite ill. Let her have her sleep through. Then you will be called."

I reached out silently to my mother. The nurse had put a hand on my shoulder (digging her fingers in quite nastily) so I could not actually go to that poor little sleeper and kiss the sweat off her dear lip. But I reached to her in spirit and found that I could not get through to her. There was the usual misty clamminess that clings a bit round someone who isn't well, but that usually lets one through at once. Here was something heavy beyond that, which I supposed was the drug they'd given her— but how very heavy it was. I pushed a little farther and knew it was not only inert but hostile. It was a malignant heavy thing, and why wasn't it left by her bed? Why had her medicines been removed as soon as they'd been fed into her? Was that the bowl the nurse had been carrying out and I'd spilled?

At this moment, the nurse began to flutter.

Zerd was in the room.

He had come silently up the stairs, like a great quiet creature used to stalking, wherever he might find himself. He stared past us at Cija on the bed, and at the same time held a hand to me. "Is it Seka?" he said. "This is actually the famous missing person Seka? Is she harmed, map-master? Has she been able to tell where she's been? Cija must be wakened to see her. Then Cija will get something better than this wretched sleep."

"She cannot be waked," the nurse said.

She sounded so definite that Zerd turned to her in surprise. "Cannot?" he repeated, an edge to his voice and a dangerous appraisal of her.

He went to the narrow bed and with a dark, still face watched the restless "sleep" there. He reached down and scooped Cija up in his arms, a pillow still under her head and a trail of tortured sweat-stained twisted linen sheet still looped around her. She flung her arm out in a sudden move almost hitting him, and muttered thickly.

"This is against orders, I am afraid—" the nurse began.

"Whose?" Zerd asked with interest.

She stopped herself. His eyes narrowed. "Whose?" he repeated gently.

"The doctors say the poor lady is to rest," the nurse said, her brisk voice grotesquely attempting to coo for her.

She began tidying the sheet around my mother, following along beside. Zerd paused, standing still, simply waiting until her hands fell. She stood looking after him as he carried my mother away. "Where do I tell Doctor you have taken the lady?" she inquired.

Zerd ignored her, but moved a hand to make sure Scridol and I followed him.

I ran along beside Zerd, holding firmly to my mother's foot. I tried to note the nature of the spill from the bowl, but it was already impossible to tell where it had been: it seemed to have evaporated off the stone, or been pulled into the patches of moss.

Zerd glanced every now and then into my mother's face on the wet pillow in his arm. He quickened his stride. He led us through a high hall, where once as I scurried along he turned to smile at me. A stab went into me with his eyes. They lingered on me, his very considering eyes, in which the watchfulness inside him bumps along at its own bidding. It would be a mistake in dealings with Zerd ever to think he is not evaluating. He will never cast a glance at any face however beguiling, however necessary to him, without summing up. Ruthlessness of his, years later, can be traced back to a single almost invisible evaluation.

We passed through a great hall in which many people stood in dark knots.

"Funeral chamber," Zerd said briefly to Scridol.

People turned to stare upon Zerd as he bore my mother nearer. At the far end of the hall, was a platform which must be passed if one were to leave the hall out of its other side. On the dark platform lay three raised boxes. These, we now saw, were coffins. In two lay men in noble gowns wrapped around them. In a great coffin, lifted high on trestles and slanting so that one could gaze on her closed face, lay the dead Queen of Ilxtrith.

I couldn't see much of her, for though there were torches held by dark-faced guards, they were some way off and flaring sullenly only. An occasional gleam was raised from her breast: she must be wearing ornaments of some kind. At one leap of a flame I saw her face and as instantly it was in darkness again. It was an egotist's face, full of self, replete with self and yet rapacious, as though it wanted still more and more—but wanted everything to be self only. I felt no sense of relief when the light left her again. I felt that if this face were around, had only days ago been alive, then no one in its area could feel relief simply because dark hid it.

My father bowed his head as he passed the bier, but did not set my mother down in order to make the proper salute of respect to the dead royalty.

A white lady detached herself from a group paying its homage to the corpse. She was heavily bandaged about the throat. She stared at Zerd, palpitating. It seems that ladies' metabolism can be much speeded by his proximity.

She winsomely named herself, and began to tell the sad tale of how she had hoped to make me comfortable in the Ilxtri-nurseries. "Then one of your bandits daggered me, Sir," she said in a rush. She waited for his wrath against Ael. "There is not one bandit in my Army," Zerd said silkily.

"Except for one," an Ilxtrith lord says meaningly, as we stride on.

Scridol danced aside with an exclamation, staring down at his feet. He had nearly stepped on a sluggish fat long thing oozing along the floor.

"Alarm! A snake!" Scridol called.

People leaned forward to look, but it became obvious from their interested lack of surprise that they knew already it was here.

I saw it now, a small wormy pallid snake oozing along the hall. People kept well away from its passage. No one would touch it. But it seemed they were solicitous of it. As Scridol raised his sword, a noble stepped forward and explained that this was no snake, and not to be harmed.

"In this big room, as you see, the Noble—" and he nodded at one of the lords in the coffins flanking the

Queen, "has just died, and this is his self-regard which has escaped from its proper place coiled in his spine."

"Eh?" Scridol was frowning.

"Don't you notice," the Ilxtrivan lord explained lightly, "how when your self-regard is threatened it writhes and chills within your spine?"

"That's your marrow."

"No, it's your worm."

Zerd called me nearer him with a jerk of his head and as I walked with him he held my mother closer against him in one arm so that he could briefly rub my back. "You can feel her vertebrae like little pearls, Seka has no self-regard," Zerd says.

He laid my mother down in a little dark boat we found moored, with several others, against the marble pavement on which very quietly slapped the waves of a sort of wide chilly indoor canal beyond the funeral hall. Scridol stepped gingerly in with us, opening his mouth wide in a silent moan of distress as the boat rocked. Very properly he had remained on the pavement until Zerd motioned him to join us: "You are joining us, Scridol, I take it."

Zerd disposed himself gracefully and comfortably in the end of the boat, picked up a broad flat-ended paddle with cabalistic signs burned into it now gathering dirt and algae, and we moved off.

Presently we were gliding through a great hall again, but almost its entire floor was water. Over the water were suspended many black silk hammocks. This room was very dark, but the few torches showed us guards in armor standing impassive, only their eyes watchful under the Ilxtrivan peaked helmet-caps, and as sleepers stirred or restlessly flung out a braceleted arm or dimpled bare leg from which drapery floated free, we saw that the room was a dormitory of palace ladies. Zerd's teeth flashed in a smile: "Beauty-sleep comes before parties."

We were soon out of this room, with its mists of perfume lying low over the water, on which lilted a scum of droppings of cosmetics.

We were now in a series of locks, but the water was up level and the gates open. Along the paved "banks" were holes in the walls like bunks, caves not much bigger than a man lying stretched out, one over another;

and these banks were bristling with soldiers. They were ours.

"I don't like the look of this," Scridol said outright now, dourly. "It looks as though you're being adequately guarded, but in fact if these are your quarters some jammy architect has designed them like the cozy end of a trap. Who manipulates those locks and watergates, them or us?"

"Why, whom do you suppose?" says Zerd, easily. "They, of course."

Scridol and Zerd moored the boat by the widest hammock, slung lowish above the black unreflecting water, and Scridol helped Zerd to lay my mother among the swung cushions and cover her very gently with a trail of fleece blanket. A sort of misery was growing in me like a chill miasma, which I remember even at the time likening to the kind of chill you *see* rising off marshes.

I hated the set of my mother's head on her body. I hated the way she drew breath. I hated her stillness, and the way she had not roused to the hot physical presence of the General. Some horrible enemy was within her.

Then suddenly in a blaze of flaring gold lights a boat had whirled into the dark echoing chamber.

There beside the hammock into which my mother was laid, the new boat rocked to its halt on the water, with Sedili arisen from its center like some mis-placed figurehead. She stood there, breasts akimbo.

"So!" she rapped out sharply. She fixed her eyes on Zerd with plenty of force. Not for nothing was she a big woman, a personage, built splendidly for confrontations.

"This is my own dower city, Zerd," Sedili said with a certain throb. She had indeed, following her own advice, worn a dress in which to discover your lord with Another. It was a simple, touching and yet stately gown.

"You are to be congratulated, madam. And we are as grateful as you to have reached its hospitality."

"Is it not seemly and politic for our Ilxtrivan allies here and now to note that you bed with your *lawfully* wedded Princess?" Had Sedili not been such a forceful speaker, I would have said she whined. But her voice had thinned at this point, it was higher than usual and had taken on a rabid reediness, inside her usual clipped Here-is-Your-Warrior-Princess tone.

After all, Sedili was Zerd's first wife and never di-

vorced. *She* had never had the opportunity to discover
for herself the truth of the old maxim that the first three
marriages are always the worst.

Zerd smiled, genuinely preoccupied.

He called guards, good men of his own household, to
watch by Cija. And remarking, "Madam, with your gracious permission," he swung me and himself aboard
Sedili's glittering craft, which was to have been a vessel
of dramatic unmasking and retribution; he motioned
Scridol to follow.

As we glided to the darkest corner of the place, where
the pavement curved into the archway out to the next
channel, a tall figure was apparent. It had not been noticeable, certainly, a moment before. It stood there
simply waiting very pallidly. It was the Ilxtrith Queen. It
was the Queen from the coffin. I heard Sedili gasp. I
knew it was the Queen, not only by the crusted golden
gemmy garment but by the cast of the greedy face, which
once recoiled from would never be forgotten. It struck
me then in that moment that there was something about
the utter *I am, I want* of the Queen's face which was kinship with the high note of hysteria inside the clipped voice
of the famed Commander-in-Chief of Northern Marches,
Sedili's voice celebrated afar for its rousing calls to men
to die for honor, a voice full of maturity and womanly
patience (for her troops so often called her their mother,
their sister)—with this thin greedy girl inside it ready to
pull any trick if threatened. Now here was the Queen
pulling her trick. Her trick was to trail from her coffin to
frighten the intruding conqueror. He must not get too big
for his Dragon boots. So she had risen from the dead at
him. For it was not in fact the Queen at all, since that
shape in the coffin had been real, a beautiful body, and
this was not flesh. Yet still it stood, or hung—for its feet
seemed more like mist on the pavement—waiting.

Zerd stepped first off the boat, and on to the pavement.

He then walked straight through the figure. He briskly
reappeared on its other side. He strode through the archway to his men.

The figure shimmered, striving to re-form itself again
in its entirety, but Zerd's unexpected action had shredded
it, and parts of it floated, ragged gaps let light through it,
and eventually in a coagulant spreading chill which struck
us all it condensed into a nucleus of invisibility.

I looked aside at Sedili. (I liked looking at her, she repaid one's eye.) She was staring with her capable business-like mouth dropped open. Pearls of sweat genuinely stood up on her brow and neck, like the "weeping-pearls" the Ilxtrith ladies had pasted under their eyes for the funeral.

"He has the insolence of the damned," she murmured.

She gaped after Zerd with a sort of cringing revulsion. But Zerd turned and called to Scridol: "My daughter is in your care, map-man," with a farewell salute, very casual; and I honestly believe that he did not see the apparition at all when he stepped through it. It would certainly be a great gambit and worthy of Zerd, to call such a thing's bluff by walking straight through it. Perhaps he'd have done that if he'd seen it. But a man as physical as Zerd is biologically ill-fitted, I think, for perception of some of the higher-frequency wave-bands of this universe.

We sailed on in silence. We turned into a wider channel, with glinting mosaic tiled banks.

Sedili re-gathered her composure. Pursing her lips in a way she sometimes had, she was gazing ahead over the prow of her glamorous craft. Suddenly she glanced aside at me. "You must go to the nurseries with the other children here," she said. "You will be looked after properly. You will be given tasties to eat. Don't eat while you're walking along the corridor. Young ladies don't eat except at table."

"I will accompany the little princess to the nursery, madam," Scridol said.

"You will attend to your proper duties, Scridol," Sedili said drily. She reminded him that the General had not appointed him nursemaid, however soft and easy such an appointment might seem to a cartographer with work to do and Ilxtrivan libraries to research in. "By all means," she said, "see the General's daughter if you will to her nursery. Then report to the General on how you find it. Whether it is clean and fairly appointed, whether the games and dolls are in working order, whether you approve the nursery-rhyme pictures on the dado." There were chuckles from Sedili's household standing about. Scridol's ears reddened desperately. Sedili's jackals and lap-dogs, unlike those of most grand ladies, being a military as well as a purely ornamental pack are mature, sophisticated and professional and it's no fun being jeered by them.

"*Then* come back to me," she added sharply.

She looked steadily at me as Scridol and I set out, with a guide, for the nurseries-quarter upon disembarking. I nodded at her. It was my solemn promise to Sedili not to run about the Ilxtrith corridors sucking sweetmeats. I knew she genuinely did not want me to let the tone of our party down.

We soon heard the nurseries. There was a subdued tranquil hum as of a well-run aviary. Little bells rang at frequent intervals, indicating as I later found out the changing-over of nurses.

From the windows of the nursery could be seen the last of the Queen's funeral. The children were grouped on the window-seats to watch, particularly the younger ones for whom it was adjudged the most educational sight; the older ones already knew much about mortality.

The bier had been lowered into the green earth, which was then shovelled again over it. With the moist turfs, the mourners' pearls (and diamonds) torn from their cheeks were cast too, as tears, upon the bier. At the very moment of her burial, the Queen must have been forming herself in the water-hall to terrify the Dragon-General she had been too late to intimidate in life.

Left alone here by the harried Scridol, I looked gravely around me at the Ilxtri-children here.

These were very quiet squeaking little girls. They were obviously obedient and obviously sly. The one seemed to be encouraged in them (if you can imagine this, you who may be reading me now) as much as the other. They wore muted colors and sat around industriously making things, anything: they sewed, embroidered, glued, cut, welded, drew, nailed, carpentered, chiselled, wove, hooked, just so long as an object emerged. What they were making were their *objects*. Any object would suffice (though favorites were daggers and lanterns and wrap-around cloaks) just so long as they had labored in the making, preferably at the time of a comet seen in the heavens, which were often sighted in those days.

Now of course that there is a moon, that new-fangled thing in the sky, which affects tides in men and oceans, these magical tools are made according to its laws—at its dark, or at its full, I can never remember which.

But best of all is during a funeral, a large funeral which is exercising the thought and mood of the minds and bodies around. This is why the nursery looked out over the cemetery. Of course a Royal funeral was not to be wasted, and the children were all hard at work.

One little girl showed me the tapestry she was making, into which nettles must be woven. Her fingers were raw and spotted like bacon gristle with blisters on blisters. She was terribly proud of these, though she kept a stern proud melancholy-face as she showed them, and I thought that surely this vanity about one's suffering was contrary to the original idea behind the concentrated labor, which must have been meant to bring on humility and a sense of self lost.

One beautiful little boy, smaller than I, with a halo of ringlets and not gray but shimmering silver eyes, showed me his knife. "There is blood in this athame," he said, unwrapping the dark cloth in which he kept it at the back of his white rat's cage. "Virgin blood of course," he added to show that he was a professional.

"You can't see the blood," he told me with a certain elitist contempt. "It was put in the athame at its making."

But I *could* see the blood. I could sense something heavy and dull lying within the object, a waiting but lifeless something—waiting, but not with any urgency, any greed, any hunger; just waiting. My eyes buzzed a little —they were not used to the adjustment you have to make when something visible in one way flakes across your normal vision.

The nurses (men and women in plain severe black clothes) now at a general ringing of bells admitted the evening visit of some of the Ilxtri-parents.

Here was the unshakeable white lady! She introduced a man to me, who gazed with poached eyes, and the pearls in her plaited silk moustache glimmered as she bent close to me, wafting perfume, and murmured: "It's no fun for a little Princess to be with big, rough soldier-men all the time, is it? The big men don't know good games to play." (I thought of saying, Ael did.) "Wouldn't it be nice to stay here instead?" She continued, "Why don't we hide when they come to get you tomorrow?"

My eyes filled with tears as I gazed back at her. Of course, I was a poor little mite, a waif, nobody ever took care of me. People forced me to learn to read and write and made me get up in the mornings. Did little children have no rights?

"Will her blood be blue," the man asked curiously. The lady smiled: "We must wait and see," she said gaily.

When Ael climbed up in the night to get me out of Ilxtrith, he met very little resistance. Our hosts, in planning their treachery to us, relied too much on their witch powers and got in a muddle. They had laid force fields and various psychic traps, which someone like Zerd tended to walk through without noticing, and someone like Ael tended to circumvent by climbing up the drainpipe anyway. "As is the way with traitors," Ael said as we traversed a narrow way where polarized light poured around us hopefully to act upon various instruments of base metal lined up like beggars to either side of us, "these Ilxtrivans are occupied with their own cunning to the extent that they have no time to suspect their victims."

While I assimilated this sentence, we had reached the window by which he had climbed in.

The spike he had hooked into one corner of the sill was still there. Ael with a practiced wrist-flick all in one movement uncoiled the rope again from his belt and snaked it twice around the spike, and we descended.

Even here, as we hung without the moth-glimmering walls, we could hear the sounds of revelry in the great halls inside. Our hosts were still feting us. And outside in the camp, Ael's bandits were holding their own carousals.

Ael's ponies had stayed below the wall waiting. He had left their reins dangling over their noses and necks, and they obeyed the reins as a surrogate rider. It was exactly like saying "Heel" to a dog.

I was pleased he had got me a pony for myself. I liked riding with him, but having a pony to myself was a mark of honor. I realized, though, with a sense of foreboding that he must be expecting me to be autonomous at some time in the evening.

Bandits were whirling each other gallantly around their camp fires, pumping each other's arms up and down and complaining about each other's spurs. But they remained watchful. Many, many sentries, eyes bent upon the walls and turrets of Ilxtrith, turned their gaze away not even when dancers stumbled against them. A little farther off, the bandits' women danced with each other.

"Warm night," Ael's lieutenant Yshur edged up beside us, acknowledging my presence with an unsurprised nod.

"Womb temperature at least," another bandit on a sad-eyed pony danced past us. His mounted partner was a slim warrior wearing black furs and black gossamer. It could have been a man or a woman but was certainly a soldier–the black gossamer floated from the handles of at least six knives of differing graded sizes, like a punctilious chef's. Fireflies had been set in the fur boa and blazed like an intoxicated gaze.

As they looked out the witchy-lords would see thousands of camp fires, and presumably would hesitate to turn on us—there were a few hundred bandits only out here, but they were good fire lighters.

Beautiful came up to us. There were handsome scars in each cheek where the arrow had been lodged in his face last time I saw him. They added to his look of warlike nobility.

"I have been detailed," Beautiful said stiffly, "to oversee the stationing of my household in the Ilxtrivan barracks to our east. I find my men constantly importuned, by the thieving and proclivities of yours." He was going on, while Yshur muttered, *"To our east,* what is that supposed to mean," (bandits only just know terms like "right" and "left") and Ael with a blank face sat in front of Beautiful, perhaps hearing him. How splendid Beautiful looked in comparison with Ael. Beautiful's epaulettes and Riverine insignia glittered in the fires' lights. "And are we not all of us here," Beautiful demanded dourly, "as pilgrims in a spiritual place? Are we not here as agents of a great lady's good faith? And are we not inducing by our behavior that very lack of faith which can only shame us and by besmirching her clean honor besmirch our own?"

"A great lady," Ael said shortly. "Ay. And so one day she shall have a carved gibbet of all her very own." Ael slapped the reins on the pony's neck and we walked on. But even I could appreciate what self-control Beautiful had called forth not to issue challenge. He really was determined not to let the side down in Ilxtrith. As the dancers again whirled past us, the slender warrior in furs and scarfs threw me a lily, picked from some Ilxtrivan arbor and thrust into a dagger-belt. On an impulse I turned and held it out to Beautiful—who received it, involuntarily. But as another of his magnificently uniformed household guard came up, leading a thoroughbred bird to take him back to the civilized festivities, Beautiful with a languid gesture dropped the lily into the bird's nosebag.

Ael took me off, away from Yshur, to his yurt—a low, much-patched leathern tent, under the roof-flap of which burned another small fire. A bandit was crouched tending a blackening pigeon, very large. My heart sank as I saw it. I had eaten up my supper like a good girl already. I wasn't hungry and to tell the truth I was beginning to be too sleepy to feel adventurous. Ael motioned me to seat myself on a sort of cradle—a carpet slung over two ropes. I accepted some burnt squab (it was tender, though so big and black) and tried to force it down, looking up at some affable tiny stars glittering in the visible sky where the felt roofing was turned back to let Ael's smoke out, and apparently other people's smoke in.

Ael was muttering to me or the cooking bandit or himself. "Spirit place," he was sneering, and I realized he was revolted by what Beautiful had called Ilxtrith. "Body place," Ael insisted ferociously. "Objects and objects' bodies they collect." *Collect* to Ael was a word of implicit disgust.

Presently the cooking bandit was given a sharp nod; he left us. There followed some things I enjoyed. The starry smoke still bellied down about us.

Ael showed me what to do with my hand. He helped me aim, and the first time he came the semen put out the candle-flame. He was so amused by this, that he had guessed it would amuse me. The second time it jetted less.

With lucky timing, just not too soon, there rose around the yurt a ghastly ragged yell. Ael ran around one of the screens of hinged leather panels which did as yurt-dividers, and almost collided with a bandit running in. They nodded grimly at each other. Without a word spoken, the bandit raced out again and Ael came briefly back to me as he pulled on his trousers.

"You will not be safe here," was the first thing he said, reassuringly. "But you are safer," he added, "than with those scrapings who would have kept you to themselves as a useful novelty at their next party. Come out with me, mount the pony I kept waiting for you outside, ride him over to the small hills, they are very near, while you have still time. The field is not yet quite a battle field. You have a few moments."

I followed him out of the yurt and was swung up on the pony. Ael mounted his own and in a second had disappeared in a terrible melee. Ilxtrith had shown her hand in the night.

My mother was in there! I hesitated, looking toward the high glimmering walls from which a miasma floated out.

Already it was darker. Fires were stamped out as fighters swayed through them. The bandits who had been carousing so wantonly had been after all in full command of their situation. The more drunkenly they had staggered before the windows of many-towered Ilxtrith, the more they had awaited the delightful shock in store for any Ilxtrivan soldiery expecting to engage with an incapable enemy. I was pleased to see, at least, that Ilxtrivans were already trickling like ants from under their stone. They were competently pursued by Zerd's troops, but as yet the exodus was no more than this trickle.

I stood there only a matter of heart-beats and here suddenly beside me in the confusion were Zerd and Clor with my mother. She lay in my father's arms, all wrapped up in a dark cape. She was still unconscious! My father caught my sick look, and nodded.

"Gods know what they have done to her," he said. "Here, Seka," he added as a carriage with a medical mark daubed on its sides careered up beside us, "this is to take you and your mother to the hills over there. Lie low," he instructed abruptly as he swung me into the carriage. "You will be sent for later by myself or by Ael, since he already showed the good sense to get you out of that fine tourist attraction."

Clor grunted at me as Zerd reached a hand and tucked a fold of carriage rug about me. Sitting silently on the seat beside me was a thin man. "A doctor who will look to you both," Zerd told me briefly, needing already to be away. The doctor simpered and clucked. Clor had noted the damp in the air. "It's pissing down," he said uneasily. "Just a small unobtrusive rain," the doctor said. Zerd, unexpectedly, said "It's a Seka rain," and they were gone. Clor gleamed and glittered, even from the rear. I could tell this was to be a worrying engagement. Clor had put on all his medals, so that his body might be recognized.

The carriage moved off, so far protected by its medical air. I found I did know where once before I had met this doctor. It was Sedili's doctor, or rather Beautiful's doctor whom Sedili had once brought to examine my mother who declined the honor.

Who had contrived that he be recommended to Zerd as a good physician?

The doctor continued to simper. He pulled the cover over my mother's face, and when I indignantly pushed it back a little to allow her air and stop her looking already an official corpse, he said "Now, now, are we to be known?" and twittered on about how the attack in the night had wounded us all deeply. I thought this was quite funny but didn't smile. He went on, maybe to shut out the sounds and sights on our jolting weaving awful route, about how Zerd's men, all primed and none asleep, had at once thrown the locks and weirs within the Ilxtrith system into disarray, having done their research efficiently in such a brief time as had been at their disposal since entering Ilxtrith. "The currents all flowed backwards," the doctor said ingenuously, "and instead of trapping us, the Ilxtrivan allies, although I mustn't call them that now, must I, found they themselves did not rightly know the ways and ins and outs of the locks and sluice-gates which we had researched more thoroughly and recently than they. The poor lady Sedili has been dumbfounded, thunder-struck by the treachery of her dower-city to her and her lord." So her name eventually slips into your conversation, I thought. "Although trusting Ilxtrith as Sedili's," the doctor rattled on, "Zerd had of course planted 'surprises' everywhere."

Blood spurted on to the doctor's uniform and he started. In the battle, a bird had run amok among its own fellows. Its rider took his broach from his cloak, set the pin on his bird's head and with his shield-boss hammered the pin into the bird's brain, the easiest way to rid oneself and companions in the ranks of such a powerful creature once it was out of control.

"Neurotic," the doctor said, hugging himself more tightly. "They are neurotic, these fowl. Excitement sends them over the edge."

I thought his endless twittering near-hysterical too. I looked at our driver. Perhaps he was better company. He had at least brought us now almost to the low hills beyond the immediate Ilxtrith plateau. Now he threw up his arms, screamed, pitched sideways. Another extra gone to the Great Sidelines. As I look back and remember my lack of real concern at these constant accidents, I remember also Scridol's concern that I was being calloused before my time.

Here were the beastly doctor, myself and my pale still little mother in her black cape alone in the pitching carriage.

The same stars fizzed above us as had fizzed up there twenty minutes ago. I rubbed my tummy. Under my shift it was still really wet with Ael's slippery come.

Here ran a river wide across a gravel bar. The water sheeted up in wings to either side of us. We were hardly splashed.

I saw the doctor was lifting my mother. I moved nearer with my hand out to make sure he didn't make her head lurch if he was trying to ease her position in his interfering way. He hurled her over the side of the carriage.

I raced at him while his hand was still on her arm. I got the tunic of his uniform—which was mainly unbuttoned—and bashed it in his face, so the blood on it was up his nostrils and under his eyelids.

But he got rid of me easily. It was bizarre that as he was beating me down from the carriage, for I was trying to cling on to its edge even though he rapped at my knuckles and pushed his hand on my face, he was murmuring in a soothing tone interspersed with croony clucks, "Oh, dear—are you hurt? Dear, dear—" at the same time as I got quite a vicious shove. It was his habit ingrained, syrupy civility. The last I saw of him he was still bending solicitously out of the carriage as it raced away with him. I crowed for breath and began to gather my wits. Thank Gods he hadn't let me fight my way back into the carriage. At least I was with my mother. I could never have put him out of action, calmed the birds (he would have a time with them) and hauled Cija back to safety.

Where were we?

The black lour of the hills broken and creased and folded about us lay outfacing me a moment. Then it throbbed and we were alone but for a war. That ridge had spewed up a thousand men.

I tugged at my mother. I pulled her into a blacker opening in the slope behind us. She whimpered. I was overjoyed. So she had not after all sunk almost irrevocably beneath the surface. I pulled her farther. Her eyes had opened, they fixed on me, she saw the night sky and the rising slopes and heard the increasing din. She helped me by pushing with her elbows and her hands, and I found that we could go farther and farther back. We were also descending. We were in not exactly a cave, more a tunnel —a grassy floor of packed earth or possibly of old paving, maybe a disused duct.

Hours before, we had been masters of our surroundings, riding high, looking down on the valleys and the hills too. Now we were below them all, and at their mercy.

3

The Darling Despair

MY MOTHER LEANED back against the wall. She was drawing deep hoarse breaths and even in the tiny light I could see she was waxy pale. Above us there was a thrumming, a clamor as though the earth were on heat. The entrance of the tunnel was some way off now and above us too, and it admitted no light. There seemed to be a bowl-shaped hole in the tunnel roof near us, a tiny shaft through the hill. It admitted the vague light of the night.

"I am in labor, Seka," came my mother's voice in the tunnel.

She waited for my reaction. She had not wanted to tell me until she was sure. She had waited, breathing, sucking the air, trying not to groan, hoping not to frighten me. She thought this must seem the end of the world to me already, this darkness, this danger, this desperation—without the fear of seeing my mother, on whom I depended, in the grip of strange horrifying circumstances which might seem to me obscene.

She thought I might not know what it meant. She spoke again, trying to sound reasonable, knowing she must keep a tight calm grip on reality for as long as she could, and direct me so that I could be carried on even when she had lost control.

"I am about to have a baby, Seka. I knew I was carrying a little baby in me. But I thought it was dead. I thought that the old woman in the barn, you remember, had killed it because that was what Smahil had paid her to do. I thought—I would lose the dead baby—when it was—time—"

139

I ran to her and she gripped on my hand, and doubled over, gasping very hard.

"But—Seka." She raised a contorted face to me, but her eyes were very clear on mine, speaking coolly and warmly to me. "I have felt the little baby stirring in the last days, while you were lost. Thank the Gods you have been found. My pearl." She hugged me. The pain subsided long enough for her to say: "Little dusk, how glad I am we are together again."

Then I had again to hold her as she doubled, groaning. "Seka, try not to be alarmed. I seem very frightening. I seem very dying. I am only having a little—live baby."

I thought of the poison she did not know she had been fed in Ilxtrith. She had been ill already, doubtless, when they took her in—but they had given her poison instead of medicine. If not at Sedili's direct bidding, then because she was the Dragon's other wife and it was too good a chance to miss. But although the fall from the carriage into the air of night seemed to have brought her to consciousness, I wondered if the poisons had seeped into what would after all be a dead baby. That might not be a bad thing, but it might depress her.

I held her hand while she was delivered of a tiny animal. Yes, it was alive. It squalled and mewed. She remained conscious throughout and was able to tell me what to do. I had nothing with which to cut the cord. She gazed weakly, steadfastly into my face. "Little Seka, listen to me, what you must do—" She seemed to drift away, drifted back and told me: "You must bite the cord. Then tie a neat knot—or your baby brother will have no belly-button. You wouldn't want that, would you?" I shook my head. I was quite willing to be as helpful as she liked. She did not add that she might bleed to death and I wouldn't like that.

Baby animal, I thought, as I gazed at it. It was mewing now. It had a scrap of body, and a little head, smaller than real babies have, so I think all in all it did not hurt my mother too much.

She reached out her arms. I picked up the baby animal and put it in them.

"It has silky hair . . ." she murmured. It had long hair all over it, I thought. It also had a most peculiar shape, a hideous face, a head like a frog, teeth which peeped out over its lip, a feathery slit. "It is female," she whispered. She couldn't say "a little girl."

I thought it must be late now. The battle might well be done. I smoothed my mother's forehead, and went up to the entrance of the tunnel. It was sealed off by something I could not move. Jammed against the entrance (not to be an exit) was this substance made of rough cloth and solidity. I thought it was the bodies of three or four men, but they must have more on and behind them, or I would be able to push them and move them at least a little.

I went back down in the dark to Cija. I made exit-blocked signs to her. She shook her head, not very interested in whatever I was telling her. She was sure it could wait.

It could wait, I thought. I went to sleep and woke with a start, thinking: "It can wait so much that when the men are decomposing and rotting we will be able to shove out past them." Then I thought: "They would not be good for my mother or the baby. Baby animals shouldn't catch sickness." From the rubble by the tunnel mouth I dreamed I dragged some stones and two big twiggy branches. I barricaded them by the bodies. This would stop the pestilence, I thought in my sleep; let us have diseased stones and twigs first.

That had been a nightmare. I felt better when I woke again and the roof-hole light was a little stronger and my mother was looking at me and smiling with her shift pulled around her neatly and her hair tugged back and plaited, and on the floor beside me, in the folds of the black cape, lay the new animal.

My mother had found a sharp flint in the wall behind her. She had broken it off and was also pulling off one of her silk boots with embroidered heels. Zerd must have found these by her in Ilxtrith, and dressed her in them. She slit the boot from top to upper with the flint, and bedded the baby in it. The effort had hurt her. She leaned back trembling, closed her eyes with relief when she touched the wall as though she had feared it were not a half-inch but astronomically far away, and lay against it as though drawing strength from its stillness.

I cuddled against her side, hoping to keep her warm. We were not actually chilly down here, but we were not warm either. I felt a lot of the natural warmth had left her because of the effort she'd been through. I missed my little

riding bird now—not so much emotionally, but because
I felt he would have kept my mother warm: he was a cud-
dly little riding bird, a feather-quilt bird.

My mother sat up. She said in a clear voice, like a
sleep-walker's:

"I know what you wanted to tell me, little Seka. We are
trapped here."

I nodded.

She was silent again, but her eye fell on the infant animal, as though she remembered it. She lifted it and it made
mewing squinting faces and twitched. She opened her shift
at the breast. Even before she had set the little creature to
it, its mouth was out in a sucker-tube, as though it scented
the milk. Its mouth, like a sleeper's limb, wavered this way
and that and when she set the nipple to it it clamped on it
so greedily and fast that it missed, catching the nipple at
the side only. Cija was watching me, I think, as I watched
the baby suckle contentedly at last. Contented is too placid
a word in fact. It was a lively little beast, full of energy,
again more like any animal than a human infant. It
grunted and worked away on Cija's nipple like a good
guest, say a good bandit guest, who would think shame to
attack a meal without belching and wiping his mouth and
exclaiming "Agh!" every few moments in the most ecstati-
cally replete of tones.

"Seka," my mother said.

I started. I had been watching, absorbed. I don't know
what my mother had seen in my face. Perhaps wistfulness,
or so it had seemed to adult eyes. "Come here," she said
gently. She held my hand while with the other arm she
continued to cradle the baby. It had sated itself now, its
head lolled back on its boot-lining, its eyes slid about sideways, its mouth reluctantly un-stoppered from the breast
but still pursued it faintly.

I know only now how hopeless my mother felt there. She
dragged herself later up to the tunnel mouth to confirm that
we had been sealed in. She must have been feeling stirrings
of sick hunger by now—she was able to feed me, too,
from her own breasts, which at least were very warm and
somewhat swollen, rather blue-veined and absolutely
creamy: you could tell from within inches of them that
they were rich with cream, like the magic cup in the fairy-
tale that was always overflowing, no matter how often it
was broached.

But she had nothing to eat. She must have thought we would die in here, that the apeling would live and die here where it had been born.

I knew my father would not find us here, even if the victory had been his. We needed help of a less practical kind than my father could give, for our situation was no practical kind of accident. I tried to have the bookshop dream again. The dream, the one I could never forget. What we need now is *that man,* I thought. He'd make everything come right. But I couldn't dream.

My mother hugged me and crooned to me in our filth and dark. "Oh, Seka's nice as bowls of rice, and Seka's good as suet pud, and Seka's funny as pots of honey . . ." and what I think was the night in this manner limped away.

When a man's voice called, "Empress! Empress! Are you there?" neither my mother nor I registered the call at first.

We had gone deaf to sounds outside our tiny dark perimeter. We had forgotten that my mother had any names. But the call came again, urgently, and there were sounds of scrabbling and a shaft of wan light hit us.

My mother opened her mouth. Sound she was able to force from herself with difficulty at a pitch the man could hear.

"Here we are! Down here we are!"

She grasped me by my arm, and holding the baby in the silk boot she hurried up the incline.

Suddenly against the light, hope-faint as it was, I saw a figure's outline. It was an enemy: it was the doctor's master.

I rushed to my barricade, thrust my arms outspread tangled in the boughs against his pushing. He pushed strongly. My left arm suddenly hung useless. It didn't hurt yet, but it didn't want to do anything arm-like at all.

Holding a burning brand, the man was turning his head from side to side in alarm at the place. He seemed very big at first: our scale had dwindled.

He and my mother stood and stared upon each other.

"Empress!" he said in an un-definite voice without edge to it now that he had discovered her, and I realized that he was sulky that he had had to call her this simply in order to locate her. This was Beautiful who had come to find us.

"What do you require of me, Riverine?" my mother asked quite flatly, since even to get the words out was almost an athletic feat for her.

"I am here to find you . . . Empress," he had again to call her this. "It was my man, my Riverine physician who brought you here. He thought to gain honor from me, and told me of the place. But it was not by my order that he left a helpless woman here with her lord's child."

My mother waited. My eyes were acclimatized to the darkness here and I could see her swaying slightly. She had been on her feet too long already.

"I am of course taking you from this dishonorable place," Beautiful said gruffly. He stepped closer formally, and caught my mother in his arms as she pitched forward.

The baby in the soiled boot fell and rolled like a longball. It caught Beautiful's eye as he lifted my mother. I tried to pick up the baby but my arm fell back to front. The baby squeaked as a new-born rat or puppy might do. "What is that?" the ignorant man asked in a sort of superstitious awe. I could not tell him, of course, and he had to make his own interpretation: "It is the Emperor's new brat, the Dragon's new spawn," he whispered. He looked at the woman, collapsed in his arm, with a new gaze. "O sweet rivers," he whispered.

He picked the infant up and gave it to me. I tried to accept, but my arm fell away again. It turned awkwardly and had begun to hurt. He said, "How is this? Is your arm broken?" He paused. I think he had remembered that it had been something my size that tried to hold him back when he broke through the branches at the entrance.

Beautiful was in a surly agony as he took us out into the light. The battle was long over, as we could tell by the state of the field. I firmly believe that he had waited to rescue us so that it should not be in sight of his cavalry (he was ashamed of rescuing us).

He was in revulsion against his rescue of us. Against his own softness and "cowardice" in having been unable to leave us to our just deserts, the fate he knew to have been his lady Sedili's wish for us (although he would always leave this indiscreet thought unspoken)— He took us in a low open riverine carriage through the dangers of the forest beyond Ilxtrith. Up into the forested chillier hills, he took us east of the Army's progress (for yes, it had been Zerd's victory over Ilxtrith). Swarming with the fled Ilxtrivans (malevolent in their last-ditch magics) and with gigantic bears and huge screaming fearless eagles as these woods were, he journeyed with us through their perils quite sunk in his humiliation—at his abject craven poltroonery in disobeying the dictates of his conscience regarding us.

At a turn in the rutted slope, where the trees thinned for a yard and one could see the plateau below, I looked back and saw the pale field.

Something like a gray ghost drifted over the field, the corpses, the ragged knots of looters. Its billowing arms outstretched as if for grabs. It was a tattered flag, a standard still haltingly held horridly grayly aloft (it was muddied and limp) by a limping searcher among the dead.

The Riverine regarded it silently. His brows lay straight over the soft spiky sooty lashes all round his savage eyes. The sight of a standard was a wound to him, a reminder of the honor he had forfeited by refusing to leave us to die in the earth.

He turned on me. "Child," he commanded me in a voice of hate, "there is a bear pelt in the back of the carriage which recently I killed. Wrap your lady mother in that. She shakes." He loathed our weakness, which bred his.

The bear pelt had not been properly cured, but it was fairly clean. The sinews and skin still adhering to it had dried like tassels. I wrapped my mother and her burden in it, as well as I could. My arm was half-killing me now. I applied all my concentration to stay out of a swoon. We lurched on up into the fragrant coniferous wildernesses.

And it was when we reached the water that our lives changed, all of our lives. Till now, Beautiful had been taking us merely to a place of safety, to the first hut or cottage where he could leave us and gather again about him, on his return to his Riverine regiment, the tattered shreds of his honor. But here, as we met the river leaping down from the crags, it took command of him too and the world would never again for Beautiful be simple. For as he stopped and dismounted from the carriage seat to

make a simple obeisance to the water before driving
through it, the water ceased to flow for a moment—and
a purely blue bird, the color of water when it runs deep,
flew out from behind the waterfall above us, at the same
instant as a blue fish leaped up from the river and on to
Beautiful's cloak as he knelt there.

Beautiful's cloak with its Riverine signs had spread aus-
picious portent prominent (Riverines often use their cloaks
for prognostication, damping them, throwing them down
and watching how they fall) and the blue-scaled fish had
skipped between two signs of the life beyond this.

He gaped and my mother leaned up on her elbow in
the odoriferous fur in the open carriage, the waters
parted and here emerged a figure wading, who came out
breathing from the river.

"How now!" cried Beautiful, going to the man and
shaking him where he panted on the bank prostrate.
"Yóu have just come out of the river, which we have
kept our eyes on this several minutes, and not seen you
enter. Yet you are breathing."

"Only just, sir, I assure you," answered the man painfully. But now there came the sound of a bell clanging
dolefully and brazenly . . . below the water.

Beautiful started, and then suddenly threw himself
prostrate on the bank beside the man.

"Sweet rivers!" he prayed. "Now I receive your miracle
which you have granted me. I realize that you have approved my humble sacrifice, my utter loss of myself, in
which I gave away all I held dearest and inmost in my
nature, namely my honest loyal honor, in order to listen
unwillingly to that which even more deeply lay in me—
namely, your sweet liquid conducting voice, which now
I know ebbs and flows between all men."

The man, who stared at this praying nobleman lying
in the mud and turf, was very impressed by Beautiful's
prayer. It is elevating of the occasion when you stumble
out of a river and the people on the bank start to pray
about it. My mother and I were impressed by Beautiful's
reaction too. We had never seen him so humble and irradiated. He seemed much more pleased about things
now.

"Come, ride with us," he said to the man.

The man was rather wet and glad enough to ride with
us in the sun. "Are you off to Soursere, then?" asked the

man, as though there wouldn't be anywhere else to be off to. Beautiful had reverently taken up the little blue-scaled fish, who had died on his cloak while he prayed, and placed it on my knee. "This little fish spoke to me of you, direct from the god," he said to me. Direct from the river, after all, meant direct from the god.

We drove through the river. It did not exactly part for us, but it rose up in two great wings glittering on our either side.

"Soursere be this way," the man reminded us gently, wetly indicating east.

Beautiful, obviously now letting himself be floated on the billows as they rolled, let himself be guided by the man's single mention of the sibilant name, and we continued until we reached a great precipice.

"Is Soursere down there?" Beautiful asked, but without doubt.

"Indeed," said the man cheerfully, and he jumped out of the carriage and pulled on a winch we now saw mounted on the cliff-edge. A great cradle, or in fact a sort of raft with little half-walls hung in a chimney of the cliff to which the man now led us. It looked from above like the floor of a natural fissure in the rock, but when he gestured we stepped down on to it, Beautiful helping my mother and even me very matter-of-factly.

The man pulled on the great ropes, which let down very easily. "You will have to leave your wagon and your brace of nice pulling-birds," the man said shyly to Beautiful. "But we can come back later for them, and take each down separately. The cradle will bear their weight thus."

"Lower away," Beautiful said easily. We began to pass beneath great boughs and roots twisted into the precipice. The birds stood meekly still in harness to Beautiful's "wagon" and watched us sink from sight.

My mother with her strange bootling in her arms sat at our feet on the raft. I pulled the bear-fur closer around her. The air was brisk and crisp but full of sun as it struck through the boughs. The man so recently de-riverized was heavy with water still, his blackened clothes like a suit of iron, the drips falling like beads on the logs of the raft. Now as we accustomed our eyes to the bright air beaming before us we saw that what faced

us in our descent was not solely sky. "The sea?" cried
Beautiful, and blanched.

From then on as we descended he stood in thought,
for so much water is master of the rivers.

There stretched a gray beach, and on it quite near
the foot of our cliff a figure stood fishing with a mighty
rod. But he suddenly raised his knees to his nose,
gathered up his paraphernalia *and ran.* There was no
sign of any other living being but the birds and quick
rodents as we now beached.

A long grim mill stood at the confluence of two rivers
and on a spit of sour grass which tongued into a gray sea.
The rivers were turbulent wooded creatures. One river
was clear. The other river was of "black" water, very
soft and acid as we were to discover during our agony at
the mill, full of peat and bark and iron ore leached into
it after heavy rain particularly. Some fish avoided it, but
the other river was full of life: in the Spring, for instance,
the entire pond would be frogs, no water it would seem,
only frogs, edible frogs, a great delicacy, crawling on
each other's backs for the breeding of yet other frogs
to crawl upon each other's backs: a great orgasm of
leapfrog. Meanwhile this was high summer and as sere
and bleak as ever it was here.

The mill, a tidal mill, was built on rock in a narrow
deep-walled estuary, fed by the fresh-water river (and
the black-water stream) from the high coniferous mountains. There was a water-wheel either side, so one could
turn whether the tide was going in or coming out; this
was a prosperous mill, a fat mill, and its brewery stood
to its rear. The twenty-foot water-wheel on the seaside
was made of applewood to withstand the salt water. It
was powered by tidal water sluiced through from the
large feeder pond replenished each high tide.

The sun had disappeared. Rain spilled down from
incontinent clouds.

"I can't wait to get you to a good place, Seka," my
mother whispered, "to get the sicky out of your hair."
For of course at one point I had been sick a little in the
tunnel: I had forgotten that by now, but of course my
neater more easily grief-stricken mother had not. When
I was a little younger I had not realized my mother used

words like "sicky" for *my* benefit and I used to wonder: Won't she ever grow up?

My arm was not so awful now. The crisp air of the cliff had stung it like needles. That, and my concentration on it, had made me feel more alive. But it would not be long before the airs of Soursere took over. Always damp, always heavy.

First the dogs of Soursere rushed out upon my mother. Before Beautiful could see what they were about, they had hurled themselves on her, slavering and yipping. Beautiful beat them off with his bare fore-arms; he had no time to reach for a knife. The Miller came striding out. "It's yer bearskin," he roared at my fainting mother. "Take the bearskin off, yer dozey dick, they think yer a bear." Only then did he deign to call his beasts off. He snapped out their names. They came to heel.

Now the horror was over, I remembered how he had walked out like a man with all the time in the world. He would not be seen to hurry: beneath a man's dignity.

Beautiful pulled the bear-fur off my mother and wrapped his cloak about her, I was glad to see. He stood there panting, big driblets of gouting blood springing up along his arms and shoulders like fountains just discovered by the dowser.

"Nearly torn apart that time!" the Miller grinned. Obviously a wit.

The man who had crawled out of the river now went to the Miller and spoke earnestly to him. He and Beautiful had been each other's miracle. The man, a neighbor here, a good swimmer, had found himself unconscious in the river, the more charming river of the two. He must have been knocked out by the shock of an electric eel. Yet when he came to, he could breathe. What had happened? It had taken him some time to work out what had happened. An old bell, on the alarm tower of a building drowned some time ago in one of the area's periodic landslides, had been his shelter, for there was still air trapped in it and he had floated into it from below. He had towed his strange host toward shore, judging by the river-bed which he knew to some extent, and in doing so had knocked out a piece of week-crusted driftwood which had jammed the clapper. As he emerged from his watery bed, the bell tolled for him beneath the racing currents.

He had emerged to find a splendid, exotic, unattended nobleman praying passionately upon the bank.

Beautiful, for his part, had seen a blue fish leap and a blue bird fly (birds nested behind the waterfall for the cool and safety where they could ambush the fish) and he had heard a bell toll as a man "walked" breathing out of the blue river.

His god, for his god was in any river, had given him a sign—a sign of approval, which had sanctioned his charity toward his enemies. (Us.)

The Miller, and his assistant who followed him out covered with dust looked at Beautiful with round eyes, yet still appraising.

"The lady is sick. She has just given birth," Beautiful indicated us. "The child's arm needs splinting. It may be broken."

"What do you pay for a good splint then?" was the miller's query. Now his wife had joined him, straddling out of the Mill with her own baby, a few months old, over her hip.

"An odd baby," the Miller's Wife said doubtfully, looking at ours. Beautiful was surprised, but bristled at her remark. "Comparisons are no part of charity," he informed her, and "Had we presumed to assess your baby?"

Cija's mouth twisted into a grin. She looked sideways at Beautiful.

"The little one must have splint of course," the Wife said. "How you done that?" she asked me. I stared at her. Beautiful explained my dumbness.

The Mill children crowded round while I was splinted, asking me questions to "test" me. The ruder they were, they reasoned, nudging each other and giggling, the more likely I would be to betray myself and let out an oath.

More children arrived to stare as the Mill's spread the news: "Ooh, fur baby, and blue girl no throat inside. Must come from Flinchwum." Flinchwum was the next village—the other side of the moor, full of strangers.

We were taken into the Mill.

We sat with rafters down around our ears like scarfs. The grown-ups sat huddled under the muffling ceiling. There was a chimney corner into which the children were herded: proportionately lower.

We ate eel, no bread. Because Beautiful was real company, the mill-wife brought a bowl of warm water for the men to dip their fingers in. Beautiful glanced at my mother, at her face so familiar to him and yet never before as colorless and pointed. He knelt, took off her remaining boot and bathed her sad feet. The Miller and his family were awed and admiring. My mother and I later realized they saw no honor to her in this action of Beautiful's (though in fact he had been quite tenderized by the fact my mother was the agent which had brought him salvation/truth when he turned his back on Sedili's feud)—the Mill inmates saw only the splendid spectacular humility of a saintly nobleman lowering himself to a servant's feet. The Mill saw no mercy in Beautiful's action. They saw only a sort of exercise in humility, which could have been at the feet of a *statue* of a servant girl. The fact that she was a female servant made her lowest of all, and therefore his humility was the most complete possible.

Servant? Yes, for Beautiful put my mother solemnly in the safe-keeping of the Miller. We would soon discover the Miller's belief that thus he now owned Cija, who otherwise was no good to him except as property.

It did no good for my mother to insist that she and I were "important." They disbelieved her—what, in that old garment? For her gown, rent and stained now, was of plain linen they could not tell was rich, and with lace they could not tell was masterly. And it only alienated Beautiful for my mother to call herself "important." He frowned and turned away at once. He had come here full of humility. She must not strut.

My mother did not push the matter. I think at first she half-feared kidnap for a ransom demand. She expected soon to be off again, with Beautiful, to join the campaign, if she went along with his mood.

The Wife, wishing to curry favor with the noble and saintly visitor, seeing that the infant apeling was sickly, wanted to "dip babby in well"—it was magic water, she explained. "Won't boil. Mothers dip sick babbies in. If they turn pink, they'll live. If pale, they'll die." My mother saved the infant which was being taken off by the loving Wife. "No wonder the water won't boil," my mother managed to say, "if all those children have been in it."

Obviously, it seemed to me, that well outside was a

speedy kill-or-cure. But Beautiful was listening hard too.
Here at least, water was recognized important.

The neighbor who had been saved by the bell under
the water started discussing with Beautiful how to return
for his wagon and brace of birds.

Now the fire fled up the chimney as the door opened
again—and I was flattened against the wall, my splinted
arm twanging, as a thick man passed me. He didn't notice
me as he entered because he was the sort of man who
thinks children unnoticeable. His face was screwed up
bad-temperedly against the wind and rain as though he
had a right to be annoyed with the weather—as though
weather hadn't any right to annoy him.

"Quar," Miller greeted the newcomer, "here under my
roof-beam sits great good noble who has brought folk here
well saved."

And the newcomer Quar flicked the grown-ups all a
glance from his eyes greenish like something festering in
his round face. He had thick brown curly hair and muscles and a *blue* cloak—he was the only local inhabitant
we'd seen who wasn't totally outfitted in the ubiquitous
river-clay pink.

My mother looked at the newcomer Quar and almost
shivered. She looked at me and said very softly, "Such a
little waif. What I drag you through."

Quar introduced himself to the Beautiful Saint. He was
a brew-house wholesaler, he said very smug, but my
mother and I guessed without a word he was also probably
a local bandit.

"Go get my team," Quar grandly instructed the wet
neighbor. "My boys will help you shift the Noble's carriage."

And Quar inquired could he furnish a guide wherever
the Noble was wishful of going.

I studied my mother's face. She was watching the struggle going on in our Beautiful Saint—for obviously he reckoned that by his action he had outlawed himself forever
from fealty to Sedili.

My arm was throbbing. I was beginning to feel like
someone asleep. I cherished the echo of my mother's voice
saying so softly to me, "little waif." Would the loving
stream pour out for the new baby too? Would it be *pearl,
joy, dusk?*

"Before I plan for the leaving of this place, I would

know of this place," Beautiful said slowly. "What does this place?"

"Makes water," Miller said, jovial. "My mill is the heart of Soursere that pumps out the bread, the beer, the biceps of our good folk."

"Are they many?"

"Our population is thirty-seven males," says Miller. (Nobody bothers to count the women. Male children only are registered.)

"It is now thirty-eight," says the Beautiful Saint without asking will they have him.

There was a pause. They couldn't in fact welcome him to Soursere, since they had no idea of community here. They couldn't imagine what difference he would make, living here. They were impressed by him, that was true.

My mother, white, drained, kept her eyes fixed on him. She had no idea either what things would be like now, or what difference this Riverine, generally in full spate, might mean to us—he was too remote from the mill to be seen in relation to it, and already we seemed drawn densely into the mill.

Beautiful leaned over my mother as he went out with the wet neighbor. "And what shall you call this little life?" he asked, touching a finger on her apeling. "Is it not Despair?" she said listlessly.

One thing at least was certain, and that was that to all intents we were now alone. When the Saint had gone, the Miller wanted the ring from my mother's finger. The ring wouldn't tug off. Miller was pulling. The man Quar came over. He raised my mother's finger to his mouth and licked it to make it slippery—drew the ring off with his teeth. He kept it, reminding the grumbling Miller of an old debt. My mother lay in her chair, the infant at her breast. It was making its mewing. "You do not feed that thing," Miller suddenly roared virtuously, "here. Out in the barn. That is where the animals wallow bare."

My mother had made hardly a motion toward the cloth at her breast. She looked up at him—though by now she could hardly see, nearly blind by now she nearly was with fatigue and starving for reality.

"I thank you for your hospitality," she said to the Miller. "My children and I shall go gladly, with much gratitude, to your barn. Perhaps of your good charity you

may permit us to stay there a day or so, when I shall be
more recovered from the birth of my baby which was
only last night, and when my little daughter's arm shall be
mending? And may I ask in the meantime, where is the
Dragon's Army? Is it spread about this area? Is it moving
North or North-West?"

Miller stared at her and went out.

My mother looked in bewilderment, hauling herself to
her feet, from the man Quar to the mill-wife. The man
Quar, himself following the Miller out, deigned to speak
to her just as he vanished over the threshold:

"No, he doesn't mean to show you the barn," he said.
"Wife shall that."

My mother gazed distressfully at the Wife.

The Wife said nothing either, except "Barn, then." We
followed her, sliding in the mud, to a miserable place
from which most of the hay had gone already, although
winter was only just on the horizon. It was not open-
sided, however, since the wind blew spray from the sea,
rivers and mill-race all about the yard, which was always
under water; and the Miller had walled his hay up well.
We sank down on the scratchy bales, which smelt of salt
rather than meadows, and I found with pleasure that I
could look down on to the other half of the barn, in which
were pigs and ponies and a popular manger. If you are to
have any moments of delirium, best to have entertainment
on which to base your hallucinations. I had that feeling of
well-being that comes with helplessness, but kept an eye
on my mother. The Wife brought left-over eel, cold this
time, and left it with us, and my mother took her time
about feeding Despair.

"Greedy sucker," the Wife says, observing its tight pull
on the nipple which had already engorged again to meet
demand. "It's feeding soon for one born only in the night.
You can't have had too difficult a time with that, no? Its
head is not a giant's. A tiny lively baby altogether. Yet
it's not right, is it? Is it not well, or not right?"

"Time will tell," my mother said shortly.

"If it lives or dies or what," the Wife said, "it will do
all at speed. You'll be in house again soon."

"I shall be off after my lord in the Army."

"Ah, no," says the Wife with a tight mouth and not
meeting my mother's eye, as though determined not to be
cheated by a tinker selling blandishments on her doorstep,

"you don't go on like that. Miller has bought you." She left us at that.

It was true. Miller had bought my mother. We found this out bit by bit, for the Miller wouldn't demean himself by explaining to her.

The Saint had placed my mother in Miller's care. And he had given Miller money. "That was to pay, and handsomely, for my food and shelter and Seka's!" my mother cried.

Wife shook her head. "No," she said. "We've heard of money. This new invention called coins—we know what it is. And it was good of my man to take it. You be grateful. Instead of asking for linen or beef or a bird out of that nice pair that Great Saint drives, my man accepted *coins* and you. And is he turning out your childer? No. How many men would have kept both childer and let you laze while you suckle for first days?"

My mother became feverish in the night at the very time that she had become most cool and determined. She had hidden slices of eel under my cloak and her own, and had bound straw round our feet to keep us warm and silent. "When the stars begin to lose their shadows," she said to me, whispering in case the pigs overheard grunting at their hollowed log filled with bits, "the Mill will be deepest asleep. Then we shall slip out very secretly, my dusk, and be away."

But as she began to toss and burn, and to reassure me in her calm too husky voice, I begged for permission to go to the Mill and wake them and ask for a doctor—or at least, she knew as I tugged on her sleeve and begged her with my eyes what I wanted to do.

She said No, wait a little, only a little and she would gather strength—until she became unconscious and then briefly wakened to say in a clearer voice: "Yes, Seka darling, go and tell them."

I hurried to the house. The door was locked. They were proud prosperous peasants, and locked out the world at night. I banged but no one came. I found a side window and slid over the lintel, and found myself in a black passage with an angle to it like a dog's leg.

The downstairs room of the Mill living-space was still chocked with dirty crocks and pitchers half full of stuff growing scum. It all smelt. The Wife now was saving up housework for my mother to do upon her recovery. I hurried to the upstairs chamber, where I could hear the noises of the sleeping family. The two levels were linked by a whole log set up against the wall, notches hacked in it. At the top of this stair I ducked into a black cupboard in the wall, and here in one milling bed slept the family; hens perched about them, beaks simpering under wings, but the more aware guard-hens outside, roosting on the log-notches, had already given the alarm.

The Wife sat up in bed and against a raucous crowing gobbling she demanded: "Eh? How did you get in?"

The Miller himself stirred and regarded me from under his blanket. He had a woven blanket with a blue stripe in it all to himself. The "conversation" was left to the Wife.

I knew she could see me easily, since the main-room window was behind me. I pointed to the barn, hoping they'd be intelligent enough to make the connection with my mother. Then I pointed to my own puny chest, rocking a "baby" but with failing gestures—dropping my head to show weakness, pressing my hand to it and to my breast and side, then jerking my head to show distress and fever. I pointed barn-wards again and waited. "The little bitch is mad," the Wife said. "Get out of our room!" she yelled at me.

I pointed urgently again.

"It's about to have a fit," the Wife said. "It's come here to show us its convulsions. You're not pretty, little bitch. We don't want to watch you!"

"It's turned blue already!" joked one of the boys with a hoot.

The Miller smiled, and dug his witty youngster in the ribs.

The Wife, seeing this, suddenly changed her tune. Once the master had indicated his mood, then she must obey it unquestioningly. But she needn't necessarily have seen his half-smile and nudge, and she was (so far) free to berate the youngster for his wit.

"You!" she clouted her son's ear. "Who asked you?" And she gathered up her breasts in both arms to keep them out of her own way, eased out of the bed, and came over to me.

"Now," she demanded standing over me, her presence heavy but no longer menacing, "what I want to know is, how did you get in here? The door is locked, ain't it?"

I nodded.

"Wouldn't that tend to mean," she continued, "that people don't want to be dropped in on in the way of midnight social visits?"

I took her hand to tug her to the passage and window. She shook off my hand as though it were a wet toad, which I have found to some people a blue hand is; but she followed me, nimbly lumbering down the log with her armfuls of breast and then stopping at the passage entrance. "Not here!" She gazed on me. "You didn't get through here!"

She held me back, running her eyes curiously all over me as though expecting to find dreadful marks on me. It was a lustful look, odd from her, as though she dreaded to see something and yet would feast her eyes endlessly.

I thought of my mother alone and desperate in nightmare, anxious about me and blaming herself for having let me out of her sight (a *voiceless waif,* unable to call for help if I had fallen). I had had enough of this Wife. I darted from her grasp and down the passage. As I dodged its zig-zagger bend in the blackness, I did notice a certain extra heavy chill in its air, and a certain faint dark tingling too, as though the air were throbbing hopelessly, and I thought, "So the passage is haunted. That's why they use it like a sort of extra guard against burglars." I pushed the window again, and hurried through it, darting off again past the hooded well it looked on to, and to the barn.

At the barn the Wife met me. She had a candle in a turnip, and some bandages and a black bottle in the crook of her apron (she slept in her apron, which was woollen and warm).

"All right, what's up?" she demanded, tramping over the bales to my mother. So she had understood my "convulsions" all the time. I think I'll take some real ones some time—I'm owed them now.

4

The Haunt in the Well

THE GOOD DAYS were the days of fever in the barn. When my mother's breast abscess was healed, we took up our duties and joined the family. We too slept in the bed—every night, just as the hens all ran in from the yard and up the "stairs," to roost on bed-head and rafters, so we eased with the children and Wife and Miller into the rugs and blankets on the straw-filled mattress. My arm was still sore and weak and apt to jump, though I do not think it had been broken. It was now much battered by sleeping partners. It became apparent that we could filch and keep a comfortable space for ourselves just as the others could, so long as Miller himself was in what he reckoned best position. If Miller grunted, Wife was up in bed throwing the rest of us around like chaff, but if she complained she had fallen into a hollow or had lost a covering, Miller ignored her and we could all stay as we were.

"The Army has long passed from within our orbit," The Saint gravely assured my mother when he visited. "While you were ill, the Army marched on and away."

My mother looked as gravely at him.

"Riverine," she said, "you journeyed from the far Northern waterlands to serve in my mother's Southern slag, and that was less to you than the saddle-leather you wore away. Are journeys now such undertakings in this new parochialism?"

The Saint would not be drawn. "The Army is far away," he repeated, "impossibly far away, and lost to us. Let us be grateful in our souls that now we are with these good simple folk."

It meant nothing to him that she had been put into service in the Mill. He too, he said, was in service to these folk, the only service worth while, and in which perhaps he might expiate some millionth part of his former arrogance.

He was clearing ditches with the men of Soursere. "The ditches must be cleaned out once yearly or choke in their own vegetation." He delighted in these nature-notes.

"Pray Gods there be rain soon," he added—it was an order.

My mother stared at him.

"There was rain not so long since," she said. "And you cannot call this drought." The sky over the mill and village always maddened and irritated Cija—it hung mottled and striped with dark gray and fleecy lighter gray cloud like some roof, too low and solid, of birch bark—"it's a sky to murder under," my mother said through clenched teeth.

It was cold in the Mill during the day with no fire left for us, and I snuggled against my mother and wished she'd think about the General and get a force field of warmth going. But perhaps she could never think magnetically again, now.

"We need rain," repeated the new countryman.

"I cannot pray," my mother said definitely, hefting to her breast her Despair, and to the other breast one of the sleek gray puppies she was nursing—for as soon as she was well enough, the Miller had given her his prize whelps to suckle too.

"When I was in the tunnel with Seka and giving birth, I prayed harder than ever in my life before. But I received no answer."

I thought myself that I had been aware, in the birth-tunnel, of our Cousin, our nearest God. My mother maybe had been praying so hysterically within herself that she had not listened for his reply.

"Yet here you are," the Saint said to my mother.

My mother lifted the puppy a little to the side for mutual comfort. "To be here is an answer to prayer?" she asked, her face white.

The Saint was not thinking of the colors of ladies' faces. "I need your co-operation," he told my mother simply and humbly, " . . . with your reading."

"I have already learned," my mother said.

"But never have I learned," The Saint said. "Will you give me your help, of your good charity? I wish for knowledge. Only thus can I be of help to our folk here. I need discipline. I shall struggle with my letters as with my sins."

"Then I ask your help in return," my mother said. The Saint bowed his head submissively to hear her, but she paused before she said stiffly:

"Every morning, before he goes to work, Miller locks his Wife into a chastity belt. And me he locks too."

The Saint lifted a wary face. "These people's customs and traditions—" he began.

"I strongly represented to him," went on my mother, "that this was unacceptable. He allows me now to be locked by his wife from and into this machine, which I think his unhappy ancestresses wore before me. He is adamant that women in his household must wear these things till they lie down to sleep. But if you spoke to her—"

"I understand your feeling," The Saint said soberly. "However we may sympathize with these folks' honest taboos, we have not yet thrown off our own culture. I will see what I can do to give you help as you ask."

It was chilly wooing that my mother now received from Quar, or the beginnings of a wooing.

Quar lived just up-river in the brewhouse. I had never thought of the brewhouse as human habitation; it had no windows. While I rinsed linen in the pond, I stared at the brewhouse. Like all these long low squat houses, it had been built not *for* but *against*. They were built against the forest, against the sea, against the elements, against the world. They had roof-beams and walls and doors and hatred—as though in this part of the world an architect always included hatred among his tools, and said to his apprentice: "Mind you've brought along enough hatred today."

These buildings at Soursere, at Sourditch and Sourbed were not for people. Openings were deep suspicious slits. Holes: you couldn't call them windows, but the brewhouse had not even those.

I hoped to our dear God we should not spend winter here. Now the water-snail was skating along upside-down under the surface of the pond, since our pond was his floor. The whirligig water-beetles were sliding over the water as though it were a mattress of transparent rubber, springing like acrobats. The water-louse (you couldn't make out his legs from his whiskers) was searching for decay—he adored to clear up for you. All the pond now was alive with little skimming popping jetting projectiles —up for air, then down again. Now the water was going wipple-whibble. Now if you looked you could see the little springs and fountains rilling up from the fine sand-bed of the stream. The sandy bank was a fretwork—lots of little black holes, swallows' nests. The mill-stream was singing high and singing low. Ferns were uncoiling like springs, like busy clockwork. The field-mouse fell into the mill-pond—he was done for. He was snapped up by pike. Now the hedges were cut down to keep the sun (although the frost too) off the fields; and this was to stop the hedges soaking up the good of the soil: there was not enough good in this soil to squander on hedges. But at least there was sun now, from time to time, enough to make a sunset sky come evening, mottled like the thighs of a fat woman too long by the stove.

And when the winter came down on us at Soursere, we should need that stove, be grateful for those mottled thighs. The clues were everywhere for the seeing. Every door hereabouts had been built short with a gap under the roof lintel; come winter, the all-wood lintel was certain to sag under the great weight of months of snow. (The gap in the meanwhile was stuffed with moss.)

In the Mill, the old tiny glass panes show permanent scars—the abrasion of savage sea sands carried in winter blasts.

"You know the taste of your heart in your mouth," Quar, watchful, said to my mother quietly at the end of the first meal we ate all together when he visited.

The Wife was not a cozy cook. Her soup was chicken wrung out in hot water. A poor little bird—it never did anyone any harm—till now. Her fire was generally out, but a sludgepot hung over it just the same. She called it her stewpot.

My mother did not reply to Quar.

"You've travelled," he said to her under cover of the general meal-babble. "You've travelled and you've learned to keep silent. I like that."

He should have liked me then, I thought utterly silently. But he showed no signs of liking me.

"What is this?" my mother said, for he had given her something.

He glanced at her with annoyance from his poisonous eyes. He reckoned that if he had handed something to a woman quietly, while generously flattering her silence, she must be a fool not to know secrecy was afoot.

In her hand lay her ring, which the Miller had stolen from her and which then Quar had appropriated. I saw her gasp as she thought of the money and possible freedom it represented, and of how she could hide it away in the barn with her maps and Ung-g's necklace. But then I saw another look come over her face. That look with which women say to themselves: "This foolish man finds me attractive. I wonder how I can turn his foolishness to my advantage, while myself remaining cool and in command as ever."

Quar noted this look, the look he had worked for. And from that moment there was relationship between my mother and Quar.

He continued to flatter her. He was in a sense quite selfless about it, since it was obvious that for him to praise was an effort. He came nearest to liking her when he was rudest with her. But this would not be for some time yet. He meant to have her.

He knew she must be approached very carefully and with all the proper contempt.

So now he lied to her, as though she were some simpleton, about how pretty she looked with a sunbeam on her head. It lit her all too cruelly in fact. She was thin. Her breasts were two pins. After hard work, her hands were mauve with saffron spots floating in them. Her knuckles stood out rather more like elephants' knees.

My mother smiled at Quar. He was for the time being satisfied.

As the men went out, the Miller knocked over a jug. The Wife, without a look of reproach, stooped picking it all up and my mother joined her. "That's because you put him there as blandishment," Miller said meaningfully to his Wife's stooped back. She did not presume to reply, though she must have been puzzled. "Ah," Miller grunted darkly. "What was him put sitting there full of flowers for? For you to show off because a visitor was coming."

"It was mark of respect because Quar was coming," the Wife quavered.

"Respect to yourself," Miller told her sternly. "Pride in showing how you can make 'your' house full of jugs of flowers."

Miller waited till the Wife and my mother had cleared up the mess. Then, to make his point, he booted the jug over once more. "And mind when I get back that shit ain't still over the floor," he warned as he walked out, free at last to meet other men in business, but having paused as was his tedious duty to have another try at the endless education of his household.

I'd noticed while this was going on how Quar had seized his chance to spit in my mother's drink. He regarded my mother then, as he left but did not again speak to her, with a grim amused proprietary air: his spit, once she drank it, would impregnate her soul: she would have no inner resistance to him, since something of Quar had already been accepted as part of her. The Wife now stopped clearing the floor, for her husband and Quar were no longer there to witness her. She pulled me forward by my ear. "You heard your master. Get it all up." She saw me pause because the cloth was already slimy. "Lick it up if you must." I didn't bother in the middle of all this to invent some way of warning my mother about her drink—after all, it wouldn't hurt her.

I thought I'd keep away from the main riverbanks where people were praying at The Saint's inspiration for the "drought" to end. But I was sent to the garden-woman at Soursouth to buy vegetables—"and mind nobody see you," the Wife added, pushing her face into mine. She meant that Miller must not see me. In her pursuit of an image of perfection, she attempted to keep a kitchen-garden for the Mill; it was a scrappy failure. But Miller thought it un-economic not to "grow your own" when you had ground. (In fact, looking back, I realize now how stony and acid his sandy mud was, but I believe he and his Wife never dreamed their precious Mill-land was not right for everything.) So the Wife would send out secretly for vegetables, and grain for her home-baking, and pretend she'd grown it all herself.

I set out with my basket. Soursouth lay inland. It was uncanny how muffled the land became once you were away from the Mill. There was no longer the grinding

of the great stones which I felt permeated the Mill air.
Then the pulse of the wheel set the whole building in an
ague. The leather grain chutes provided a constant rustle
—and a warning bell would ring quite often when the
supply of grain stopped; else we'd have been set afire
by the revolving stones, the terrible runner stone spark-
ing on the gigantic bedstone if they ran "dry."

Outside, on the shore-wall of the Mill, the air was always a moan. The sea was a way off, and quieter than
the sands themselves. The villagers called them "singing sands." The grains were of silicified wood. The dunes
here blew all about anywhere and lay sloppily, flabby.
The villagers had spoiled their original slant-shape, they
could no longer resist winds and protect the shore-
houses. For so long the peasants had grazed their cattle
on islands just off-shore (because that saved them building cattle-walls) and had cut the timber—so there was
no resistance left in the shore now. The sand was no
longer held together by roots and lob-lolly pines.

I gazed at the lurid colored cliff out there beyond the
harbor. It rises almost sheer from the farther waves, who
beat terribly on its base. It is forbidden. No one moors
there. It is Old Land—land that was thrown up from the
ancient places beneath the sea. Also, these peasants are
too stupid to get away from land. A few yards out, that's
all they can manage, driving their poor cattle and rotting
their hooves. They can't swim or row much. Only one
man, I heard, had rowed near the foot of the Cliff: "He
don't talk of it."

Shoulderblades tingled.

I knew I could fly there.

I'd fly *above* the high elemental-filled waves which
had kept him fiercely off the base of the Cliff.

I took a deep breath of the ozoney sea air here, where
the red slippy sand combined with the salt. I felt my
lungs were full of health to last me past the head of the
mill-race as I turned inland.

Here the breathing was sluggish for everything. Blackened trees seemed to hang on the sour acid air, rising
from dazzlingly green moss which was bog. These were
poisoned trees because they were Soursere trees.

The river by me seethed. The tadpole of the hill-
torrent frog had suckers to avoid being swept away by
water-fall. The caddis fly larvae built cocoons which they

weighted against the current by adding sand particles and even tiny stones. Like the peasants building *against* the elements of their world, the water and its occupants were enemies, in constant combat. Around it all patrolled the venomous freshwater stingrays, hoping for stream-bed crustaceans, ready to unsheath a terrible spine into whatever enemy appeared. Was this what the Saint meant by the Communication of River?

I followed the river where the two-colored streams mix, though for a time they run along flowing side by side.

I knew it was the "black" water, which had drained heavy-forest and leached much dead leafage, that the Mill Wife's haunted well consisted of.

I knew there was something troubled and venomous, a sort of indoor stingray, in the dark passage which looked on the well. No one in the Mill would go in the passage if they could help it. Even my mother had quickly pulled me out of it once as I seemed about to enter. "Not in there without a candle, Seka," she said to explain herself; but there was a pulling draft where it zig-zagged, and candle-flame could be undesirable, surely.

I cut through the forest to scrubby hillside, land despoiled by Kings and other predators.

There on the rise ahead of me lay the vegetable woman's cabin up to its eaves in cauliflower and cactus.

It was hung about, like a tinker's cart, with goodies she hoped would attract a customer's attention—the ubiquitous fir-cone toys, gaily painted farming implements which had faded in the weather, tooled leather aprons crusted salty from the sea winds, wine-flagons in string cradles from whence all but a grapey stain had long departed . . .

I walked up the lane. In the fields, the working women wore visors, kerchiefs over their nostrils and mouths to save them breathing in dust and seeds. Their eyes swivelled at me over their visors: like me, they were speechless just now. Other women near the hedges, their hands steeped in green slime, were busy crushing cater-pillars on the branches where foliage was being destroyed.

"Jolly ho! Where you to here now, cuntlet?" one demanded of me.

I appreciated her insisting on advance warning of my invasion. But I could only nod at her, and walk on.

"A very madam-nod he gives me!" she roared, and she hurled on me her basket of caterpillar-pulp.

At this, all the other ladies followed suit. I stood there, quivering, emerald slime across my face and dress where some of it still writhed.

There was another sound suddenly, and I was seized up in the air and whirled around. There was an arm round my waist. A strong big arm, and the sound was a roar of an utterly different strength from the women's— here was the yell of a full-bodied fisherman.

I was enveloped in the smell of salt and sea, before even I turned and found the grizzled face of the man who had lifted me. He was brushing me down, calling to the fieldful of women: "Faithless! Ye faithless!"

I thought he was another kind of Saint. Then I saw that though the women were wincing aghast, cringing automatically in apologetic fits because here was a male, he was yelling:

"Bitches! Ye promised yr'insects to me. Do y'expect fish from me at any time these dry months?" He continued to brush me down, salvaging off my clothes as much squirming slime as he could and scooping it into one of the small wicker pouches hung on and around himself. He wore feathers with hooks on them in his ear-rings, ready for baiting the end of a line, and his cuffs were silver like a lord's—for they were bright with fish-scales.

He continued grumbling about the waste of caterpillars. I was to discover later what a terrible time he always had getting hold of lugworms. The peasants never would keep proper compost, in which the lugworm so softly and blackly flourishes if only given a chance.

He took me back with him to the vegetable-woman's cabin. He thought I would scrape off more easily there. He was currently passionately committed to the vegetable woman. She was a squat, square-hipped muddy woman, a taciturn very female person with a great richness of experience and compost.

When she appeared, and Fishhead had become rigid with intensity as she entered her cabin—he flushed in his beard and side-curls, and then stood up and took her very shyly and strongly by the pubic curls through her canvas smock and kissed her on the mouth, not to be denied—she took the green-smeared list from the bottom of my basket.

The Wife could not write of course, but it would have been useless if she could—no other woman would have been able to read what she wrote. The shopping list was scrawled in a series of signs. The vegetable woman grunted that the Mill-wife's cabbages were always indistinguishable from her carrots.

"I'll give her some of both," she said. "She wants milk, mm?" she grunted at me. "Wants jam? My jam very lovely right now, she'll want it."

I didn't think the Wife wanted these extras, but I couldn't say so, and as I accepted the extra burdens I hoped I would not be rewarded for humping them all the way home by a screaming and beating.

The vegetable-woman's cans of milk had always been watered down. You weren't supposed to know, and I think the Wife genuinely didn't know—she seemed to stumble round among objects as a foreigner. Degrees of quality were alien to her. But water would have been more drinkable than this pap. Her jam was already fermented. It was runny and patched with mold. Yet the cabin was idyllic. It was *pretty*—a commercial come-on. Each sill was a basket of flowers.

"You'll want your cans back, darling," Fishhead said watchfully to her.

"No," she stated. "Mill-wife welcome."

She wanted of course, as usual, to charge for the use of her cans—the longer they stayed at the Mill before she collected them, the more she'd charge.

"You too generous with your utensils," Fishhead said to the vegetable woman. "I'll accompany child on way. I'll carry cans, heavyish they are. I'll bring your cans back right and tight to you straight away."

The woman glared. She would sooner he was out on some waves earning some daily luxury. "He's strong enough to carry cans," she grumbled, feeling my arms.

In this language where women were so implicitly inferior that they must not share with men the same verb endings ("I sit" said by a woman was quite different from "I sit" said by an actual man) (and people greeted a man with "How are you?" whereas if a woman were greeted at all it would only be with "How you are," spoken as a statement, inviting no information) women themselves tended to feel they must not say *she* or *her* too often, since those feminine words had taken on a feeling of indecency. Girl children were referred to by women as *him,* until they wished to scream an insult. Men were at liberty to speak out in their coarse harsh masterful fearless way and say *her* and *she* from their position of unassailable maleness.

Fishhead had already seized the cans from me. Oh yes, that was more comfortable.

My arm was shivering, helpless with relief, after he took the weight from it.

Fishhead swung out of the door and down the lane and I followed before the woman could stop me.

Fishhead had his own ways of approaching Soursere. The world to Fishhead consisted of coast.

It had been Fishhead we'd first seen from the raft lowered down the cliff, I realized, the fishing figure who had suddenly doubled up his knees to his chin and dashed leaping away up the bay.

Here we were on this same recognizable bay, Fishhead's principal bay. We passed his boat, sixteen-foot and clinker-built, pulled up high on the beach. The wind was pushing waves into the milk in the cans. Fishhead's thick fuzzy hair, the kind you can't get a comb through, was leaning in directions. His pieces of cork jewelry were bobbing like buoys around his neck and waist.

"So you live Mill," Fishhead said wistfully. He always invested with romance anyone else's *"home"*—he saw himself as a perpetual outsider.

"It's good, yes? To live at the Mill and be with the family? You need a family in this world, you do.

"I'll tell you a story about family," says Fishhead leaning into the wind.

"Once upon a time, you see, these brothers (sons of course of a poor fisherman as heroes are) went into the world. To seek their fortune.

"First brother sees a beautiful valley with kine, river, vines—and it's a natural fortress. The owner tells him he can have the valley if he labors seven years and builds up a house (a stone house be best, with moat, brother decides) and business.

"End of seven years come, and brother sees lovely girl

bathing naked in pool and rapes her. You know what rape is?" Fishhead broke off anxiously, hoping he wasn't wasting his story on an ignorant listener. "Owner reveals she's his daughter. He banishes first brother, who has to go away into wilderness.

"Second brother meanwhile has set out along same path. At once sees beautiful girl weaving tapestry in flowery meadow and singing. He wants to marry her. Her father says 'Yes, if you woo her seven years and help her finish tapestry.' Seven years' wooing? That's nothing to romantic brother. At end of seven years here she comes led toward him in white veils, smiling sweet. Her father says: 'One thing.'

" 'Yes, yes.'

" 'Be gentle.'

" 'Yes, yes.'

" 'Must tell you,' says the father 'the poor child, she was raped by a laborer today as she bathed for her wedding to you.'

"In horror the second brother flings away her hand, which he won't touch to be contaminated by. He hurls off away up on the hillside, he sees a unicorn and flings himself on its back. But it bucks him and he is dragged over rocks, tangled in its mane, unable either to let it go or mount it properly.

"The third brother, he's coming along the path from their father's house. He sees the unicorn terribly dragging his own brother. He catches the unicorn after a chase of seven years. He throws his brother (who cries 'Help me— give me water') into the valley near the stream. He mounts the unicorn which recognizes a master and soars off into the mountains and high kingdoms."

We pressed on into the coast-weather.

"And the moral of that is," said Fishhead after a pause, "that most things take seven years to accomplish."

I thought this was a very silly moral, though I had been moved by the story. But Fishhead said this in so didactic a way that whenever I thought of the story, which I often did, I thought of the effort of the brothers' seven-year patiences.

I began to wonder when I'd get home.

Across the river I could see the women who been toiling in the meadows, on their way back up to the village, a pattern of giant shadows. Mules wandered from the light

to the already dark side of the mown slope, looking now
dun or now brilliant pink.

We stopped in twilight at a roadside stall selling heaps of
fresh toadstools. They were still stuck all over with pine
needles. Fishhead bought some, paying with a piece of
tasteless-looking squid he just happened to have about
him. The starlight struck through its gelid surely ice-cold
gelatinous bones, and I admired his good taste in keeping
it as currency only.

"Whist!" Fishhead held up a peremptory hand. I halted
obediently and listened with him.

"What be that?" Fishhead demanded dramatically. "A
ghost, a haunt, wandering the twilight land. A grieving
mother-soul mourning her lost babe."

He started crossly when I ran forward, cracking a twig.

I hoped I could guess the direction accurately. It was so
maddening not to be able to call out a guiding reply to
Cija.

She cried out and seized me, making noises like several
wood-pigeons.

"You be this one's mother," Fishhead said, finding us as
my mother rocked me in her arms, to and fro against her
waist. "I've brought Mill's milk."

"You are a good kind man," my mother said fervently,
seeing my placid look and my fistful of fungus.

The noble Fishhead was inspired at once. He took from
his pocket a smooth-planed wooden "tooth," and fitted it
into his mouth before pulling out his pipe—since otherwise there would be no sound (he'd lost his real tooth in a
fight, he would tell me later). To the lilt of his tune about
motherlove, we arrived back at the Mill yard. There was a
rainbow around the mill-wheel. The stars hung rather
close, as though we were their business.

Miller was not in yet, but Quar had come to visit. "I
was just coming to find you," he said gravely to my mother,
though in fact he looked very much ensconced in the high-
backed settle.

The Wife was hurrying round, her face somewhat
clearer than usual and her shoulders less tightly defensively
hunched in Miller's absence.

My mother too looked better. I watched her blossom
falsely, singing at her work, roses in her cheeks—because
of Quar's interest.

"This good gentleman escorted my little one home," my mother indicated Fishhead. "She must have lost her way; the market garden after all is a long way for a child to go on an errand." She looked at the Wife.

"Then let me introduce you to the gallant in question," said Quar sardonically. "Meet Fishhead."

He said the name as though that in itself should show Cija how ridiculous was any possibility of taking its bearer seriously. But the Wife pressed Fishhead to share our food-trough. And when Miller came in, obviously from some social occasion, with his hair sleeked down over his forehead, looking very smart, he too was in a host-like mood.

The Saint arrived, breathing hard after the hill-lane, proudly bearing lighter models of chastity-belt. He responded to the Miller's hearty welcome, then held these out to my mother. "So," he said gently. "You see I have been able to help you, as I promised."

He turned to the Miller. "Sir," he said, "let me entreat you to give your consideration to these versions, so much kinder to a gentle arse. Your wife and his good lady, for whom I still feel regard and responsibility, would undoubtedly go about their tasks more easily in these."

He beamed upon the Miller so wonderfully that the Miller delayed his agreement a moment so that he could bask a little longer in The Saint's intensity.

"Of course I shall have the best in my Mill," Miller said expansively, accepting the free offers. "You'll wear this, Wife, you hear? You'll wear this, woman," he instructed my mother.

"You have not introduced me to your friend," The Saint was looking with respect at Fishhead's ethnic accouterments and his big grizzled chest, the kind of chest you'd like to run through, barefoot.

"You've heard of our sea-fisher," Miller said. "So this is he. He likes to do funny things to ladies," he added as extra information (women were always properly called ladies) but without disapproval—anyone could do anything to females if interested enough.

"Ah!" cried The Saint. "So this is the man who rowed out to the Colored Cliff."

Fishhead remained mute. Miller said, "He said he'd go. He disappeared. We all knew he'd gone there. Then he came back—changed."

The Saint regarded Fishhead with burning inquiry, but met no response. "What did he say about the Cliff?" The Saint asked Miller.

"He didn't say. You don't think we asked?"

"How were you—changed, Fishhead?" my mother asked, though Quar made a restive movement of disgust because she spoke to him outright when men were present. (In such a gathering, a good woman should talk only to her own man, or to other good women.)

Fishhead raised his deep eyes to her.

"The unicorn it stamps its hoof,
"how mysteriously aloof,"

                    he said,

"and umbilical.

"I came back able to speak in poetry, madam."

"And there is gray in his hair," the Wife added.

Fishhead frowned. He hadn't been going to mention that.

"Let me tell you, sir," he said to The Saint quietly, "that I did not go to the Colored Cliff by boat."

There was a stir throughout the room. It was obvious that he was breaking a long silence.

"I went on the floating island. It came, and to those to whom it comes it obviously is meant. I turned no back on it accordingly, but set foot on it, and was taken where it took me."

The Wife had gone white. Mention of anything supernatural seemed to affect her with nausea. But every one else leaned forward staring. "What island?" beatifically asked The Saint. "What island must this be?"

"The mystic floating island," Miller said like a guide-book. "Is said to appear off-shore in times of meaning."

"Of meaning?" cried The rapturous Saint. "Why then, so it now is! A time of meaning it now is!"

Our Saint's glorious eyes were shining like star-shot smoke. But before he could ask the grizzled Cliffer eager questions, Fishhead himself interrupted:

"It is a time of piscatory garbage. It is a time of tracking the scaled pigs of the sea and harvesting their hate. It is a time of working hard for your neighbors' necessities and hoping they will of their hearts reward you with a crumb, a crust scented with the sweat of the ladies who make the bread in the crowded female bakery."

The Miller was used to Fishhead, his never-ending battle with his enemies the fish, and his predilection for detail even if it were female detail. Amazingly, as Fishhead courteously went to the Miller's Wife, and adjusted one of her breasts for her while he talked, because it was falling over toward the soup, the Miller placidly placed the towel around his own neck before embarking on the evening's brew.

But Quar did not like all this chatter while Cija was listening. She might become interested, she might get above herself, which he felt was all too likely with her.

Quar rumbled at Fishhead: "You—" (and Quar paused to find a belittling word) "feckless untrustworthy indigent."

Fishhead smiled, then swiftly shrugged: "But what cares I for praise?"

He wasn't going to allow himself pleasure at such compliments from a man he was against as much as he was against Quar. Fishhead was very against the Miller, very against Quar—but accepted drink and work from both, and said then what good chaps they were.

He would say genuinely and sincerely to my mother, "Great chap he is. Great family man. Kind good miller is is." That was when he'd recently supped with the Miller. Home and hearth held great mystique for Fishhead. So did hosts and guests and sharing of ale shoulder to shoulder until it was rolling on a floor next morning belly to boot.

But in fact there was something he loathed in both men, something as antipathetic to him as fish. Men like Quar were for watching and stalking and thinking about sideways, which was why when Quar started to talk "business" (smuggling) with Fishhead, promising him good pay for his boat and pilot-skill, Fishhead said yes yes and hardly ever turned his eyes on Quar. Quar showed him a chart which Fishhead studied: the chart was covered with tiny numbers and arrows. It looked extremely sea-faring to me. Fishhead raised a brow: "Well, I'll be there."

He didn't want to talk to Quar any more. He stared elsewhere, and appeared not to notice Quar's leavetaking. Quar told my mother: "Good night to you, Cija. You are too pale. It is summer. Other women are brown and attractive. You never get out. I'll walk out with you—tomorrow."

He handed her a fruit, a gourd he had in his purse. Her

face lit up with joy. When my mother peeled it, the spray of juice was so sharp it spat straight through her old woolly shift and when she took it off that night she would stare at the pattern of delight around her navel.

"Oh, there are orchards in the world still," was all she said. Though she might well have gone on, "though not for me."

She had become, indeed, very despairing of her own nudity lately. Like most women even when they get every chance to bathe, she was hourly convinced of her fetidness, her unventilated hung gaminess; I've a theory that there are times of the year when any man can flatter any woman without being in the least aware of it, simply by sitting beside her for a while as though entirely unrepelled.

The contraption was irking her more, and more.

Her nymphae, we were to learn, were all but mashed.

We had heard those tales of the sooterkins that are "born" from the thighs of the women of the Seres after they have sat on the stoves throughout their winter—the "infants" of soot and womanly slimes, changelings which find their way out "to do mischiefs in the world" through the squeezing slats of the contraptions. Cija had me and Despair already.

Quar went out now.

Left at trough-side with me, Fishhead frowned at the chart. "I'll never be able to read these sea-maps," he grumbled.

Sure enough, my mother began getting out more often— and while I was in the middle of one of my reading or writing lessons with her, along would come Quar and order her out with him. "But the child . . ." she would say uncertainly, while I quietly closed the lesson-paper, knowing she would go anyway.

She would stumble on, about how she spent so little time with me anyway, what with the work about the Mill.

Then he grunted. Did she want her health?—for that was what he was offering. Take or leave.

(Quar and The Saint had both already intimated that to teach a girl-child in my situation to read and write was not only unnecessary, but snobbish.)

She patted my cheek, her hand lingering, "Little heart. Go on learning. I'll be back soon." Yes, she would be— but she'd be at work another three days solid with no moment for a sit-down with me. My book was bound in sacking; it had been agreed with The Saint that would keep me humble.

I was humble anyway. I knew my lessons were the least of anyone's worries.

How how how could I learn something like how to *speak?*

I took my book out into the branches of the nearest climbing-size tree. I hid in the droughty branches with leaves all edged brown. I had stolen something to suck too, hot bread with beef drippings.

There were so few trees around here to choose from.

The villagers *hated* the trees—as Fishhead hated fish. They cut trees clumsily, untidily; destroying them even when they meant to keep them alive for future use. They hacked and spoiled, partly because they had no idea how to preserve objects; any physical act brought fringes of spite and malice from them; they felt some sense of enormous personal power as soon as they did anything physical. At once they sought around for ways to misuse it.

"There are too many around anyway," they grunted when they found they'd mistakenly killed another tree. There was constant battle with the forest, from their point of view. They felt threatened by anything too vivid.

This hot bread was good. Mostly I'd stopped bothering to eat. It was too much trouble. I might grab a green crust or a dollop of rancid stew now and then. It was such a battle for my mother to fight the Wife's habitual squalor —even the dirt was dirty. A filthy pot, all grease and old scum, would also have acquired *on* the grease an edge of old hairs from heaven knows where visible on its original edges as you lifted it. If something were spilled one evening, three evenings later what was lying spilled, having never been mopped up, was obliterated in any case by what had been spilled over it since.

It was a careless household, my mother sighed once to The visiting Saint, that couldn't even keep its dirt clean.

"You expect the wrong things of these honest hardworking people," The Saint told her.

"You impose on them your own expectations, your own culture and capabilities. You have been surrounded all your days by servants and slaves who had nothing more to do than scour for you."

I remember my mother at that point smiled, not inter-

ested in recounting for The Saint her history of servant-
hood. I knew that my mother had a certain weary amused
pride in the experiences that had rolled over her like
great wheels. At least, she congratulated herself, she accepted buffets of fate like a bending womanly reed, without resentment. See, now she was poor. Very well then.
She would chaffer for necessities with door-peddlers, conserve candles (blowing out the flame as soon as it was not
needed)—be very careful paring cheese rind. Then she
saw with amazement that the Miller's wife, often bewailing
the Mill's poverty, was careless and profligate, left candles
burning and sliced the potatoes off with the peel—
although in constant terror of the Miller's rage when
coins were short. (Not that the Miller understood coins
and what really constituted their shortness. Money in this
neck of the world was wild and young. Nobody had it under control.)

So my mother realized yet again, it must be in some
natures "not to niggle," as my mother put it, "and it is a
worry to them to be told they *should* niggle."

At such an observation The Saint would nod agreement.

"The peasant nature is spontaneous and generous," The
Saint said, making reaping movements in the air. "How
else can it remain in tune with the rhythms of the earth
and waters, as it does?"

He was learning to reap, and my mother sometimes
rubbed his back when it got stiff.

I leaned back in the boughs. I saw my mother and
Quar come along. They sat under the tree. I stayed very
still.

He had a handful of hirsute gooseberries. He was always feeding my mother. That was one useful thing about
Quar.

"It looks like rain," said Quar under the black sky.

I wondered how he could have lived all his life in this
area and still not know those clouds were going too high
and too fast for rain.

"I'll make you cradle for your baby," Quar said. "I've
a nice log at brewhouse, in yard. I'll hollow it out and
swing it off ceiling for your baby. Then you won't have to
carry it everywhere."

My mother looked down at the squirming Despair.

"Wife won't want her room taken up by cradle," my

mother said—adding, "It very kind of you, Quar, though, to think of such thing."

"Wife do as she told," Quar said loftily. "She do as my brother tell her. And he do as I tell him."

"You are Miller's brother?" my mother faltered. "Oh, I never knew. How fascinating!"

How boring, I thought in the tree. But my mother sounded thrilled and excited and Quar actually looked important and pleased. Perhaps she *thought* she was fascinated.

"You travel, Quar, don't you," she said shyly as though the miles round about were great horizons undreamed of by such an ignorant little stick-at-home as herself.

"Town to town, selling, buying," he said laconically, punishing her for her interest now he had it—giving no information because he knew that was what she longed for. He didn't mean town to town anyway, but hamlet to hamlet.

And what he bought and sold was liquor, Fishhead would later tell me. "Buying, selling," sounded very lordly and professional. What it came to was puddles of "mild" and vomit on every ale-house table on Quar's glamorous route.

"I am desperate to leave the Mill, Quar," my mother said softly. "I must get my children away."

"A place to leave, you think?" Quar said. "Not too sophisticated a place, maybe? Is that it?"

"The Saint is in love with the peasantry," my mother ventured, knowing Quar did not equate himself with peasantry. "He exhorts me to spend a wholesome life here to the end of my days. But, oh, Quar," she said very appealingly, "my children will be starvelings by the winter."

"Winter indeed is cruel here," Quar said viciously, going on with such a bland appearance to tell her of the interesting turnip-parties in the winter (bring your own turnip, sit on the stove) and whistling whining winds which even the separate outside-walls, built like a double-screen on to the houses in the autumn, could not keep out—the walls just blew to pieces by mid-winter. Then it was too bitter to replace them—easier and more sensible to huddle by the fire "while the women and children wish they'd a fire too," Quar added.

"The peasants last out the tail of winter sleeping on

stoves," said Quar. "That's all. If they go out, the hairs on the backs of their hands instantly whiten with frost: that's inside their gloves.

"You can blow whole windows in the air," says Quar, explaining how each breath hangs frozen then. "My brother went out with a nose-bleed, and blew stained-glass windows.

"But no. The children wouldn't survive too well."

My mother cuddled Apeling.

"Why don't you run away?" Quar suggested blandly.

Instead of saying where to? and how?—my mother very expressionlessly said: "I must do my duty here."

"I respect you," Quar suddenly told her. He said it very weightily. My mother, startled, had actually merited the Quar seal of approval.

When my mother and Quar had walked sedately away, not touching, after Quar tried to tweak and maul her and my mother quite sweetly and firmly resisted him, I climbed down from the tree and Fishhead climbed down too.

"So was you up there?" he cried incredulous at me (I was about to say the same to him, till I remembered as usual that I can't speak).

"Well, well." He pulled a musing hand through his three fuzzy plaits. "Let a ferret in at a pile of logs. Pretty soon, you'll smell the scent of rabbit baking."

I stared at him. Was the Mill the pile of logs they'd let Quar into? Was my mother the little rabbit who was hunted and harried? Fishhead was shaking his head in some disgust.

A little river-eel wiggled past the stones in the water. I bent and pulled it out between finger and thumb. It struggled—it was total muscle—and Fishhead sprang to take it from me, wrestling it and beating it around the head and strangling it.

"Ahar," he said, threading the eel on to his hook with a slit in its pulsing gizzard as though he were making a daisy-chain.

He patted me, unsurprised. "I've heard of folk can do that then, stick their hand in the water and pull out the plum."

Fishhead went on, "I'm not handy with the beasts. They coil up at you from among the ribs of wrecked ships under the lagoon. Have you been out there? Beyond the shore, before the breakers, and before the Colored Cliff?

"I'll take you." He interrupted himself to bring in a fat fish which sure enough had bitten on the eel.

"Hah, joy, delight. If a brontosaurus saw us, what would he say? He'd pray. The cuttlefish is sweet and wet," Fishhead shouted, "and what she is, is what she'll get."

Fishhead was so pleased with my skill that he certainly did take me shore-ing as often as he could. From now on he explained to those in charge of me that I was a tool of his trade. If they wanted fish, they'd have to give him me.

The Wife grumbled, but she liked fish, or rather she knew her husband liked fish. She lent me to Fishhead whenever he called for me. The vegetable-woman was not so generous with her occasional lover. She warned my mother about Fishhead and his "likings." My mother thought, decided Fishhead was good for me, sighed and said nothing.

Now the thrash of the deep-sea rain was often my lullaby. That, for Fishhead kept me out late, and his silly songs.

> "Whale so pale and dear as ale
> In the low waves washing wet
> Tender rock ye in the water
> Like a palest little daughter
> And I'll come and find and get you yet."

All Fishhead's songs had "sweet" and "wet" in them and lines about fish obliquely sneaking into neat nets sweetly.

We pulled a female cuttlefish behind the boat so the males that rose to her would be scooped into nets.

But sometimes she attracted bigger prey. Then it was uncertain as to whether we might not end up as prey ourselves. Fishhead was always sure it was the end of us. At the very least he would go through several pairs of gloves when hauling in a big fish—because of the burning of the line past his hands (you could see the smoke off the line). Fishhead would curse and insult and hate the fish while he held on the line and the fish leaped and fought, every now and then coming up like a peacock-kingfisher, all spun blues and greens and flashes of gold. The boat bucked like a rocking-chair; this was no vehicle from which to win at tug-of-war.

A big fish in the net could break it, that must never be allowed, so we had to be watchful. We'd have to cut the net and let the beast go. But once a big fish was on the line—you could tie the line round the short samson post at the transom end of the square-nosed clinker-built little trundler boat, and let the fish tire itself while you stayed in the front of the boat to balance the weight. (If you were Fishhead, not if you were me: but out on the sea hour after hour, we'd think of each other's weight and dryness and so on unconsciously, as though we were each other as well as ourselves.) A fish-hook through its gills later, when the fight and go had gone out of it, kept it at the side of the boat, traveling in the water with you, if it was too heavy to lift in alone.

But how you had to be sure. We caught a shark—we didn't want it, it insisted—a huge shark, or seemed huge. Fourteen rows of teeth, said Fishhead, and when it was tired (that took a long time) he leaned over to try to cut its throat from the boat.

That thrilled it. It smelled its own life-blood ebbing. It turned with the thrill. It turned, it was thrashing, looking for *itself*—all lust for blood.

The boat was turned and tossed with it. Fishhead was screaming the unfairness of it. "Die, you pig, die!" Fishhead leaned over dangerously and shouted into the shark's snapping great head. I sat huddled by the samson, sending my thought like a dull metal pick into the shark. Fishhead was quite right, the only thing for all of us was for the shark to die. It died. Fishhead wiped his gloves across his plaits. He was slick with sweat and salt and the shark's blood and froth and the light of the sun which set well, like a jelly.

"It died," he said. He said hoarsely, "It died, the pig."

We had hauled the shark half up the beach when Fishhead said, "Fuck it. Leave it. Why should we tire ourselves on the pig? Leave it drop."

I looked at it. It was good meat; he would get plenty of money for it.

"Aagh," he said. That was that. Someone was walking

toward us over the beach. It was The Saint. He walked elegantly, with a dark broad-brimmed hat on his head. He stopped beside us, making a peasant's gesture of good-day-and-welcome to Fishhead.

"A great catch," he nodded at the shark.

"Filth," Fishhead said, and kicked it. But just as when you boot a pig, however hard, in the side it hardly notices, so the shark lay there frothing, bloody, un-noticing.

The Saint was interested at once. "You are not proud of your catch?" he queried.

"Proud of shit," Fishhead said moodily (it was a fine shark). "You try cutting it and skinning it and chinning it and salting it."

"You'd trust me?" The Saint shouted at once. And that was how The Saint first moved in with Fishhead.

Fishhead, when he was not visiting his adored vegetable-woman, lived in a tiny timber tower which revolved on a little platform he'd built on its hillside overlooking the sea—he didn't like the view, but for his livelihood he needed to know what weather was coming up. Generally the tide was coming in like steel, that was all, but sometimes the warming drying salty sun shone, and then Fishhead (or The Saint) would jump out of the tiny tower, and shove it round on its well-oiled un-squeaking platform; it would follow the sun around and be in the good gold shimmering plank-loving warmth all day.

The sunlight would catch the rows of golden herrings hanging below the roof to be cured in the smoke of family fire. For it was a family now—Fishhead and The Saint.

Now that things were settled for some of us—for The Saint and myself anyway—I wished that somehow they could be settled a bit more for my mother too.

Life stretched her unmercifully. She looked tight and scraped. I remember how Fishhead came round suddenly one night for an unexpected "conversation" with me. My mother had had some water over the fire all day. At last it had nearly boiled, and I was ready shivering in the tub. My mother invited Fishhead cordially in (Miller sprawled with a mug of ale, Wife was mending) but he primly refused.

"I'll stay outside," Fishhead said in a very ladylike voice.

And he talked to me through the half-closed door. "Your mother looks tired, Seky—" He wasn't saying it for my mother to hear. We were just having our social chat. He shouted again: "Your mother looks like a lady that's been winded up too far." Wife looked up, Cija tried to laugh. Small spontaneities were difficult for her now. I often saw her swallow hard before she got her mouth open to make the lightest remark. Miller roared, "Come in, let's see some drinking." Fishhead put his fuzzy head in, made a good-luck sign and went away.

He'd got it right. Cija looked wound up too far, like clockwork springs, that if you touched might snap, spring and be quite ruined.

The Saint used to be very wound-up as well. Now he was so much softer. He used to stay with different peasants who all vied to play host to him for a while, but since he moved in with Fishhead he just never got round to moving on again; and he slowed down and stopped getting in quite such states.

Before, coming to the peasants and to God, after seeing that blinding white and blue vision which made him give himself up to religion, he had been convinced he loved beauty, sweetness, light. He had turned one of his good hostesses out of doors when she objected to his building a shrine in her washing-hollow (in her own inherited part of the river-shallows). Having taken a solemn vow never again to shoot deer, which had been his last "noble" activity till he discovered it upset the deer, he had no way to channel his violence at all. So he took to bashing around cleaning out the loft of the farmer he was staying with (having thrown out his wife). He'd realized he'd broken the wing of a bird sitting on a nest in the loft. He was heartbroken. He wouldn't kill the poor little bird.

He took it to the doctor, who was useless with cows in labor-dilemmas and certainly couldn't think how to help a broken-winged bird. So The Saint, deciding on a prescription of therapeutic warmth and love, carried the little bird in his shirt against his heart for two days. It died. The Saint was furious. He tore the bird wing from wing, hurled it against the shrine. "Why did you die? Little bird, you knew how much I was doing for you. You knew what love I was giving."

Now he was channelled by the sea. It roared, it heaved, it crept like silk to his boots.

He was quiet and chewed dune-grasses. He gave out fewer penances. He advocated understanding rather than instant punishment.

"You have to mentally think," he would say to a wronged farmer, "what it was that was in your enemy's heart."

He frowned when he saw a drunken man beating a child. "A male child, too!" he said, and "Is this any way to bring up a new man? Bruises unto all generations? What bruises are cast on the waters, are washed back to you." He spent hours studying the sea, reading its messages and interpreting its philosophies. Once he would have said, whatever the peasant father wished to do he must be allowed to do, since the peasant instincts are always right, intuitively utterly correct and should never be warped by the sophisticated hand. Now the sea was suggesting otherwise, was suggesting a huge control, a huge rhythm of tolerance allied to control and awareness.

He broke up a drunken brawl. He began to turn all local feeling against frivolity (it was already that way inclined). Then he outlawed alcohol. Only Fishhead went on drinking right under his nose.

Miller and Quar, neither at all frivolous, continued their illicit distilling and selling while the Mill was officially for the grinding and production of bread.

The Saint still equated "frivolity" with City-slickerism. But he no longer worshipped instinct as much, and he was beginning to show signs of kindliness which startled even himself—he wondered if they were wrong, and would analyze them anxiously afterwards to make sure they hadn't broken any rules to do with the nature of water.

I felt sure that if my mother would go to him now, would talk to him again, she would begin to be his friend. And then he would find himself helping her to get away from here. But she had given up. She thought of him as an enemy, someone who amused her but of whom she must be implacably suspicious.

Instead, because she knew Quar was playing games with her, she remembered that games are for winning, and she started playing games too. She teased Quar and persuaded herself he didn't know it was teasing. He let her think she was winning, so that she would continue playing; both were placating and patronizing the other. At least The Saint had been straight. I wished I could get her to the shore.

One night I noticed a look passing between my mother and the Wife, sitting both at the Mill kitchen table shelling peas. I knew what they were noticing—and each felt it must be her own peculiarity, a headache, fatigue, those shifts in perception people are ashamed of and ignore and never mention to other people—the kilter and camber of the Mill had shifted while it remained simultaneously perfectly level on its own ground-plan and its own proper decent built foundations—the Mill had keeled to one side and no angles in the kitchen, the walls nor floor nor beams nor the table-edges, were in relation to each other as they should be.

I might as well straighten things back again, since we were all feeling uneasy, superstitious and also seasick. When I set that portion of my brain against the force, I found it was not evil but it was very *wrong*. It was selfishly, wildly, venomously, bitterly, sullenly *enraged*. It was a thick tangible (or anyway to that part of my brain completely tangible, like touching a howling jelly) agglomeration of something old, stale, decayed, black and constantly fed. It was total self-pity and frustration. When I flattened it out, the Wife gave a sharp sigh as though hurt, and another breath as though eased.

"Something odd happened just then," the Wife said. "Perhaps the ground shifted a teeny bit. Did you feel it?"

"Uh?" the Miller grunted.

The little cat, also alarmed, ran across the Miller's knee and off again.

"He likes you," the Wife said in a clinging, whining, congratulatory voice. And again, since her husband hadn't even looked at her the first time she said it, "He li-ikes yew!" Roughly translatable as "Please like me."

The Miller grunted again. His grunt meant "Yes, animals like me. Don't know why, I'm only a rough unassuming chap. Perhaps it's my naturalness and modesty. But I'm masculine, so don't sugar me up you syrupy sentimental cow else I'll grunt at you to put you in your place. Don't ever stop flattering me either or I'll have no use whatsoever for you. I've got to have someone to tell not to be sugary about me."

The Wife settled back to the pea-podding. She hefted her breasts into contented positions on the table. She had fulfilled her function. She had drawn from him some acknowledgment of her womanliness, her syrupiness, the fact she "worshipped" him, the fact she she she was always there to flatter him, and who but she. She could bear being ignored for another few days.

"Your Mill is haunted," my mother said in a level voice to the Wife.

Wife stared at my mother, hung her mouth open, and began to scratch one of her nipples all around anticlockwise.

"Last night," my mother said, "the blankets on the bed tried to strangle my baby. The blankets."

Amazingly, the Wife agreed: "And one of my good husband's shirts was spoiled in the wash. It boiled all patchy. There is something in this building doesn't want things go right. My husband's shirt. Now how would it know my husband's shirt was in that pot? It was mainly all childer's wash."

The Miller heard, but made no sign. It was still woman's talk. When the shirt was presented to him, he would roar. It would become a personal affront, punishable by marital law. Till then, it was woman's problem.

"It's the well-wife; that's what it is," Wife said hoarsely.

"Well-wife?" my mother repeated. And my mother, far from ill-educated in these out-of-the-way matters, added, "You mean a nixie?"

"Darkness in the well," Wife mumbled, almost in tears. "A dark in well. It's well. It's well." And while she blamed the well, I thought of the Moor which lay beyond the well. The Wormingend. WorminGend, the peasants pronounced it. Out there it lies, hissing like a snake. (All reeds and wind.) Had something crept off the Wormingend and into the Wife's well?

It was worse, much worse, having mentioned the haunt. Mentioning it had in some way sanctioned it.

Again and again in the night, I woke to find my heart clench. This was genuine attack by fear, not inside me, not created by myself, an attack from outside, an attack of etheric fear. The chill trickled down, vertebra to vertebra. My stomach felt as if coming to the boil. I could not command my body. Yet the horror was only in the body. Certainly I was under attack, as the infant ape had been, as the Miller's shirt had been. But I could go ahead with my mind quite calmly to deal with it. My mind was my own.

I would calm the crawling vertebrae, one by one if I could do it no other way. It occurred to me that it was like having the emotional idiocy that the daft superstitious witchy-nobles of Ilxtrith thought was a worm in your spine. A sort of physical bodily emotional whimpering that was nothing to do with you yourself—a thing that would flare up in righteous anger, or sulk, or stand on its rights, or cringe in horror, or crawl in loathing, or sneak in syrup, or flutter in ecstasy—but was not your mind, not your self. It was that which could be attacked. But *you* could disengage it.

You, not being its slave, could tell it to stop lying there wallowing in its ooze of fear—just as you could disengage it at any time from the other oozes—of implacable hatred, of deathless love, of now-or-never, of once-in-a-lifetime, of this-is-bigger-than-both-of-us, and all its other shallow deep-ends.

I was so interested by my fear that I forgot about the fear-*attack*. I presume it went away. I didn't notice it any more that night.

But next morning, as nearby birds started clearing their throats (you couldn't call it a dawn-chorus) and the dawn leaked like mildewy flour into the chutes and bins of the "spout-floor," and the chains squealed as they raised the sacks of meal to put through the sieve, my mother raised a wail; a low carrying hopeless *bored* wail, a wail she knew would do no good, would not be listened to, could help nothing and no one.

I ran to her.

She was sitting on the recently emptied "bed," apeling in arms. She rocked and rocked it and held her face to its soft strange little head. She turned dry eyes at me and tried to hide her pain from me so I would not be alarmed.

"Apeling is ill, your baby sister has a tummy ache I think," my mother babbled. Then she drew me against her and held us both tight.

The Wife sidled in. She had heard the wail. She bent

over my mother and the lifeless scrap. "Not breathing," she said. Again, very heavily: "No breath."

Miller was heard treading up the "stairs." He came in and stood staring. He did not look interested nor concerned, but he did not look hostile. The incident was a traditional tragedy.

There was nothing innovative about the death of an infant followed by a household's wailing. Nothing to make Miller uneasy or aggressive. The period of female wailing was in this case an honorable tradition. Ingrained in Miller's stumpy experience of life, so his mother and aunt and grandmother must at times have wailed, not to be denied for once, and so his father and uncle and grandfather had stood with solemn faces, swaying in wooden doorways, acknowledging the females' perfectly proper social right to grieve.

I did not know what to do to comfort my mother. I held on to her. I tried to pour comfort and calm into her but she was trembling so hard with the old dry effort to impose calm upon herself for my sake—she was creating too much simulated calm in herself to accept any genuine injection from outside. Oddly, I did not think, I just did not think of trying to heal the scrap of limbs and fur. The hairy infant with its flat face and eyes like watchful vulnerable currants, it never had been alive or real to me, except as something my mother needed.

At this moment, it was the Wife who truly was creative. "It's not breathing," she said again, as if settling into one of those mourning-chants. "It's not breathing here. But here is not a place to breathe. Perhaps the mite would breathe, somewhere else. Somewhere not here. Take the mite to The Saint. Take the mite to breathe."

The Miller blinked a slow scornful look on his Wife.

Then he said venomously, "Breath does not depend on *place*. Breath does not leave because of a *place*." He had been insulted. He would not leave it alone till he had flattened the insult to his Mill. "Breath is hearty," he said, "in a hearty Mill."

"It difficult to breathe here," the Wife said. "Don't you notice? No," she hurried on, still without flattering him, as he had been warning her it was time to do, there had been now half a dozen sentences from her in front of his face without a word of flattery to him, "You don't know it difficult breathe here. *You* at *home* here."

She did not actually say, *You* make the breathlessness.

The Miller swung out of the door, delivering an educational clip around Wife's ear as, baffled, he went out to his cronies.

Wife laughed gaily, flirtatiously after him, acknowledging his witticism.

She pulled herself off the floor. Staunching the blood from her cut lip, she said to my mother:

"You take babby to Saint then, at shore."

Gulls beach-combing on the gray ribbed sand. Gulls found small marooned fish and molluscs. Cold-toed, following my mother and her armful of Despair, I combed to good effect too—for suddenly I see a gold coin washed up amongst weed and rocks. I keep it in my sash-band.

That gold coin was like the one Ael had given me that I lost to the Mill-children.

Gray. The first sign of habitation for miles appeared: a long barn. A bird wheels over its roof. My mother has stopped. I catch up with her. She is gazing over the apeling's head, gazing at nothing much, gazing at grayness. She pulls a blind hand over my head. She sits down, cries. Walks on.

We reached the Saintly towerlet. It was inhabited. We could tell by the clack of large needles as The Saint practiced his knitting, which he had recently learned from an old woman.

I followed my mother and her armful into the cabin doorway. The Saint rose to his feet and gazed mildly and yet very deeply upon my mother, his smoky violet eyes running full tide in the dark.

"My child is dead," my mother said in a low, listless voice.

She leaned her head on the Saint's lintel and closed her eyes.

The Saint stood un-moving. He stared at her and at me. I don't think he looked at the apeling.

Down on the fore-shore there was a beautiful singing. Resonant grumbles with repetitive grumbling cadences full of rain, wind, weather and resignation. A man wearing a small kayak had pulled up on the beach. The rain began to fall, falling like diamonds from the sloping eaves around the lintels of the little tower. The elastic timber sang as sweetly as Fishhead, thoughtful sensible timber which moved where it was wanted under the pouring heavy water. I turned my back on the still-life in the cabin and watched Fishhead, his head bent under the weather, climb the slope.

Fishhead blew in through the door with the rain.

Tossing fish he had been carrying on to the logs scooped out like baskets for such prizes, Fishhead stared in his turn. His stare was short. He touched the infant and it stirred. My mother glanced unbelievingly but suddenly started. Faint shallow breaths parted the apeling's snout. Its pathetic nostrils, marred by their human chromosomes, dilated into a hesitant rhythm.

"Your Despair is dead?" The Saint said slowly to my mother.

Only he and I, I think, had remembered the bitter abusive name. My mother convulsively held the little creature to her heart and sank down on the rain-spattered rugs. The waves rose and beat hugely on the shore.

"The long walk from the Mill revived your faith and its spirit," The Saint said, touching my mother's shoulder. "So result essentially all pilgrimages."

Fishhead rubbed my hands between his to promote life, piled sticks on the fire which bristled up at once on its flat shore-stone.

The shore and waves were hidden and misted.

The air thrummed and beat as though we were tossed on an endless ocean.

As Fishhead made a hot soup for us all, I saw my mother beginning like a traveller returned to notice her surroundings. I saw her glance rest faintly on the scarf The Saint kept dropping stitches in, the clay bowls he had decorated with uninspired peasant daubings, the shrine-boxes he had bodged together with Fishhead's hammer.

I saw the smoky wet cabin for a moment as The Saint felt it to be. Until the great battle was won, and Gods could be faced with pride, no home could be anything but borrowed, no home could be a man's place as of right, for no man yet has anything as of right.

The Saint was based on this cabin as on a raft, a precarious perch tossed on the wide perilous oceans of the universe and the consciousness, a little fort constantly under siege, where sometimes he might recuperate and gather strength between bouts with the Enemies, evil and temptations from without, weakness and temptations from within.

The raft tipped and sped down one great breaker, paused, hung, did not fall, climbed up another dizzy hanging crest.

The water was sparkling shining out like jewelers' ransoms pouring from drain into gutter.

"Thrutch up, now," says Fishhead, meaning "Squeeze up for me." He had finished his cooking. He handed out the soup to us.

"Have you seen any stray travellers?" The Saint asked my mother.

"Those you fear lost?" she roused herself to take the bowl, staring into the soup as though wondering what soup was for. "And their local trading and worship lost too? The peasants think they have gone over the Flinchwum." She spoke the word now as the peasants did, sounding not only bleak (as though upon hills whistled by winds) but also as though it was at the end of the world, Flinchwum, the place you wouldn't dream of going beyond.

I remembered how once, a long time ago, on campaign, she had savagely said how she hated the intonation of ignorance, the way that the unimaginative in any part of the world distrusted speech and style and would play safe and heavy by giving equal emphasis to every syllable in any name.

Certainly, now that she was speaking so herself, it made the names of god-forsaken places *sound*, even, heavy and hopeless.

"How you find Mill now?" Fishhead asked my mother.

She glanced at The Saint. She had not met him for some long while now. She knew she wasn't supposed to complain about Mill. Saint didn't like it.

I think by now she could have spoken out—and perhaps would have seen a great thawing of The Saint's sympathy and a definite decision to aid her.

But where once, in the beginning, my mother had been bored and amused by The Saint, now she had started to "god" him. Just as the Wife had bought peace from moment to moment by treating the Miller to godhead on earth, so Cija had given up the fight and for the sake of a little respite from time to time, she had started to think

"The Saint should watch me now and notice how by his lights I am doing well and trying hard at the things I despise."

So, asked how she found her life in the Mill where she had just found her own baby suffocated, Cija hesitated.

Finally, she said:

"Wife thinks Mill is haunted."

The men laughed kindly at this evidence of wholesome femininity. But then The Saint said, "There are dangers of disembodied spirits. If they cannot occupy a body, which would be their ideal, I suppose they might settle for a well surrounded by bodies."

Thus The Saint. But would a haunt have enjoyed a well half so much, or at all, in the home of a happy contented family where the wife did not accept blows as though they were bouquets, where she did not have to turn herself inside out to lick spat spittle as though it were social wine . . . ? What happened to her inside when she had turned it out? Where could it roost? Since she had disowned it, since she had denied its tender rawness, perhaps it had gone to skulk in the well, where it could brood on the wrongs she refused to recognize.

"There is no air to breathe in that Mill," Fishhead said, enjoying his soup. "It gets all sucked off."

"Maybe it is sucked into the Well to feed whatever keeps on dying in there," said my mother.

"You will have a wet going of it," The Saint courteously bade us farewell as we prepared to set off across coast and fields and back to the Mill.

The rain had cessated, but the ground wallowed.

I stared at The Saint, but he did not suggest we stay and ride the raft any longer. He had refused to help my mother, in spite of her faith in him manifested by the breathing of the baby brought to him. And my mother had forgotten how to ask him to help her.

She had lost the confidence for asking.

Fishhead had gone down to the little bay and pulled on his kayak like an old overall. But as he saw The Saint was not escorting us, he disembarked and came clambering up to us again. "Brought up as a nobleman, he is not used to looking after ladies," Fishhead without irony apologized for The Saint. The Saint's dusky eyes opened in shock. Fishhead took us over the fields.

The huge muddles of broken branches in some trees

were, Fishhead claimed, "bears' nests." And as my mother laughed, and the apeling turned its trusting snuffling face and trusting currant eyes to her, trying to decipher this unfamiliar sound, we saw the giant withers rippling away under the branches on-shore: a bear; "or a wood-demon," Fishhead went one further.

"I have met the giant wood-bear," he said. "I wanted his big fat fur-coat. I went down that cliff after him, digging my knife in at an angle all the way to give me fifty hand-holds." But then, he said, as he lifted the dead bear's head to lop it off, he saw down inside its red mouth and there past the powerful and white and experienced tusks, past the crimson stinking tongue and all the way down inside the gaping yawning throat, he saw the beautiful face of a lady gazing up at him. "I could see her eyes shining like two quick bright stars fixed on my own face as I stared down at her, and their light and the daylight at the bear's mouth lit her two breasts and her nude foreshortened body."

He dropped the bear's head and its strange inhabited body, he said, and he ran. "But I often wonder how the lady found her way out. And I hope that she did. Otherwise she would have remained to this day, I suppose, a captive of her own bear-body—as are we all," Fishhead added as afterthought.

He landed us on a stretch of sand my mother recognized.

"Fishhead, it was you we saw when you were fishing here on this very strand! We saw you from that high road. You looked like all the calm free masters of destiny. And then suddenly you doubled your knees up to your chin and dashed away alone. What had happened?"

"Oh, that," Fishhead said, "was because the current in the quicksand had turned."

My mother's feet on the sand shifted as soon as she heard that. But she did not want to go back up the hill to the Mill-land.

"It is a glad good morning," Fishhead said, watching her face. "But you look like a woman who slept in a kind place but with a machine without a key locked around her sweet bottom."

"Thank you for your kind place, Fishhead," said my mother. "What have you in that basket there?"

"It is my crab-basket." He shook it obligingly to demonstrate, and the pink crabs scuttled and whistled.

"Fishhead, you don't keep a lid on it? They'll all get out!"

"You don't need a lid on a crab-basket. When one crab starts climbing up the side of the basket to the top, the others always reach and pull it down again. You can trust crabs as you can trust farmers. They don't let each other rise far."

My mother remained silent.

Her eyes began to cloud. She turned ready to trudge Mill-wards.

Fishhead said conversationally, "You know, the babby won't be able to breathe again in the Mill. It did be a sign, you were taken to The Saint and our little shore. Let me go back and ask him to come back with me later today and we'll take you out of that unkind breathless eel-manure."

My mother shook her head. She had a habit to keep going—a wish to "retain The Saint's good will" in case unthinkably she lost his "good will." "He wouldn't like me to ask," she said.

She walked up the hill. I followed. She'd lost the simple truth which allows a request for help. All she had left was a faith in crooked games, in playing one desire against another's desire and coming off "the winner." In the stifling Mill, she was convinced that only tricks could win. Within a month, she was married to Quar.

5

The Blind Bed

MY MOTHER'S WEDDING when she married Quar was a
peasant affair, a traditional celebration, but since The
Saint officiated at it there was also much Riverine about
the ceremony.

My mother had asked The Saint about this.

"You know I am wedded to my lord, the Emperor,
Zerd . . ." A foreign name on her tongue. But if she mentioned the foreign impediment to the wedding, might she
not even now oh gods be swept up and away by The
Saint. ("Go, my child, go from here with my blessing and
my aid to your lawful lord.")

But The Saint said the Zerd marriage was no marriage,
a lawless fakery, since Zerd was married already to
Sedili; myself, I was a bastard, of course. "Why not give
your little ones a real father at last? This will be your
first and I hope your true marriage, Lady. Here you will
thrive, with your good man, your good simple active vig-
orous man who will bring you thoroughly into the rustic
community."

And The Saint reminded my mother how many presents she had already received from "this fine simple who
loved her."

"The fine simple," my mother replied, somewhat
strained, "counts his increasing right to me with every
gift I take."

The Saint told her she was not seeing clearly, but when
Quar joined us, and confidently with a sweet smile lifting
his lip like a llama-camel's showed The Saint yet another
bangle for Cija's arm, The Saint snapped out:

194

"You buy reality with objects?"

And left us.

"He must still have a yen for you," Quar grumbled, "and is sorry he can't have you himself."

My mother said restlessly, fiddling with the bangle and not putting it on: "He has never *wanted* me."

Quar said: "Of course he did, or he would never have rescued you in the first place." While believing this, Quar also thought he was complimenting my mother and putting her "in a good mood." He believed everything had a value, but a neat negotiable value.

"Seka," Quar said, "out you go. Go and catch us a tasty fish. Your mummy and I have our wedding to discuss."

"Or not our wedding," my mother said, going to stare from the window. "Don't forget I am already married."

"Oh, we can discount Mister Zerd," Quar said.

And as I went out, he slipped a wheedling arm around her, set his bold handsome face to her ear, and whispered to clinch the matter, "Who else would I marry? It's you I love so sweet."

But at the wedding, after Quar at the feast-table had told Cija, "So now we've done it, eh? I would have died, you know, if I couldn't have had you," she became very pretty and fetching in her locally embroidered new gown, and yet Quar was not noticing at all because he was a very deliberate eater, as a matter of fact, and his eyes followed his fork almost into his mouth with each bite. Quar was so careful and watchful that he always missed a lot.

Perhaps, I thought to myself, watching in my turn his slow forkfuls and his eyes that missed his bride on their one historic night, perhaps that's a tip I could remember for the future. He'd be less dangerous if I could get him eating.

Quar reached over a great pie that lay open between us and chucked me under the chin. "I am going to adopt you, Seka."

"Adopt the infant. You can't adopt Seka," my mother told him quietly. "Her father has acknowledged her."

The Saint stared at my mother. Under cover of the festivities, he said, "Why mention him, madam? You need never again think of Zerd. You were no better anyway than his whore."

"Whores," she said, smiling, reaching for a fruit, "get something for it."

The Saint tucked in his beautiful lip. Being a woman, she shouldn't have spoken that word.

My mother got up to dance with her husband. She whirled lightly, her cheap embroidered frock floating on the wedding breeze. Her chastity-belt was part of the past. Isn't it worth getting married, to get rid of daily locking into a grinding chastity-belt?

At this point I stole away absent. I went away to Fish-head's beach. I stared sadly at the piece of old liver in the sawdust and bran outside Fishhead's door. He had left it there hoping it would fill full of useful maggots (bluebottle, not just house-fly) and his hope was apparently not in vain. Here were the brandlings, the smelly yellow worms from the compost, and here the ragworms with sharp pincers, and here in a compartmented basket the live crabs and the tiny squid he used as bait.

"Is it all a great party, a great twisting of torsos and shouting of boasts?" Fishhead inquired with interest. I turned to see him. So he hadn't attended the party. He wore his old corks and working-clothes silver with a king's ransom in scales.

He was carrying a great eel, one of his greatest enemies, which he dumped in a dust patch to clog its nervous system.

"Come on, little fellow," he said to me. "I'm going back for a turn around the ocean before bed-time. Coming?"

I took his outstretched hand. We went down to the boat. He lifted me in. The day's warmth still lifted off the swelling water on to us.

"Hey. You never talk to me, do you?" Fishhead said seriously to me as we pushed off. "Cat got your tongue?"

He went on, to himself and to me, "You'll have had plenty on your busy little-lady-mind lately. It's strange to lose a Mill and gain a big dark pig." I presumed the big dark pig was Quar. I liked that, and I smiled. Fishhead suddenly stood half-up. "A strike. A shark. Already. Grist they are to the mill—excuse me, you know what I mean, I hope." The shark thrashed, leaped, pulled away, jumped, pulled again in obvious emotion. Fishhead crooned, "I know . . ." reeling him in.

"Little one, I know," sympathized Fishhead.

As the twilit clouds built themselves up above the still-glowing sun, and my head nodded, he could have been crooning to the shark or to me.

"The pink clouds fluffed up in the sky
like beaten custard high and dry
while beneath
the whales
went spouting by
—they're not to be trusted

and WE KNOW WHY . . ." The light on shore struck a waterfall high up a cliff. Floss stood quivering out from the fall.

A cormorant spread wings like a cape.

Fishhead yelped to a seal. It bobbed from its cave at his call. It stood up on its tail in the deep froth round the boat to "kiss" him. He bent over to make smacking sounds above its questing whiskers. Now we were going through the sound—a narrow channel, where the water was higher one side of the boat than the other. The water stayed lop-sided tonight even past the sound. A big swell, standing at times twenty feet above our prow. But the swell fell. It melted away in the breathing blue warmth left over from the blue wedding-day. Now we were on a table-plateau of glassy water, slightly higher than the racing little waves surrounding us everywhere in the wider sea. The plateau was full of plug-holes—all whirling round—and the plateau itself was circling itself—an embryo maelstrom. Now we approached the standing-waves. They stood perpetually six or seven feet in the air, a "wall" or "fence" of waves licking air, their tops ever curling and never falling, held up perpendicular for ever where two opposing tides hit each other.

The whales knew Fishhead's song. The calves surfaced from under the boat, each with a massive playing tail coming up from the depths to slap sea. Spotting the whale he had to chase, Fishhead interrupted our conversation about marriage (his monologue was our conversation, for I think he never knew I never spoke)—and he cried: "There he goes! The poor spouter with the ravaged mouth. A kindness to kill."

Somehow still alive, the giant was a hulk, a swimming wreck, neglected and avoided even by the other whales,

who do not as a rule shun their troubled or deformed. He
was to an extent not there at all, though he had managed
to fight off the sharks, four in a pack, who deliberately
rush a whale, hold open its mouth by hanging on its jaw,
while taking it in turns to dart into it, eat its tongue, and
be off again.

"Fish!" Fishhead cried aloud, snarling in a kind of
pain, as we followed the great hulk.

He had fought nobly. He had turned the attack again
and again, and had lost an eye and the side of his head
to the bone. I think this was no chase for a child. But the
night seemed such cruelty to me in any case, I was so
wounded and dark inside myself, and the wounded darkness shouting its terrible protests out in silence seemed so
gigantically echoingly all pervading, that the chase of the
whale, with its merciful purpose, seemed something better.

I must add that had Fishhead "cornered" the whale, I
think he would have killed him. He kept throwing-
javelins in the narrow forward hold, which he had manu-
factured in the boat. The tip of each was smeared with
something deadly. These were not harpoons. Fishhead
did not want the whale for himself, did not want the
blubber nor the amber nor the glory. He wanted to kill
that one whale. I do not know that we wouldn't have
been killed too, but I also think that Fishhead knew we'd
lose the whale. The "chase" was a gesture, a wild hope
for extinguishing some of the misery Fishhead felt in the
world and for avenging some of the evil his enemies
wrought. He was sure his enemies were the fish, the
sharks for instance, though perhaps he was beginning to
suspect that they were the safest nicest possible enemies.
The whale eluded us blindly, easily, and led us on to a
sandbank. We were marooned. It had happened very
suddenly and Fishhead flailed at the bank with a petu-
lant oar.

"What does this mean?" he cried at the sea.

Fishhead told me how difficult it was to get off a sand-
bar, once on it. "Waves," he said, "they swell up on a
sand-bar, you see, like pregnant serpents. Even a little
change in the weather means big waves breaking, which
you can't get through, not in a small boat."

He was crooning doggerel to me as I lay in the crook

of his arm. "You need some comfort, Seka, I need some comfort," he said. "So the sky was blue and sweet and still
The stars went climbing up the hill
They did not know
Where else to go.
But sleep, little one, the day is not here yet, the stars are still trudging."

In the morning he fed me squidgy strong-tasting mussels he prised out of their long blue shells, and tried to comb my hair with a piece of salt-bleached twig. "Today you go to your new house, don't you?" he said. "I hope you'll like it. I don't know are you looking forward to it or afraid? You never confide in me, Seka, do you? I've noticed that. Don't be afraid of your new house. It will be better than working like a slave in Mill."

He held up a hand. "Listen! If that dog keep barking, we can find our way to shore by his sound." But the morning mist cleared, the swell lifted us, and we found our own way through the table-water and past the standing waves, to Fishhead's cove.

Here a great crowd of people waited on the shore.

"They come to welcome us," said Fishhead and clove forward through the sparkling brine.

They had indeed come to welcome us. They had smashed Fishhead's kayak already—the shards and splinters lay along the pebbles. They had erected a gibbet made out of one of The Saint's shrines dragged from the river-bank. The Saint must have given them permission.

Already they began squawking and crowing like chickens on the dunes. We could hear their thin gurning across the amiable rolling vasty sunny warm soughing of the sea. The sound of them was thin as their souls, a squeaking of cockroaches who should have been at home under the skirting-boards, not risking themselves out in the lovely morning. Yet it was obvious the sound was meant to be an ominous rumbling, an awesome gathering storm of righteousness, and that was how it sounded to its makers. They had recognized our boat, for Fishhead had a peculiar and rakish way of handling a craft, a personal and individual manner.

I do not know why Fishhead landed. I think he did not know they were waiting to lynch him. I think he thought his friend The Saint had arranged for a lynching to be celebrated in their cove, so that Fishhead could watch close to home, without having to trek a long way to it. By the time the men began to wade out into the water to meet us, I was hanging on Fishhead's arm. I wanted him to turn, to turn back. He was free, he was strong. But he said whimsically, "Now, now, little mer-girl," and the men shouting waded to us and hung on his boat's prow like the sharks hung on the whale, and we were dragged to land.

Miller stood by the little tower, and on a rise by the tower stood The Saint.

My mother ran into the water: she still wore her wedding dress, and now she was spoiling it in the waves. I realized she had been up all night. She clasped me in her arms, she almost dropped me in the water as she tried to pull the men away from Fishhead.

"Leave him alone!" she cried. "Let him be! She's all right, don't you see?"

"Who knows what he did?" said Miller's somber voice.

"I'll take her in the tower!" my mother cried. "I'll see if she's all right."

"*She* won't be able to tell you what he done," Miller said.

"We know why he had her away!" the vegetable-woman shrilled. "We know why he had her away all night. We know."

What did she know, I thought? Had I really not been safe with Fishhead? Maybe Fishhead had been lulling me all this time so I should not be surprised when he killed me.

Like a dull baying, the farmers from Souredge who had come over the hill to see justice, now deepened the cockroach-squeaks and chicken-squawks. "String 'un up," they advised. "See. Child's dress be ripped."

I had become real to them since Quar married my mother. Even my dress was *property* now.

Cija feverishly questioned: "Did he touch you, Seka?" I nodded. "Did he touch you—personally?" I thought of the crook of his arm while he crooned to me, and I nodded again.

Fishhead seized one of his planks which lay in a lumber-pile by the shed. The plank was part of a consignment of pine-timber which, on its way to some trading post, had been swept off a wrecked trader-vessel. Fishhead had spent two long days hauling the planks to shore. I had not been able to help. They were heavy, saturated with seawater. But Fishhead, leaving them in their stacks to dry out, was delighted: "The salt added to them," he said, "will seal the burrowing termiters out. They have already been seasoned." Now, from their previous experience of each other, the plank and Fishhead understood each other. Fishhead was able to lift the gigantic thing, of which he had the knack, and he whirled it around himself like a broad-stave of entirely unexpected dimension. Two farmers tumbled back, one with a cheek gashed half-open, the other with his shoulder hanging. Others approached warily. The Miller's biggest boy hung on the end of the plank as Fishhead wielded it; it went down like a seesaw and Fishhead staggered. They tore the plank away from him.

Fishhead staggered up again. He had his head down hunched under his shoulders like the hunch of a hunted animal. He was almost under the pack, as they dodged massed lunging about him. He stumbled across the conger eel lying in the slough of dust where he had tossed it twelve hours earlier. Suddenly with a honking bark the great eel rose up. The man who had followed Fishhead across the eel had Fishhead in a jeering grip; his grasp fell away, he himself fell away, and as the crowd and then, more slowly, he began to scream I saw what happened: with one swipe the eel had bitten off the man's leg. The eel lay in the blood, swaying from side to side, half-raised. It had been shamming dead all night. It had known it might need to conserve its strength after the first shock of capture and dry air.

Now my mother could make herself heard.

"He must have a fair trial," she shouted.

"After what he done to that little innocent?" Miller yapped. "I feel responsible for that sweet child. She been in my home, under my roof, many a night and month now and it grieve me she be molested."

Quar cracked out: "Fair trial! I demand fair trial!"

He put his arm about my mother.

The eel had hooked its other end coiled round a rock. Its head lay panting in the blood, the teeth all exposed and ready. It looked as though a horse would be needed to pull it off.

"They do that, you know, eels," Fishhead called unnecessarily to The Saint. "They sham dead for hours, then they let you have it. Wow! Bam! Splat!"

At this one added item of education, The Saint stirred on his knoll. His smoky violet eyes narrowed behind their sooty lashes. The people quieted again at the sight of his beauty in the slightest mobility.

And as they turned away from him and toward The Saint, Fishhead sprang. He leaped for his boat. The sail was up. The sunlit breeze bellied into it before Fishhead was properly afloat. The waves creamed against his prow. The sea first licked, then lifted and led him. The villagers screeched. They ran out into the water. They shoved each other near the conger. It leaped as Fishhead had leaped. A man fell, his leg hanging stupidly as my hurt arm had hung.

"Be good to my widows. Find 'em out and be good to 'em," Fishhead's voice sang back over the blue swell.

My mother pressed me against her. "He will be all right," she said after a long sober pause. "He will be all right, Seka." She knew Fishhead never hurt me.

Quar did not like the necessity my mother and I had at times to quiet and cure each other. That was our last pause for a long time. Quar took us each by an arm. "Everyone has had a late night," he said. "Seka, your mother is tired. She will come to bed with me. My grandmother will see to you. Be polite and obedient with her and she will love you as we do."

There were no windows in Quar's house and I was from now on to have no friends either.

Quar had paid Miller a lot of money for Cija and she was treated with full respect accordingly. When Miller came to supper, and found Cija presiding as his hostess over the long table in Quar's dark neat tidy house, he behaved as she dictated, sluicing his hands in the water-butt outside the door before sitting to eat, not spitting his meat on the table nor even the floor.

Miller one day called her a "fine good cook." She must teach his Wife, he amazingly said. He had never had between his teeth and tongue anything that tasted as good as here.

But Quar was ashamed of my mother's cooking. Basically, he had only ever eaten with any respect his grandmother's cooking.

When my mother in Quar's house first ate the steamed

over-boiled meals his grandmother served, she looked pleased. Here was something she could better, to please Quar and keep herself inventive.

The grandmother, a tiny woman like a terrified spotless doll, cringing before Cija as though expecting to be relegated to a corner or sent out to be left in the woods for the bears now she had been supplanted as housekeeper, used not oil but rancid fat for cooking in. She boiled all vegetables to death so that they all tasted exactly like each other; the taste "vegetable" in Quar's house equalled the taste of rag boiled soft. Quar, when Cija took over the cooking, was always asking mildly, with as much patience as he could muster for he knew she was a novice, that she take his vegetables back to the kitchen and "give them a little longer." He sweetly explained that they were "a little raw." Sometimes he said the carrot was too tough; he meant it did not disintegrate in his mouth, but was crunchy and he had to chew it a little. He almost gagged on Cija's cabbage. It tasted, he said—it tasted—he could not find the words, as he sent it back to the kitchen, but he meant it tasted of cabbage.

"Raw" vegetable in fact was a sign of savagery. Over-boiled to mush was civilized. The Saint's feelings about simple rustics' oneness with nature would have been abused.

My mother gave Quar and the grandmother a delicate grilled fish with herbs. Quar ate in silence. After the grandmother had left the room, for he was too conscious of decorum to rage in front of her, he exploded:

"Fish! Just like peasants eat! My poor step-brother may have to eat fish from his everlasting waters but we have no need! From now on let grandmother do cooking for dear heavens' sake."

My mother and Quar slept in a very big black bed. It had four big high posts and a huge dark sagging canopy.

The canopy and coverlet of the high bed were maybe crimson that was almost black that was almost red. I had to climb up at the full stretch of my limbs to get up on to the bed to join my mother there. Once I tried to see what was under this tall bed; Quar stopped me "meddling." It seemed to have a solid base rising direct from the black old plank floor. The candles burned all the time in the black room. No one would ever be able to see in or out of the black room unless it were blown wide open. I experimented in my head with vast wall-killing devices.

Quar's little old grandmother was frightened of Cija till Cija went out of her way one day to do something both difficult and kind for her. From then on, the grandmother looked at Cija with contempt. Another person who despised Cija.

For Quar despised Cija. He paid enormous attention to her. She was his great interest. He was thinking of nothing night and day but how he could shape and mold and indoctrinate her. One mission in life was to get Cija to stop giving. "You don't do it to really give," he would point out painstakingly, again and again. "There is no such thing as generosity. It is a word people invented to flatter themselves with. You 'give' to feel nice, and make people like you, and see yourself with smug image."

"You are generous, Quar," she insisted. "You have given me so much."

Eventually he burst out: "Presents were only to *get* you. Don't think I could have cared less if you had nice things. They were to make you see only I could provide what you need." He reckoned himself her savior. He would save her mind, so dangerously on the verge of a sort of softness he found repulsive in his bed, however he appreciated her "aristocratic grace."

She continued to give—to me, which he said in exasperation was "spoiling the child." Finally he forbade more gifts to me. She gave to Wife, alleviating conditions for her and spilling over on her some of the respect Miller accorded anything from Quar's household.

The summer was heating toward full harvest, and the decline into the winter my mother had feared more than anything else, more than marriage in a house with no windows: the Winter Quar had filled her with bogey-tales about. It could never be quite as vicious a Winter as Quar had told it.

My mother had hoped to "coax" Quar into taking her away on his trading route. But he had tricked her with her own bait. He had her on his pin now.

The pigs were fattening for the fall of the year. The boar at back of the long low blind house, with his tiny blind-looking eyes sunk in marketable pedigree flesh, at two years of age was three times the size of the young pretty gilts going to boar for their first time. He was already really too big for them, he could crush or hurt them.

"Where will you obtain new boar?" my mother asked Quar. "Will you go to trade?"

"Always after thoughts of Big World," he ruffled her hair.

"Would you not now take me with you?"

"I'd be afraid you'd be after news of soldiers and sergeants and—" he paused deliberately, "generals in gaudy uniforms strutting fancying their high-step with lesbians, and those other things you are romantic about."

"I am not still romantic," she pleaded.

I turned from my lesson-book and stared at her. To me that sounded like a coward's repudiation of all that had been magnificent in our life together. But then, Zerd had been my father, not hers.

"Still," he said, giving her his big boots to polish, "you have a house of your own now. All you see here is yours. You are its mistress." "All is yours," piped the echoing blue-eyed doll-grandmother.

My mother made a dye from roots, as we had seen Scridol do on campaign, and with it we painted stylized flower-designs on frayed cheese-cloth we found, and hung it over the back door of the house that was "ours." Next day we found the cheesecloth had been washed in the night and duly re-hung. My mother did not bother to challenge the washing—she knew the disappearance of her flippant flowers would be excused as an accidental casualty in the sacred unquestionable cause of cleanliness, the cause of washing cheesecloth. I think that in not mentioning her defeat, although it was simply that she disdained to, my mother compounded it.

For I think that was the last time she treated Quar's house as "her home."

If there had been windows, however, what would have been visible?

Yes, the Moor. The Wormingend.

The Saint living alone in his gazebo was finishing his knitting. On one turn of the towerlet, he looked out over sleek fields, on another over slippy seas. On the norther side, The Saint could look out over un-drained fen-land and marshes, fowling, fishing, rough pasturage in summer.

"That's what they have called Sedili," Quar interrupted The Saint's account of what could be done with the bog-oaks. "The Great Quag. That's what I have heard the soldiers call her."

"What soldiers?" my mother said wearily, for without loving Sedili she liked to hear true gossip, not make-believe.

"Even deserters wandering, they would speak with pride of Sedili. Her army loves her, they haven't known such another woman," my mother insisted.

The Saint sat silent. He was a changed man. Sedili was no longer his pride, he had no lady, no allegiance but to waters and earth and their people. But his jaw tightened along its superb line.

"See the gulls!" my mother changed the subject. "Fish-head would find a plenty eggs."

"Poor scavenger," Quar snorted. "Gulls' eggs and little dumbies."

My mother quickly said to Quar, "Oh, don't be silly." But oh, little mother, little mother, she said it in that voice I cringed to hear any woman use to any man—an aren't-you-a-big-man-to-be-such-an-original-*rogue* kind of teasing voice which connives at the "silliness." If the man were baiting a cripple, the woman (whose first consideration is that she has no intention of really upsetting him, *she* doesn't mean to lose him) will object if at all only in that most terribly treacherous ugly and vain of voices. He must go on being her admirer, because she will always give every sign of being his admirer. How glad I was I had no voice, and would never be able to employ such a voice.

My mother always thought of herself as arrogant. "I am too full of pride," she would say to me.

But put her into one dreary summer, I thought, and she's at the end of her world—if someone takes some notice of her she can only give them anything, thinking "what a lucky girl I am."

Oh, dear little Cousin, somewhere away outside my head and wherever little gods live, please get us out of this.

Quar's tiny neat grandmother set me to work chipping salt blocks. They were big blocks, very heavy for me to carry. There was a cut in my hand. The salt stung in it.

Quar had bought my mother a blue bead necklet with a quartz clasp.

The Saint admired my mother's blue beads. "Because

they're so blue," my mother said. "No," The Saint said seriously. "I would admire any color . . ." He was becoming very broad-minded. "Do not mock your ornament," he warned my mother. "You have a good man," he told my mother. "You have done well here with these ignorant folk. They did not know nor care for your station in the wide world. First the kindly Miller in his age-old homespun wisdom, he made you welcome in his own family—and now this local trader, this shrewd unassuming rough diamond Quar . . ."

"My grandson *assumes,*" the grandmother suddenly said. "My grandson Quar assumes a great deal; not like other stick-in-the-muds around here who don't know how to assume."

It was so like what my mother had been thinking about Quar and assumption, I believe, that she laughed. But the tiny grandmother wasn't in the market for comedy.

"My grandson Quar," she said, finickingly cleaning her own beads, "assumes what people are good and what people are stupid, what people deserve to live and what people deserve to die."

It made The Saint blink, and he began to stammer a sarcasm about the apparent superfluity of the Gods, but it seemed to me an ordinary enough summing-up of a local philosopher. After all, I had always thought that was what The Saint did all day: decide those things. He had sentenced Fishhead by making no move to investigate the people's prejudice.

"When the traders come here," the grandmother continued, "we entertain them, we give them good food and good wine—" she winked at The Saint, who had made a motion of distaste at the mention of alcohol—"and then we put them kindly off to their sleep in the trick bed and—" A tiny genteel laugh escaped her, not one of those laughs that can be *heard,* too vulgar.

"*Only* if we've disapproved of them, mind you," she added, sitting delicately upright, her spine straight as a princess's. "Only people we have not thought well of. If they've revealed their wrong thoughts during evening conversation."

"In which bed," Cija asked very carefully, "do you put those travellers you do approve of?"

"We would put them," replied the upright grandmother, "in the closet-bed, if there had been any yet."

My mother waited for The Saint to lead the tiny woman into more disclosures. Apparently she was proud to talk, thinking that her grandson had already shared his little joke with his bride and his moral guardian, who would approve of a severe young man's judgments in ethical niceties.

But The Saint said nothing now. The grandmother turned her attention to her jewelry. "There's nothing like making everything clean," she sighed.

"What happens—to the travellers?" Cija asked.

"Clean sheets every time," nodded the little woman.

"The trick of the bed? What is it?"

The Saint took a newly-polished blue bead from the pile awaiting thread. "Each physical object cleansed," he said thickly, "can seem to raise one up as a minor god, virtuous, because pettily victorious over matter."

"Why are you both talking about housekeeping?" Cija stared from one to the other. "Can we not question this lady about the travellers who come here but do not apparently leave?"

The Saint leaned back on his spotless settle. After silently observing the tiny busy grandmother for a while, he informed her that she was deaf—"deaf," he said, his words a little slurred, "to dirt."

The old woman looked up at mention of the thrilling word.

"You are not letting dirt tell you the things it wants to." The Saint was not looking at her, nor at me nor Cija. He was looking at nothing in the room, and though his gaze was fixed on the waving grass of the outside meadow, he was like a man in a little fever; he appeared blurred, blotched, restless.

"You know dirt's nature well," The Saint seemed to tell Quar's grandmother. "You know that in this world dust becomes grease, and that if you cleanse it away today, cauterize it with acid and amputate it with your scrubbrush, tomorrow like a monster it will grow into grease again. Yet you don't let it tell you that it can show you contentment, that since you can only be satisfied from one cleansed moment to another cleansed moment, so you should not be sharp and sour as though you marched forward in a straight line, but you should be mellow and easily placated since life (like dirt) stops and starts and lies not in the un-plannable future. But in the moment, in the moment."

He shook his head sadly in her direction.

"You are not being," he said, "a proper peasant." And on that most sorrowing of notes he stood and left us, bowing his head under the old lintel.

I believe that not in the tunnel where Despair was born had my mother felt so alone. She did not turn to the old woman and question her further. With a protector who found the ethic of dirt interesting but who seemed bored by the thought of murder in his host's home, my mother obviously felt the grip of utter fear. And the force, the logic of pursuing a policy of utter inertia.

As The Saint disappeared striding determinedly up the lane, his head full of good and of evil, and of the rightness of letting the people's own rustic mores however savage hold sway in a thriving community, my mother took me in her arms, guided me shuddering past the tiny grandmother, and into the heart of the black killing-house—our haven.

Quar continued to shower my mother with blue beads, quartz clasps, and pink beads. The purse was willing; however, there was very little around in the way of variety.

"You give me so much . . ." Cija faltered, noting how with each gift his rudeness to her increased, his bullying as of right.

He smiled. "It makes you pretty. Don't you want to get prettier?"

It was no compliment, but Cija tucked in her chin, hoping to lead him into a mood in which he could fancy himself as a lover—he was always more gentle and playful then. He was still fascinated by her. I don't think I can decide how their bed-making went. He would not let me much into their room, and I have few memories of their togetherness there now to piece together any knowledge of whether she had comfort in their physical touching, or whether for that matter had he. Did she not miss those magnificent genital spurs?

Sex to me had always seemed something that happened on the move—in the saddle, in the tent after one day's march and not long before the next—it still shocks me when I understand that people go into fixed dull rooms and flatly do sex. Perhaps that was part of the

dank horror that (to me) attended my mother's living
with Quar—the ceiling that was the same night after
dank night.

"You think I am prettying, Quar?"

"You pretty every week," he said, and it was true. She
had not been good to see in the Mill. Now, in spite of the
strain, she was granted her femininity—it was the daily
reason she was here.

"The bed is glad to see you now," he added. "At first
the bed held out its arms to you, but turned its face
away. Now you light the bed like a couple of candles—
two little white candles," he slyly flicked them, "flaming
pink flames."

"Which is your trick-bed here, Quar?" she asked.

A terrible look came down over his head, a long
straight helmet, a mask.

I had a moment of wild joyful hope that the grandmother was about to find herself in real trouble for having
talked of the bed.

"To whom has this been mentioned?" he asked in a
voice of grating rock.

"To The Saint."

. . . My mother felt constrained to add (humbly, helpfully, reassuringly) "He was not interested"; and thus
she placed herself alongside Quar; her husband's ac-
complice.

Instantly, although I think at the time he didn't know
it himself, he knew that she, anyway, need not be placated, explained to, wooed round past the horrendousness
of the situation.

She added, "What is this bed? A trick you play on
your guests?"

Quar tapped me on the shoulder, his big hand came
round to my view, it jerked a thumb in the direction of
the door. "Out."

I went out. I listened at the door.

The bed tipped sleepers through a trapdoor when
levers were manipulated—into a stone pit slopping with
the acid needed in distilling.

Their packs and baggage were then Quar's property.

Quar too, like the grandmother, made the careless
point that he would listen carefully to conversation of
the traders at his table. "You would never believe what
dross they are, how they chaffer, what—" he spat, "what

little-minded uncharitable shopkeepers they are. Not worth the saving."

"The *saving,* Quar?"

"The very bed," Quar said clumsily, "on which we shall please each other this night." He said earnestly, waiting for her response, eager to arouse her, "I have been waiting to tell you this is the bed I chose for us. There are beds in this house I have never used, and until you this was one of them. I would have told you on our bridal night that this was our bed's peculiarity, but as it turned out I did not know how to broach the subject . . ."

His voice trailed off. No, I thought, that was the time Fishhead was to be lynched, and it interrupted the ambience the poor bridegroom had planned over the greedy months of waiting.

And my mother in pain cried out: "But this is perversion!" But automatically her voice had changed by the end of the sentence. She had thought how we were alone with the murderer in his house, she had thought how presently he was on our side and could be coaxed to remain so. She seemed a little, a hint congratulatory, even sexually conniving. I could almost hear past the door the answering proud agreeing twinkle in his green curving eye.

"You were planning our night in advance?" she said, almost listlessly—the words themselves certain to flatter him.

And Quar, seeming to shake his head at himself: "I am glamoured by you."

The house seemed more windowless after we knew this about its bed. One night I woke in the black and there on the pillow beside me lay something. I could not see it of course, so I brought up my hand to touch it. It could have been a mouse, a rat, or something placed there by one of the grown-ups. It had a familiar shape. It was a face! There was no corresponding body in the bed with me. Why was there a face on the pillow beside me? At first I thought it must somehow be that Quar had placed the severed head of one of his victims for some reason on my pillow. But that seemed silly, and as the head continued to yield its features to my tentative fingers, it seemed to me that I felt life in the lips, almost a sigh as of a sleeper, and breath at the nostrils. And I knew that pudgy nose, those coupled chins, that troubled jaw. It was the Wife. Why should I find the Wife's profile on my pillow? She seemed not to know that she was there. She was unaware of my hand. In truth, she must be not here at all, but where she really was—in the Mill.

Next day I went to the Mill to find out if the Wife had slept all right. Since I could not ask her outright, and heard no one mention the night, I do not know. But on the side of her face, the side that had been turned away from me "on the pillow," she was blue and black and purple and green and sported a closed swollen eye; the corner of her mouth was a belch of flesh, where it must have been bruised by a ring from outside and her own teeth from inside. The bruise looked settled, it looked to have happened yesterday. She went about her work calmly enough, as though she had noticed nothing in particular. But it must have been even to her a traumatic beating. She must be very churned up by it even now. Her ears must be deaf and thick, her heart must be fast and then sluggish, her hands and shoulders must tremble from time to time, her nose must find air like salt. Her eyes must ache, light must splinter. She must be thinking. She must be thinking, do I go on making a life's worship of this wise, kindly, all-pervading Miller? The profile that had transported itself elsewhere had been the untouched side of the face, the side that was still itself.

Why had she come to my side? What link was there between us, of which the waking Wife was certainly utterly unaware? Was it that I had wrestled with the thing I found in the house? I had amazed the thing by not accepting its spite, not being spiked or curdled by its malice, I had walked the black hate-soured passage without a candle.

I wandered on the hill. I could not go to the shore now, there was no Fishhead to play me his flute once his wooden tooth was fitted in his mouth. I heard a galloping and rolling. A party of coaches with a large armed escort drew up beside me where I sat on the knoll of gray grass. "Which way to Northeryex from here?" I could not answer. "Come, come, we shall not eat you," bullied the caped coachman. I found later it was no whimsical remark. "Point us the way through the hills, or tell us you know nothing." I knew nothing, but could not

tell him so. "Idiot hill-brat." The man made a swipe at
me with the whip, and I rolled back on the hill, my hands
over my face, my feet curled to my bottom, like a hedgehog. The huge crested harnessed birds honked and barked,
the carriages rolled on. Through my fingers I could see
in one of them sitting a girl my age—warm, safe, cos-
seted, above all with hands not sore whatever she touched
because of chipping the salt.

After seeing the little girl, days later I was still making
a certain gesture. My mother finally said, "What is that
you keep doing? Don't do it, don't keep doing that thing
with your hand in the air, Seka, whatever it's meant to
be—you look silly." (She was always very careful that
people would have no way to think me a cretin—since
once they really thought it, and said it too often, it would
become official and she couldn't easily ever prove otherwise.) I would do it alone only after that, repeating in
the empty air the gesture by which the little girl in the
carriage-window had held her hand for a clean white
hanky and received it, smiled, sniffed, and patted the
nurse who gave it to her. The exact blend of coquettish
yet throwaway secure fond lightness with which the little
girl expected, and received, something which had been
washed and pressed and kept ready and nice *for her*.
Not by a nervous frightened woman to whom she had to
be protective when she accepted anything from her, but
by a calm safe prosperous settled smug *safe* woman.
I went up on the hill, watched the clouds and flies, and
practiced my beautiful gesture, getting it perfect.

My mother as Quar's wife wore nastier clothes than
she had worn as a servant in the Mill. In the Mill she
had worn disgraceful ragged things—but at least they
were remnants of fine campaign gear—flashes of exquisite embroidery amongst the grease.

As Quar's wife she wore rubbish—respectable genteel
dresses you could shoot peas through, sewn by local
sempstresses with one sleeve set higher than the other,
and a bow to one side of the neckline to look "classy."

Now she was a slave indeed. She had come, as usual,
through her Test of Dreariness with the colors of defeat.

If there was one thing in this world that my mother
detested and deplored, despised and feared, it was dreariness—and for this reason she apparently was fated, presented with this test again and again. She never endured

it. While she thought she endured, she fought—but not with her inner strength. Merely with her resentment that *she* the scion of a Divine house should be subjected to this ultimate loathsomeness—the bleaching-out of her days, the color withdrawn slyly from her life: "wasting" it away. None of what she considered her inalienable right—speed and surge, the lifted chin and the instep high, the boot, the spurs, the purple; the violet passages, the haughty mini-victories, the easy tug o'war and the sleep of exhilarated satisfaction: above all, the "emotion."

She said often how she loved quiet. But by quiet my mother meant blue and gold and daisies and cream, the surge of happy days, and nights speeding to the stars as on the prow of a lonely ship. Certainly she did not mind being alone, she rather preferred it, since she found that with people arrived more general dreariness.

While she thought she endured and was adaptable and humble and submissive disguised as the ragged scullery-maid in the fairy-tale who will be recognized in spite of all, she fought. She fought not with her soul or her sense, not with steel and backbone but with aching angers and wistful tantrums that were none the less tantrums for being silent. She was overtly "submissive," writing her "humility" into her Diary, burning with her inherited petty-aristocracy and arrogance. She would "god" anyone who came near, anyone attracted by the force-field of such an overt victim. She would convince herself that her shining inner princess-hood was revealed through the disgustful disguise to anyone who showed any interest—and that Anyone himself was transformed by necessity so that he fit into her fairy-story without distorting it: he became a Prince as in all good stories, or at least true Observer, a pair of eyes clear with truth (the better to see *her* with) and unobscured by any of his own human failings, to which he had no right at all. She had in fact chosen to be Quar's victim, and he would never forgive her for it.

As the summer wound to an end, Quar came home one day to the dark house with a consignment of mirrors. They were poor mirrors, they distorted, but the people of the Sours did not know that, since they had never seen themselves or each other in a good mirror. Quar apologized to the people for the price of the mirrors.

But these, he said, were almost impossible to make, and came a great distance, wrapped in gauze so that they would not scratch, and then great bundles of lambwool so they would not crack. They had travelled in fact stacked clumsily in jolting carts ˏ separated from each other only by their job-lot carved frames, and our house was full of the shards and splinters of failed mirror.

The women of the Sours prevailed upon their men to buy a mirror for the house. They prevailed not upon their men's good nature, since the men had so little to prevail upon. They worked on their men's consciousness of how grand a mirror would look.

The air had been electric, a storm and a downpour was on its way, and when the people saw the price for which the peddler from Flinchwum was selling the same mirrors, they gathered together in their exasperation, and marched on Quar's house.

They chucked a stone or two, but that made no difference since the house had no windows to break. They chanted "Come out, Quar. Come out, Quar."

The Miller roared: "Give us back our stolen *price*."

Quar was disgruntled with Cija that day. He thought it very funny to go to the doorway, lean in it and roar back to Miller: "You give me back *my* stolen price. You charged a lot for this lady you sold me."

Miller's face empurpled and inflamed. He had always held it against Quar, obscurely, that Quar had not enslaved Cija after buying her, but had married her.

The gray sky hung low. The thick air itself was sour. The peasants stood shoulder to shoulder, their pockets aching. Quar smiled. Miller screamed: "Look in his house! Look under his bed! That's where you'll all find your stolen price!"

Quar's face changed. He glared murderously at his brother. He continued to lean in his doorway, looking heavy and strong.

"Good people," he said winningly, "believe me, if you are not satisfied with your furniture, then I shall be only too glad to refund your price. It is at the moment invested in a bale or two of silk from the worm-forests, but believe me when I have eggs and bacon and pennies enough, I shall pour them your way."

The people felt the sneer. The blacksmith, always a good leader of a lynching since he looked so metallic and meant to the people a clanging rhythmic power, bellowed and plodded up the slope. The blacksmith's plod was like a bull's rush: it could not be turned aside. The people followed. My good people, Quar began to say, but instead he fell back before them. The house was full.

They stumbled over each other, they blinked. They put dirty footprints over the grandmother's neatly washed floors. They staggered in inky corners, they fell down the stairs. They knocked over a flaring squeaking oil-lamp, which sent a thread of flame across the freshly waxed wood-plank floor. The grandmother stood at the top of the stairs, twisting her white apron in her hands like a hamster's, wailing soundlessly. She would have liked her wonderful grandson Quar to put them all to bed. But her wonderful grandson was barricading the bedroom door from within.

Miller yelled, "We can see if we've light." With this simple truism, he lit a brand (a chair-leg) from the creek of fire in the living-room floor.

He led a charge up the stairs, stumbling on the way against Cija, her baby and myself. He looked very big to me as he swayed there, pushing his face in my mother's; though he was not a big man. He told my mother: "I hates yer not." He went past her and the Soursons followed him.

The grandmother was knocked off her feet. She screamed, a high needle-thin song of outrage. My mother did not go to the old lady. "Let them do what they like to her," she said as she saw my glance at the grandmother in danger of being trampled or pinned half-hanging on her bannister. "My babies are all I've time for."

But we were separated by a surge of good people. Past heavy boots, past swishing petticoats, I dodged and ducked in a loud trampling fetid dark, and got to my mother's little closet on the attic-landing where the stair twisted, where the old cheesecloths were stored and where Quar and the grandmother had never thought to poke around. This was where, I knew, my mother had stashed her only precious things—her cold maps, the necklace fished for her from a forest pool by the apeling's father. I threw my apron over these. I raced down the zigzag back stair with them to the pantry. There was a lot going on in the kitchen, where they were turning over the cheeses and churns. But in the little stone pantry, reached by an outside door, there was quiet: nothing alive but me, and the pulsing cold of the maps, and the warm buzzing flies, and the stirring of the dough, which had been rising in a dresser drawer for two days.

I found the string. I tied the rolled maps (they throbbed quietly against my fingers) and the necklace very firmly, with several knots, to the two biggest weightiest blocks of salt. I ran out of the pantry with these.

I dodged across the meadow-ridge and down past the Mill-race to the Mill-well. I sank the great chalk-like blocks in the well.

I turned. Huge tongues of hot flame were seaping out of the black house. It was blind no longer. Its upstairs walls were collapsing. Rafters and joists were criss-crossed between the red glow of fire. I could feel the heat from here. The good people were racing out of the house, down the ridge. They clutched looted goods, small tables, a figured glazed jug we had used for wine, a tasselled counterpane, a clock from far lands. There was no sign of Quar, or the grandmother, or my mother.

Suddenly the whole ridge of the meadow, across which I'd just scampered, seemed to shake itself and rumble. It seemed a giant mole had raced along below it. Then flames shot out of the Mill beside me. The Mill exploded, collapsed. The upper stories quivered and collapsed, one into the other. I could see through to the grain on the millstone: it all rose up alight like sparks, fire-flies; the small natural concavities on the great stone's grinding-surface—for the stone was of silicious grit, brittle and rather open in texture, good for grinding, and containing many quartz pebbles—fell into long shadows. The canvas granite-chute charred as long flames licked it. The river's behavior I could not understand. It had turned here to a river of fire. Far from being an overshot wheel, the groaning great wheel seemed now to be an overwrought wheel. I discovered later what had happened. As the people fired Quar's house, the flames had spread to the Mill—through the tunnel used for contraband liquor. This tunnel, of which we had never known, had linked the brothers' buildings.

Since The Saint had forbidden liquor, and its distilling, Miller and Quar had kept it stored under-water beneath the Mill dam-stones. The flaming spirits were what had turned the pool and river itself to an inferno. Up went the great drums of malted corn The Saint had thought were for loaves to feed the villages. The Mill's upper roof itself, touched by a spark and the heat-draft, went up in a moment. Since that was where grain was kept, it had been kept very dry (or else the flour would have been ruined) and after the summer it was ready to burn hard. I saw a little bird flying above the fire. Its wings were scorched from beneath and it too fell.

Miller raced to his building, his pride, his identity. But beams were crashing down, showering swarms of sparks, like forest trees in a fire. One beam tumbled and thudded and there was Miller trapped under it. He appeared perfectly hale and un-crushed, but he couldn't lift the thing. Wife, unable if she had wished to dart in among the flames and attempt to tug and shift the wood off him, suddenly screamed out at him in a great voice: "Miller, you fool! Have you left me?"

The whole well, pausing in astonishment in mid-air at the sound of her berating her man, leaped from its hole in the ground. The great splurge of white water gouted on to the beam, quenched the fire as it reached Miller, and he began crawling free and Wife ran to him over the space that had been their floor, the little flames like beads still licking here and there the black dripping timbers. People said later how the shift in the earth, caused by the caving-in under fire of the subterranean tunnel, had caused the well to gush forth and quench the flaming wood. But I had seen a shape in the water, a nothing in the water, not white where the water was white, pass back into the Wife. And from that day on, whether because Miller had lost his pedestal, his shell, his Mill, or because she had become a whole person again, Wife dared to nag Miller.

I had not enjoyed the fire as it deserved. It was indeed a magnificent holocaust, a poetic fire, a dear and ironic and wonderful fire. Miller had set it off himself, as Wife would now never tire of reminding him, what with his secret distilling and his breaking-into Quar's house and his knocking-over of his brother's lamps.

But I was looking for my mother, my little apeling-child sister Despair, my mother, my mother. I ran back up the ridge, the earth and grass were charred under my feet. The ground was still heaving. The Saint had arrived. He ran down toward me. He held my hand. His boots had got greasy and charred and bloody.

I was panting and gurgling nastily. I looked up into his face and gobbled like a pig.

"Yes, yes," he said. He had become very kind. The old Beautiful could never have reacted to me like that. "We shall find your mother. Come."

Big black specks floated in the air to meet us as though we approached an oven in which an accident had occurred.

There circled a smell, too, as of steak broiling.

The world had gone quiet, as before rain it does. There was the little crackling of the embers in the black ruins of the black house. I became aware of the blisters growing like toadstools on my feet—that was from running over the hot grass spine of the imploded tunnel.

"Quar's good grandmother," The Saint seldom spoke to me but now he did so, "can face her Maker— He knows she's never let the oven get grubby."

I had no hope that his sarcasm could mean he knew my mother at least to be alive. The Saint had no taste; no sense of fitness. In any circumstance, he would say anything. He laughed "grimly" but in fact with plenty of satisfaction.

The black bed had fallen through into its own pit. It sizzled in its wallow of acid. Here were old bones, pitted and eaten away like leaf-skeletons. Here was a recent skull, a face of a sort still adhering to it, and a glass earring—not interesting to Quar, overlooked in his pickings.

Quar lay in the bed where the peasants of Soursere, Soursouth, Sourditch, Souredge and Sourbed, numbering in all about twelve males, had strapped him when they broke through the door of his black room which he had barricaded from within.

They had activated the levers they had found in the room to its side. As the levers burned, they lowered my mother's bridal bed, in which on so many recent nights she had lain, into the pit of old flesh and terror. They had lowered the hard mattress with the warm impression of her body, they had lowered the sheets and blankets that carried her scent.

Quar still lived but he was dying. The acid had not much reached him, there had been little of it in the pit at this time. But the levers had broken as they burned, and the bed had fallen a great way with all its weight, and Quar's back was broken.

He turned his eyes, poached very white and green, up toward us. I must have been a wavering dot on his hori-

zon: but he fastened on me with a vicious energy.
"You," he said, "give your mother a message. Write for
her that she is not—she is *not* to let herself think I loved
her. Her and her whey face. I *saved* her. *For her own
good*," he shouted to me, to the sky.

The Saint and I walked on. I think Quar died at about
this time, in this hour or the next. Later they buried him.
By that time I had found my mother. Despair was still
in her arms: she stood looking down very quiet and
alone on the place where Quar lay. I don't know whether
at that time he was dead or still alive. When they buried
him the acid had bared the bone of one of his arms, on
which he had tried to support himself.

I wrote the message to my mother when we had
greeted each other wonderfully, freely, and eaten with
the Mill-family, refugees, in The Saint's shore-yard.

She read the message quietly, just once, and then
wiped it off the slate. She kissed me, holding me very
close.

"I am a widow now, Seka," she said. "Autumn is on
its way, and I am very glad to be widowed. We shall be
spending the winter neither in the Mill nor in Quar's
house."

And she was right, for The Saint had been walking up
and down before the waves, up and down as with others
of his regular disciples we ate in his forecourt, which was
paved with small mill-stones, the confiscated hand-mills
of local peasants—they'd been discovered using them to
grind their own corn at home. The Saint had decreed
that all must carry their corn to the Miller for grinding,
for bread, to compensate for the "loss" of his distillery.

Miller had the grace to hang his head when The Saint
returned from his communion with the waters and stood
above him.

"You have disobeyed the Law," said The Saint.

"That's true, he disobeyed," said Wife, who dandled
her youngest fretful teething homeless boy, her hand fiddling up under his skirts to pacify him. (Miller didn't
know how his son got pacified.)

"I showed you great understanding, but you showed
none at all," went on The Saint. "And you have destroyed everything."

"Everything," said Wife, sucking her thumbnail, which
was a ragged hole through to the flesh, where she had

been pushing needle through leather in order to mend Miller's split boot.

"I have been very ugsome," said Miller, putting his hands over his head, and rocking back and forth on his arse and his heels.

The Saint tightened his jaw. His ivory fists clenched. "You have indeed," he informed Miller.

He took another turn around the little yard. "We are going to Northstrong," he said. "We are going North, to meet the Army. We are going to bring Gods to the Army. I have done all I can do here. I have given of the utmost of my strength, the strength possible," he got a little muddled, having embarked on one of the long sentences he had never even listened to when he was just Beautiful, "for me to give all of here. And you have let me down. Now as penance you shall accompany me. You, and the others of your fashion, shall crusade with me. We shall go." He paused, looked about him at the open mouths fixed toward him, and turned to address the ocean. "To Northstrong!"

"Northstrong!" A ragged chorus from Miller, from the men in the courtyard.

And they left the Sours. They left their crops and harvests and the long enmity with the trees, and the long fear of the silicious sands biting their houses in winter. They gathered their carts and their wagons and their wains, their scythes and spades and neighbors, their flint-sickles (impregnated with the harvest-glow from scores of years of cutting of golden corn)—and their wives, if they liked them. They were not going to be left in the Sours without The Saint. He had been let down here to such good effect that he could sway their wheels and heels on to whichever road he wished. Now he was on his way to Sedili, to his Lady again, but it is doubtful whether he thought of her at all. He knew only that his time here had been burned out. They knew only that his smoky vigor was something they followed, they would not live again without it.

6

Journey North

CASUALLY, DURING THE preparations for taking off, The Saint asked my mother if she too would like to travel North.

When we set off with The Saint, the distance became a beautiful color.

We all set off across the Moor. The Wormingend.

As we passed what was left of the Mill well, I pointed and my mother said "What is this? Look!" She scrambled over the banks and came back tucking things into her cloak. I knew what they were—of course. Her maps, with so many metallic threads in them none the worse for their wetting, and her necklace which once before had been pulled from a pool. After the salt dispersed and dissolved in the well-water, the treasures had floated to the surface where my mother finding them could say "They must have been thrown here by some thief in the looting."

We passed the twilit farms, fewer of them as we trundled northwards, each with its house glimmering like a puddle of spilt milk not for crying over.

The women, and the few men who were not with us pitchfork in hand, came to the doors or gates to see us pass. Some of them had the courage to cry out to the men who rode with us on their wagons, pitchforks ready as though we were to have to press our Faith upon our first victims around the bend of the next rutted lane, "Why you leaving us? Why you go-oh-oh?" And the mournful wails mewed like following gulls.

The men in our wagons twisted their mouths straight, and sat up tall. They looked ahead, squinting into the norther light. A man must do what he must do. A light tenor wind began to serenade us, here and then gone, there now and now gone. The air still brooded. The wandering-star lay big in the sky close over our heads.

Not till the ensuing night did the storm break. I thought of the Sours' women racing out to bring in their washing, their hair plastered down over their eyes in an instant, their nightgowns saturated about their fetlocks.

Here their men set their teeth and endured, as men must. There is nowhere wetter than a Moor on a wet night.

I remembered how once Quar my step-father had warned "Cross Wormingend only if you know the land, and then only in thigh boots." But Fishhead used to cross it barefoot.

We had camped on one of those higher ridges precious in hollowy un-drained fenland.

This was Fishhead's advice bearing fruit in The Saint's head, I thought. I crouched under a haycart with my mother and two other women with children who rashly had accompanied their men. One "wall" of our black and silver room, fitfully lit by the storm, had sacking tacked over it but it was sodden and filtered a chill. We hunkered on more sacking, indistinguishable from the mud. I thought of Fishhead sailing away in his boat with his song spiralling up over the foamy crests:

"When will I learn that it is no use expecting others
to be
Even nearly as intelligent as me."

Now if Fishhead ventured back to his villages, he would find them denuded, the men off on good works indefinitely; no one much around but his favorite people, women.

Would he have come with us, since obviously we needed him? I imagined Fishhead very clearly, standing by the sodden sacking, his fuzzy head a little bent with the three plaits sticking up among their cork combs. "No, I'll stay and keep looking," he said, "for my Floating Island."

Then he looked at my mother, who sat beside me, her

own face glimmering like milk spilt, unaware that I had imagined an address to her.

"Of course, *you* want me to think of *you* as a sort of a Floating Island," Fishhead asked her, "don't you?"

He peered through the rain and dark, almost as corporeal as they.

"You'd like me to get a yearn on for you and be always wistful for a little more of you than you'd allow me. But I'll stay here."

I heard him whistling wandering off in the wind. He wandered off whistling all night. I tossed my head restless on my mother's soprano breasts. The wind was flapping the sky, I heard it too. It was crippling the trees, what there were. "The storm is blown direct from the anus of the devil," whispered the peasants, rocking back and forth, covering their heads, determined that nothing should be normal and wholesome.

But out in the dark and gluster, The Saint lifted ecstatic face to the heavens. He saw rain and the Government falling.

It continued to rain as we trundled through Wormingend. Every night I heard the rain drippling and dribbling about wherever we had made our rest. Away went the river muttering to itself. We passed the very last of The Saint's altars, set up where river-current perpetually formed the initial of Saint's god.

Someone was crouching on the altar. He watched us, his head turning to follow us as our cavalcade disappeared in the floating mist.

It began to get better because we began getting used to it. The Saint had brought the bog-oaks with him to burn. The "oaks" The Saint had found in the fenland were very hard, ridged and dry—all the moisture movelessly pummelled out of them by the motionless fist of time. They burned like coal, flaring up like logs.

One day we were in woodland and it was still wet.

We found an ancient temple, obviously of great value, but The Saint destroyed it because it was heathen. We could have sheltered among its fallen colonnades. Or wandered sight-seeing the deep moss-furred inscriptions on the urns gathering floating leaves like old rainwater butts outside a farmer's backdoor—crusted with snails waving their translucent amber horns in the wet, and with old emeralds. But The Saint was distraught at the sight of the place, he could hardly widen his nostrils to admit the air there, and we were set to work smashing it all. He killed the great snake guarding the ruins. "No," cried my mother as the great body reared up swaying, thick as four men's torsos set upon the other, glaucous in the raining; and one of our archers set his arrow in the nock. "See, he is blind!" But the arrow flew, whining a little for the wet, and pierced the great whitish under-belly where it stuck aquiver. And others followed—fing! flk! wheenk! and the great snake reared and twisted and now flung itself sorrowing from side to side, its scales sliding the one to the other to our sight, green as ice of spring. His hooded whitened eyes finally opened in death. The Saint made a gesture of stern restraint but my mother ran to the giant sensuous body. We found a necklace of exquisite coils, a twin to the necklace my mother wore, ingrown about the snake's lower head. The Saint would not let us touch it.

A much smaller, thinner snake glided out like swift water falling from a ruined wall. The Saint stared in the anger of one who has gone to a great deal of trouble and still been disobeyed. He picked up the thin snake while he was giving orders for departure—cracked it like a whip, and broke its back.

Miller and The Saint hurried the women getting our packs together. They didn't think of helping them to get ready for leaving urgently.

But the Wife could now nag the Miller. She did so with the juiciest joy, gleeful glittering streams of nagging. The Saint was much shocked by Wife's un-humble be-havior. His lips pursed, his hand rose in a movement of distress—but Miller never availed himself of The Saint's championship; Miller bent his head and grumbled just in the way of a willing man, and did as Wife wished.

It was possible to see now why Miller and Wife had first fallen in love (for love matches were allowed in that area)—each must have seen in the other the features they found best of all in the world—those they'd so ad-mired from time to time in mirrors and streams.

For Miller, less horrible, revealed a softness of expres-sion reminiscent of Wife's—and with some determina-tion her soft jaw and blobby nose took on the look of Miller's.

We came to signs of civilization—not of old, gone civilization; but fine newish old places. A big mansion, its railings destroyed, stood empty in our path. "Soldiers have taken those railings for their lances," said The Saint, testing the rusted stumps. I wondered how Fishhead had taught him this, till I remembered Beautiful and his birthday present, the army his grandfather had given him. At the mention of soldiery, The Saint's throat took on an eager arrogant *glutted* curve, and the fine knuckles stood up on his hands as though his skeleton were spiking. I spared a thought of pity for the misguided heathen who would shortly find themselves in our way.

In the meantime we picnicked in the empty mansion. I embroidered my mother's hessian cloak (made from a vegetable-sack) for her with seed-heads and corn-stalks.

Some of the younger men had backed a girl who had accompanied her father, once the dairy-man and now our fletcher, against the stone gateway with its chipped-stone woman-breasted dragons. She was giggling. Miller, ever pure, frowned at the youths and girl.

"The mistakes of adolescence," Miller said, "make for misery."

But Saint said, "Misery may sometimes be not a bad thing at all."

Miller grunted, he had to give up, he was beginning to find his own voice always in short supply. The girl giggled and we children dangled legs and the stone dragons' woman-breasts gathered in the warm air in intensifications of midges.

Soon deserting soldiers were finding out our camps and listening to our fervid explanations of why we marched so irresistibly upon Northstrong. They heard how the sounds of the River would be brought to all hearts, how all armies would fail unless they hearkened to us, how the walls of Northstrong would fall to us and our might. Since we were so small and weak, they knew we must have a great secret to speak in this way, and they flocked to our cause, to our River-ornamented banners and our bread and cheese.

The Saint knew our provisions (for we continued with great resource to make our own as a daily and seasonal routine) were an attraction to his converts.

Twice, when he sent away men he thought "the wrong sort" and I saw how they could hardly swallow their own saliva, and how the little white sores clustered round their mouths which were shrunken and sunk, I thought of giving away my gold coin from out my sash-band. But I always kept it. I would glance at my mother, sitting apart from the women generally, and think: *I don't know when we shall need it*. The apeling now would cling to a proffered finger with its hooked feet. *It will need food one day*, I thought, *and for some reason Beautiful won't supply it*. I was beginning to think of him as Beautiful again. He was so warlike now. The camp-followers of the Northern armies straggling now about us thought him beautiful too. He was preaching one day when he broke off suddenly to say sternly to a girl sitting in the front row of his congregation on its tussocks and tree-stumps, "Don't stare at me. Shut your eyes, stare at the altar. I am nothing except what I tell you of. You come to hear my words, not my face, not even my voice."

Later he sometimes smeared wood-ash in his hair, hoping to be less personable. I do not think he realized he was one of the land's loveliest sights; but he knew that young women will be interested by men with impassioned jaws and vivid eyes.

He felt soiled and shamed by this, as though he lent himself to something yet should know better. I noticed him talking with women, how he talked solemnly, with pauses, damping down his energy as soon as he noted the conversation going with a sparkle—afraid his magnetism was catching fire.

Now the camp followers began to leave the other armies; whose soldiers after all were in a bad way, making shoes from their hats. We heard the battles sometimes as one commander or another deployed near us. At one time we could have crossed the river on the bodies of the fallen; it hardly mattered who was winning, who was losing: it was no longer a clear-cut case of Zerd and Sedili versus Progdin and the Northern King. According to our sources, factions had split off, the Pig fought the Bee, and Zerd by all accounts lay low, entirely inactive martially, foddering his birds, who were never at their best by the end of summer when they did not know whether to molt or put on featherage, or simply run amok, snapping off the kneecaps of all men around. Sometimes we heard them giving their bronchitic barks, far off away over the lower river.

A man came once through the wood. He held my mother's hand, wept, went away. There was nothing to say.

There were signs at times of Zerd's passing before us. We heard of the decisions of Zerd's Master of Cavalry; the lizards the birds mainly fed on were now sloughing their skins (the fresh skins were bad for the cavalry-birds' craws, and though they still ate smaller quantities of the lizards they suffered diarrhea and needed to be rested from being saddled). We saw the clearings he had chopped in the wood, the efficient trench and blockade system he had at one time employed here, so different from the haphazard arrangements of the fighting factions.

While we scoured the chopped clearings for brushwood, we saw his fires raising their russet plumage across the river.

Zerd and Sedili were conducting their armies together, and this was why my mother did not go over the river to him.

Every day peasants and pilgrims were in and out of our camp with flowers, offerings, prayers, requests for advice, blessing and gods. Gods were what they wanted most of. They were very grasping of gods.

Saint's confidence was being fed as by daily honeydew.

He began to think quite hard now about how he could take and reform the King's city. He wanted a base of his own, he decided—not just a camp in the woods, but a place of his very own. A roof, strong walls, arrow-slits, that kind of thing. He looked about him.

Overhanging the river on the point of one of its great twists, loomed a bluff. Built into this was a laboratory. No steps led up to its gates, since the Northerners had never quite discovered the principle of the staircase, but giant logs had been laid up the slope, and notches cut across the grooves running down them. In the grooves, the wheels of carts delivering goods could run easily; in the notches, the toes of the pedestrian could cling as he climbed.

The laboratory housed a collection of scientists leading a rural and investigative existence, and now it housed us too.

The scientists were the first people I had ever met who remained unimpressed by The Saint, the first such people I'd found ever since he became A Saint. But they put a good enough face on our take-over of their residence, and continued their experiments in the main hall. They were experimenting with the re-generation of muscular power. They had hooked frogs' legs up to a porcelain concentrator and the energy in the frog's leg, thus "concentrated," would make it jerk and kick even though life had left the animal itself. The question was, could the power obviously inherent in the Muscle (if of frogs, then of other species too) be linked up in massive concentrations to drive wheels when wind or water would not suffice.

The laboratory had been regarded as quite sacrosanct by the marauding and skirmishing petty-armies, for after all they were all of them Northerners one way or another and science was paramount.

But The Saint burned with a different worship, and he assured the scientists they were his respected hostages; nevertheless, they'd better make us welcome in their dormitories and corridors and the tiled spotless kitchen.

It was the scientists who first mentioned Clor. "A proper sort of a soldier." Apparently they approved of him because he did not try to talk pseudo-jargon with them, as so many commanders and nobles would do.

"How do you know Clor?" my mother asked after a pause.

"His sorties frequently end in our area, and when he has marched in circles awhile, we entertain him and consent to set him on his route."

Clor turned up one autumnal evening. The river dawdled by like beef-tea. An anemic sunset leaked through clouds, golden but insubstantial—like the future. The leaves were whirling and skirling along the ground and up the slope with Clor and his forage party, fallen leaves twittering and tinkling like dry bells.

Clor pulled off a long woollen scarf and grunted a greeting as one of the scientists greeted him in the wide porch with a mug of mulled ale.

The ale never reached Clor's moustache.

It was thrown to the porch floor where it foamed as Clor saw me, strode forward and picked me up more or less by my ears.

"Little princesscule! Is it you?"

I didn't know what my mother's present policy was. Rather than nod, just in case I was supposed to be incognito, I gave him my usual grave stare. He put me down as though fearful he might court-martial himself for having laid hands on my person. He bowed.

"Your Divine Mother the Empress is here?"

The scientists, three of them here in the porch, were looking carefully and listening cautiously. They had known my mother these weeks only as a sort of rather under-zealous lady curate of The Saint's set-up. They began to smile, however, at the corners of eyes or mouths; they could see Clor was pleased and moved.

My mother had heard the big unmistakable voice. She came out, wearing her hessian cloak and walking on bare chilblains. She extended a hand as Clor sank to one knee before her. "Clor! Have we not met in too many places to stand by ceremony?" She embraced him as he kissed her hand. "Sirs, is there another cup for the Commander?" She noticed the smashed mug on the floor. "Let us go in by the fire. I shall require of you your news. And Clor—" She glanced at his men. "They are not to spread the word or the rumor about your camp."

". . . The rumor?"

"Of my being here, here. I want no one to know, Commander."

Clor looked rueful and alert. "No one?"

My mother repeated her ban very firmly, although it was not hers to make to an officer of Zerd's. And though Clor agreed to nothing, I believe he told no one about her. She had always been one of Clor's favorites, or perhaps his only favorite.

I am sure Clor understood, and possibly shared, her uncertainty as to whether even Zerd could or would hold her safe from Sedili; as for the ogre of her youth, the Northern King of whom she had heard nothing but obscenity, to go near his claws was out of the question.

I sat at my mother's feet and caressed them to get them a normal texture, while the flames bounced in the meager hearth, and my mother talked to Clor, the fur-baby on her lap. She did not introduce this infant to Clor, and of course he made no comment: perhaps he thought it was a sort of local kitten.

"How goes the war, Commander?"

"No war, madam, but for us a lull while the fowl are readied for winter campaign: for the city of Northstrong, however, and its King—" Clor just in time thought better, in this company, of spitting matter-of-factly at the name —"for them, this is a siege."

Clor peeled off another scarf and explained how the huge hens of his cavalry detail were restless and wouldn't stay put, although not fit for any march. "It's rogue season," he said glumly, shaking his head. "To keep 'em at base I've given 'em eggs to sit, though they're only old 'dead eggs.' I've had a hole drilled in each egg, and introduced a big worm into it, so she can feel the movement in the egg, which keeps a hen satisfied where she is, a bit. But they will get up and roam about looking for eyes to peck. One huge hen is too good a mother—she'll sit all the other eggs, rotation, and the hens all know it."

"What is troubling you, Commander?"

"I came here to announce to the research folk, madam, that I must burn this place."

My mother sat back and looked at Clor calmly. "We can't have that, Commander."

"Madam, we understand there is an interest in this place from the point of view of the North-Marshal, the Northking's Marshal. He'll be thinking of coming here to destroy the place and use the site as a look-out over the river. The site mustn't fall into his hands."

"He already has an island in the middle reach of the upper river, I believe, Clor. He will not be bothered with us here. We are only a few women, peasants, children, the men of science whose experiments should not be upset—and a religious revivalist who will keep trouble at bay."

Clor nodded somberly. "Very well, madam." He stayed for supper, with his men, was introduced to The Saint afresh, and talked over old times a little with him, admiring his knitting: it was getting very vast now, and The Saint had begun to think of parting with it, piece by piece, cut up to make blankets for a few of his peasants. Clor saluted my mother, and he and his detail clattered away into a drizzling dusk.

Within days we were paid a stiff visit by the Northking's Marshal.

"The rebels will be here," his lieutenant rapped out. "For your protection—" he was addressing the scientists, "we had better take the roof off the place and remove the wood. The rebels will be thinking of burning it, you see, as they always do."

The scientists conferred a little and then soberly informed the lieutenant that they preferred to keep their roof, since the weather at this time of year was inclement.

"We shall be no target for the rebels," they said. "Don't forget that even though they are rebels, they are Northmen too; they know an important experiment when they see one."

The lieutenant rapped his riding-boot with his cane, nodded shortly, adjusted his riding-cape and picked his way with his men down the ramp again.

Clor soon arrived, sighing. "What it is," he said, "is that these learned scientists here regrettably might decide to signal to the Marshal's camp on the island. That's why I'll have to evacuate you from here and fire this place."

"What would they make signals about, Commander?" My mother placidly threaded a needle. "About your coming to burn the place down?"

Clor saw her point. He searched the laboratory and dormitories thoroughly for signalling devices, found nothing incriminating, and went away.

The North-Marshal's lieutenant brought a prisoner whom the Marshal wanted the scientists to keep safely mured up here. He was a thin heavy-eyed man, unsteady on his feet. The North-Marshal had given orders he must not be fed more than a cust once a day, gravy twice a week: "He is recalcitrant. We want him amenable before we see him again." The scientists received the instructions and did not feed the man more. He was kept locked by their gardener in a tight room. They listened to The Saint's words, impassioned as these were, about the man's free time and his soul, however; and they allowed a young peasant woman of The Saint's persuasion to visit him daily, although their "jailer" searched her for food or any kind of weaponry before she went in. The young woman reported favorably to The Saint on the progress of the pisoner's soul.

The lieutenant's men set up a beacon on the laboratory roof, so that it could be fired as a signal in time of distress. "If you are in danger at any point," they said, "we have only to see this light and we will row out instantly to protect you."

Clor came and found the beacon. He regretfully moved all human souls from the building, and set fire to it.

The Northern Army saw the light. They presumably set about rowing out to our rescue, but they arrived far too late. We were already gone, taken off toward Zerd's camp where we were all to be evacuees.

The North-Marshal's contingent knew we must be prised from such a fate. The scientists were too revered to fall into Zerd's unworthy hands. Besides, there was the prisoner who must be kept hungry. A short sharp engagement as the North-Marshal's lot, outnumbering Clor's men and falling upon them from behind while they were weighed down with our clutter, prevailed—and to make sure of our future safety, we were escorted not to the island but inside the King's Walled City of Northstrong, where we were, all of us indiscriminately, promised a new laboratory . . .

7

Northstrong

THE KING'S WALLED city bombarded us with leaves. Fallen leaves, millions on millions of them, kept up a murmur and whisper like that in a seaport-town, so that there was never quite silence here, not even in the small parks and gardens. Leaves rattled against the doors at twilight, and down the chimneys at midnight.

My mother and I were housed in a hole in the wall, for there was not sufficient in the way of living-quarters in the laboratory. But I went to the laboratory every day to work. My mother did not work. She could not leave the baby, the scientists told her they would give me enough pennies a week to keep us, and every second night I was given a loaf of bread and a sausage. The Saint came often in the day to visit my mother and ask her advice as he set about the conversion of the King's city; sometimes he came to supper, and brought when he remembered things he was given by the poor people of the place: a good-hearted cabbage, a whole roast pigeon wrapped in thin bread.

The hole in the city-wall was not a safe locality. Only pence were charged for the rent here. My mother and I both curled up on the shelf before the window, every evening when the curfew had been sounded and we knew there could be no visitors, no hurrying out to the street-vendors for a forgotten necessity, no wandering in the little parks to watch the litters and bearers and beggars all among whisking leaves. We folded up a bed-cover and sat on it to make a sort of cushion, and forgot how dangerous our place here was; we would not for anything have exchanged such a horizon for the dreary empty streets outside "safer" windows.

The window did not at first yield more to us than a bit of blank light on bright days. We were allowed to use a lamp or candle in our other room, but not in this one because "the enemy" could see it from their naughty peering-posts. But my mother said if we were to use no artificial light in this room, then we must have some real. We unstuffed the rags from the window, chipped with a knife at the metal plate bolted over it, and could see out to the "siege." Also beyond to the true North—rolling hills on hills on hills, land steeped in sour rolling melancholy. It was obviously a land where many men still haunted, here. Later we heard that area called Battledown—and were told it was forbidden wilderness. It was an unpopular place of old defeats against the Blue Tribes now rampant in those hills, entrenched out there, in control.

The "rebel troops"—Zerd's, Sedili's, the Pig's, the others—did not come round often to this North curve of the King's city, in fact. The fires I once or twice saw gleam high up and far away in the hills were the Blue Tribes' fires. I put forth my mind and sent it flying into the dark rolling spaces toward the little quick lights, and met a confused alert warmth—met something. They were after all my kin.

We saw blue people in the streets in the day, but they were not much fun. They were city-bred, heavy surly slow blue people. They were big, they were strong, they were not very bright. They carried the Northern ladies' litters aflutter with ribbons and mirrors. I saw a herd of blue people in pens at market. I went up to the fence to return to one big female the baby left on the straw and dung when a soldier had taken it out to pinch for plumpness, then put it carelessly aside. The mother grunted. She was almost hysterically grateful to have the baby back, but could not say so. I realized two things. She did not see me as blue, in spite of my small stormcloud look: I was outside the pen. And she had never been taught to speak.

As I became more used to the life of the Capital, as I found my way from ramp to ramp grown with plants

and hung with "drapes"—great weatherproof canvas
monstrosities once "elegantly" painted to provide areas
where the civilized could shelter from the elements, now
cracked and creaking in every breeze, throwing shadows
like crazed pterosaurs at noon—I could differentiate
more between the lives of the blue people and ourselves.
The blue people were not slaves. They did a lot of carrying—they lifted litters up and down the ramps, they
even carried high-born children up and down the hilly
streets on their backs. But they were not *told* where to
go, for most of them could not speak. They had merely
learned directions and certain homes or stables, as a
horse learns. And that is what they were. They were
beasts, they were fodder, they were fed well—and when
they were needed, they were eaten. The Northerners, so
clever with their science and knowledge, had killed off almost all their "real" cattle with insecticides and chemicals
introduced to improve either the soil or the cattle's flesh.
They were finding it oddly difficult to breed more, and
here after all were cattle, blue strong protein.

What scandal! What license! More, what avid greed
for the Princess Sedili to mate with the blue body.

Yet I saw how many brothels were staffed with blue
bodies, (for we passed through a street of low open
brothel-windows on our way to our rooms in the wall).
And I saw how plenty of soldiers too, in Northstrong
parades and barracks, were blueskins.

And I realized that the Northerners now saw in the
blues a sort of silent secret inadmissable salvation. They
lusted after their energy and virility. I met blue people
who *could* speak. They lived in palaces, much at their
ease. They were entertainers, athletes, long-distance
javelin-throwers, tireless cocksuckers. Only the old-
fashioned ate them. It was considered progressive to be
very polite and honor them behind their backs when
there was nothing they could do about it, to their faces
lust after them and their new blood, stamina, "freshness," "robustness."

For the Northerners' own peasants were not good to
look at. They were pallid, puffy, dewlapped. Northern
peasants eat far more meat than peasants elsewhere, but
look pastier, weaker, more rotted from within. They have
poisoned even their poultry with chemicals, in the great

surge of "science" which saw also the flooding with air of Atlan's old clean private vacuum.

Yet nobles and scientists looked healthy. Why? They had bred a special meat, non-infected.

No wonder the Northern King was humiliated at being vanquished, his Army led, by stud beef! But how proud Sedili must have been.

I saw Sedili once, from our window—Sedili directing maneuvers out on the river-delta. She rode a white bird (of course) and a veil of muslin gauze misted from the crown of her helm. She darted around rising in her stirrups again and again to point proceedings (so easy on the mount). She was the very essence of modern princess-hood, rebellious-new-generation, passions unfettered and muslin gauze unfettered too.

The two rooms we lived in were very bare, and unpromising in texture—things were damp, no matter how we brushed the very old rug, which had mortised itself almost into the equally soggy floorboards, it could not take on a nap—it was more like dank paper. But this is one of the best times I ever remember for my mother. She was living alone. There was not one other woman there to spill where she had mopped, or to smash where she had placed gently. If she kept things neat so did I, for I shared her affection for placement. If she kept a remnant of old brass, polished up with the right kind of soft rag, by the hearth even when most of the time no fire could be lit, I knew why: she used it as a symbol of the way it could reflect the flames if ever there just might be any. If she placed a chip of broken blue glass in front of our window, I kept it there: I knew she loved to see the waxing or waning light throw its blue little pool on the ceiling or the "cushion." She began to be happy.

Her face became less thin. She began to look young again. Her movements became quick: she was sure of them, she knew they would end up wherever they'd been planned for. Someone would not appear to change all her directions.

I think she knew she was happy. Suddenly this was the life she'd always asked for. I read her Diaries after they were returned to her, and before she burned them. I read how she had always asked, Please, could she be let alone, could she be not her mother's chess-game, her husband's waiting-game. She had always said, All I want is to be left to *be*. She began to sing as she worked, and to stew truffles.

Since one day he noticed her bare mauve feet, The Saint gave her his old boots: "There!" he said, standing back so they could both admire her. They were the ones that had got fouled in the Quar ending. They were too big for her. They slopped and shuffled even when she stuffed them with rags and thrown-out stable-hay we found on the streets. But it was too cold to take them off. The Saint now wore officer's boots again. After all, undeniably, that was what he was.

I knew my little Cija wanted nothing more in the whole world than a decent pair of shoes. She felt that slopping and flapping and dredging and slipping around with her ankles sticking out of these grotesque stained things degraded both her and myself—it didn't, but she felt it did. She had made me a little pair of soft canvas slippers, stitched to wooden soles the carpenter shaped for her for several coins. She could not afford the extra for an adult's soles. I saw her adding on sheets of paper and they were all different ways of juggling into our budget a pair of adult-size wooden soles. But that didn't work and she held my face in her hands, softer again now, she looked lovingly into my eyes, and she said: "If only you could walk down the street beside a mother with proper feet!"

I thought again about using my gold coin. But it was not economic to use it. I would never get the right change for it in this part of town—and being a child, particularly a child unable to speak up. One day we would need all the coin could buy, not just part.

I felt it was still the coin Ael had given me on my silent tongue. It might very well be the same exact coin. What after all would the Mill children have done with the coin, once they had taken it from me, but throw it down and lose it again? For looking eyes to find once more?

There was at the laboratory a very golden boy, a thirteen-year-old noble who had from infancy been brilliant scientifically and whose presence with us now was one of the main reasons for the ultra-protection enjoyed here by the scientists, since the boy's parents were related to the King's something or other.

This boy began to think that I was perhaps extraordinary.

I was sent by him into the laboratory with the key, on an errand. This was to the part of the laboratory which was still used as a cell, since it was very bare but for cupboards with phials stacked in them; in it was still kept the prisoner we'd been donated and who was supposed to be kept hungry.

We were still dutifully keeping him hungry. Every now and then someone official arrived to check up on him. No one told us what he was incarcerated for. He seemed quiet . . . not surprisingly, I thought.

As I unlocked and walked into his "cupboard," the young woman who visited him from The Saint "to fill in his soul-gaps" gave a scream. She seized one of her own breasts and aimed a jet of milk at the candle: out went the flame. But not before I had seen her suckling the prisoner, the prisoner's tired patient furrowed gray face pressed to her breast, working at the nipple with his mouth, his eyes closed wearily as she herself held the creamy globe creased almost double as she too worked on it with her fingers to ease the nourishment toward its exit. The way she had aimed that spurt made me think of the bandit Ael and his magnificent aim at the candle-flame.

The young noble came running in, knocking a retort to the floor: it crashed and splintered. "What? What happened?" he cried.

By the time he had lit the candle again, the young woman had pulled her coarse demure gray mourning over her chest, and the prisoner lay slumped on his bench, his eyes still closed.

"Why did you scream?" the golden boy rather impatiently asked the young woman.

"That child who walked in—" she faltered. She was trying to think of a lie I would not contradict. She did not know I could not speak. "She reminded me of my own dead daughter," she said hesitantly.

"You seem confused, madam," the boy sighed.

The young woman would not be bested. She stood up and in a great voice cried: "I tell you that child is a spirit."

The golden lord—his ringlets, his experiments, his

amber eyes were all golden—he looked at me and winced. "Into the other hall, Seka," he said curtly. And then as he saw over my shoulder the river at which I had been idly gazing through the window as I waited my dismissal, his eyes sparkled in shock.

Below the narrow slit window of the laboratory-ward, the river had begun plunging and curvetting. It was jetting like semen. I had been thinking of Ael still, and his beautiful control, and my nails had been digging into my smock. As the boy gazed from me to the river, and I realized what I had done, what a messy liquid commotion I had caused and how the fish must be leaping churned up in dismay, I dropped my gaze in confusion and the river-waters fell away, curling upon each other, and subsided. The boy did not fail either to note this.

Sometimes the golden boy's illustrious parent came to visit him here at the laboratory, to pause before the humming phials and turn on one foot and say, "Yes, interesting . . . Now tell me—" and then take his son out to eat better food than we could provide. And on one of these visits, after the golden boy had spoken quietly to his parent, the parent came over to me and clapped a hand on my shoulder.

"Little lady," he said to me, "now you, you must come to the temple with us this feast-day morning coming. It will be a pleasant ceremony and since we have asked our son which of his colleagues here he would like to accompany us as his guest, he has named you. He asks if you would like us to ask permission of your mother, so that she knows you are away for that hour or two in safe hands."

They did come and ask my mother. The parent cast judicious eyes about our dwelling, and raised one brow very, very slightly. He was more cordial than ever to me after that. He was surprised at, but proud of, his son for being so democratic. The golden son noticed nothing: he did not notice social bits and pieces.

On the morning of the feast-day they fetched me from our hole in the wall, to which "we shall deliver her home in good time," the father assured my mother. She smiled. She kissed me. She had dressed me in clothes she had mended very carefully.

The streets were full of proud, clean, fervent religious feeling. The temple we were going to stood on a hill. You could see it from most directions. Ramps led up to it, hung today with flags and striped silk awnings.

We sat on low plain wooden stools. My hostess passed me some candy. She tried to give some to her son too, but he didn't notice.

In a very short while my back was aching and so was my stomach, for the stool was pretty low and you had to dispose of your legs in trailing tangles. I thought the others, taller and bigger than myself, must be pretty uncomfortable. But that was what they came here for, or part of it.

The great gaunt echoing temple was filling up around us. I could see what a fashionable temple it was. Officers were coming in, braided with gold, leaving their swords with their servants at the first entry-arch. Officers don't go just anywhere to church. Ladies were here, their hair braided with flowers, looking very good, in high-necked dresses only a little accidentally tight.

The entire congregation on its uncomfortable wooden stools shifted and turned as two entrances galvanized the temple, one from either end of the high hall. At one end the priest in a great cloak of black and ivory was lowered seated beneficent smiling in a tasselled cradle of rope-of-gold. A huge hidden choir of boys' or eunuchs' voices swelled in a crashing of paean on paean. At the other end of the hall entered coincidentally a young couple obviously much celebrated socially, whom everyone wished to see: they always knew what the priest would be wearing, but this lady's church-attending attire must not be missed, for later it must be commented upon, compared with, costed, a little admired and much tittered at.

The lady, who was small and skinny except for a good high shelf of torso, like a soldier's breastplate, was wearing a drift of yellow on yellow, with yellow flowers pinned here and there. Her escort, an officer in the 18th Golds and thus resplendent already, had tucked a yellow flower into the shako he held, too. Naturalness was very important to the Northkingdom society and nobility at this time. Flowers had begun to die out of their gardens, their city and its purlieus, which were increasingly difficult anyway for them to reach, and had become symbols of all that was strong and poignant, as the blue people had become.

The lady's gown was of fine linen too—gods knew what that had cost. There just was no linen around. Perhaps she had found it folded in her grandmother's closet. In this case, she was wearing it illegally, which was very elegant of her. To encourage the synthetic clothing industry, a law had been passed and never repealed: any garment over ten years old was a punishable garment. The only materials really available in Northkingdom were those synthetic stuffs of which the shop-keepers and main middle classes were still immensely proud, but which the nobles were beginning to loathe—they were made very cheaply and fast, employing the maximum number of laborers who were still called "weavers" but who once had been craftsmen and were still somewhat bewildered by their retained name and vanished trade, by boiling and refining a mineral which was mixed with the smallest possible residue of genuine linen; long fibers were then pulled out of this coagulant, coated with a preserving chemical and shaped into garments. Because they were not spun, but more or less glued together, they did tend to fall apart at the slightest stress, and were never happy in rain. They developed odd weaknesses, hems hung and drooped, the color lost in patches. A new garment was then needed, and readily available. The North had been very proud of its prosperity, the endless production, the immense wardrobes of its ordinary people. Nevertheless, rain had never been welcome in the towns since the synthetic stuffs; and this partly accounted for the awnings and "drapes" over the streets, ramps and boardwalks, to keep the weather out of the city. In consequence, the soil had suffered and plants become sickly and rare; also the chemicals were pumped back into the ground—some as waste, some as "miracle earth revitalizers" which burned out the land. The leaves of the trees fell almost before they had grown.

This was one reason my mother despised Sedili, a Northern pullet strutting on a chemical-wastes heap: an honest dungheap would have been better, and my mother's sporadic efforts to like Sedili, to understand her and admire her for whatever was splendid in her, might then have been more successful.

The priest settled in his benignly swaying hammock, and began to intone a prayer.

There was a lot of standing up and sitting down and

sometimes we all had to throw ourselves to the tessellated floor (room had been provided for this masochistic extravagance in the lay-out of stools) and lie there humped and whimpering responses to the priest's castigations. With my nose on the ground, I opened my eyes wide and stared about me.

I discovered down here inordinate numbers of ladies' slippers. I supposed they took them off, as people do at a lecture or theater, to ease their toes. But I think it was yet another form of coquetry too: the slippers all smelt like heaven above, soaked in attar of chemical roses, or in ambergris and musk-oil, flower-petals had been scattered inside them so the wearers walked upon (crushed) flowers—sprigs of aromatic herbs had been stitched to their sides, or pinned with quartz brooches to the ankle-strappings, and I realized that I was crouching amongst a piled-up wealth of the very thing I had been yearning for.

If the ladies wished their shoes to be noticed, then noticed they should be. I searched around among them each time I was dashed to the ground by the example around me.

I settled on a pair not far from my right elbow. They looked the right size. I would be surprised if they weren't. And they looked new and were lined with spotless kid—yet they were gray, a demure church-going color which would not prove too noticeable in the street on another wearer. They were unobtrusive stealable shoes.

It was easy to scoop them up with me as I regained my seat. With my foot I started to stir up the slippers around me. When the owners came to sort them out, they would think them all a little disturbed, that was all.

Sure enough, hours later it seemed, we left the temple, leaving behind us a twittering of ladies all helping each other look for one pair of kid-lined shoes. I kept the bulges under my cloak in the crook of my right arm. This was difficult, as my hostess, the golden boy's mother, had insisted on taking my hand—but I had managed to get around her to the other side, and smiled confidingly up at her.

We emerged into melancholy autumn rain, the unclean rains of the city. The grit underfoot was unpleasant, even for the shod. I thought of the lady who had lost her shoes. I did not think emotionally, I did not think

with pity, but I did think of her. Nevertheless, the wheel
had turned, my mother had been many months through
a nightmare of grit and blisters, and her turn for the soft
kid lining had arrived.

There was a great deal of greeting of other temple-
leavers to be got through. The discomfort, and the greetings in the courtyard afterwards—I was at that time clear
in my mind that these were the lures that drew the
church-goers.

With his one plainly-dressed servant following sedately
behind him, my host seemed the least obtrusive of men,
yet everyone wished to speak to him. Talking to my hostess in a very relaxed, affectionate manner was the star
of the congregation, the lady in yellow linens; and here
beside her, heels together, following her words with a
grave, interested, pleasant expression was the resplendent
officer of 18th Golds. He looked down at me. He said to
my host, "And is this a new beneficiary of yours?" "Let
me introduce little Seka, who works at the laboratory with
my son," my host replied. "Seka, this smart gentleman is
regimental lieutenant-colonel—"

It was Smahil.

He had become rigid with the thrill he suffered. His
body and bearing retained, by familiarity, the ease and
nonchalance of a social celebrity, a military foppishness,
formal and yet simultaneously ironic. Smahil was very
graceful. He had fixed his eyes in a line to my face, again
and again exploring my features, in case he had got any
of them wrong, in case I was a different dumb blue Seka.

He was terribly, painfully excited. He could not believe
that I was true. Yet he would as soon see me thrown to
the dogs in the street, or in some unspecified but final
way torn from my mother, as he had torn my little apeling sister from her (or so he thought).

He bowed to me, making sure everyone could see
the bow was ironic. They all smiled as he made the ex-
aggerated courtesy.

"Which way are you going?" he said.

"We are taking this little lady back to her mother on
Northwall," my host said, "or presently her mother who
so gently loaned her to us for the morning will become
restive." They were going to eat next, but they would not
eat with me. They had taken me to temple for the good
of my soul, for the sake of their son who this social morn-

ing had asked for me, maybe because I was silent and would let him work equations in his head throughout the service, maybe as a test for his parents' vaunted liberalism. But they would not dream of eating with me.

"Good, Larita and I are going that way, we shall accompany you and hope that you will eat with us after," said Smahil.

The linen-draped Larita was nudging him, and half-turning away with airy movements of her fingers in what was not quite a yawn. She did not want to be stuck with the golden boy's family. However illustrious they were, she was in no need of their particular glow. She cast plenty of her own. She certainly did not want to tag along to the miserable Northwall on a dreary errand, and could not conceive of why Smahil was wishing this horror upon them both.

But Smahil had become blind. He had become a rotten escort for a pretty charming and famous girl who had never deserved to be dragged to Northwall.

The awnings over the ramps were sodden and many of them, you could glimpse, supported heavy pools of gray water.

I had racked my brains to think of a way of stopping Smahil coming with us. It wouldn't have done any good, of course. He could have asked the golden boy's family, any time, carelessly, whereabouts on the Northwall lived the little waif to whom they had been so delightful? Oh, *that* part—what a hole, there . . .

My mother opened our hole to us all and she became very white.

Without a word she stepped forward and gathered me to her. "She was very good," said my hostess, caressing my hair. "We can understand why our son takes an interest in her, and we are proud that he does. She is a dear little soul."

The father laid his hand on my shoulder, warmly on my little mother's, then on his son's and turned away with his family. The golden son briefly raised his slender clever hand to me in farewell. Smahil paused before my mother's doorway. Before he had finished his flourishing bow, she had firmly closed the door. As she shut it safely, we saw his face coming up from his bow, the pale face sharp and foxy, the eyes pale as a bird of prey's.

Our room smelt of autumn leaves.

My mother sat down before the window. Over near the delta, where the agriculture of Northstrong in some sort struggled along, clouds of mist rose: they were spraying the ground with repellent of some kind. Bird-repellent, butterfly-repellent. They couldn't manage a rebel-repellent, although they had all prayed so pompously this morning for the overthrow of the rebels.

"Seka," she said. "Here is a piece of slate." She was searching around. "Here is a scriber. Tell me, for our Cousin's sweet sake, how did Smahil come here? Was he at the temple? Is he a friend of your friends?"

With my two nods, there was no need for the slate. She put her head in her hands. My little sister mewed in her crib, a grocery box stuffed with paper. I opened up my cloak at last, it had become almost welded to my arm, and placed the good pretty shoes on the coarse drugget matting before her.

I went over to my mother and touched her knee.

She opened her hands, seized my face in hers, and kissed me on my eyes and cheeks and ears.

She stood up to go to the kitchen. Only then did she stumble over the shoes. She stared, caught them up, yet half afraid to handle them—"Did one of your friends leave these . . . ?" her voice trailed away. I stood over the shoes in a protective manner, made her put them down, made her take off her terrible Saintly boots and slip her foot into the gray good leather, the soft hugging loving smoothing kid. I did up the laces for her. The shoe fitted like magic. "Seka, write for me on your slate. Where do the beautiful shoes come from?"

I wrote, "from Smahil."

I had wanted to write, "from Church," but now I knew she would make me take them back, not because she was guilty—but because of her fear. She did not want me branded, helpless and dumb, as a thief. She drew a deep breath. "Smahil."

Now began Smahil's visits to us, for he appeared on our door-slab that same evening. He set just the edges of his fingers, delicately gloved in tasselled kid, across the door-jamb. It was enough for Cija to be unable to slam the door, unless she also wished to be arrested for the assault on a military hand.

"I could see, my dear sister," he said, "how overwhelmed you were to find me here at your very door this morning. Or did you perhaps not recognize me?"

"You are recognizable," Cija said tightly.

"Let me look at you. How tired you look. Come here. Let me kiss you." Cija stood rooted to the drugget. She shook her head. "Brothers kiss long-lost sisters, my dear. Must we be so unconventional?"

"Please leave us alone, Smahil. Please do not visit us or harm us again. The shoes are very beautiful. Thank you for those."

"The shoes?" He raised his brows. He saw the neat gray laced shoes she wore, he looked aside at me. "Oho. A dismal shoeless maiden this morning did not slip and slide in vain. I see good work was afoot. It was not I, madam, who found your feet for you. Your sensible child stole these shoes. Do you want me to tell you from whom?"

She hesitated.

"You want to be kept in ignorance. You want to rest assured that I shall loyally remain silent, that no one shall ever know to what depths my family sank this morning. Why, madam, I believe I know something that could make you afraid of me."

"I am afraid of you anyway, Smahil. You mean me nothing but harm—in the past, now, later."

"I love you, Cija." He put a hand each side of the doorway, looming over her in spite of his small size, pushing her backwards, following her into her dark room. "You are mine."

He pushed her toward the bed.

"Smahil, you can have whatever you want, me on my bed if that is what you want. I am too bored to fight you. But not with my child here." He turned a blank, expressionless face to me: "Then tell it to get out."

"There is nowhere for Seka to go. This is all the home we have."

"You shall both come to live with me. I have space in my quarters—"

"There are three of us, Smahil." She indicated the "cradle." "I remained pregnant. You were incompetent.

I think your luck has changed, Smahil. You begin to bungle."

He stared across at the cradle. He was not interested by what was in it. He may have forgotten that desperate abortion in the barn.

"You will come to live with me," he said. "You are mine. I have found you again. I always find you again. Haven't you noticed that, Cija?"

"I notice that I always manage to cut clear of you. You are a stain, following me, easily wiped."

"You will be mine for ever now. I will not bring you to live with me until you are willing. But how else shall you and *these* survive? You look ill."

"I was ill. I am much better, and shall be better still. I am happy here."

"In this squalor? Something has happened to you that was very bad and deadly, madam, to make you set your sights so low."

"I am alone here. That is what I like. I am in control."

He sneered. "Of all this? Well, let us see." He re-strapped his belt. He left us, swaggering, his hand all over her, his gaze questing into her very skin. "I shall give you nothing, Cija. No money, no clothes, no food, no help, no *shoes*. And when you know you cannot survive without me, come to me."

Sometimes she forbade his almost daily visits. Once she said she would call the city-police to keep him away since he was harassing her, but he laughed. Another time she announced she would go to the golden family and ask for help: "They will believe me, they are good people as well as powerful and influential, and you after all are only the Army."

He threw her on the bed, or took her against the wall, and my mother with an icy face motioned me with her hand to go into the kitchen for my own sake. She had told me after the first and second of these assaults: "Don't be frightened. Whatever you are, perhaps angry as I am, don't be frightened, Seka. It is nothing. He is nothing."

I think she learned to enjoy the assaults. I know she had never been able to find his body unattractive. I think she deliberately took what pleasure she could in his embrace, while shutting her mind of him before and after his touch. She tried for several days to keep the door

closed to his knock, to any knock, so long as I was safely
in with her. But he brought a sergeant-at-arms with him,
and they banged and banged, and told the startled neighbors who came out to inquire what was up with my
mother: "She is refusing us lawful entry. We have a warrant on her."

Finally a thickset man left, and returned with our land-
lord, who spoke through the door: "Open, madam, or you
will be evicted."

"We know she's in, we saw her come in an hour ago,"
a spindly woman said. My mother opened the door. She
smashed Smahil squarely across the face with her hand.
The red mark flared across his white face and his eyes lit
up. Before she could strike him again to the gasp of sheer
horror of the assembled neighborhood, Smahil had caught
her wrist. "In with you, madam." He was unbuttoning his
trousers already as he pushed her into her home. The
sergeant-at-arms turned to grin at the assembled audience, and lay his solid finger beside his thick nose, and
walked away swinging his club.

What could I do to destroy Smahil? I had not at that
time heard of making waxen images and sticking pins in
them with many piercing thoughts, or I should have obtained somehow plenty of wax and many terrible pins. I
knew I was not strong enough to stab him, and if he were
poisoned my mother would be arrested: everyone knew
now how she was an Army whore.

We received a little news of the camp outside. People
were much more willing to talk to my mother now that
they knew she had a military lover.

The rebels were still having trouble with their cavalry.
The "poultry," as it was called, had caught a fungus-
infection. It was confidently expected that the siege was
over for the winter. Quantumex, the Norhern King, was
retiring his own outside-troops to winter quarters.

Quantumex was a gentleman as well as a king. He did
not ask Zerd's nobles to desert Zerd's cause—only, of his
generosity offered free passes to those rebel Northern
nobles who wished to go away and look after their estates through winter.

After all, many of them found themselves in just the
right spot. "Their estates are so *near*," Quantumex was

saying. "Those great estates are not to be ruined if we can save them—for their owners, certainly, since their owners will save them for posterity. We have no quarrel during the winter with the owners of Northern estates."

One by one, one by two, Zerd's nobles left his camps beyond the delta. They entered the city of Northstrong, tended to their mansions and enjoyed supper with Quantumex before receiving free passage on to their estates. "It is not," Quantumex was saying, moving rings from one finger to another, "as though I were depriving the General of his men. Naturally, they will return to him. Just, one is sure that no general in his senses would campaign in such weather as is coming up—and certainly not with this nasty infection these lords are telling us has been caught out there past the marches."

It was Quantumex who years ago had sent Zerd out to conquer the continent—with an army of rabble, of rubbish. Zerd had conquered the continent. He had also decided to keep the army, since it was he who had turned it into one; the rabble had been meant to let him down, to mutiny, to fall apart. Either way Quantumex should have won. He should have won a continent, or lost a troublesome general, sucked under by his own rabble. Quantumex was still expecting to win.

I was tired of being in the laboratory. I played truant and went out into the streets to wander.

I found rows of old quiet shops where rubbish was sold—quite literally, old green glass bottles with nothing in them, which could be used to hold dried flowers (who could afford real flowers?) or broken statuettes or saucers with cracks in them. It was not the desperate rubbish of the Dictatress's market-place. It was friendly, mellow rubbish, which could be set to pleasant useless uses, an understood secret between you and the vendor. I had not seen shops like these in Northstrong before, where it seemed everything must be new.

There were very occasional browsers here: I don't know if anything was ever bought, but gentle-looking people turned the things over in their hands and minds.

I found a shop that had revolving shelves of old books outside it. I looked at the titles, but they did not make me happy. Northstrong only made books for people who did not like books. Here were books *about* things, nasty

things like How To Make Bits of This Out of Bits of That
—books which made out they were about something
when they were about how to waste your time—books
with titles like *The Gods Decide* when the books were
entirely about people deciding—picture-books where the
"illustrated myths" were enacted by glamorous stick-
people with sloe-eyes and sloe-mouths and no bones under their bodies.

But as I turned the pages, a little wind blew spangles of
sun from outside on to the print, and I noticed that the
wind riffled the page over at the very instant I wanted it
turned: I did not myself have to make the vulgar effort.

When a good thing happens in a day, gracefully, you
know something else good and graceful will happen to
keep it company: good and graceful little miracles esca-
late, they pile on each other like happy contagions.

I opened the books, hoping and hoping that each new
opening would be The One, the one in which I would fall
in love, and know that here in Northstrong in this gritty
solid unloving unromantic exile there had been manu-
factured something wild and warm. Finally I opened a
book which made me pause. My heart beat faster, but
with hope only: a wilder, stronger moment of hope than
usual, but disappointed still. The pictures in the book (an
old, shabby, leather-bound volume) were of warm, loving
good things indeed; but they had been drawn with a slick
quality that pulled your attention more toward the artist
than toward his professed subject, and the print-register
had slipped, the engravings were fuzzy. You had to
scrinch your eyes to get them clear.

I knew, however, that this book, maybe this book alone
of all books in Northstrong, would reward long hours before a fire, taking us away, both of us, from the mean
room and the winter and the petty tortures and the dull-
ness that was most unrelenting of all: for now that home
was no longer ours, but invaded, the little rhythms of the
sunrise and the sunset and the blue broken glass and the
high window were nothing, they were ash on the tongue
and a whining in the hair.

It was unfair to reject the book. It was better than all
its kind, here. It could not know that elsewhere, in other
lands, other kingdoms, were books far more wonderful. I
walked past it one way. I walked past it completely the
other way. But it looked sadly at me as I refused it, so I

slipped it under my waist-sash and the bookseller arrested me.

"Hey." A heavy hand, a pause. "The police shall be called."

I could not bluster and whine, nor could I coax and charm.

I stared up at him. He removed the big warm book, which was to have been a friend, from under my cloak.

A man who had been reading with his back to the street and to me, turned. "She is with me," said a man's voice. "I'm paying for the book."

A great gold glow beat up around him as I beheld the man. His keen gray eyes observed me straightly as he counted out the coins to the grumbling bookseller. His hair lay in curls above a flesh of honey gold over shining bone-bosses. He was very beautiful, but all in all, all beautiful, beautiful as an entity: you could not single out the detail of him, he was not to be piece-mealed, he was warmth and strength and safety and truth and clarity, and anyone who looked at him and could not see this was a fool seeing through muddy eyes.

He was an ultimate, he was a climax, he was things put right. He was things not being wrong any more. He was the man in my dream. He had stepped out of the picture-book I had once dreamed about. He was real. He was true. I was grateful to him.

He put on my shoulder a safe light dry comforting hand, very different from the bookseller's menacing paw. He seemed to know that I was voiceless. He had summed up all that was to be summed up.

I offered the book at him.

"It is your book," he said, "a fairly decent book. Listen," he said, "I shall escort you to wherever you live. I think that would be a good plan. You are far from your own place here, are you not?"

I nodded.

"If you know your way," he said, "lead me, and I shall escort you. Thus, you and your burden will be unaccosted." He almost smiled.

He was right. I should have been challenged in the streets. Children were not meant to walk with bulges under their cloaks. Big people, or big rough boys in crowds, challenged them and took their object. The afternoon was darkening and the trees were shaking and shivering. Soon it would be curfew.

He waited with me while I knocked on my door and waited for my mother. And she cried out as she saw him, in the street-dark I could see the wild rose flame up in her face, so different from the waxy look she had taken at sight of her brother Smahil. "Ohhhh, ohhh—" she said now. Did she recognize the beautiful man? Well, we could do with a decent coincidence. All we'd had were the kind that did nobody any good.

"Who is it?" Smahil asked abruptly, sharply—and he came out to the doorway. He stared from his sister to the stranger. He did not recognize the stranger, with whom leaves had blown into our room, but he saw that Cija did, and his eyes drew together in a swift meanness.

"You are this lady in this dark wall," the stranger said, taking both my mother's hands—I could feel how his touch must strengthen her. A crystal ring sparkled on one of his hands like a caught sea-curve.

"Your daughter has a gift for you," he said, "Beloved."

Smahil's hand cracked down over the stranger's knuckles. "Let go of my sister's hands, stranger," he said in an ugly voice.

The stranger smiled. He had summed Smahil up and had hoped Smahil would hit him.

The stranger did not even move. But Smahil reeled back. His face was gaunt with shock, the bones sucking the flesh against them, his fist still out before him in the gesture with which he'd touched the stranger—he could not unclench the shocked fingers.

"What do you want to bring with you, Beloved?" the stranger gently asked my mother.

"Am I coming with you, Juzd?" she whispered, her eyes as gaunt as Smahil's face as she began to query, her voice gathering warmth and almost strength as she ended.

"Do you wish to? I would much wish you to."

"And my little ones?" "Of course," he bowed very sweetly.

"My—*two* little ones?" She hesitated. She went to the "crib" and pulled out the hirsute apeling in its shawl and was half-about to show it to him, like some sort of bounden revelation which she thought might change his mind for him; he forestalled her by taking the thing in his arm. "And what else shall you bring?" he asked. "Shall

you want the cot?" As she hesitated again, he answered
the question she thought it too greedy to ask. "We can do
better than that for you."

"Then no." She became very businesslike, piling into a
gray frayed sheet (our best) in the center of the drugget
flooring the few possessions we perhaps might wish not to
lose. She included her broken bit of blue glass. Smahil
slowly had lowered himself to a crouching position against
the further dark wall. He took his eyes off her once or
twice to stare at the stranger. He said in a hoarse voice,
"Cija, answer me. Who is this? Is he someone of Zerd's?
For if he is, you know you will be drawn and boiled and
quartered in the city."

"I am no one of Zerd's," the stranger said.

This did not seem to reassure Smahil. He crouched
there, pulling at his lip, his eyes sick on Cija.

"Where shall I find you?" he said. "I must know your
address."

"I do not know," she said, straightening from her amazing light-headed work. She pushed her hand through her
hair, which was curling damply over her lovely thoughtful-
child forehead. "I could let you know, of course, the absolute minute I know . . ."

"You 'must' not know her address," Juzd said, drawling
a little, not putting much bother into his words. "Why is
it 'must' that you know her address?"

"I am her brother," Smahil said, drawing himself up
with a challenging hauteur.

"And she is obviously very tired," Juzd said. "What
have you, or what have people of some description, been
doing to her to make her so tired?"

He took the bundle my mother offered him, and re-tied
one knotted corner more tightly for her.

Ah, what at this moment became of the ground below
us? A great ragged terrible yell went up outside the window, and we heard the clash of arms. It rang through the
room, of which the air had already become chillier and
emptier as we began to withdraw our habitation, our ac-
customedness. The melancholy last-light fell on the hairy
infant in Juzd's arm. It screwed up its eyes horribly, rolling the livery whites, and mewling, throwing its arms out
with their simple almost un-lined palms uppermost. Juzd
did not look at it. The room, vibrating to the ghastly

sounds, was the scarlet of old wounds, of stale sunsets, of the lost corner of a cloak.

My mother after a moment went to the window. She looked out. I joined her. The busy slaughter was fore-shortened down there.

This was one of the times the fighting had closest approached the wall. I sometimes could not see why Zerd did not take the city. It seemed at times he would not when he could. It seemed at times he held back.

Suddenly a youth was spitted on a lance. High it lifted him, lying horizontal, impaled, like a standard on a windy day—he was raised toward me like a flag on a holiday —his eyes, they met mine, his breath panting—he died —he was lowered again as his killer's triumphal lance slowly fell, the killer's turn now to be split with some axe or other away down there. This visitation, brief though it was, from the battleground below, unsettled me.

A bell tolled. It tolled again. Dark chords fell across the town. The sunset-beam had faded into a nasty gray. "Curfew." Smahil stood up and smacked his riding-crop against his boot. He looked from Juzd to my mother and laughed at them.

"Shall we dispose ourselves," he inquired, "for our night here? Shall we put down this bundle before we look quite ridiculous? Shall we perhaps talk this hasty action over?" He went to my mother and drew his hand lightly up and down her arm, then slipped it around her throat and down her neck. I saw her shiver and so did he. "After all," he said, "who is this man? Let us talk sensibly now that we are all here together. How do you know he will treat the children decently?"

This was too much for my mother. She picked up her own bundle and said fiercely to Juzd, "Is there a way through the curfew?"

"But of course." He nodded. He had only been waiting for her.

As we descended the dark stairs I noticed a faint glimmer around Juzd's hands and head; I realized that if his feet had been bare his honey flesh would have cast a honey light there too.

As we reached the street door, which was locked, my mother rested a hand on his shoulder and breathed, *"He* will follow us, you know."

"But of course," Juzd said to that too. And the lock fell

off the door. I was delighted. Here was a master I could follow at last.

As we emerged into the dirty cobbled streets, I was twanging inside with the thumping joy of the discovery. My whole body seemed huge and light, a limitless caravan without its usual tensions and boredoms.

I was seeing the picture in the book come to life, just as I had resented and begrudged it for not doing, having no possibility of doing, in this drab little world. I was stepping along in the vision at last. If a grown, honey person with a trick of telling one's mother very truly what to do for her good *and being listened to* can lift a great physical here-I-am-and-here-I-stay lock from a landlord's door without a quirk of his hand, or a mantra spoken, then the universe is indeed perking up a bit at last.

The curfew-watch, men renowned for their vicious execution of the bureaucratic and almost absolute power residing nightly in them, were walking parallel to us down another of the mean streets, talking in their un-loud, un-hushed iron voices. Suddenly at a cobbled junction they were before us.

A truncheon was swung meaningly, with indecent vigor. "It's curfew, madam, sir."

Juzd bared one of his knuckles to the man. Beside the ring that glittered in the starlight, the lantern-light and the honey-glowlight of Juzd's own nightly flesh, he wore a ring I had not noted, so insignificant it seemed: a curiously twisted dull gold ring, like a seaman's knot worn for mockery.

The watch motioned to his men, and they all stepped aside, touching their hat-brims good-naturedly. "And good night to you, sir, madam."

"Smahil will get past them too," my mother whispered to Juzd as we hurried on. "He also has a ring—he is Grand Military."

Through devious back ways, and climbing upwards through the moaning little winds, we were presently near the Palace on its hill. "You have a good address, Juzd," my mother laughed.

"Impeccable, dear one."

For we were about to enter the Palace itself. This was no back gate at which we found ourselves. It was a side-door, but mighty, a great door of immaculate red giant-pine which must be polished daily. As we with our bundles mounted gleaming mosaic steps curving in a high crescent to the door, guard after guard in the royal Northern livery put up leather-tasselled lances in a salute. We were in. My mother drew a deep breath and took Juzd's arm. "You have rooms in the Palace, Juzd? You have announced yourself to the Northern King?"

"As an important man, Beloved."

"You are here, Juzd, as ambassador," my mother guessed, "from Ancient Atlan—not from Atlan, which still adheres to Zerd."

"Indeed."

"You went to Ancient Atlan when released"—"By your fine and courageous hand," he interrupted her. She went on: "You left the prison by your secret black route, which to you was clear as sunlight, since no blackness is where you are. And as spokesman for the strange throbbing heart of that continent, you are here to confirm for the Northern King the welcome news that you and Ancient Atlan will do all possible to prevent the entrenchment back there of Zerd."

He nodded to her over her bundle and her impossible infant. "You deduce, madam. The ancient heart of Atlan is indeed throbbing to a rhythm long unaccustomed beyond the saving seas. But the seas ceased to save on the wild night that you and evil entered our continent, madam, and Atlan's heart-beat is becoming so loud they hear it almost in the towns."

"Juzd. If Smahil follows us— He too will be authorized to enter the King's Palace, you know."

"I am sure, Beloved, that he is an esteemed caller, and an asset at afternoon tea."

My mother held my hand more tightly, looked behind us, at the soaring archways under which royalty first learns it need never ever bow its neck, and she said with resignation and with deep doubt: "I suppose he will not find out your rooms particularly."

Starlight falling through high windows now showed us very little of the great hall we began to cross here, but my mother, glancing down at the faint glimmer cast to the ground by Juzd's hand gesticulating as he spoke, gave a start. I thought I saw just why, as I looked down too. What we traversed now was a hall paved entirely with gold coin—in some places mashed, in some softened by the passage of countless feet out of all recognition, but in other patches still clearly coinage, the head of Quantumex the King visible in its familiar hauteur, the thrusting profile, the lifted chins (three of them, very regal) of which his subjects so well knew this one side only, as they chaffered over it and exchanged it in Quantumex's marketplaces.

As we left that hall, moving into more darkness, I thought that my little sisterling had begun mewing. But when we started up a giant stair, and the racing flares of the esconced wall-torches showed me my companions' faces, I saw that it was my mother who was crying.

And when in later years I read my mother's rediscovered Diaries, I remembered her tears as we left this hall. For Smahil her bother had quarrelled with her when they were both children in the Dragon-General's train. Neither of them had seen the North, probably neither expected ever to see it, but Smahil had told her that the tales of the Northern King's hall paved with gold coin must be lies. I believe her tears here at this moment were her final farewell to the brother of her first sweet fierce fresh discoverings.

We heard a sound behind us, and again, and knew that we were being followed on these stairs too.

But as we wound around another stair-corner, a mesh of pure gold curtain lay across the steps, depending a rain of glory from a pointing arch, and behind it was glimpsed another curtain, of wrought-iron links. Before it stood five guards, very well awake, their arms glittering in the great fleer of torch-light reflecting gold.

The guards did not cry out such remarks as "Halt, whoso goes before the King's private rooms!" or so on, but I think that my mother and I straightaway knew where Juzd had brought us, for there were Northcrowns on the guards' spears and on the breasts of their hauberks, and they were uncommon guards, with alert noticing fine faces. Distinctly hand-picked faces.

They quirked the corners of their mouths at Juzd. They liked him. They flourished him into the private place, lifting the mesh of gold for us all, and the mesh of iron, both of which could be raised on metal cords.

And as we climbed on up the narrowed intimate staircase, with its worn soft exquisite old carpeting, mismatched and over-lapping, and its quaint smiling gentle conceits of emerald-ended stair-rod or little leering inquisitive faces carved in diamond on the baluster, we heard behind us the quiet challenge of the guard and no more. Juzd looked at my mother. "I know," she said submissively. "We cannot be followed here."

"My—personal—turret." Juzd led us up a final steepish flight. We stepped into an inexplicable warmth and translucency and a quiet plainness. Oddly we found the stars right above us. And yet there was a roof, a ceiling here . . . "Your ceiling is glass-panes," my mother said in a great glad *relief*, as though what she had all her life ached for, while finding this out only now, was a ceiling of glass-panes under a high, high night-sky starscape. And we looked beneath us. Down there, there too were stars. There were one or two very soft warm wool rugs, of unbleached fleece, which seemed to be floating among the stars. "Your floor, too, Juzd, is of glass-panes!" my mother began to be amused. "You had this built?" "To my own design." Juzd bowed.

We disposed the bundles. We laid apeling down on warm fleece. "How is it that your place is so warm, Juzd?" my mother asked. He opened a plain small cabinet and poured for us from its beakers of a fiery, bracing, exhilarating clear spirit of fine flavor. He put sausage into good bread for us and fed some into my mouth. He had correctly assumed, I was very tired.

"The sun stays in my glass," he said.

"You mean the sun of the day? Collects in your glass and stays for the night? But how if the day is overcast? You have no fire-place that I can see. Do you sit and shiver, or go out? Can the King not give you a brazier?"

"My glass is double and triple in places, and it is shaped to peaks as you see which slope to collect the sun in troughs in which it wallows like the gold in a precious treasury. When it is hot, I pull cool serpentine wooden curtains over the glass-panes within. But it is never cold. I can open panes to let in the breath of stars. Tonight not, I think, the littlest one is in need of a solid comfort, am I right?"

A central column in Juzd's room was always of a definite temperature. He was to explain that this was full of water, into which his "troughs" at the top of it directed and beamed and concentrated sheer sunlight, which heated it all and thus the room. He had also some arrangements of mirrors, which showed how much in honor

he was held with the Northern King, since glass is hard
to come by but mirror in such quantity is a princely gift
indeed. He made my bed, of soft rugs, up by this column, and I sleepily snuggled it as he and my mother in
low relaxed voices waterfalled conversation on and onwards into the blue picnic of the nightsky.

I was surprised when I woke. We were no longer
among stars. I had forgotten a sky can contain daylight
too. It was an overcast morning, with twinkles among the
mists. A strange effect when I looked downwards. My
rolled fleece blankets literally seemed to be flying me
across the cloud. Then I realized that clouds were scudding by beneath us, lit by reflections, beams and shafts of
sun here and there.

Juzd came and crouched by me, smoothing the night-
tousled hair off my face with his cool dry capable hand.
He offered me a glazed-earthware bowl of hot bread,
honey and milk. My mother came over, wearing a soft
ivory-color fleece gown, rather big for her, presumably
one of Juzd's. She looked very good in it, calm and elegant
and fresh. She had been given a blue-tinged creamy flower
from the big pot of creamy flowers on heavy angular twigs
growing in a niche. She had stuck it in her belt of twisted
yellow linen. She was carrying her own bowl of warm bits.
"Are we happy?" she asked me. We nodded at each other.
Our faces were shining.

Juzd's floor was made of panes of glass, doubled indeed
but most of them quite clear or nearly so, some plain and
some blue. My mother delighted in this. It was like the
culmination of all she had ever loved about her piece of
blue broken glass. This she kept, propped up on one of
Juzd's countless small thick sills.

I was to wake myself specifically, in future during our
stay here, to watch the sun-rise through Juzd's floor. I lay
with my face to his panes, my bottom no doubt in the air,
a stumbling-block for Juzd as he went about his few tasks
—he was an early riser, needing a few hours of sleep
only. The sun irradiated the floor. Flights of birds went
winging by beneath us, their wings tinged with pink and
gold. Sometimes if Juzd had opened a pane or two, we
could hear their dawn cry as they sped across their vast
domain of massing air. Once or twice a bird would fly
through a "window" into our home, and eventually settle
on the creamy plant, or on Juzd's arm or shoulder, for

creatures were fearless and happy with him. Meanwhile the airs gathered for the day. We could see the coagulations of warmth, the intensifications of light or weather, the beginnings of rain, the birth even of lightnings far off.

Juzd's home was supported on pillars of stone and wrought-metal, built up from the main roofing of one of the King's various towers. "I shall introduce you to the King," he said to my mother and myself, "as soon as you are strong enough to withstand such a boredom." He glanced at my mother's look of dismay. "I think it indeed good that he should know you at last," he said steadily. "You are no enemy of his. He will always bear in mind that one day you may be useful. It is good to be borne in the mind of a King."

"I could be useful if harmed," my mother said soberly. "He could bring pressure to bear on Zerd, he might think, by imprisoning or even mutilating me. He will know the legend of how our marriage was a love-match."

"Legend?" Juzd lifted a brow.

"I have no clothes," my mother said, "for the meeting of a powerful King, and I do not think that it is the sort of thing you can obtain for me, Juzd."

"I think I know a good lady," Juzd said, "who will lend you some garments. She is older than you, but small. Shall I ask her?"

"If you would, Juzd," my mother said after only a moment's pause.

Juzd took my mother to meet the lady and I was left with strict instructions to take care of the awful baby while they were gone. My mother came back with two armfuls of silk and cotton, including little stiff dresses and trousers for me. "These," my mother said, "are a present for you, from the lady's niece, whom she says you must meet. The niece apparently is a very brave little girl, who has undertaken long arduous difficult journeys between parents, since her parents live in separate cities and both covet her. She is apparently an adventurous experienced child, and you might like her."

I had amused myself in the afternoon in Juzd's tub, behind its sinuous wooden shutters of piney slats; in which one window-wall was wide to the birds, who came and put their heads on one side as they clustered on the outer sills, trying to peck at the greenstuff and ferns and great thuriferous creamy magnolias Juzd grew in profusion in his generally steamy washing-place. Now on our polite evening visit I felt so clean that anyone touching me ran the risk of perforated eardrums from the resultant squeak.

This smug, uncommon, nose-in-the-balmy-air feeling of freshness made a difference to my manners at the visit. I behaved with a great deal more prettiness and pleasing-ness than I usually did, mixed with a little consciously-graceful over-confidence, waving for a servant with a dish she had not given me quite enough of, flirting with my mother and my hostess. They were all enchanted by me, including my mother, who had always been afraid the world was sure to overwhelm me. I was a brat, simply thanks to my smelling all that sweet soap on myself at every turn, and I shone. I outdistanced entirely in moppet-ness the little girl I was supposed to make friends with. I thanked her, by signs and condescending smiles, for her clothes which I was wearing, and I remember how pleased I was to discover, after racking my memory a moment or two over her extreme familiar quality, that she was the little girl I had once seen hold out her hand for a handkerchief from her nurse in a carriage travelling past Soursere. It had indeed, as her admirers said, been miserable and painful terrain over which the little heroine had so dauntlessly journeyed on wheels. I was glad to meet her and find she was (I decided almost instantly) *totally* boring.

Who shall we conquer next? I remember was my last thought as Juzd carried me up the turret-stairs and wrapped me in fleece among stars again. *Tomorrow, maybe the King.*

Juzd remarked that tomorrow night we were to attend the King's great table, for a banquet was scheduled celebrating the sudden arrival in Northstrong of a particular visitor.

Thoughtfully my mother chose a gray dress, all her instincts for understatement coming into play at least.

One had the impression that she thought invisibility the most refined choice of all.

As a flight of great wild geese flew past, flapping the air audibly against our panes, and giving those familiar cries of harsh yearning, yearning they were doing something about, I drew together a courage (because it takes courage to ask about the thing that matters most) and I wrote to Juzd:

How was you able to make the lock fall off our land-lord door?

(It had not occurred to me in those days that tenses took any preferred form in speech. Not employing them myself, I had never once been corrected for early offending the adult ear.)

Juzd smiled and looked at me very lovingly and seriously. "There comes the time, little darling," he said, "when physical matter no longer awes one. I have been in the world so many times, in this world and the others, that physical matter has stopped evoking any response from me. The more I am involved in people, in thoughts and actualities, the more vague and un-impinging the things have become that young souls, still caught up in things to touch and be thus impressed by, still call 'real.' "

I wrote after a thought that this might be impertinent, *Have I been in the worlds too? Long?* I added so that he should not think me insanely conceited: *I can make things do things sometimes.*

"I know you can," he said. "You can 'make things' much. Or best of all, you can make *things* little."

After all the banquet preparation, our guest was late. I mean, Quantumex's guest. Prince Progdin, who was the guest's escort, was late too. There were uneasy whisperings. Had Progdin, *even Progdin*, that black-browed broad-shouldered taciturn careless callous inflexible soldier, not come through the enemy-infested night outside us? The King did not exactly forbid our starting the banquet before Progdin's escorting-in of the guest, but he himself toyed with a piece of bread and a peeled fruit—so while everyone waiting before the magnificent spread followed his example, we could watch him. I saw how my mother's eyes darted to him, up sideways under her lashes. This was the lurking legend on the edge of her life since first she lived. Quantumex the Northern King was tall and fair. The back of his head rose straight from the back of his neck like a great knotty club. His blue eyes bulged a little. His fair moustache dripped gracefully and curvingly down either side his generous mouth. His cheekbones were high and rigid, angles under his high chess-player's forehead. He was Sedili's father, Zerd's father-in-law and mentor, patron and debtor, enemy. He was the North, the monstrous North of which Cija had been told tales as she shook in her childhood's tower. He was Juzd's admirer now, and we sat on the angle of the high table which bent back in an uncompleted square from the angle at which Quantumex himself and his lords were seated, and we could see from here too the entire banqueting hall with its lesser tables and its battered floor of gold coin.

The guards at the far end of the hall sprang to attention with a clash of arms. Pennants on saluting spears waved as in high wind. Through the great doors minced a hairy giant, a young mammoth, almost an infant mammoth, with great wise thoughtful obedient innocent eyes shaded by forests of shaggy lashes in which still skittered gnats and midges and fleas from the outside marches, and on its back rode a solid bejeweled bedraperied figure in a saddle like a chair, wafting sequinned ribbons and painted leather fringes.

Prodgin on his dusty black bird, accompanied by his tough personal guard, rode in beside the mammoth as escort. Progdin and his men dismounted at the great doors so that their tired beasts could be led away, but the figure on the mammoth continued on through the hall (where the banqueters or would-be banqueters rose to their feet and began cheering) and up to the center of the three-sided high-table-square. Here, facing Quantumex who had risen to his feet (and how tall he thus towered! a kingly height) the figure was assisted to dismount by Progdin, who himself had kept a hand on the young mammoth's lead-rein on the journey up the hall.

The figure, in long dagged skirts over fat leathern travelling-trousers, now revealed itself as a woman. As a very familiar figure. And Cija, casting caution cleverly at last to the winds (for there could have been no better moment to give in to spontaneity, and she was not her mother's daughter for nothing) sprang from her seat, placing a reassuring pat on my shoulder so that I should be unalarmed, and darted around the table and up past the mammoth to the guest. Here she paused a moment to show her face to the guest. The Dictatress responded by hurling her arms around her, shaking her, flinging her from side to side, and half-lifting her off the ground (for my mother was still very slight and underfed).

There was a clamor and furor at the high table. Quantumex, smiling, was demanding who was this stranger at his own table who claimed and was claimed by his honored guest with such joy and abandon.

Progdin, who had stood by with a look of sudden shrewd unsurprise, for he never could be presented with much he did not at once understand and besides my mother and her patterns were known to him of old and fitted his own patterns, Progdin now presented to my mother his dusty travel-stained black arm. My mother, with a look at him, placed her hand on it. Progdin led her up to the King, saying with a wide and courtly flourish toward the Dictatress: "Sire: our honored guest the Dictatress. And may I, Sire, introduce her daughter. Her daughter Cija."

"Her daughter!" shouted the King.

He reached over the table and flagons, grasping both ladies' hands in his huge paws.

"How can I tell to you, sweet lady," Quantumex roared at the Dictatress, "what happiness it is to have you here at my own table? How was it her daughter Cija was here and I not knowing?"

A huge livid smile was turned on Juzd. Juzd said calmingly, "Majesty. The lady Cija was discovered by me not many days since in your wall. In your Northwall of your city."

The eyes, like great blue poached eggs, were turned upon Cija. "But how is this?" the King "murmured" again. "In my city and I not know? And how Northwall?" He had begun to croon, as though it were all a dear and interesting pain.

"She had been living like a pauper, Majesty," Juzd said. "She has been long separated from her husband, she has not seen him for near a year. But by strange and limping means she arrived at Northstrong."

"Limping . . . ?" the King stared. "You should, dear madam," he addressed Cija, "nevertheless have announced yourself to us. We are your host here."

"She is in a difficult and unique position as the General's wife, as you, Your Majesty, may well imagine," Juzd said.

"I could have thought you a spy?" Quantumex turned to Cija.

He boomed a laugh, patting her hand. He filled her goblet with his unique wine. "I could have kept your children as hostages. Are your children with you?"

"Indeed, Your Majesty." Cija beckoned me lovingly to her, "Come, Seka. Your Majesty. My daughter Seka. The younger child sleeps in Juzd's apartment."

"So?" The King smiled, but without offense. He obviously had no illusions, nor wished to have, about Juzd's uprightness.

"I had believed," the King said, with a puzzled look, "your elder child to be a boy, Madam. But my intelligence is stale now, and likely I was misinformed."

My grandmother the Dictatress was meanwhile making much of me, feeding me from her plate. "Well, well, Seka, and how do we find ourselves? It is a strange delightful good joy for my arrival here among mighty strangers to include a meeting with my dearest little family. Ho, ho. If you are pleased to see me, you squeeze my hand, and I will squeeze yours." We squeezed each other scrinchingly. "We are both great travellers, I see."

She looked travel-worn, but not tired. Her entourage, scattered around the high table now in places reserved already (room had of course been made for me by the Dictatress, for my mother and Juzd at the King's left hand) included only one lady, a ladylike lady of sensible countenance and uncertain age. The Dictatress's travel-cape had been flung off over her chair-back. It was thick with rain, which now began to pour off it and to send steam into the air around us.

There was no sign of the essential famous train. Away from her country, she obviously dispensed with it.

At times, as Cija charmed the King who set himself to delight her in turn, I saw her eyes scour the hall. I knew from the pinched tension around her mouth at these searches, she was looking for Smahil's sharp face in the crowd. But he was not here, and for the rest of the Dictatress's sojourn here he would be not allowed within royal purlieus. He was Progdin's companion, but not at a time when the Dictatress was here: now he must be kept out of sight, for the sight of him would be odious to the Dictatress who had long ago issued her own edicts against him.

The mammoth had been led away to comfort. I wished I could ask my grandmother about him. I hoped that when we had a chance to talk with my slate and scriber, maybe tomorrow, she might say "Yes" to my polite question and let me have a ride on him.

She had hurt her foot, this was why she must ride even to the King's table, she explained to Quantumex. But the hurt was nothing, "a throb," she said bracingly. She did not even recollect how it had happened.

She was here, it became obvious, to form some alliance with Quantumex. Ever one (as Quantumex knew of her) to gird her loins with strong allies, she had evidently fretted that Zerd had left her with what seemed to her too little protection.

We were present the next day in the intimate salon, all down-stuffed cushions and gilded twiddles, in which Quantumex entertained with wine, sweetmeats, a string quartet and politics his principal officers, the Dictatress, and her principals.

"I need an ally in that quarter, it is true," Quantumex said, amid the graceful drawing on huge curly parchment-pieces of many doodling maps of his part of the world and ours and of the lands between (he was remarkably well-informed, far more geographically aware than his daughter Sedili and I could not help thinking how he would better value Scridol, who presumably was still out there preparing for winter siege with Sedili tantruming).

"But you must let me say, dear Madam," to the Dictatress, "that I need an ally on whom I can depend not only now, not for a year or two, delightful though that sort of relationship of course can be, but for ever after. An ally who is really, let me say, tied to me. I feel, if I may put it this way, that a Dictatress whose blood-tie is with the Dragon—your daughter, Madam, your dear daughter has after all been married to the General whose good taste we all understand—such a Dictatress can not in the greater analysis and the fullness of time be considered totally trustworthy."

The Dictatress, who had stumped around the salon twice, now stopped and snapped out at him, "Exactly. Yet you need me. What about marriage?"

There was a pause. Quantumex blinked slowly and one of his lords sat up and drawled: "One would suppose a marriage might well be one considerable solution."

And marriage was now considered.

I'm not thinking that Quantumex *seriously* considered marrying this preposterous woman. But it was now a public possibility, and a long preliminary "courtship" began, the sort of courtship which only royalty can enjoy, where everything is in the air and nothing is exactly afoot. Quantumex adored guessing games and riddles. He was quite abubble with this courtship. His blue eyes twinkled constantly in his big healthy tanned head. His thick lips pouted, pursed, leered, persuaded.

He knew how invaluable the Dictatress's land could be as a base. He knew that if he had both Juzd's friendship, (and thus the alliance with Ancient Atlan herself) and full and entire permission and co-operation in basing himself on the Dictatress's mountain-protected peninsula with its unparalleled access to the route to Atlan fastness, then Zerd would be intriguingly out-maneuvered.

He played his game with the Dictatress for all it was worth, his "maybe" game. He was used to charming and bullying people into having crushes on him.

The Dictatress meanwhile played by all her own rules. She had advised Cija so many times on the infallible means by which to ensure a man, any wanted man. Now she utilized her own rules. She flatteringly let Quantumex win at chess, but displayed an interesting skill at guessing-games. She was awed by all he showed her. She was useful —she cooked little possets when he was out of sorts, she entertained at his private suppers, she displayed all her tactical brilliance and they discussed details of old battles (in which they had been on opposing sides) till late into the autumn dark.

Also, I have never known anyone like my grandmother for wearing her jewels all the time, and the awful thing is that it was effective. One would have thought that any royalty of Quantumex's standing and experience and so-phistication would have known that another royalty owned a few jewels, a few decent heirlooms, just like any-body else, without their having to be on any display. But the more vulgar the Dictatress's attire, the more she ap-peared at breakfast in a crown or two and diamond ear-rings and a broach of the finest water and the size of a thoroughbred pigeon's egg pinning her dressing-gown to-gether, the more Quantumex muttered asides to his advisers about investment. This was a King who prose-cuted, for instance, if any of his subjects was foolish enough to recover from a suicide attempt—they had at-tempted to deprive him of a body and a soul.

*   *   *

A new development was the autumnal Northern determination to put an end to the siege. "He is sitting out there," Quantumex restively said of the Dragon, of his son-in-law, "like a man applauding opera."

The conundrum was put to the scientists, and to protect their cogitations an extra wall or two were built around the laboratory, created of bricks from houses which had been torn down for the laboratory's sake.

A demented scientist arrived one day at Quantumex's salon, demented and stuttering and jerkily paralyzed because in his old black rusty gown and clumpy boots he had no idea how to behave socially with a King. However, he was to tell the King in person what plan he had conjured up for the discomfiture of Zerd.

A long-range spray had been almost perfected by this genius, which was to coat (if sprayed when the wind was exactly right) the thorn-bushes through which Zerd's main body must pass on their regular reconnaissance, with a sticky insidious and deadly poison. "Thorns being particularly excellent for this purpose, Majesty . . ." spluttered the scientist. He had brought a sheaf of diagrams showing the way thorns press into flesh, or into garments or even the fine mesh of mail-armor, later to become worked into the blood-stream itself.

I was watching from my favorite place. My place was a step on the ladder scaling one wall of Quantumex's salon, which was lined with books, those useful draft-excluders. I munched a pastry and recognized the scientist who planned my father's undoing. A nasty un-doing.

The scientist was a shy ferocious stale-clothed teacher of mine who had been known in the laboratory for his smackings. Once in a while, when wrong had been discovered, he would appear in the doorway to his study and rap out a name. We all knew that we would not see the criminal for a long time.

Once this lonely gentleman had smacked me. His study had skylight-windows, high up in the drafty plank-paneled room. It was raining that day, and the gray runnels sluiced down the skylight panes and tapped and pattered endlessly. Occasional chill drops blew in and plopped on the papers shuffled between test-tubes on his several desks. He stood there sternly without a word and indicated to me that I must bend over and lift my skirt. I

knew what I had done that was wrong—I had spilled
precious liquid—and I bent over.

I was sure his hand must smart. His arm must ache. I
was in no doubt that it was a heroic action of his. He
must know the sniggerings went on behind his back. The
rain pattered on without any sign of hope of ceasing, and
here I was in this man's power, not too terrible a power,
a fairly mild and occasional power, but for this afternoon complete—for no one would come in, he would call
no one in, he had locked the door, he was intent on my
punishment, intent on justice. Justice had set in for the
afternoon, and my bottom was getting sore under the
regular slapping *crack!*—as regular as the rain.

I noticed a protuberance in the venerable black old-
fashioned voluminous trousers at my upside-down eye-
level.

I thought "This could go on for ever, and presumably at
the end of it all, when both of us are bored and exhausted,
he will still be miserable and puzzled with himself."
I reached out kindly and gently, so as not to alarm nor
insult him, and very gently and fast un-did his trouser-slit.
Nothing popped out. It did not know how to do that, it was
quite un-used, obviously, to being handled. I had to reach
one or two fingers in and grope about a little for it. The
smacking hesitated, uncertain, but he was into his rhythms
half-hypnotized while the strength of his arm and the
drumming of the rain should last, and he did not stop my
fingers. Soon he could not have stopped them had he been
dying, had the door opened and a whole classful of stu-
dents and colleagues appeared in the doorway. The
smacks became eager, melting, shy, cruel, pitiless, grateful, amazed, transported, inexorable, controlling his arm
as a tail wags a transported dog. There was a smell which
amused me and which I liked too—as though this had till
now been utterly private and was suddenly released from
long isolation. Sweet busy private veins stood out and
quickened. He came magnificently, frighteningly, from the
depths of the matted crispy curls which lately had begun
thrusting out fully from the rusty academic slit that had
seemed so secretive. Presumably he came from plenty of
depths. I straightened up. He stood panting, staring wildly
at me. "You need this," he croaked harshly. He handed
me his big folded spotless kerchief. I regretfully wiped off
the velvet-soft globs, wishing there were some way to

transport them back to my mother—she had begun to worry about her dry under-nourished complexion, and I knew this would moisturize wonderfully.

He had hardly righted himself before he had hurried me to the door. But before he hurried me out there was a little tap on my shoulder—not a silly tap, but a warm though hardly-perceptible, swiftly-curtailed tap—he had understood me and my understanding of him. Ever after in the laboratory day-to-day life, he had been very strict with me, if he could not avoid me, and I thought that once in perspective my action had become an intolerable memory to him, and I hated danger, even though I am voiceless. But once he had been kind when a student was teasing me; he had frowned very blackly, and said to the student: "Go home at once. Do not return for a week—which fee will not be refunded to your parents—or, if it takes longer, until you have learned manners."

Now, I thought, "my appearance on its own will fairly discompose him. He will never have forgotten me, no matter how changed my attire and circumstances."

I kicked the ladder so that it fell, and I hung by one arm to the bookcase, unable to cry out *Help, help!* but hoping nevertheless to be noticed.

Indeed, I was noticed. The scientist looked up and saw me. Two amazements chased his face—surprise at the sight of a small girl hanging by one arm from the bookcase above his head, and surprise, deadly paralyzing surprise, at the fact that I was me.

I dropped toward his papers, hoping to snatch up while he was still bemused the crucial paper—the one I had seen which was covered with his spidery notes in terms of the preparation of the spray-mechanism. Of course, he would have others, but this one was his fair copy, and would take a long while to get together again.

Quantumex cursed and sprang athletically backward, both kingly heels together, in one bound. I had pulled the bookcase too hard. The shelves had come away from their wall. The books rained, poured, pounded, thundered down upon us. Men ran to help, beating their way through the banging books. "Help ho!" roared Quantumex. "We need help. Mind our spines. Our spines." He was well out of danger anyway, and did not mean my little spine and the poor scientist's vertebrae. He meant the

spines of his leather-bound volumes. But the scientist's
spine was cracked. When the books were cleared off him,
he was still not to be roused. A little froth ran into his
beard, that was the last sign of life they drew from him.

His papers were shuffled together. The crucial paper
was missing and they could find it nowhere. It was not to
be found copied in his laboratory either—he had hidden
his notes when he came to the Palace so that his colleagues
could not root about among them.

Quantumex became jovial, in general, with me after
that. I had not until then existed for him except as an
abstraction, the Dictatress's grandchild, Zerd's daughter
(though possibly not of absolute marketable value to
either of those forces). Now I had become real to him. I
was the person who had killed one of his scientists. In
the middle of a conference, what's more, about one way to
defeat the enemy. Quantumex had not failed to note that
the enemy in question was my father. Quantumex had
noted the disappearance of the crucial paper. He would
never forgive me, but he had been shocked in a way that
rarely happened to him, and thus I had delighted him.

He was more careful, however, about where I was allowed. I had to sneak around a great deal more in order
to be where I might see or overhear anything of the slightest interest.

In this way, what I did find out about was the *inform-
ing* life of the Palace. Here many doors were opening,
many shutting. The back stairs were in places worn almost
away. Each spider, devouring flies in tortuous torturous
webs, was a fly in somebody else's trap. I was glad that
no one could pull me into all this. My words never can be
held against me, not twisted before nor behind my back.

I was able to repeat to my mother and Juzd, on my
slate, what I heard—the behind-doors of the siege and
who was jockeying for how much honor at the ending of it.
What was certain was that the North had decided that
Zerd must in some way be destroyed—Sedili did not matter so much, she would cease to battle once Zerd was
dead, her reason would be dead, her teeth drawn.

It was amazing to walk in the lanes around the Palace
with Juzd, who gave coin to every beggar, just as the

Dictatress withheld coin. Juzd, noting my surprise when he gave to some who seemed as well-heeled as he (for he did not look rich) said to me, "I'd sooner be 'made a fool of' several times and incidentally give to those who need it, than turn away possibly one in need among others 'making a fool' of me. How can I be 'made' an anything of?" He helpfully added that if I wanted to keep my gold coin, I mustn't give—or I wouldn't be real anyway, just storing up hatred of the beggars I had been "forced" to give to, as the Wife had fermented a tangible living haunting hatred of the husband she had been "forced" (by her self-image) to worship.

Juzd began to re-dispose his mirrors. Instead of arranging them to catch sunlight, he began to send sunlight with them. He could send sunlight at great intensity—long distances. He could direct it into beams that hurt. He could dazzle. And finally, he directed the beams during an attack, which we could see very small and bustling, at one wall of the city of Northstrong—Eastwall. I saw the patch of dazzle Juzd aimed, flickering over a wooden tower to our own nearer east. I saw it settle on a particular spot, which I suppose looked dry and tindery to Juzd, and then he brought in two more mirrors and concentrated the day's noon light on this place. Being autumn, the bright dry day provided only just enough heat, but I saw a thread of smoke rise thinly from the spot. Presently a flame followed it. The clangor of battle continued in the background. The wooden tower was deserted—an old warehouse I think, Juzd had picked it with knowledge. Its roof began to blaze. I watched band after band of the seasoned wood take. Juzd stood behind me with his hand on my shoulder. The baby mewed in one corner. My mother was not there. She visited away often now. Many people wanted to entertain her.

The wooden tower fell to the slant-roof of a hall beside it. This too began to burn. A pall of black smoke rose now into the pale shining air.

Huge flames now were hurling themselves into the pall. The side of the second building took. It was of brick, but on a timber frame. It was some kind of public building, close to our part of Eastwall. Bricks were spat out from the building as from a masticating giant maw. We could hear now a sound of screaming. From now on, water was brought and efforts made to stop the fire, but they did no good. The flames had taken hold. They spread rapidly now to Eastwall. This was where the enemy had been able to reach nearest, though the wall winding on its high mounds with their ancient well-kept trenches was famed as impossible to approach effectively. These walls contained a great deal of timber. Beams, balks and bulwarks. The wall burned. It did not burn down entirely— most of it stayed standing—but breaches were created in it. Men were leaping about the breaches attempting to fill them with anything to hand—rubble, canvas, more timber —but nothing was to hand that would repair the damage really. The tide of the battle over in the distance down the length of Eastwall began to change direction. Word had spread of the breaches in Eastwall. The fighting became very fierce just below us. The "enemy" were bringing up reinforcements. What had been a routine engagement on the wall became a major launch. I saw a flash of red, a skirl of red cloak. Here the fighting was massed. A ragged cry went up that even we could hear in its hoarse multivariety. They were through. They were through! They were in Northstrong. Zerd was in Northstrong. The siege was broken. We were taken. We were occupied. "Your father is less likely now," said Juzd wryly, "to be poisoned in his camp, yes?"

I started to write on my slate, "Why you do when you want no Zerd in Atlan?" but my scrawl trailed away as Juzd said, "Come quickly. Let us get your mother. She is visiting one of three people I guess at—but I could not wait till she was safe with us, the heat and brightness of the year was dying, and with that attack so near on Eastwall it was now or never."

He caught up the baby, so that it should not be in some place where the rest of us were not, if a crisis struck.

As we hurried down the stairs, the Palace was already in uproar. Juzd never cursed, but his lip was caught between his teeth. "Panic begins fast," he said. "I lost time. She will no longer be where she was." But we stayed on the main stairway, though at times with difficulty, and found Cija pushing her way through, climbing up toward Juzd's room. She fell into Juzd's arms, shivering, groping for me. "Seka. You are all right? You know what has happened, Juzd? He is in. Zerd is in."

"What do you want to do?" Juzd asked her.

She thought a moment, shaking, clinging to the stair-post.

"Do you want to stay with Quantumex?" Juxd asked.

She shook her head. "No. No."

"You want to go to Zerd?" he asked her levelly.

She thought more carefully, her hand pushed against her brow as though to keep the thoughts in.

"If that is my other choice, then yes, I suppose yes."

"You have other choices. We can make for Atlan. There is a way from here, not locally known."

"Then, Juzd, get me to Atlan. I can think again there. I cannot think that to cast myself on Zerd's kindness now would do me or my little ones any good. Sedili is with him. This is Sedili's home. She has allied herself with Zerd, and he with her, for a reason. She is still invaluable to him here."

People were jostling against us, people shouting and trampling, carrying great bundles of gilt and enamels and the luxuries without which life cannot be lived.

"Everyone is making for the Citadel," said Juzd.

"Then let us make there for the time being," said my mother. "After that, when the way is clearer, we can leave Northstrong altogether."

The Citadel, the center of the nobles' barracks adjoining the Palace, was already occupied by Quantumex and the Dictatress. Progdin was out in the streets, directing the Northern defense. Quantumex stood at a high private window, staring out over his occupied city. His big hands were quite quiet on the sill before him. He looked very interested. The Dictatress grabbed my mother. "Thank all the Gods, you got here. I have had men out looking for you." "A habit of yours, my dear," Cija said; and they consented to laugh at each other.

A server brought wine and Quantumex sipped carefully.

"Here rides my daughter," Quantumex said. The Dictatress was not interested. But after a moment my mother moved to stare down over Quantumex's shoulder, and I saw past them.

We were not over-high here, and could see in some detail the big woman on the white bird. She was accompanied by a small force, but no one was fighting. That she had got thus far was significant.

Truly she was Quantumex's daughter. She carried herself with a solidness, which she thought was style, but she looked like a housewife returning from market after beating a neighbor for a bargain. She looked unutterably pleased with herself, it was true: she put a hand on her hip from time to time, or on her waist, which with Sedili was much the same thing, she pivoted, she let the poncho she wore (composed all of the skins of those little Northern gnawers called mink, where each hair has a sparkle on its end, so that all became like black fur stars) slung over her wide shoulders flirt up in the wind like a dancer's veil.

Quantumex almost sighed.

Sedili did not look up. She ambled on toward the Palace, although it was doubtful whether at this point she would try to make her way in: it was still heavily guarded. She wanted to look on it, with whatever thoughts we could only guess.

Her wig of burnished turkey feathers shone in the waning afternoon light. So little time had elapsed since Juzd lost the war for Northstrong.

Leaves rattled at the hooves of her horse, scudded and scattered again.

Flames still flickered here and there in the vicinity. It was odd to see in the day all these shadows, like the night-flambeaux of a great courtyard where feasters' carriages are expected. Quantumex's Citadel, of which we could glimpse another wing, was fronted by pillars of brass on which were sliding shiny reflections dithering all over.

Quantumex held his cup for more wine. "Send runners to the street," he said to his advisers. "Ask my daughter to come in. Tell her I am here. Tell her she is free to come and to go this one time. Take her this ring as my signature."

My mother made a move to leave the private room (the Dictatress made no such move, she had no intention of leaving the hub of activity, which in any case she connected with her being there) but Quantumex signed to her not to leave.

"I would sooner leave," my mother said quietly.

"Then as the King in this room," Quantumex said whimsically but with a note of stiffness, "I *ask* you to stay . . ."

It was a royal order. My mother could have faced it

out. But with a look at Quantumex, she remained. She saw, I think, what I thought I saw too: the King's almost desperate insistence that someone be here who could channel away the aggression of Sedili from himself. He knew that Cija, as Zerd's latter-taken wife, was a thorn in Sedili's side more bitter if longer-lasting than those thorns which the scientist had designed for Zerd's last thicket, Zerd's last fence. My mother had no slightest wish to benefit Quantumex, but she had become curious, to see if Quantumex's little fear of his daughter Sedili could be turned to advantage.

"And you, too, Juzd," Quantumex said, "we all remain. Is that fair? Why should any of us seek other quarters? This is to be no private meeting, of that I can assure you."

I remembered that kings cannot enjoy what is not public, that in all my experience your common-or-garden royalty has lost the capacity to act except for an audience. This was after all what my mother had always begged to excuse herself from.

Soon we heard many feet up the stair, and Sedili paused on the threshold. She made us all out, ticking us off behind her eyes one by one, and made her entrance.

"My lord." She fell to her knees before her father. A guard of seven men in her uniform stood behind her, and there were twelve more in the courtyard outside. It had been brave to come in with so few. Obviously she had disdained not to accept her father's challenge, and had thought how ridiculous she would look if too many men bunched up the stairs behind her. Again I thought, a splendid woman.

"My first-born." So far as we knew, Quantumex had no other-born. He raised her to her feet, and she stood there tossing the black fur poncho and then pulled out her tobacco for a way to retain face as she continued to stare at everyone. She carried her tobacco loose in a pouch now and kept a narrow box of thin brown cheroot-papers. The economics of siege: Sedili had to roll her own.

"So we are all here," she said wittily.

She blew smoke as she succeeded in manufacturing the sort of cheroot, throwing out one hip and pointing a leg. As she gestured, ash fell on everyone but Sedili; Sedili at least was never ashy.

"You remember, my dear," Quantumex said, indicating the other royalty present, "the Dictatress—soon my bride."

Sedili's heavy eyelids flickered. She shot a look of pure malevolence at my grandmother. She was a jealous woman with a great sense of possession: people "belonged" to her as soon as they had much connection of any kind with her, and that her own father, despite the fact she had spent the last few years trying to defeat him in a war of family devising and trying to wrest his kingdom from him, should be about to give himself away to a woman she instinctively loathed . . . this was life's treachery to Sedili personally, it was destiny's little mistake.

But the Dictatress too was alarmed. If Quantumex had expected her to be gratified by this capitulation, he was out-of-date. "No, I am afraid not," the Dictatress said firmly. "No. No question of it."

Quantumex stared, stretching a hand out to his recent treasure. Sedili, hooding her eyes swiftly however, stared too, losing ash fast; she did not altogether like this turn of events. Her family was not to be rejected.

Sedili knew how important was this bluff, bustling personage's one asset: the mountain-ringed harbor which gazed along the sun's ocean-reflected path direct to Atlan.

Now she blinked anew at the Dictatress; and drawled: "Are we perhaps now hoping to make new overtures to the re-instated Dragon?"

"If Zerd is back," said the Dictatress briskly, not stating where exactly he had ever been away, "then my land is his. I am his chosen regent. I thought he had forgotten me —to some extent. But now I must wait and see how he will wish to dispose of his—"

"His midden?" Sedili raised one brow and blew smoke directly into my grandmother's face.

Quantumex paced around the rooms and back. His advisers muttered together. Wine was brought, tardily, for Sedili. She tossed it back. The Dictatress sank down on a low couch, hefting up her leg with both hands to get it among the cushions. "Your foot is troublesome today?" Quantumex inquired of her. He went over and sat beside her and "with your permission" eased off her purple slipper.

"The old cut is rubbed and re-opened," he said competently enough and sent the server for bandage and warm water. At the end of the room, dancers had appeared. Whirling in fine coordination, they made little yelping wheep-wheep sounds like silk ripping. This for some reason generally had an electrifying effect on men of the court, including Quantumex, but now he stared at the pudgy foot before him as though at the hand he had all but lost. He rubbed a thumb along one of my grandmother's toes: she kicked to show her irritation at fuss, and he gazed at her. A thought occurred to me: the spoiled Quantumex had met his match in the uncaring Dictatress —he had got a crush on her.

He wound the bandage round her foot for her with a certain love-sick langor.

The Dictatress did not notice his look, not even to suspect him of putting it on. "Well, young lady," she firmly addressed Sedili; "Where is this husband of everybody's?"

Sedili went through her repertoire, pivoted, raised a brow, puffed a smoke. ". . . Husband?"

"This well-known husband-about-town, the Dragon, the General, your friendly neighborhood husband." The Dictatress lifted her foot from Quantumex's limpid grasp and he eagerly helped her to up her ankle-straps and buttons.

Sedili quickly laughed her sweet, mirthless laugh, as at social naivety nobly born with.

"Why, where do these Generals be," she inquired, "but where they are bred to be, grinding down their heel? And now place your fatherly hand upon my brow, my father, and bid me sweet skies," Sedili said, "for I have much in the city here to do."

"Can the lady your daughter Sedili," his advisers muttered to Quantumex, "not take messages back to the— hum—Dragon . . . We can give him," they said very low, "the feeling of a certainty regarding the Dictatress's treachery to him. And thus he will repudiate the Dictatress, and she will have to ally herself with Your Majesty . . ."

Quantumex's blue eyes stared over their heads like marbles. They trembled and clustered a little, knowing they had done wrong, yet not knowing how.

"Stop," Quantumex said deeply to his government, "playing politics."

Rebuked, they gazed aground.

"Besides," Quantumex slowly gazed around, his finger playing on his by now impatient daughter Sedili's sleeve, "my daughter is not leaving us."

Sedili's head jerked back. She gazed in angered crisis at him.

"Oh noble King!" she whispered. "Oh, ineffable majesty! What honor, what a clean pride."

Her father smiled at her, showing his teeth, but pleasantly enough. "A King," he said, "is not about to sacrifice his people so that he can keep a promise or two, prettily, to the enemy."

His daughter blinked at the word, its finality. She could not shut nor open her mouth on it.

She cried, scornfully: "But your word!"

"What's that, a *word?*" says Quantumex. And he invites her with a slight little gesture to see the capture of her men in the courtyard below, and the silent grim men, many of them, in his livery and well-armed, who have appeared behind her men on the stair. Her men wait for a sign from Sedili to set about us and die in the attempt toward freedom. But she is in fact her father's daughter, and thoroughly bored with this honorable concept of death. She shrugs and flashes an icing-smile, this time sweet as preserve.

"Are you not two neat hostages, fitting as mantel ornaments or dovetails in a joist?" Quantumex said gallantly, bowing first to my mother and then to Sedili. "His two wives, so cherished each in her own way. Whichever of you is the more important to him no one quite can tell, one invaluable in war and one in peace. But here we have both birds in the hand." He chuckled and turned to put a fast riddle to the Dictatress.

Sedili frowned at my mother. Sedili had not thought of this: that she might be a hostage, taken because others considered her important to Zerd, and yet as an adjunct to the weight of this scrappy scrubby accident still known by the world as married to Zerd. Quantumex roared a dry great open-mouthed hack of laughter at the Dictatress's busy pin of reply pricking his riddle, and threw a sequin-coin as tip into the chief dancer's navel, which greedily closed about it as a flower sucks on a bug unwary. Quantumex had dismissed the dancers; and he had had his show with us, too.

"Now," he yawned, suddenly matter-of-fact as stone, "I shall leave you here, daughter. Since we are short of rooms here, perhaps this can be your room . . ."

"But it is an ante-room," she said, "and entered by a public stair."

"Perhaps a trusty guard at the door," he said, "will keep the tourists away. Shall we all," he suggested, as if sweeping us up, "leave my daughter to her meditations?"

"I would like—the Empress Cija—" Sedili snarled with a jaw like granite, "to stay here to speak with me."

"I suggest that this should be so only," Juzd said unexceptionably, "if I myself stay here with the Empress too."

"As you will! As you will!" Sedili, following her father's example, yawned and turned her back on Juzd, fluttering her cape off her big round shoulder and undulating away to the window with a great scorn. It occurred to me that she was excited by Juzd.

Turning on my mother, Sedili cooed: "My dear, we have seen so little of each other for so long— How are you? How do you feel?" Lowering her voice delicately: "Has the war been good to you?"

I saw my mother's eyes reflecting the hole in Northwall, any war-wife's nightmare, when a look of amusement crossed her face as suddenly she realized that what Sedili meant was, "Has the war brought you this interesting blond man as lover?"

My mother looked around the ante-room. "This is not bad, I suppose, Sedili. Where will you sleep?"

"On the floor, if necessary," Sedili crooned. "I am used to campaigning, don't forget."

Not, her voice said, *like you of course, you poor soft cat.*

"In fact," Sedili considered, "this couch here looks very welcoming . . . since a certain monotony would seem for a while to be mandatory. Will you join me . . . ?"

And she loosened her tunic, so that the chemise popped out all in a solid bundle.

"Are you going to sleep now and ask me what you wished to ask me later, or speak to me now and sleep afterwards?" my mother inquired.

Up went Sedili's ubiquitous brow at this rendering of the perfectly easy social situation. She had of course nothing specific to say to my mother. She wanted to feed on my mother, to lick her, to roll on her, to get out of her what she was doing, what she had been saying, what she had been wearing, who she was friendly with, who she wanted to marry or reject whom in the Quantumex-Dictatress case, whether she still intended to remain Zerd's wife and Empress, all Sedili's prurient curiosity was on edge and she had expected my mother to be social enough to skirt around it and dip her toes in it. For like all jealous women, Sedili was sometimes more fascinated by her rival than by her lover.

"I am unique, I suppose," Sedili said mournfully. "I find myself here because, most of all, of the great love in my nature. I have given up all to my lord, the General— all, all. My father, my home, my birthright. I have given up all to cleave unto my lord, the clinging female unto the rock-hard male, and go with him where he will.

"It is my nature to give, to give recklessly. I have always been a great giver.

"You remember, Cija my dear, how I even gave you my dresses?

"I do not pussyfoot," Sedili said, as if ah, she would if only she could. "I do not pull my punches. I can only plunge, and dive, and quaff deep.

"Courage is the keyword in life, though perhaps you do not agree? Many people do not agree. Such as I," she said with a gesture meant to suggest recklessness, which set her bolero bumping, "need stronger stimulus, drain deeper drafts of Life, than the more easily affrighted. Do we not all recognize these truths about ourselves?"

Sedili rolled herself a cheroot and tamped it hard on her clitoris, which stood up ready to be of use. "Well," Sedili drawled at Juzd, "are we going to talk or not? Are you going to discuss the weather, or tell me before you lose your tongue, what is the state of play here in our mighty capital of state?"

"Neither," Juzd said without apparently being aware of there being any bush to beat about.

"Beloved," he said to my mother, who looked worried and duty-bound to be standing around here like somebody's party-guest, "I shall take you away now."

Sedili's hand seemed hardly to have moved, but suddenly there had been a blur, and what had flighted through the air had been not the untidy cheroot, but a small enameled dagger that had lain loosely in the strapped pouch by her waist (or belly, it was all the same, since with Sedili there's no difference between the two rolling spaces). It went straight for my mother's eye—for what Sedili had found least forgivable, apparently, was that someone should decide to walk out, or rather to drift out, from what was to have been Sedili's salon.

As swiftly as it flew, however, the dagger was deflected. I could not see how Juzd did it and I found myself making a firm mental note, almost as if making my request then and there on my slate, to ask him how indeed he had done it. But the dagger circled, slipped in its own flight-path, and fell back into Sedili's cheroot. Sedili gasped and croaked and gasped again, the cheroot fell to the silken cushions and she began beating it out with her bare hand as sparks and charred feathers flew. She was cursing in her outraged way, and Juzd ushered out past the bewildered but not un-pleased guards my mother and myself.

We met the Dictatress waiting in my mother's apartments. She was not, of course, alone—there were the usual slaves and paraphernalia.

"Zerd . . . Zerd . . . !" My grandmother clasped and reclasped her Dictatressly hands, moving the huge pearl rings from her fingers on to other fingers. "Zerd—" She growled, she gritted her jaws (you could hear the grinding) and she shook one of her slaves.

Juzd stood, amused, waiting for explanation and beaming light. My mother clasped her own hands. To hear her husband's name growled so emphatically, when even Sedili had not spoken it although it had vibrated in the air between them both unspoken, struck at her involuntary center. She gasped in breath and was able to say, "Calm yourself, Mother. What has this General to do with you, that thus you should growl and pray to him?"

"What is he to do with us?" my grandmother cried in a passion of some kind. "Nothing to do, it appears! For how do I get word to him? He is outside the walls of Northstrong. Northstrong is now all but his. And yet I cannot get word to him. This—" she paused as if to spit but was too caught up in her spate of words—"This *King*—" (for she was helpless to think of anything as bad to call Quantumex) "keeps me mured here like a—like a suspect."

"Why, Mother, no. Like a betrothed."

The Dictatress snorted and tossed a pearl in the air.

My mother caught it, and before it slipped again she cried, "Mother, the King has given you these pearls! They are fabulous. Look at them."

"Pooh," my grandmother shouted. "What are pearls, anyway? Only old fishes' bones."

She began to flap her dagged sleeves about in a moody manner. "You would have thought," she said in a momentary sourness generally foreign to her, "that an inland King would have had plenty of decentish diamonds."

"Perhaps because he is an inland King," my mother shrugged, "he thinks pearls a rare and all but—"

My grandmother made a rude noise and stamped up and down the room. The fountain in the corner drifted aside at her peremptory passing. Outside, massed storm clouds were visible and the ugly sounds of hand-to-hand fighting (and hand-to-hand looting and rapine) could be heard. My mother shuddered and pulled away from the window.

"I shall be abed," she said softly and without expression. "It is all there is to be. Do you stay with me, Mother?"

"How can we find Zerd?" my grandmother demanded of her.

"There is no way if Quantumex refuses exit to your men," mother shortly said.

"Would he listen to me if I found way to get word to him?" the Dictatress said insistently. "You know, Cija, you know the creature, the man, whatever he is."

"I know no thoughts of his, Mother." My mother turned away restlessly, but when she found that in this way she faced the darkened window, she shifted.

"Not only is his heart ice, drift-ice it is," my grandmother said. She struck a slave's shoulder to emphasize her remark: "Who knows where his wants are? He looks for power, power only."

"Do I leave you, madams both?" Juzd bowed. His face softened and he smiled at me. "Madams three?"

"I shall come with you, Juzd," my grandmother said briskly, gathering cloak and slaves about her. "Do we eat? You do not join us, Cija? Seka? We shall see you then in the morning. And gods know what that shall bring us all." She kissed my mother. She kissed me. She smelt of infant mammoth. "But for me to make union with Northstrong—pho, pho," she said, "would that at this stage not smack of necrophily?"

In the night the windows blew open. The rain spat and plashered in, beating my head into the pillow with a sort of friendly savagery, like the rough play of a ruffling hand too big for one's skull. The thunder rang round the sky in a great long loud bellow, and rang round again. A ball of lightning rolled into the room. It lay in the thick electric air midway between carpet and ceiling, oscillating slightly, regarding me as I lay there staring it back, a big fat savage amiable mighty jovial *amusement* in it: it was radiating laughter (or merriment, I suppose, though I feel like sticking by the word laughter, since it was a definite joviality, larger and swifter and more amused than anything at all except laughter) and it was saying *Well, then. Ho, ho. Well, then, small one, is this not the way to conduct a good storm?*

When Juzd, recognizable because as usual in the dark his flesh cast a blond glimmer, hastened into the room, I paid such attention to Juzd that I did not see the thing, the lightning, the storm-laugh, at the moment it faded and "went."

My mother woke. "What . . . ? Why, Juzd! Yes?" she whispered.

"Yes!" Juzd answered. "Come, both of you. Come, my beloveds. We are able to leave, under cover of the storm."

My mother did not doubt him. Juzd took winding ways that held no guards and yet many locks; but it seemed that some fusion of the electricity and the simple power of Juzd himself had combined to loosen metal and liberate linkings.

Through the streets afterwards, it was the same thing. We went up alleys and through private gardens; always the locks opened for us. I do not know whether they opened silently: the storm was too jubilant for the hearing of a grating latch.

There was fighting and looting, yes, in the taverns and the mansions. The storm quenched any fires which briefly flared. But there was a dark tide running in the gutters, and even on a private lawn, slick with private fragrant rain, we stumbled across a prone figure in uniform. Another figure stepped out of the trees and challenged us with a drawn sword.

Juzd, who had bent above the body to help my mother up after she half-fell over it (and had no intention of examining it to see what the uniform was, or what the state of life or death might momently be, for he was no time-waster) raised his gaze to the newcomer. And shrugged, the shrug of a temporary resignation.

A flash of lightning and the white preying-fox teeth of Smahil's smile coincided.

"My family—!" Smahil crooned, not sheathing his sword. The leaves skirled about us. "And my family's protector. My travel companions from now on, I presume? Since I presume you are on the way out of this hospitable township?"

"Are you not guarding this—gentleman?" my mother, leaning on Juzd's shoulder, inquired.

"This—gentleman—" Smahil toed the body, "is less than the dust to me, now that my—travel companions— have arrived to claim me. My duty was all and everything to me when I was alone, here, with my small band of men yonder, banished as we were from the King's purlieus while your *family,* madam, were visiting; banished we might temporarily be, since our poor faces did not fit, but our duties meant something still. Now, however, I shall away with you, no longer a soldier, only a traveller, a companion; my priorities are quite clear, you see. I would be a deserter to my true being were I to stay with my adopted army, instead of cleaving unto my own." And he stood himself alongside my mother.

Juzd looked to my mother—but she, trembling, said nothing.

Smahil, before now anything could be further said, produced from a clump of trees (trotting forward to his whistle) three tall birds silhouetted against the sopping sky.

Juzd again, almost imperceptibly, shrugged. He had not been able to provide mounts, that was true; and we were nearing the edge of the city. So we mounted in the deep cupping stirrups. The birds shifted restlessly. As we kneed them (Juzd had taken me up before him so that my mother could hold her baby) these birds broke into their jogful lope, and cries of "Hai!" broke out behind us—Smahil's fellows discovered the theft.

Smahil smiled in the half-dark. "Death before dishonor? Well, death is so monotonous."

We forded a shrub-shrouded river with a private rather ornamental landing-stage, haphazardly lit by lanterns in curly wrought-iron sconces, and moments later were in the mean winding back-alleys where the rich tiled back-walls of mansions had already been in many cases broken down.

The birds, well-trained cavalry-birds, were shying and honking. I guessed the lightning and thunder had unsettled them. Then I remembered how this was the rogue season, and how they had the pleasant habit of without warning turning a giant long reptilian head back toward the rider and snapping off a man's kneecap.

A great air, it now seemed, flew in our face. It was the unaccustomed freedom of the plains, blowing in upon us—for where for centuries had stood the city-wall of Northstrong, here lay the jumbled black charred and still smoldering and blood-seeped stones around a gap, nothing, just the night and the unimpeded view of the long hills.

Over the plains stretched the fires of the "enemy"—of the Northern Misappropriation, as the gathered hordes of Zerd and Sedili were known. Brands were massing toward us and beneath us as we stood on a slight rise with looting going on in the poorly taverns around us. The storm had turned the landscape to mud and Smahil remarked of the Army's tread, "Sounds like the approach of massed cunnilingus."

But what could be heard above the squelch and rain were the drums—the massed beating thrumming *winning* black drums of the North. They beat from the plains, they answered from the beseiged streets.

Smahil rode knee to knee with my mother. As our mounts jostled each other in the narrow windings, his inexorable ineluctable hands would come out to touch her, then not for moments leaving but gripping and thumbing, taking advantage of the geometry of the street to slide immediately into her dress. We could hear the troops of the King forming and marching down behind us. They were not, we imagined, in our street but in one broader and parallel with ours. We looked about for shelter, for cover. Really, there was none; the doorways were not deep.

Yet ahead, less open to view now that we were in a hollowed street-dip again, lay the plains. How often I had looked out on this edge of Northstrong—The Bat-

tledown, with its melancholy sunsets and its air of bit-
terness. It is ever so, where men have died and realized,
in their last breaths, how needlessly.

The thunder and rain had cessated. Already we could
hear the wind neighing over the plains.

Juzd conversationally told Smahil, "When we reach
the city perimeter I shall turn and cut your face with
my whip if you have not left us."

And he spurred our bird; my mother followed suit.

"Do so," Smahil replied on the instant, and he too
spurred forward.

I was worried now that Smahil would trick Juzd by
attacking him first pre-perimeter. The black sky continued to fall upon us.

A cavalcade of soldiery was loping toward us up the
narrow black street—from the gap. They were not
drumming.

We were seen.

Clor, detaching himself from the van, rode forward
and stopped in the darkness beside us. He untangled a
scarf from his epaulettes. He was dismounting in order
properly to bow to my mother. "No, Clor, well met and
stay in the saddle," said my mother. They held hands,
arms and elbows, gravely and firmly. A great gust of
leaves blew rustily, wetly about them. The faint glow
from Juzd, silent beside my mother, lent her emphasis:
her thin, honed face, her eager eyes, warmed by the
Army meeting, stripped of many layers by late months.
Layers stripped away, as though she were a recent ghost.
But levels added. She looked thin and almost dangerous,
still and deep-levelled, like a human well to be drawn
into.

The officers again parted ranks. There was a stir. The
big figure in the red cloak rode through. "Sir," Clor
said, "the Empress is discovered."

"Near Northwall and the new laboratory, as you expected," Zerd held a hand toward my mother. Unlike
Clor's extended hand, it was a gesture, not expecting to be
taken. The starlight pocked the edges of his scales. The
dark face was limned, the eyes after one efficient glance
judging us all, again fixed on my mother, but not staring,
instead taking her in, her cloak, her bed-gown, her
shakiness—the infant in her arms.

"Zerd!" my mother greeted him as firmly as she had

Clor. "You have won your city! Have you won your war?"

"What is that you hold?" Zerd asked her.

"My conqueror?" My mother held up Ung-g's sleeping baby to be seen. "This is a pet of mine, my lord."

Zerd would not be drawn. "I am no conqueror of yours," he said, "but as conqueror of this city, I direct that you be taken to safety before I see to the sweeping-up here. There will be much dust flying here for a while, and it will be an unhealthy place."

"You will send me to the safety of your camp?" my mother inquired, her brows up, the impact of meeting him nevertheless augmented by the fury of her expectation.

And even Clor cleared his throat and edged closer. "The lady Sedili at camp—"

"My camp is of course no place for you," Zerd continued to speak to my mother. I liked the sense of his concern for her safety. I wondered how he would react when he found that the lady Sedili was currently detained at His Majesty's pleasure.

"Clor," and Clor saluted and was ready for his order. "May I detail you to conduct the Empress to a place of some privacy in the hills immediately to our North?" Zerd requested. And he began to give directions. My mother's eyes had gone bleak. He might call her Empress in a dark narrow street with seven officers to hear, but he was swiftly getting her gone.

"The barrow lies beyond the watering-place, due nor'-nor'-east." Zerd was instructing Clor, when suddenly he said, "Clor, start the clear-up for me here. I'll take the Empress myself."

"You'll escort the Empress?" Clor almost stammered.

"I'll be there and back in a day. I'll ride hard, harder than you because I know the area. I need you here, and I don't want to be waiting while you stumble around the norther barrows. Madam?"

He looked inquiringly at my mother, his reins up in his fist.

"My lord?" she did stammer.

"Are we ready?" Zerd set off at a gallop, or whatever you can call the birds' lolloping top speed—I know only the military words for it, and they are all words of command. He had snatched me off Juzd's saddle and I was righting myself on the pommel before him as the stars streaked overhead. Looking backwards, I saw my mother's white set face. She too spurred her bird. As Zerd leaned backwards, he roared: "Arrest those two men!"

"Zerd! Zerd!" My mother came up beside us, not panting, her hood and hair lying on the rhythm of her speed. "I will not go if they are arrested."

"You've gone." The left side of Zerd's mouth twisted. We glanced back. The street had vanished. The tavern-fronts and black doorways had vanished. We were down the hill and through the gap and the soldiers, soldiers marching, marching, slouching, bearing in the dark the gleams of serried torches, blades, grinning teeth, parted for us and saluted and shouted: "the Dragon!" in celebration as we reached the next hill-hump. "They will be safe, under arrest," Zerd bothered to assure her, perhaps too speciously. "Where else would they be as safe?"

"Where are you conducting me, Zerd?" my mother clung to her privileges, her bare rights to know what was becoming of her.

"To my mother," the Dragon-General told her.

The stars slit the sky as we dashed under them. "To your mother? The giant blue—?" she bit herself silent on the word "reptile-woman," I knew she had been going to say that, this was what she had always been told had spawned Zerd for the illustrious killer his father, and Zerd knew she had been going to say that, too. He laughed. "She lives in the hills. So fear not. I know the way pretty well." This was of more than ordinary interest to me. My Dictatress grandmother, the only grandmother I had ever thought to know, was of far less interest to me than the female whose blood, whose flesh, whose scales were the essential beginnings and initial blamings of my strangeness, my blue-dusk, my difference from the people around me—oh, as was my lack of voice too, of course. So often I forgot that my certain sense of watchfulness and isolation was due to this silence. I had not chosen.

We hastened into a light tenor wind. The storm had dropped already up here in the foot-hills of the Downs, where a hitherto successful human race failed to carry its curiosity and its surveillance, where only the wind was wondering about the horizon. Zerd laid a hand on my mother's bridle; obediently, the bird loped within two strides to a halt. Zerd tied my mother's cloak into a sling for the apeling, its creased eyelids still sleeping over its raisin eyes, and made it easier for her to attend to her reins. "Is the child heavy?" Zerd nodded at the apeling. "No," she answered. "It lies very light." "Is it my child?" he asked. She looked at him and shook her head. "Is it yours, Cija?" he asked very low. "Yes, Zerd. It is my fantasy child. It is the child spun of chimera in the forest. It is the product of a hope that was possibly sentimental, therefore seeming to have been mistaken." He thought, he slapped the reins on the bird's neck and it quickened and lengthened stride, and he said: "Not for me is it mistaken, Cijaling. You have hoped and you have had courage to act on your hope. Perhaps that was all we ever allowed you room for, space of your own for." "Hope?" she echoed him, not sure she rightly heard his wondering.

Zerd silenced himself, as she had silenced herself when she was about to mention his heritage. A look which could have been grim closed his face. We rode on. It was not too dark now, there were after all stars and a wind. A swooning throbbing fragrance rose up under our birds' claws and filled the night. We were loping through thick large flowers, frenzied by the wind, and the stars spikily lit the flowers' dementia.

I looked up at him. He glanced down at me and our eyes met. "Good evening," he said to me. But I quartersmiled at him, that was all. I would not give myself to his kinship till I knew what he was planning for my little mother.

Up on the deeper inner hills' ridges, in that inky velvet liquid-lit blackness not long before dawn, we saw dark excrescences risen in wait in silhouette. Cija's lips trembled: she may have murmured a talismanic remark to herself, since these were barrows we were approaching, a deadly area, ghosted and thickened, the graves of old kings.

Zerd drew in a breath. I had never heard the Dragon almost-sigh like this before, and I think neither had my mother, for I saw her glance at him curiously. It was as though he had said, "Home."

The dark entrances of the barrows in the hill loomed up ahead of us as we drew nearer. Zerd stood in his stirrups and cupped his hands around his whistle. He let out a mournful piercing harsh cry, with a long whistle like a swooping bird of prey in the center of it.

Something appeared, almost at the same moments, in almost every aperture. My mother and I by a process of association expected corpses. But the things that rushed on us from the holes were very un-corpse-like. Each was mounted—not on a bird, nor on a horse exactly, but on what I suppose is the primitive version of the horse—a small angry thyroid-eyed ponyish creature with long flaring swishing sweeping fetlock feathers and three spreading elegant *toes*. Oh, yes, I know about thyroid. I know about virus too, and so to its cost does Ancient Atlan—the virus of sick yearning defeat.

"These are my mother's sons," said Zerd as the wild riders rode upon us.

The foremost brother halted within inches of us. Like a monkey, his smile was his warning. He dismounted and came forward, his face extended blank on his neck to Zerd, but as he looked at us smiling a warning.

"This is one of my brothers," Zerd said to Cija, very properly introducing the gentleman first to her—which, outside of Court and civilization, at once seemed strange to me, though I found later how this was something of a matriarchal society. The brother was not introduced by name, for he had none: his kin was all he needed.

"This is my wife," Zerd told the brother. "Its name is called Cija."

"Keeeya?" the brother smiled.

"These are its children."

"This one is blue?"

"Blue. Mine . . . I am told."

The brother sniffed at the apeling in Cija's arms. She managed not to draw back.

The brother's blue scaled short snout-nose wrinkled up. He still smiled, and the stars glittered his residual tusks.

The other brothers gathered about us, not dismounting, silent, sniffing, scaled snouts wrinkling.

Was this safety? Would my mother not have been a thousand times safer in Sedili's and Zerd's camp? Yes, this was safety. I have never felt so safe. A warm tide ran over me and through me while I tingled yet with the

present peril. The danger from the brothers' suspicion
and distaste was real and palpable. But at the same
time I too, like the Dragon, had come home.

By the hearth in the barrow, the grave, into which
we were led sat an enormous woman. She was bigger
than Zerd, bigger than the brothers—though their size
was hard to gauge since all of them except the first to
meet us remained on their absurd fierce beasts. By the
light of flickering fire, her deep blue could be accurately
assessed. Her tusks overhung her lower jaw: they were
ringed with gold. The hearth consisted of a clay platform
fenced around with shank-bones, stood upright, a great
spit turning a beast no longer with any credentials. I
was to find in the morning how the meat thrown out
brought daily wild dogs, bald vultures, and other sani-
tary engineers.

She received Zerd with a high-pitched scream into
her arms, and he fell among her bosoms. She glanced at
us without smiling: that was all right, then. Through the
open doorway of the barrow I could see the brothers,
all dismounted now, going out to the place they had met
us at, and taking out their blue dark penises and urinat-
ing ceremoniously on the territory before leaving it, to
allay trackers who might follow our scent with dogs—
"After all, two of them are animals," I heard them say
to the mother as they came back in, and I knew they
must mean Zerd and the apeling. So that was all right
too.

I woke when the sun was high. It still looked like the
inside of a grave as the daylight poured in. Zerd's
brothers, gathered around the hearth, were wearing
anyway what I had not recognized last night as real
garments at all—in fact obviously plundered from
graves round about. The brothers wore women's bod-
ices, silver or horsehair stomachers, tiaras, parasols.
The brothers were belching in appreciation of the
breakfast. Zerd ate on a nearby bed. In a zither of light
on the bed (a construction of sticks and reins) lay my
mother still asleep. One of the brothers looked at her
gently, stuck a flower (these grew on the barrow earth-
walls) into a piece of meat and laid it on her coverlet as
breakfast in bed. He took a mouthful of the hot runny
berry-alcohol they were drinking and spat and sprayed

it from his mouth all over her face to sweetly waken her.
Zerd wiped her face and looked amusedly, not smiling
except for a quirk by his mouth, very excited that she
was awake. I had understood last night what the brothers'
terrible smiles meant, and I realized at last why Zerd
smiles so rarely, and why when he does there is an element of *learned* courtesy in the smile, or else why it is
hardly there at all.

The mother sat immovable by the roasting remains.
She might have sat there all night, I expect she had.

"We are looking after your fowl, brother General,"
said the brother who had first dismounted to (greet?)
us. "They are good fowl. Not picturesque. Fowl are just
fowl—but horses are like nothing else in the world."

"But what you ride are not horses." Zerd stroked my
mother.

"Nor what you ride? We saw you ride late!" they
hooted all together.

My mother smiled shyly.

They stared at her assessingly over their meat-fringed
bones. She had not thought to curb her smiles. They
thought she had been offended, and wondered whether
she could be nasty.

"There is a high wind out there," one brother said,
"blown straight from the anus of the devil." "Such a
high wind, even the moss ripples on the stones," agreed
another, thrusting a knife-blade in the wall of the tomb,
revealing wriggly grubs, and so eating while talking.
"What wind has blown you to us, brother that is General? What is happening in your places? Can we kill any
men that are Generals for you?"

"I am killing only left-over men today and tomorrow,"
Zerd said.

I wondered how long since they had seen him, picking
up where they had left off. I wondered how often secretly he had visited the barrows during the Norther
campaign.

"Are you hunting with us today, brother General?"
they asked him. "Is your wife with the name hunting?"

There was a sister, or sister-in-law of some denomina-
tion, obviously "hunting today." She was sharpening her
knife on her jewelry. She wore odd ornaments—old iron
chain-links. It was later explained by Zerd to my mother
that they were part of the chain in which her husband af-

ter subjugation to Quantumex (her husband had been another "civilized warrior") was found dead tossed out on
the Downs. "My wife stays here," Zerd said, "and my
children stay here" (so he acknowledged not only me but
my sisterling) "and I stay with them."

What was all that, I thought vaguely but pleased,
about going back immediately to clean up his new restive property?

"Was that buried with a child?" Cija asked with her
usual un-morbid curiosity. The youngest brother (nine
or ten years of age) was playing with a large doll. He
looked pleased that she had asked him specifically a
question. I guessed he was pleased because of the way
he gravely blinked very rapidly several times before
answering her. He told her lovingly (it was a story he
loved, as Fishhead had never quite loved his tales) of
how the *doll* was buried. In the tomb of an olden-days
pretender to the throne who had died very young, so
told the inscriptions, the brothers had discovered the
silk-dressed doll. The real baby boy obviously went free.

"What, dear named lady," they wanted to know of
Cija, "is your baby?"

"It is wish come true," she said quietly. And I realized this was not just something to tell them, she was
not just being difficult. The baby had been a joy to her,
something that needed looking after (as I looked after
her)—something small and ridiculous, a memory of the
time, a *proof* of the time, when she had been outside
the politics and pawnshops of the world she had otherwise always been considered necessary in. She had been
a stranger (as she almost always seemed to be, once she
got outside her political identity) but for once wanted,
for once precious as herself, and for once brave and
reckless and ridiculous for (as Zerd had said) hoping
and telling herself of happiness. Zerd gazed at her and
fed her. He understood, without any explanation, the ker-
nel of what the apeling (and its conception) were about.
I don't know if he accurately imagined its other parent. I
myself have never quite been able to imagine Ung-g.

"What is this?" Zerd had taken her by the pubis and
stared at her in the flickering, observed in alert sympathy by the brothers, the cats and myself. "You are
crushed and blunted here—and here—along your sweet,

sweet lips—" His flickering blue face hardened. "Who in all the outlands did this to you?"

"It is only long bruising, not calloused. I am sensitive and have joy as ever," she said, "if I still please—" Zerd brought his hand from her there, to her other lips hushing her at once. She quickly closed her legs. "Who?" was all he said. "In a place I lived," she said, "I for some time had to wear a wooden belt between me."

Zerd's face whenever he looked at his wife would never again be the same. He would wish to know her every experience in the long parting: her pains and her fortunes and had she been by them changed in any ways, how she felt regarding him. For it would become real to him that she had been warped and wed, cut but cauterized.

My mother and Zerd, distinctly, were looking upon each other in the manner of two people in trouble because they were not at this moment able to tear with their teeth large pieces out of each other. I stood up with my feather-cover, and trailed it to my mother's bed. She rubbed my shoulder, saying: "This is a weathery day, isn't it? Can you hear the wind outside?"

Yes, I could, and I could hear the creatures that had arrived to launder the outside of the hill-barrow. They stayed generally a fair way from the "door"—which was a slab of turf with a latch formed of part of a jawbone, the teeth sprung to clamp shut. What looked like human skeleton fingerjoints had been gripped around the hinges to keep us more or less shut in. But when we went outside, the brothers hooting and howling to horrify the animals who made off to a safer distance, the wind seemed immaterial. For the sun up here was baking. Moreover, a brother had a brazier of fire (for a torch would have scattered everywhere) with which he signed the spines and spikes of a few towering spongy cacti, so that his sheep and "horses" could eat of it without needles sticking them. These fierce long-legged hill-sheep were a very different kettle of cattle from your average flocks— active—always up and bollocking—rams mounting ewes or butting each other with a sound that gave you a headache just to hear.

I remembered how beautiful had been the hands of the shepherdess who wandered with the flocks near Mill

—near Soursere. The natural lanolin in the fleece had given her hands a queen wouldn't know how to get. But the scales of the youngest brother, who herded these rams, would never soften—these wools were scabbed with burrs and blood.

Zerd with his brothers, on foot, examined the few trees about. Obviously, they had been planted (and were still carefully nurtured) by the brothers. One, bearing only miserly fruit, Zerd advised they arch. I gathered that the tusk-marks on the trunks showed where the bush-pigs had been advertising territorial ownership. Then I looked at the ivory in the brothers' conversational snarls, and I thought again.

The soil, it appeared, was pretty fertile in spite of its barren aspect. It was thinking soil, augmented soil, soil on which things had happened, soil enriched as it is when battles have been fought there. I had seen a captain once crawl away on his own with the blood coming from his mouth. At first I had wondered why he didn't stay with his men because they could have helped him, eased him, been with him. Then I knew that he could not have been helped, that he had an urge not to inflict his indecent melodrama on men who could only be embarrassed by the blood coming from his mouth; he was crawling away to die out of sight of his men.

This was soil which had been manured by deaths like that one. And the trees grew, on the whole, nourishingly.

When one brother spat on the ground, he scattered there the seed-heads he had pulled from the last "oasis." The next morning, we woke to find, where he had spat, enough cereal for breakfast, had we wished.

Yet the brothers did not cultivate grain. They were not prepared to sow and hoe and harvest and winnow. They had, thus, no real alcohol: they could ferment wine, of a sort, from summer fruit, but there was nothing to sustain them through the long winter—when, as they said, "nothing is here to drink stronger than melted ice, unless it's your own urine."

Instead of drinking, the brothers had an amusement for the long cold dark nights. The amusement was, they told us and reminded each other, laughing and looking forward to it, that one brother would grip the scythe blade and challenge other brothers: "Get it out of my hand." They'd try tipping it from the point, leverage, sneaking away his attention with ribald tales until while his concentration wandered they could jerk the scythe from him ("Aha! I have it still! You thought I had slackened grip")—the terrible joke being that if it shifted at all, it would razor his fingers off at one slice— but each brother's grip was of course iron.

"So then you have scythes!" my mother exclaimed. "What do you indeed cut with them, since never yourselves?"

"They are from the graves," the brothers said vaguely. "We keep them honed."

It was still our first day here when my mother tried to talk to Zerd's mother. But the gigantic blue mother would not speak. She gazed on Cija with flat semi-circular eyes, each apparently as ingrown as toenail, each so far off from the other eye that apparently it could claim a whole radius of vision for itself. Cija had tried to ask, very courteously and only after helping at the hearth, if the mother were glad to be away from the Court (where, as a strange perverse strong-tasting plaything of Zerd's father's, she had dwelt)—"or are you glad," inquired Cija, "to be here in the wind and good air with your sons?" (There was no sign of the older tusked blue male or males who must have fathered these full-blooded sons. Perhaps, like a matriarchal lizard, she devoured each mate after use.)

For the air here was good. The royal human corpses in the barrows had long since withered into cleanliness, as do dried petals.

The mother's eyes, each of them, flickered from Cija to Zerd and to the hearth.

She continued to poke the fire with a rod that resembled some scepter stained with domestic function.

Zerd did not laugh.

"She is like Seka," he said, hunkering there in his red cloak by the hearth. Our silences he meant. It was as though he implicitly, at these hearth-moments, which recurred unexpectedly through our three twisted lives, acknowledged me.

By the evening, after the sun had disappeared into a big bag of fog, my mother was holding me close for comfort and looking at the General waiting for him to stand, stretch, and saddle up ("A fairish ride before

Northstrong and Clor.") But he remained hunkered, grunting or joking with his brothers (it was the same thing) and telling them how desperate he was to pay his troops—he had been paying with fistfuls of salt, which was worth an awful lot more than their wages, most of them, but at least limitedly available where coinage now was not—or with rum. He had also arranged a system by which each man had a fixed amount of "imaginary money" with which he could, however, purchase genuine articles "on sale" in fallen towns—it saved a little on the looting. The brothers were interested in this and detailed other examples of argumented arithmetic. Zerd hunkered on yet, accepting a further three helpings of the simple vegetable meal (a beige meal, for rather than trust the terrible water of the region, water in which foreign bodies abounded, mostly dead, the blue tribe drained off a little blood from some beast of burden and boiled the vegetables in the blood) and the stars sped into the sky ("God's sperm!" said the brothers in hushed voices, awed by the regular proliferation) and Cija gazed very widely upon Zerd, thinking she must fix him in her awareness so as not to lose him when he was gone, and he did not go. He had no intention of going.

Bats clustered, fanning themselves from the baking of the day with their wings—making the nearest tree into a treeful of fluttering flags.

A little cat, with a very evident ribcage and a look of eyes bigger than its entire pointing face, sidled into the barrow and leaped up on a brother's head and as he talked it finickingly groomed itself; Zerd reached for my mother's hand and as she let him take it, a blush one could see even in the gathered dark flew up in her face.

After an hour, she whispered to him, and he leaned closer: "Again, Cijaling, I did not hear you."

"I said, 'Are you staying?' " she whispered, shamefaced.

"Yes, of course I am staying a real night with you. Last night was no night, it was dawn."

The little cat had forgotten which was itself and which the brother, and groomed delicately its own fur and his mane at the same time.

*   *   *

Now did my golden, brazen, grim, martial, relentless, ambitious, all-embracing, simple, unpretentious, scarlet and easily contented father, the leader of destinies and the destroyer of known demarcation-lines, find my mother sexually satisfying? I think there is no doubt that he did not. I think there is no doubt that she left him ever and ever on edge, grasping for more, for the shimmering mist over the horizon, for the substance of the laugh half-heard in the dark—just as he grasped ever for the power and the total and utter devastating victory just over the horizon. But I do not think my father was a weak man. Don't think that I discovered weakness ever in my father. He was a leader: Those vast armies needed such a one. What else would they have done, wallowed dankly in endless night maneuvers, without such a one? There I agreed with the "callous" Sedili and disagreed with my mother and her "integrity" and her "horror" of him. He was a soldier, for whatever reason the gods would show in bigger worlds when his experimenting here was done.

My father in one great essential is a giving man. He gave his loyalty to the shimmer beyond the horizon because nothing else, *this* side of that horizon, is worth such loyalty. Not many such bluff unsentimental extrovert soldiers know that.

If I have seemed ever unkind about my small, vulnerable and yet perhaps through no fault of her own unreachable mother, it is only that I wanted more than anything to do what I knew from the beginning I could do best—protect her.

This was about the time I began to be a different person, taking on a keener edge of vision, like the beginnings of a new light just around the corner at the edges of a prism.

I know that my mother and the General came to a conclusion and a hiatus.

And yet here now was this woman, who has subjected herself and her children to every rigor rather than be aligned with this man, and here was this man, who had fought three or four, or five or six, campaigns to be where now he had left someone else to "look after things" before ever he entered and claimed his utter key possession, this man, or whatever he was, who had married at least two princesses other than my mother to ensure his ultimate taking of the place he had now left to itself for not one but two whole nights—and they were looking at each other mainly, and murmuring a little about things like the wind outside and the blanket and whether it had caught a spark from the hearth. The giant blue woman sat by the hearth, looked at me, almost passed me a bowl of something, and decided it was not a point over which to bestir herself.

The brothers' ponies were fighting, maneuvering to get back to back and kick each other's testicles off, when we went out to saddle them. The brothers said, "There you are, we left them too long without riding them—" (it had been a matter of hours) and while reproaching themselves and shaking their heads, separated the "horses" (for they always called them that) and put upon them their bridles with the bits in three pieces.

My mother had finished sewing her dress where ash from Sedili's cheroot had scorched a hole (the giant blue mother had gut-thread and chased silver needle) and put the dress on. The wind blew our clothes against us. I gathered we were going to hunt today, because we needed food for the hearth-spit and the scavengers—they lurked about at a distance, tails down and rigid with hatred, heads turning from side to side to avoid our eyes when we showed signs of glancing their way, great yellow orbs coming back to us when we were busy among ourselves: what were we about, not to have provided food today?

We were bound North again, I saw—going Norther into this great lonely terrain—where distant storms that could not be heard could be seen toppling tons of rock off the tops of mountains.

I was glad though that I was not to be left, and neither was my mother, alone all day with the blue grandmother by the emptyish hearth, where apeling was to stay.

The General must have wanted Cija with him, and she must have insisted on my accompanying.

"The Norther you go," said the brother who mounted me in a deep bucket of saddle before him (I gather it was taken for granted my mother would need all hands free for the "horse") "the deeper go those barrows."

"They are very deep," said another brother. "They are lined with wood." "They form frost-hollow," Zerd joined in this accustomed brother-descant, in which they formed rhythm for each other more than providing a hearer with information. I could imagine the refrigerated contents of these isolated barrows. How had their builders and their occupants struck so far north anyway? Who would indulge in battles where were no cities?

After the dissertation on the local necrologic, the brother seemed less cross with me. He had been cross with me earlier because when I found a tortoise on its back outside the barrow, obviously to me an unhappy tortoise, I had righted it. As it sped away with all the suddenness of one who has only a year or two to kill, this brother had caught sight of its back legs trundling into an earth-hole, and he had dug around in the hole with knife, hands and eventually teeth, and with no success, then looked very much as if he were going to hit me. He explained, savagely, how this tortoise had been his "larder," helpless on its back, it would stay fresh till he decided to kill and eat it.

But now, since he was the brother who had undertaken to ride with me, I guess he was the one a bit interested in children, and that was why he had noticed enough to be angry with me.

"We shall make our way to the great Highway," said the brothers. "There," said one brother, "there," added another brother, "is always game and traffic."

At the mention of traffic my mother looked (though bit back) her alarm. Were we to brigandize some caravan? Zerd did not see her alarm. The General had his own controversy with the brothers. Their hope was that he use his venom, his gift of being able to shoot poison from the pocket in his mouth. He was telling them he entirely refused today—even if it meant no evening meal to gather around—and I feel his reason was that it seemed an ugly thing to do before these "human beings" —my mother and myself.

Why he should have this gift if his brothers did not, is another biologic and therefore philosophic puzzle I consider important. For I too, in my mixture, am in some or many ways more complete than either of my types of ancestor. The mingling of the ways has produced a hybrid of a certain richness and some power, as the arching of the woody plant, which my father recommended, produced the fuller richer fruit.

Now the rind of the land peeled back. We were skirting mire, ground which seemed firm enough, yet every now and then sent up bubbles. The brothers nearly though not quite halted their horses at the mire, and hooted around it, as though jeering it or simultaneously sharing with it a discreditable joke. "Much is born in there," one brother sneered interestedly. "The things down there don't breathe in air as do we. But inside the bog they breathe nevertheless. They make marsh-gas." "The gas in the bog-deeps bubbles and balloons." "It rises very fast when it does rise. It bursts up in the moor and traps whatever is on the ground, old horse-bones or a young hare or a wandering warrior, in huge eddies and bubbles, and pulls its guest down into the darkness." "But also it sends up to the surface its own bornings. It pulls down a warrior to the deeps of the bog, and uses his sperm, and makes a marsh-hybrid from it, and sends the changeling up to the world to breathe of the day." "And the changeling is very *strange!*" they all hooted in unison and clapped spurs to their "horses'" sides, and galloped on.

I had seen my mother wince visibly as they came to the part of their tale which ended with—"And the changeling . . ." for she had thought involuntarily they would chant, "And the changeling does harm." For this was the song Smahil had crooned to her in the abortion-barn. He had told her how he and she were changelings, since they carried through the world their father's bad blood. In actuality, it was only Smahil who was a changeling. His mother, after all, had been the witch. But changeling was a word, a concept, that cut my mother's insides. Each of her children had been hybrid. Her blue and later voiceless daughter, her apeling infant that meant something to her of a peace and purity it could never actually bring her; and the most beautiful child, or so I gather, the pale ash-haired son with violet eyes, it had been the child of crossed blood, the child her brother Smahil fathered on her. Her womb had been a waif she'd carried around the known universe, keeping it hidden in hut and cottage and hole in wall and even under-hill, yet never safe.

But the brothers spoke of the marsh-hybrids as if they

knew them, and met them, perhaps at times to pass the time of day with, and they mocked them; that was all.

"Who are the marsh-people?" my mother asked Zerd.

"They of course are sheer fantasy," he raised a brow.

"How do you disbelieve in them, even if they be fantasy?" she countered after a moment leaning on the glassy wind. "You are fantastic enough."

She meant of course that he was a creature of legend and almost of myth. But he pretty obviously thought that she meant he was a monster, and that venom lived inside his jaw, and he almost flinched, as she had winced at the word *changeling*, and yet he kept his eyes on her.

The river now came roaring past us. It churned and frothed and birds swooped low into it, pecking at the logs tossed along on its currents. I saw that the logs were hollowed out and contained—"People!" my mother cried. "There is a man lying in that tree! Can we wade in and rescue him?"

"Dead, dead!" the brothers cried.

What they meant, it appeared, was that the river was in its own way another grave, and the hollowed trees were coffins, in which the Riverines (The Saint's people?) placed their people for a last resting, a last turbulent taken-awayness.

"Each Riverine is lying," a brother said, "in his personal tree, planted to mark his birth, and to be his own coffin." "A floating feast-table for the birds," said another approvingly. "And for the scavengers, who can swim out to them," saluted another, as we galloped past this idyllic scene, the sparkling sun and water and foam, all bucolic, rustic, with the floating bird-tables. As the Riverines returned into river.

And the brothers sent their spears flashing into the tangled brushwood where they had seen a furry rearing.

"What is it? What are we killing?" my mother asked as we grouped around the opening in the wood.

"Bear," Zerd said. "Bear," said another brother, and another.

My mother rode back a little way and reached out her arms for me. The brother holding me gratefully lifted me out to my mother. "Thank you," he said politely. He thought she had decided he would hunt more easily without me as impediment. She held me before her and breathed deeply. "The bears here must be very terrible," she said.

Indeed, the height at which I had glimpsed something in there seemed vast. My mother waited for Zerd to give her some sign. He said to her: "Don't follow us. Wait by the river, at this point," and they disappeared into the trees.

PART THREE

1

The Melancholy Plain East

WHEN THE GROUND opened beneath us, we thought both of us at once, I know, of the marsh-kings abducting wanderers. But it was a chute, very smooth and marbled, down which we slid. Once down, we thought as we fell, there seemed no method of scrambling and clawing out again: our ingress was too smooth.

"Yes, to be here, you must be a friend," said a voice in the darkness. "You are at the mercy of those inside, whenever you enter."

"Inside where?" my mother said in the gloom. She held me and her heart beat into my ear.

"You are under Saltfalt," said the voice. "Under the battledowns and our river."

"Are you Riverine?" my mother asked at once, at the words 'our river'.

Something shuffled forward out of the gloom which our eyes were adjusting to. But it could not be this that had spoken to us. This was the coiling of an immense snake, standing up on its own lank body, a snake with eyes that saw us well.

There was a very long and wearisome silence now, which my mother broke by saying to me, "Seka, try to scramble up this chute. I will stand at the bottom here. Brace your legs against my shoulder, if you can." There was no reaction from the snake, which remained swaying ahead of us in the darkness, nor from the voice. But I could not climb the chute. It was too smooth. Neither could I see much light in the opening above. It was obviously pretty high above us now, and at an angle maybe.

I slid down again by my mother. The snake wavered. It collapsed itself on its coils, and at one point rustled thickly and longly away into the darkness, its pin-head gliding before it half-raised, at another point returned.

"We are tired," my mother said into the dark. "We shall not sit down because of your creature. We'll lean against the chute you brought us down."

We thought the voice would not answer, that whoever or whatever it was had gone away. Then: "Sleep," answered the voice.

This then became the last thing we wished to do. We tried as the silence wore on to remember what the voice had sounded like. But we could not recapture the sound. "It sounded hissy," my mother said at one point, but that because she was tired and was thinking of talking snakes. We dozed, with our backs half-sloped against the icy hard chute, and woke to feel sure we were not here; we had been in odd places, we must be so still, but not here. Yet here, whatever here was about, we were.

"You do not feel, Seka," my mother anxiously, lovingly whispered, "as you did in the tunnel before Mill-time? This is not as bad as then. Zerd and the brothers will come soon. They will hunt for us, and they will call —we can answer." (She could answer!) But the dark had arrived up there, there was no day up there now, and we listened with all our heart but heard no shouts. My mother mentioning Mill-time had sent quavers into me, and a hatred that that must never happen again. That had been worse than the hole in the Northwall. That had been worse than anything. I thought of the cold Quar, of the new-hatched chicks half-dazed tossed in a bin on top of each other alive, and the Miller's neighbor who had spat his wodge of leaf-chew in on top of them: "runts," he said in contempt, punishing them; of the dog picked up by one hind leg by Quar and hurled downstairs because he was tired of it lying in his room; of the vegetable-woman crying longingly for the lynching of her lover Fishhead though she knew he had only taken me out in little boats on blue days; of Quar taking Cija out for a picnic when it rained, and instead of courteously regretting the weather and then enjoying it with her, saying every time a gust blew in their faces, accusingly: "You should like this, you're so romantic."

All this swept over me when my mother assured me

we were not beginning another Mill-time: Wife as all burned, shrieking "The Well's fault. It's the Well's fault." Quar saying soupily to me, his hand-grip like iron, after I had written him a note, addressing him as "Mr. Quar": "I'm your daddy now."

Cija was most alarmed when I began to cry. I could not remember the last time I had cried. At Mill I had never cried. In Quar's disgusting house I had never cried; I remembered it as permeated with disgustingness, not because of what we discovered later about the fooled travellers, but because of the fooled Cija and her horrible marriage.

I leaned heavily, like the night against the window, against my mother and sobbed into her little breast, the last dear safety, and very small. A few inches in the world. I was racked; it seemed the sobs tore my lungs as they came up from wherever they come from.

I could not quite understand why my mother had stopped petting me and seemed to be looking at me, holding back from me; through the blur I could see a smile on her face at times. I sobbed again, sobbing my hatred of the Mill-time, and then wondered if my father and his brothers had arrived, or if my mother had at last gone mad and become my enemy. "Seka, don't stop crying," she said. "Don't stop crying. Keep on crying. Now, while you please keep crying, listen to me very carefully. *You are sounding properly*. Can you hear yourself sounding?"

Sounding? I listened to myself. Instead of the whooping gasping choking sounds I had always known myself capable under stress of producing, I was making sounds as real people do. I was making a strange natural sound.

My mother held my face in her hands, the tears running down all over them. "Now listen to me, Seka," she said, "and, darling, keep crying. While you are still crying, don't draw a different breath, but try to say 'I.' "

I produced a beautiful clear vowel.

"Now 'Oh,' " my mother said in the same tone, but obviously terribly excited.

Next I produced a tiny sentence, to her orders, with consonants in it.

I fell to crowing at the consonants, and they almost took my breath away. My mother's face clouded and fear entered her eyes, though she tried to hide it: the starlight was cold up there, we became aware again of our known square feet of surroundings, and she was afraid she had taken me too fast and lost me my miracle. She said to me, "Say 'I am Seka.' "

And clasped me, crying herself, as in a voice I recognized as a child's (though in my head I'd never spoken as a child) I said it.

It was very strange to hear my own voice. It was as though a third person had joined us. Although I kept exercising the voice (till my mother said to rest it, she reassured me I must rest it and that I would not lose it now—though I knew again she silently feared) it was uncanny to hear this young girl talking with my mother in the dark. We did not feel at all lonely any more.

The goose-pimples ran along my arms as I heard a fourth voice, not the voice long since sunk into absence as the voice that had informed us we were under-river. I knew the wonderful voice: it was as miraculous as my own.

"Juzd!" I cried. He would not know who it was down here that called to him with a child's clear voice—not too firm, as a matter of fact, on the hard "z" which I had not used at all before. In the minute starlight my mother stared at me bemusedly: "Juzd? Are you dreaming, Seka heart? Juzd!"

A man's figure came scrambling down the chute foreshortened and purposeful toward us. My mother and I stood away, treading carefully, thinking of the snake; the figure was slight, it stood beside us, it was Smahil.

"Up with you both," he said in a very sane voice. "Cija, take your child in your arms and I will heft you both up with me together. Let's all get out of here at once."

He tugged on the rope.

Juzd, who had first heard my mother's voice below ground drew us up.

Out of the gloom appeared the wan snake. It swayed, its head up, regarding us. Smahil gasped and tugged the rope again, for more speed, as he saw the gigantic thing; but my mother and I, curiously, remained unalarmed. The thing had not come to us till we were all but gone. It now watched us go, as it had greeted us.

We sat under a tree, exhausted, once we had limped some way from the place, yet hoping it was not too far to intercept Zerd if he should arrive. Smahil offered us each a drink from his bottle, apologizing that whoever he had lifted it from had kept it too warm. We watched the starlit spurling spume of the rapid river, still bearing its bleached-lit cargoes, and we discussed the situation. (Once or twice the Seka-voice spoke even. Juzd would smile and touch my hair in joy each time Seka spoke.)

Cija said she was too uncertain of the direction of the barrow. She wanted to stay here, even if Juzd and Smahil wanted to continue their own trek. She thought Zerd would come sooner or later, probably sooner. She thought he must have searched already, and we had not heard him, but he would search again, here.

"What if he has gone to Northstrong?" asked Juzd. "He will have to go, Beloved, sooner or later."

"He will send his brothers to look!" she said of course.

But a storm erupted. It genuinely erupted. I think this was the overspill to the mainland continent of the atmospheric disturbances which had begun in central Atlan.

A ball of lightning rolled on to and down the trunk of the tree under which we were sitting. The tree burned and we ran. The lightning remained in its ball—it was an actual sphere of lightning, as the one which had laughed on my coverlet—and was amused at the burning tree and our escape. It was amused, then presently dispersed.

"Here at least is the Highway," Smahil said.

I looked around. Wilderness, and sighing starlit lightning-stabbed grass. I looked down. A thin wavery uncertain straight track beaten as by single file passed upon several times. I remembered how Fishhead had always followed his own track, as though unwilling in the wild ever to show his having passed more than once; since to show that he had passed once was unavoidable, his tracks would tattle no extra tales.

The rain had not yet struck. But before it, came a sibilant subterranean hiss—"the termites," Juzd said, with some affection, "vibrating their abdomens against their underground network of tunnel walls to warn each other of approaching danger—in this case a storm from the ocean."

"How far is the ocean?" my mother asked at once.

"Over those hills," Juzd said at once.

"We must wait here," my mother said definitely. "Till Zerd or his brothers come. They have my little one in the barrow."

"Where is here?" Juzd asked, as my mother had asked of the Voice in the earth.

For we were nowhere. We were on the Highway. But where on the Highway? Where was the Highway?

"You know the way back to Northstrong," my mother said to Juzd, "since you and Smahil have so splendidly laughed at the locks there and arrived here. You passed the barrow there."

"No, Beloved. We were not looking for you. We were on our way to the ocean."

"You are bound for Atlan, Juzd? But you are taking my brother with you?"

"Your brother escaped with me. Your brother was imprisoned with me by your husband. I had doubts about allowing your brother to journey only when you were with us. Your brother vampirizes you."

Smahil smiled. He stood beside us lightly.

"You know the way from Northstrong. You have come from Northstrong," my mother insisted.

The hail hit. The branches started falling around our heads, breaking off, cracking—the hailstones the size of sheep-knuckle-bones beating them off the trees.

Juzd had no intention of taking my mother back to Northstrong. He never did answer her remark, and the (for him) extremely timely and obedient hail drove us, it would seem, ever farther over the hills, step by sodden stinging step.

We took shelter as we could, under tree after tree. But as each tree became entirely inhospitable, we faltered on to the next tree and always to an observant eye in the same un-Northstrongly direction. I had an observant eye, since I believe such had been trained into the dumbling, and I did not speak out: it was a habit of mine to be quiet, I suppose, as well as having been a physical disability, and besides I trusted Juzd.

Slowly the hail cessated. We stood on the brow of a hill and saw the great sulky water ahead of us all churned up by the hailstones.

"Oh, no!" cried my mother, in pain.

I think Juzd suggested that we shelter here for the night, since we all were either weary or astray, and wait to see how the morning would look. I think he said things like Tomorrow is another day.

"We have nothing for you to eat, little-one-with-a-voice," Juzd said to me as we sat in the furze.

"I don't think I am interested in eating. It is a while since I have eaten," said my lovely Seka-voice, speaking slowly in its pretty testing-out way.

Juzd looked at me searchingly. "You are refining," he said. "We are all changing in some way. We are getting ready for something."

A circle of gold light lay still under the burnished leaves here with us as we sat, as though we had a lamp switched on in here in the tree-calm. Juzd was now giving out a little of the sunlight he'd gathered in and stored during the day.

Smahil and Cija were talking, he as guardedly as she, for he seemed very edged and sanded-down out here after what must have been a great long walk with Juzd in wilderness. They spoke of the escape from prison—the same lock-loosing we had seen Juzd so adept with—and the state of the Capital.

Up there, Algol giving its wink. "Every two and a half days this star fades from one magnitude to below the lesser," Juzd said. My mother shivered.

Juzd saw at once that she did not want to ask either Smahil or himself to huddle her for warmth, but that after her long vigils she was chilled to her bones.

"We must light a fire, my friend," Juzd said to Smahil.

Smahil waited to see what must be done, like a horse with the reins over his muzzle. "Obedient" was the word I kept thinking of for things and people tonight to do with Juzd.

Juzd made my mother sit still against the bark of the tree, while the rest of us gathered twigs and fallen boughs. "But these are wet," Smahil said equably to Juzd and into the wind.

"Pile them," Juzd said, and we did.

The water-drops slid along the grain of the twigs. Juzd set his hand on them, not quite touching, just over them, and grimaced a little as he put himself into them. The glow from his slender naked palm (it was always very noticeable when any of Juzd's skin was naked) flickered and then fixed again and suddenly the pile ignited—all at once, a rose of exquisite flame, and the water-beads still trembled in the fire as the flames grew. We sat around Juzd's fire as people do round any camp-fire, and gazed. It was alive, it was warm, it kept out the wet dark and made the sound of the sea sigh less, and my mother clasped her arms around her knees and looked helped and relaxed.

I thought, each log, each stick *is* a memory of boughs in a gale, or twigs in a hail, or leaves in frost vivid under rain or stars or sun or creatures. The logs crack their green discontent, and the sticks each crackle their stories.

"Juzd, tell me a story," said my voice, after I had told it to; stumbling still only on the hard sound in his name which seemed impossible to rehearse.

"Shouldn't *you,* little-one-that-is-speaking, first tell me a story?" he suggested.

"This morning I could never speak," I began . . . but I could think of no more story.

Juzd waited, then laughed. "And that is the best story any man ever heard," he said. "My ears are glad to hear that story.

"Now, what shall I tell you?" Juzd leaned over his fire, holding his hands toward it—and while it warmed him, it leaped up biddably at his nearness.

"Now once upon a time, these three brothers, they wandered the world to seek their fortune. The eldest brother was dressed in red like the earth, and he labored seven years to earn a valley he coveted; he built a stone house in it, and thought he would farm and grow prosperous. But when he raped a girl he saw bathing in a valley pool, the owner—you know what rape is, Seka?—the owner of the valley was disgusted with him, and said 'That is not the way you build up a home, to spoil with your greed' and the brother had failed: he could never have the valley.

"The second brother was dressed in yellow, like joy and hope, and when he arrived in the valley he saw the fat kine and fat vines and the sight made him sing a little as he went on his way. He saw a girl, and because something in her laugh and her frown hit on his heart, he asked to marry her. 'You must woo her seven years,' says the owner of the valley, the girl's father. Seven years of aching and longing and pining were sheer delight to the brother, just what he had always wanted, and eventually the girl was led toward him looking like dreams come true for her wedding. 'But,' her father said, 'you must be kind to her.' The brother liked the thought of being kind to her, and he agreed enthusiastically. 'The reason,' said her father, 'is that this very morning, her wedding morning, she was raped by a man in red.'

"The brother was wild with grief. What a tragedy! How could destiny have treated him in this way? He ran away into the hills, he mounted the unicorn he saw browsing, and started to ride it away to a better valley, but the unicorn bucked him and dragged him, and he was unable to control it or to untangle himself from its cruel mane.

"The third brother, who wore blue like thought and intuition and like you, Seka, he was coming along the path to the valley. He saw how horribly the unicorn and his brother were harming each other. He chased them for seven years, and for him they were the worst years ever a brother had spent."

"Worse than for the brother being dragged?"

"The dragged brother had only to stay passive and think of each bump as a tragedy and destiny's game with him. But the brother in blue had to stay on foot and master the unicorn and at last un-tangle his brother. His brother begged dramatically for surcease so he threw him toward the stream. Then he mounted the white unicorn, which bowed to him, and they soared to high valleys."

I looked in his fire and I asked rather sadly: "Do the brothers always be not friends?"

I meant that I had heard this story once already, and I had hoped this time in this telling that something nicer would happen. But Juzd anyway said, "No, they are not mutually incompatible. They are mutually necessary, though too often the earth-brother and the hope-brother are entirely self-indulgent. The hope-brother can be as gross as the earth-brother, and all too often the blue brother has to work terribly hard all on his own."

"Will my father's blue brothers come and find us?"

"I doubt it," Juzd said and gazed around.

"Do all families have the blue brothers?"

"Yours has the blue daughter, yes? Do not apeling and your father the General wear red? Are your mother and your uncle Smahil wearers of yellow each in their fashion?

And you, Seka, don't you think and aren't you all intuition, little observer, calm little analyst?"

Smahil now withdrew from us a moment, with a bow of apology, and went through the fine lessening rain in the night down to the rock-pool where he must have placed his bottle, and was lost to sight for a little.

"You are fairly happy, dear one?" Juzd asked my mother on whose face his fire cast flickering bruises.

"Seka's voice makes me happy," my mother replied.

My mother added against the whispering rain, "Zerd has gone. He could not find me. He is with Sedili now, isn't he, Juzd?"

"Yes," Juzd said after a pause, presumably a pause of seeing far.

"Is Smahil evil?" my mother asked.

"No."

"You called him a vampire of me."

"His is not a good soul," Juzd said.

"Not good like—like your golden Atlanteans *are* good?" my mother tried to think of indisputably proper people.

"Yes, they are good, but," said Juzd, "without complexity, without structure and strength to withstand storms. Those golden nationals are young. They have not yet been through the centuries of being bad-souls most of us have to go through, according to our ways and twists, before we can fight and force ourselves back to good with all the added experience, and strength of the enemy—knowing how the enemy is to be conquered, because the enemy has been knotted within us around our vitals, and yet has been conquered."

He added that the "enemy" he mentioned was not evil —"Evil," he said into the night-rain, "hardly enters this small essentially buffered incubatory kindergarten of a world. Evil is more in a disease virus, which is foreign to the natural lessons of our kindergarten, than in hate, revenge, cruelty—which are only warped good, love and self-love we have not yet learned how to handle, by which our yellow brother is still dragged along. Now see," he looked up as Smahil strode into the fire-light, "your brother Smahil has decently chilled his wine in his rock-pool."

Smahil passed the bottle around—we all drank, even I was allowed. It was cold enough to be warming.

"So are we going on to the coastal Atlan way?" Smahil

asked, conversationally. "Or does my sister want something else again? What does Cija want? Tell us, Cija. We've never known."

"Whatever I get," she began to say, "is a little bit what I want . . .

"I was going to say that whatever I get is non-right. I think what I want, whatever it is, is very little—a place of my own to be busy in and make Seka happy and busy in. Not a crumbling castle buried in a sick, secret shoreline— no one could suppose I should have been contented with that, I wouldn't have been a good mother to be contented in that place.

"Maybe my mother's palace—though that wasn't in any manner mine, my mother's ways are foreign to me, perhaps I should accept them, but they're also unpredictable and dangerous. Neither I nor Seka could ever rest where the person in control could jump up any moment without warning and send us here, or send us there, or somehow use us without telling us why.

"And that," she said in a level voice, "is why being with Zerd is not right either. He or my mother, it's being in the presence of too much selfish power."

"In your last life," said Juzd, "you often would be sitting complaining of *that* husband, that last life's one. He was your *one*—your true soul-mate, your utterest brother, made for you and you for him." (Smahil here took a startled gulp, staring around the bottle.) "But you were dissatisfied because he was so loving, kind, too bland for a greedy adolescent palate. You prayed to your little god till he granted—for only by granting, it seems, could he finally give you what you really need, by first giving what you *think* you need and sickening you of it—so now you have been given one who is almost impossible to possess."

"*Almost* impossible, you say," Cija said after a sobered pause.

"Yes," said Juzd, "the Dragon, like every other soul, has needs—he does not know of them himself. But it is just possible you might be the person who could begin to show him. Good can come of any wrong. Nothing is ever quite a mistake, though it may be the slower steeper path than the one originally offered."

"I find this un-locker of locks unutterably smug, Cija," Smahil said and rose and walked out into the rain, pointing his toes a little, strolling, dissociating himself from the conversation.

"Smugness is in the eye of the beholder," his sister said quietly after him, and I fell asleep.

When I woke, my mother was asking Juzd why since somewhere her "one" was waiting for her *like a brother* if she "journeyed truly," why did Juzd disapprove of her incestuous relationship with Smahil? Juzd told her about the vortex of mating bodies in which all three "selves" of each —the red self, the yellow and the blue—reach up into the intenser planes where for instance a Nal can be snatched into the vortex and be suddenly conceived; I just remembered Fishhead saying "A successful parasite never harms the host." Smahil, I thought huffily, was generally an *un*-successful parasite.

Smahil was still nowhere in evidence. I now thought I would like something to eat. I looked blearily around the firelight-edge. Out there in the darkness were eyes. The scavengers again, kept at bay by the Juzd-flames? Would Smahil be all right? I remembered something suddenly delicious and wonderful that swept over me like hot gold. I flexed my inner throat. If Smahil or anyone were in trouble, and I knew, *I, Seka,* could call out helpfully. I felt a throbbing pride and love of the universe.

I could make out, now, the shapes around the eyes companioning us. One shape was quite tall, taller than we as we sat, and shaggy around the head, with burning eyes like lamps. Several shapes near me with little eyes reflecting the dance of flame were very small and low to the furzey ground. I stared at the nearest one. It was a hedgehog. It looked away from Juzd, to whose cadences all the creatures were listening lovingly or as though fascinated perhaps, hypnotized, and looked at me. It trotted away and when it came back to my feet, right into the firelight, there were fruit and berries all over its spines—it had rolled by fallen fruit to make itself a walking dish.

I pulled off the berries and ate them and felt good and reflected how everything was turning into rhyme such as my nurses had told.

"This," Juzd was saying, very warm and easy, "was the very reason Ancient Atlan was so keen on your son Nal. It was prophesied long ages ago he would come at the right time to be their Emperor. Ancient Atlan—not the golden youth people around the coasts—had often thought

of purposely making 'a double blossoming' but to be the
given Emperor he must not be made deliberately."

"Smahil and I knew what we were doing."

"But not thinking at all of a child or of Ancient Atlan."

"Is my son Nal still alive?" my mother asked after another very deep breath.

"Yes."

I went to my mother's knee and gave her some berries.
She took them without seeing them. "In Atlan's city," my
mother said, "my son was *christened*. But it can't have
had much of an effect—he was dedicated to my own little
Cousin, just a private god." "That Cousin's name," Juzd
said, "is a glory of all the worlds, and this world in particular will come to think of him as more and more *private*."

"A Saint I knew," my mother said listlessly, "had a
fairly good god. He saw great splendor, a beaming, a 'vision of the light of the river' after his repudiation of an
old hate-feud."

"And plunged in frantic religiosity thereafter?" Juzd
guessed rather wearily. "If only people would realize it's
perfectly ordinary being put into a state to perceive or
notch-in to the permanent light (not usually seen when
our red self is busily in control)."

Juzd and my mother were both tired by now. The stars
were fading. My mother laid my head in her lap. We all
slept around Juzd's fire.

I woke in a seeping silver gray light to hear my mother
stir, and Juzd stir alert. My mother moaned and whispered.
The marathon continued. It was like a wheel that must roll
over me, I thought, piteously, now that it had turned at all.
Now I knew why there was still no sign of the incestuous
Smahil. It was one thing to commit this thing called incest,
another to hear all about its place in limitless patterns.

"Who are you, Juzd?"

"I wander, dearest one."

"Why did The Saint and I wander together?"

"You have a nature that accepts, or sidesteps. You are
being taught, I would think, Beloved, to stand and face
and look in the eyes. And thus become un-anxious, and
become thus detached. And your somewhat religious
friend, who presumably is over-rigid by nature, and too
intense, and too greatly the slave of his yellow self, he was

being taught I would think by the *same events* to reach
the same freedom (detachment) by a different route—
loosening up. To see that all have ideals and most have
some form of integrity."

The rain had stopped, I noted. Presently in the paleness
I heard a rustling. The termites were coming out and repairing the earth-work turrets damaged by the rain and
hail and lightning-balls.

"In my life in this world," Cija said almost sulkily, "I
am buffeted."

"When you go next in another world," Juzd said, "anything that happens to remind you of this one will fill you
with nostalgia. You will remember all this as so lovely
once it is unattainable—piercing, poignant."

"No I won't," Cija whispered. "All I want is a strong
dependable sensible world where everything is solid, reli-
able, tamed, like a middle-aged husband."

She added, "This is both dreary *and* un-predictable—
I can't think of two much more repellent characteristics
for one's biography."

Juzd, laughing in his whisper, understood her. "In some
worlds," Juzd admitted to her, "life is a surge. It is hurled,
or hurls itself, upon you. You wake most mornings from a
dream which partook, as usual, of vision and before
breakfast note the quality of dawn—where all dawns are
of the *essence* of dawn, the dawns men in this world only
dream of when they hear the word from a prison cell.
No 'real' dawns in our present world's space-time are as
real as those essence-dawns are. In your morning mail
there will be one big surprise, one small. If there are oys-
ters for breakfast, one may include a pearl. Before lunch
you are sent on a high quest to a meadow—and there the
meadow is as much essence-of-meadow as the dawn is
essence-of-dawn; or the blues of such a world sing in your
eyes, and the greens are different again, and the scarlets
are to the greens as a trumpet blast to a whispering evening—"

"So what is the purpose of *this* kind of trudging plod-
ding world where even adventures un-fold with all the
shock and thrill and urgency of rice pudding?" asked Cija.

"Why," Juzd said, "in this sort of a trudging world we
can detach ourselves from our greed for sensation. We
may sulk for a while, for several lives even, because we're
not getting the quality of life, with its speed and color, to

which we feel we're 'entitled.' We may disappear into pretenses of our greed. We may dream or drug or pervert a life or two. But eventually we'll have to start using our self—after all it is always there waiting quietly to be made use of—and that is when we can begin to manipulate for ourselves the essences of what qualities we *do* find here and now. We can start to exercise our powers at last, to pick and choose, to take this path or that, in a cool amused detachment. Then at last we shall be nearing our adult-hood, and be able to go into the rich colored fast high worlds as of right, not as infants being swept along."

It was light. We could see in a gray spray. With the dawn—a little wind running as fast as it could get, across the plain and away from the city, whispering, whispering of the sorrows of the day to come.

A great lion lay revealed at Juzd's feet. Its mane, bleached of anything but a certain warmth, spilled over his travel-rimed boots.

Juzd chuckled, aloud this time, and the lion opened great eyes, amber I think, and blinked upon Juzd's face. Juzd sat up and drew from his jerkin sandwiches of bread and cheese, and offered them to myself and my grateful little mother. Juzd soothed with his stroking hand the trunk of the tree he disturbed, by sitting un-invited on its roots. He perched there, sharing his cheese sandwich with a lion.

The sky was blue as milk.

The shadows of the straight trunks of nearby trees were cast, like barrel clasps, around the auburn trunks of the pines here. Juzd could be seen practically gathering in the sunlight around him, so it was intenser and more golden immediately about Juzd. He somehow was attracting it, was storing it.

My mother did not try too hard to keep me away from the lion. She could see how respectfully it shared his picnic with our wanderer.

"Are we fairly happy?" she suddenly asked, as Juzd had asked last night, but with a world of difference in her thought, her mouth full, eyes gazing out over the crawling pulling-itself-together ocean.

"Do you find any uses for happiness?" Juzd smiled.

"Even in this dreary world?" said the woman with the picnicking lion between herself and a daughter with a

brand-new voice. "I suppose," she said, "it can be used as
incentive when one is not otherwise strong enough to reach
out for strength."

"Where is Smahil?" I asked.

They turned at the clear young unfamiliar voice.

"Look, there are his clothes!" Cija pointed down the
beach. "He must have gone for a swim."

As we watched, a long pallid worm darted out of
Smahil's clothes.

Cija shuddered and turned away.

From a third direction, Smahil was leading soldiery toward us, across the beach. In the growing sun his uniform
was shining. He had cast away only his hood and cloak
and dead bottle. He looked very bemedalled and epau-
letted. Anyone in the same army, or even a different
army, would be much struck by him and feel privileged
to follow him across any spit of sand.

2

The Mystic Floating Penis

THE RAGGLE OR at any rate taggle Smahil was leading to us were Sedili's, and they were perfectly all right, except that they had been left manning a shore for a long time. They were delighted to be seeing a bit of action at last. Here we were, the people they could guard Sedili's shore against at last.

They had salt on their collars, and they led with them their asset—a young mastodon, an alienated-looking pachyderm with lavishly-blinkered eyes and many reins and snaffles, and carefully sawn-off tusks, and sparse hairs on end here and there on its loose wrinkled pachydermy skin.

"What shall we do?" my mother asked in alarm.

Juzd's lion had come to its feet and barked a warning—or barked a cough, a deep rumbling sharp yet reverberating cough in its throat, that seemed to echo off the sea. It leaned forward into the scent of the approaching mastodon; its lion-voice rumbled again.

The mastodon, blinkered and up-wind, had the sudden wild thought that these salty men were leading it toward an actual lion. It thought again about the whole situation: this was no calm little outing. The mastodon, getting bigger every moment is it neared us, put up its trunk—oh, what warty pneumatic extravagance—and charged.

Juzd, my mother and I ran down the bright beach and into the handy shadow of a cliff which had hove alongside. "The Mystic Island!" my mother shouted, in spray-spattered capital letters, as we splashed through the very blue water in a rock-pool, splashing slightly alkaline, so blue and warm, we licked our splashes as we ran, and

then out to the creamy spurling wavelets and then the
purple green mauvey pinky heathery silvery mass of the
cliff up which Juzd helped her scramble: I followed as
agile as anybody's small daughter with a tongue in her
mouth to grip against her teeth. I made moaning grumbling noises for my ears alone, and said, "Oh, really" at
knotty tussocks, for the pleasure of moaning and grumbling which I had watched only other people enjoy.

Smahil saw. His eyes widened and narrowed. He hurled
himself through the water and as the island set off, Smahil
grabbed the heathery roots and hauled himself up, hand-
over-hand up the cliff. A wave of white spray hit high at
us. The involved lion, the mastodon, the sailors diminished
on the beach which became a strip.

"Baby ape," mother said to the vanishing shore of the
continent.

The island glided very fast. There was salt in our eye-
sockets. Foam as I looked down curdled on the sea-
hollows. A vivacious sea. The sapphire waves, and the
amethyst waves, and the deep emerald gullies, and the
opals flashing up again, and there the backs of dolphins
sleek as steel. The morning intensified.

My uncle lay face down breathing deeply on the weed-
soft grass. Presently he rolled over, his hands behind his
head, and squinted up at the sun and at Cija.

The slim young woman sat with her spine straight, her
hair fluttering and her garment a yellow linen rag by now,
fluttering also like a flag to the sunlight. Her left hand caressed me but her eyes, smoke-distant, were on the shore
as it became our past.

"Will the Island bear us to Atlan, Juzd?" she asked.

And she added, as though to make Atlan seem more
domestic: "Seka was born in Atlan."

Smahil slid a malevolent glance at Juzd. "Doubtless we
shall go wherever this fair sweetheart of ours wishes us to
go. It has not escaped my notice that I was allowed to join
you on this monster. If you had wished to keep me away,
I should be in one of those dark shining troughs by now."

My mother now looked at Smahil, and she looked sadly.
I knew that out here, in the salt and air, safe with Juzd
beside her, so that she need fear neither herself nor
Smahil, something in the cadence of his voice in his adjectives used youthfully as though they meant something,

in the set of his soul, she recognized (as he did forever) the set of her own.

"We go to Atlan," I said uncertainly.

My mother paused. "My destinations have always been the same place," she said, and though the tone was clear, the words were (I thought) sullen.

"Have you not been to different destinations?" Juzd asked mildly. "You have been to heart-warmth, and to independence, and to generosity, yes, even for your husband."

"My husband!" she said and sat stilled. "For Zerd?"

Juzd said very gently, "You can still reach him."

"I will have to send out my thought, Juzd, and I have no psychic strength."

"You can reach him."

I can reach him, I thought, if we should ever actually want to reach him. But why should we want to now?

Huge white birds arked high and low over the arching frothy waves, their wing undersides a delicate blue like the inside-wrists of an anemic girl, reflecting the blue of those turbulent waves.

The wild winds, sweeping the waves southwards. They swept the sun away from us. Soon the sting of gold had left the day, though the air was still wet and warm and white birds cried by us. "I have lost all my dreams but you, Seka," my mother drew me into her dress. "Seka is your only dream," Juzd said un-emotionally. "The others have only ever been shadows."

"Shadows, Juzd? My fair boy and my forest baby?"

"Or totems—as the Miller's Wife you told me you met had made a totem of her Miller, a totem whom in her case she must never displease—mainly from vanity, herself really being the ultimate god, who must never be found displeasing."

"I had no vanity about my children, Juzd."

"Vanity is only one aspect of the shadows. The shadows have many names, but none of them is real."

"Then can a dream be real? You call Seka my dream."

"Seka is your only dream. And when you have dreamed fully, and to all the levels of the dream, then you will be as real as Seka. And she will be as real as you. Already she has a voice."

The island sailed on over the waves, at times dipping a prow of cliff deeper in the dark salt.

"Shall I always be with my mother?" I asked Juzd timidly with my voice, later.

"Your mother will not again be alone, not till," he answered, "not till she is born."

He interpreted my glance. He never misinterpreted it.

"No, not 'till her next life.' She hasn't yet become herself at all, and these 'lives' are only sleep-walking in limbo. Just as all our 'lives' in these physical worlds are spent mainly waiting for ourselves to be born."

I saw in the middle distance a great ray leaping from the sea again and again and with each leap releasing a newborn ray—thirty-two in all.

In the curdling waters Smahil, gazing over the edge of the sailing cliff, seemed to see something startling, or almost too fulfilling. He drew back with a muffled exclamation, and turned his gaze blank, but not before I had looked where he was looking and seen a face in the water, disappearing as he drew away. A reflection in rolling seawater, I thought, that's good. It had looked very like Smahil, an inner version of Smahil, as reflections so often seem to be the inner succubus pulling one inwards. That is why it is dangerous to pause too long before mirrors.

The sun set, bleeding.

I realized I had not eaten all day. But I was not hungry. I thought my mother was not either. The scent of salt and heather-honey seemed enough.

At night, I started awake to glimpse another island floating past, lit by ocean swirls of phosphorescence and on it a man or creature standing upright gazing.

I wanted to shout "Yaw this island into the wind!" or orders to luff the island. Or somehow to stop our island ignoring the other island, losing it. The sea was all on fire with stars.

I leaned over the side of the island. It was steep, and its surrounding tangle of floating transparent vitreous roots hard to distinguish from polyps, anemones/organisms— there were things on the move down there, but which might only be the creeping transparent snail-like plants.

Some things were climbing up the side of the cliff. Golden pale silvery hands with creeping fingers lit—I think, lit from within—with the finger-joints visible within, very delicate, gelatinous bones.

I sat up and looked back at the sleepers with me on the turf. Smahil, my mother, Juzd in his cloak between them, scattered sleepers, a fold of Juzd's cloak around my mother's right side to keep her warm in the night. I could speak. I could tell them things were climbing on to our island out of the sea. But I wanted to see the strangelings from the seawater.

Two beings climbed from the· sea on to the island. A male, a female. Juzd started gravely upright and regarded them. He wrapped in his cloak, the traveller, the man: they in their nakedness and shining wet, the sea coursing down their lit limbs, literally shining—they regarded each other, they pulsing a vivid light, he pulsing quietude.

My mother, caught in the warming gentling fold of Juzd's cloak, she rose when Juzd rose, and leaned there in his cloak, eyes closed till slowly they opened and were met and held, astonished.

The male—I could not see his eyes, for they were presumably part of the intensity at the center of his (in the night) almost unbearably bright face—seemed to see Cija. He advanced toward her, holding out his hand.

With a charming gesture, as of a hostess in her own world making welcome without prejudice an inferior, Cija at once made to take his strange hand.

Juzd warned her. He held her back by his cloak, and pointed directly at the male's penis. This was on the rise, then on the wane, then on the rise—and arching toward her like a giant worm. Lit veins trembled in it. Obviously it was greed-filled on its own account—it was alive, and unpredictable.

But Smahil too had risen now, and was staring at the people who had climbed from the sea.

I could see the mer-female's eyes for some reason with less difficulty than the male's. They were fixed glowing on Smahil. What did she want of him? She wanted what he wanted of my mother.

The female was little less difficult altogether. She looked more visual. I only say she *looked* more visual—she was less a dazzle, she was less a puzzle perhaps, you could look at part of her without your eyes sinking into her as if into forever. I saw Smahil staring at her shoulder. There was a mark where her shoulder began to slope to her breast, a livid mark, almost opaque, dead flesh where the rest of her was alive, a mundane burned-tissue scar where the rest of her was translucent. She has been burned, I thought, by a sting-ray or electric eel. And as I wondered about her flesh, a yearning for Fishhead swamped me. Fishhead would have told us what her wound was.

"You have been branded—there." Smahil stepped forward and touched the female's pectoral. As his finger contracted her, you could see all the blood in her race to the touch of him—or so it seemed.

She spoke. "SsssSS . . ." she said, a wavy indeterminate sound. She looked very wonderfully upon Smahil.

"Do you want them both to go?" my mother uneasily asked Juzd.

She was now occasionally glancing in trepidation to the male's penis, which stood right up from time to time and made sucking sounds of its own—as though wishing to get its teeth into something. Perhaps it even had teeth.

The male advanced steadily upon Cija as soon as she referred to him and his fellow-visitor. He smiled a smile of concentrated blandishment. I relaxed. I knew everything would be all right. If there was one thing my mother in her cautious and impulsive nature distrusted, if there was one thing that never got anywhere with her, that was charm. The meanest grimmest creature might get in with her, so long as he had no charm.

Juzd himself smiled—and the island began to falter on the sea, as though bowing to a new tide. I saw that Juzd's smile was sad.

"We have reached Atlan," Juzd said.

My mother looked at him in amazement, Smahil took no notice.

"We have been only hours upon this sea," mother cried to Juzd.

"One day," he reminded her, "and one night. But they reach Atlan who have journeyed to Atlan. You have journeyed, and are here. I have journeyed, and am ever here."

"And Seka?" my mother cried.

"Seka," he said, "as you pointed out, was born in Atlan. Of course Seka is here."

"And—Smahil?"

Smahil at mention of his own name, and surely (I thought) he has been in Atlan, he turned a savage face upon my mother. "This is your last chance," he cried at my mother. "This is my last threat, Cija. If you do not belong to me as I wish, you have lost me and our blood-tie entirely."

"How do you wish?" my mother asked him. "How do you wish me to belong, Smahil? With every breath I take, every sneeze—?"

She would have gone on, at a loss for words as she momentarily found herself, but he sneered and stopped her.

Now here came the dawn as white as lies. A beach lay before us sparkling. The dawn struck stars of light from the crystal boulders upon the beach.

The island lurched, and grounded upon a rock.

Juzd firmly took my hand, and began to lead me down the island. The island on this side was less high, it was like an earthy rooty heathery gang-plank running down into the sea. Cija followed, hitching up her rag skirts. But then she turned to look back at Smahil. He was with the mer-female as he'd "threatened" to Cija. He was leaned upon her as she swooned with him, down, down over the side of the island she was pulling and pulling Smahil. "Smahil!" Cija cried sharply wildly.

The mermaid turned and regarded Cija. Her face was terribly like Cija's. For a moment the three of them could have been triplets—exactly that—the pale brother and the two Cijas. When the mermaid shifted you could see the marks her nipples had already made in Smahil as they suckered on him. But Smahil's face was fixed in fierce "triumph" on Cija. He was "saying" "I warned you."

The male leaped before us. The island too seemed to be descending. It was pulling itself down into the water as the mermaid was pulling Smahil. The male merely glimmered, interestingly enough, in the rising strength of dawn. He urgently took Cija's hand peering lovingly into her face. Juzd made no move, but watched her. Cija fell to her knees. Now she and I were both leaning over the edge of the turf—the sea swirled at us—and we could hear the grunts, howls, barks of the fish under water.

Cija wrenched herself free.

The male already mopping and mowing in the water sure he had won, ejaculated a cloud of serous black ink, and with a furious gesture made off into a darkened sea, polluted thickly under the strengthening sun. The island submerged on Smahil's triumph.

We waded ashore. As we scrambled up the crystal boulders popping curtains of seaweed to which we clung, my mother's garment was pulled from her. I almost screamed

—I think long habit kept me silent—I thought it was the mer-male.

But it was only a dolphin whose smiling beak disrobed her. It half-surfaced, all silvery in the morning, tugging away her golden rag, then let it go and the sea brought it back to her, froth-garlanded with glass bubbles and weed.

My mother stood on the crystal promontory, on Atlan, the morning striking her, the wind flaunting at her scrap of yellow garment.

How could this woman, after so much recent pain, look so alive and lit?—yes, like the mer-female? It was obvious that to Cija, after her ups and downs, one mastery at least belonged—pain was just another of the things that could happen to a body, to the "doll"—like heat or cold or spiced cheese, which left no spiritual *nor even emotional* lines.

Turtles huddled—like immense benign tumors on the beach.

It was a giant dawn. The points of crystal rock were glittering and glickering. Atlan was giving off great vibrations—like iron warming up under the sun.

We climbed off the beach. Over fallen autumn leaves, the air was warmer than in the mainland-continent we had left. "Even Zerd," Cija said to Juzd after we had walked awhile gazing, "says Atlan is alive. If a plain looks harsh, that is because it is harsh. If a wood is lush, that is because the plants and creatures feel lush within their deep hearts."

We were still real. Hunger and thirst were by now almost a problem, and both were assuaged at once when a beautiful beast, a long waddling legged serpent with many udders and a sidelong eye, stepped into our clearing. Juzd halted her with a gently raised hand. One by one we knelt to her wobbly udders. A wiry gold hair strayed across one. The milk was rich. I know how being fed by an ape lady had once been degradation for Cija. Now Atlan, freely, fed us, we were nestled at Atlan's welcome.

Later, we were charged without warning by a huge beast, from a thicket we must have been too near, but had time to crouch as Juzd quietly told us, and roll like balls right toward it and out between its thunderous back legs. It cantered off, presumably still looking for us.

These two incidents inducted us into Atlan, and we

were un-surprised by the gathering galloping. The riders were presently upon us from over a hill.

They were friends of Juzd's. They were glad and amazed to see him. They were very polite to the woman in not much yellow linen and to her daughter. If they guessed at once who Cija was, as I believe they did, it was not because Juzd told them. He introduced us merely as travelling companions.

The main occupant of the chariot I rode in was a girl some years older than myself, with broadly-plaited braids in which flowers were twined. She was controlling the reins, slapping them on the necks of the white mules pulling the chariot. The other occupant of this chariot was a small white snake. It lay curled in a basket on a cushion and occasionally reared when we hurtled over a bump. My mother was in a chariot driven by an old woman; Juzd in a chariot of which he himself had taken the reins as he spoke to the woman who had been driving it. I guessed we were coming to an encampment which men had left for war.

I was not excited only: I was apprehensive. This girl would be the first child I had ever spoken to.

The sound of the hooves of the mules, of the wheels, of the wind of our passing through the gold land, proved intractable—we could not speak. After I had been handed down by Juzd, the girl re-appeared at the camp-fire with a wicker-held bowl of soup: "Will you have soup?" she said very ordinarily. So this was what real girls said to each other! I said, "Yes," overcome, and relapsed. I sipped and watched the fire bloom, and saw the mules had each a horn on its head and violent-veined velvet genitals and must be those indigenous Atlan centers of story—pure ruthless unicorn.

I saw my mother's face. It was white in the dark. She was alive in Atlan, and yet a yearning lay under her contentment. This was the first time I decided to really call Zerd. I sat by the leaping fire and I consciously called very hard: "Zerd. Come. Come to her. She needs you. She wants you. We want you. Come."

There were harmonious singing yet mechanical sounds in the air. I thought they were kites made of reeds that the encampers had raised in the air to establish territory so far as the bell-like flute-like sounds could be heard, and maybe to frighten strangers.

It was not till the next night that I was to find that they were *men,* not kites, up there and they were flying.

The talk was of the bitter fury of Ancient Atlan, and against the possible arrival of Zerd. The talk was too bitter, I thought. Emotionalism had run riot even here in the world's heart. The intensity of Ancient Atlan was fermenting, turning in on itself. There was a piper here, and he did tricks, which made Juzd smile, concentrating for instance on water to make it boil faster. The piper said something to Cija about "and there in the interior lies still the safe purity, the ancientness, your son and the old ones—"

There was a quietness. Then my mother in a voice very strong for her and yet very uncertain, said *"My* son?" And as the piper bowed his head, she repeated: "Nal?"

Before the wildness could come into her, the desperation lay hold on her, Juzd said: "He is Ancient Atlan's, as he was born to be. Look on him not as *your* son." But he had presently to begin talking to her. "Nal, Smahil," he said, "are passion, destructive."

"Because I allowed Smahil . . ."

"You allowed Smahil."

"When I was married. But ah, Juzd, my friend, I was lonely."

"You were lonely because you wished to be 'loved.' "

"I did not wish to be unloved," she said proudly.

"Zerd did not un-love you. Even at that stage, you could have changed it all yet you allowed Smahil—you caused Nal—you are causing the downfall of Atlan. But," as she made a movement, half toward him and recoiling too, "it is not your fault. Atlan would have fallen anyway. Except you need not have been involved. You wouldn't have been involved. You would have been happy and safe instead of always talking about being happy and safe."

Cija paused. "I am wanting Zerd," she said quietly. "I want him to love as Zerd. How can I find him yet?"

"As soon as you forget your myth. The very instant you forget your myth."

"What is my myth?"

"Your 'self.' "

Cija by the fire frowned, the "kites" melodiously chimed overhead.

"I must not lose my self, Juzd."

"You must cast off your 'self,' Cija, your specter. Only then will you be whole. Then you can begin to live, and Zerd too, at that moment. This trouble and it is a very hard one, is hubris."

"That is Zerd's trouble," she said steelily.

"No. He is a soldier. One day he will fight more than men in battle. Let him learn. Let him learn his trade."

"But Zerd has self-love. He's above men. He manipulates."

"He leads. He is young, yet he leads. You suffer hubris, as we all must before we strengthen ourselves into our true selves by casting it off. Forget your 'integrity.' Get on with what is already in front of you, half-asking, half-ready, half-love."

"Shall I get Zerd?"

"Do you remember when you were very young, when I first met you, how you said fresh from your immurement, you felt your self would be revealed after experience did not add *but stripped away* faults and ignorance? Paring you down to you? Do you remember how when you emerged from your Walk across the plains, you were faced once more, you said then, with the weariness of your own importunate personality constantly getting in the way.

"Each man's specter haunts him. Till each man can strip it off and stand clean."

Cija and I slept in each other's arms. The air was crisp but not comfortless around the fire which stayed through the broad night.

I dreamed of high funnels in the sea.

I dreamed I was a man and fighting the mer-male in battle we "said" was over the mermaid but was really over our rights. We fell in fight into a pool like a box, very damp, very high sides. We rolled over and over fighting. We realized a long time later we were chained together, by entrails, our own old insides. We'd each thought it was the other hanging on to us so we couldn't stop wrestling. We'd been dead a long time, still rolling around, still wrestling joined to each other by our rotting. I woke very heavy, very terrible. But a voice said, *Not your state, his.* Then I knew, with relief, I had not been me in my dream. I had been Smahil, and the dream showed me how Smahil had found his only salvation, which was that he had been obliterated at last with his reflection.

Smahil at last to rest. Sucked in by the most female

orifice ever. For the mer-girl had taken Smahil right into Ocean. The only rest for Smahil—so restless, a succubus himself. On journeys, he had constantly been going to Cija: "Look, look." He wasn't *sharing:* he was sucking. He was leeching on to another being, to possess even its every reaction to whatever it sees. He was constantly: "What I've done for you. What you've done for Zerd." He was horribly Cija's twin soul—her specter. With Smahil gone, Cija could be at rest and turn at last to Zerd—Zerd the constructive soul.

Of course, my mother had always gone on about how she "must give up greed for Zerd," as she put it, since "Zerd is not pure."

But now, I thought suddenly, Cija had reached a point where she could give and take without need of return. And so Smahil had disappeared into his own specter. Smahil had so grossly over-developed his own sucking, that he could only be "sucked." When he placed himself (sexually) in the mer-girl, he had a sensation of adventuring into lush wallow, into easy grab. I could feel it still.

We woke and were given last night's thickened soup. The striped horses fought and danced in the dawn, a zither of light. They fled with the day into thickets.

I felt no sensation that my father had heard my call. Perhaps because of his skeptic quality, he was unable to hear. I lay in grass and new light, in that feeling familiar to most of us, that "thickening, broadening" as though we were bigger in every joint and limb and with a vibrating perhaps "blurred" outline, which happens when one is just moving out of one's physical body. I recalled myself before I could whip off to Zerd. I withdrew safely into my body and drank soup.

The girl older than I was plaited her hair and with a smile took the flowers I brought her to twine in it. In the wood the trees were remarking, commenting to each other quite obviously sentient (whishaawiffa) and I found a crystal egg which must have fallen to the ground. I picked it very carefully and tenderly up and placed it in a nest on a gold branch. I was sure I saw an unwinking and innocent eye regarding me from the cloudy pulsing interior of the egg.

"Atlan is a place of marvel," I said.

"Atlan is poisoned." The girl repeated what she had been hearing. "The trees took thousands of years to grow.

They are cut up for toothpicks. The Atlanteans are glad."

"No, you aren't."

"We are not Atlanteans. We are Ancient Atlan. They are the stupid golden people by the coast, the people who submit in delight to your bad father. We are pure. Rather than submit ever, we shall die."

Die or destroy, that was the strength of it.

A woman later at the camp said, "Even unicorns in the woods now are ravaging maidens."

Juzd laughed. He said, "At last! After all the years that maidens have ravaged unicorns. Perhaps things at last are righting themselves."

Snakes mated beside the encampment. They mated for nine hours continuously. The reluctant female couldn't get away, as the male was equipped with spurs for hooking himself into her. "They would never have done that so near the camp once," the woman said. Juzd did not laugh this time at the immodest snakes.

With handfuls of nuts for the fire to pop, the girl and I ventured back through thicket. No longer daytime wood— so different! No longer dark as in day. Amazing bluish lights and in different degrees of intensity—drifting or darting. I realized: they were *beings*. And at dance. But attached to the trees. Attenuated out from them or concertina-ing back into them. The spiritual emanations of trees were at dance.

We splashed out of tree-light and through a pool glowing like a dozen peacock tails. We popped the exploding nuts in the flames.

"Something" was being grown, in a giant ruined temple. Where the light of perpetual lamps ever coldly burned, the tiny dragons were being bred. Each could dance on the head of a pin. Dragons to fight the Dragon.

"All this, that is too much," Juzd said. "You are growing imitation life. You are growing what is called virus. It is blasphemy, it is parasitic copying of the body-dragons it will suck on and destroy."

"It is orders from the Emperor," they said proudly.

"How does the Emperor in the Interior talk to you?"

"He sends messages by the yulven." Wolven.

"What are those syllables overhead?"

"The sounds are men, flying."

And another said: "They are flying to take viruses to the

coast. Those are wandering cells—cells which migrate in the body."

Juzd turned a face of totality on my mother. "We must stop them, Cija. The only way, to demand it of the Emperor."

"The emperor of Atlan loves me not at all," Cija said.

"The real Emperor, I mean. Nal."

The campment had not, one would swear, heard anything amiss. They pulled their coverlets over their heads and slept in fragrant Atlan which they would "possess" with all such destruction as that must mean, rather than surrender.

Cija sat up under the big Atlan stars, fingering nervously the snake-necklet at her throat. "Let me see," Juzd said. He always meant what he said. Cija showed him the snake-necklet, but it was the maps she wanted to see, the cold maps she kept in a leather pouch under her rags. "These are maps of Atlan's insides," he said.

He was very interested in her cold maps. He took them and examined them, and she said, "Keep them, my friend. I do not want them back again, any more. They trouble me."

"They shall trouble us all." Juzd sat and closed his eyes.

As we made our way, Juzd, my mother and I, Juzd having decided what we must do and where we must go under the singing "kites," I said to Juzd: "How that Golden one in the laboratory, in Northstrong, would have loved such knowledge."

"Is that noble-boy very far on his path of lives, to own such genius?" my mother asked as we saw the untidy ruins loom up between the stars.

And as Juzd answered, I wondered again what dovetailing gift of past humility had brought my mother to this life freshly crippled. For my poor little mother had this crippling disability, that she felt it was the biggest possible compliment if someone was able to desire her; better than to be trusted, for instance. Anyone could trust her. She had been let out of her cage in her youth only on condition that she should awaken greed for herself in my father. This had seemed difficult (he is greedy, but he can control and direct his greed in a way foreign to most men). So my mother had emerged with a feeling of awe if anyone ever should recognize what she saw in herself. Her contempt of most people (all the countless noisy creatures she had passed on her journeys, who bewailed life and claimed that life was "breaking" them, and yet did not push themselves as she did, nor endure as she, nor observe nor rebound as she)—her contempt of most people was automatic, just as was the General's control. But when she met someone who seemed worthier than most, and who saw in her those steadfast qualities most people on her path abused or ignored, then in a rush of amazed gratitude she would "god" that person, returning their compliment as though it were all a matter of courtesy of souls. And so she found herself rushing too fast and too gladly toward them; and had established with them a pattern of courtesy and gentleness which had placed her in their power.

It was the Quar nightmare, the nightmare of my life, for all that it was her doing and only my seeing.

The Mill children had played "wishes." "Wish for wealth, wish for health—wish for breath or wish for death . . . all bend down."

I had lain in the tangled rugs and wished for a mother exactly like my own except it would say, could say "NO" to the people mine said Yes to.

She had done her best, I supposed. But her Quar had shadowed my life like soot, like soil, like shame.

I felt as though he had always been there, in the time before the dirty months with him. Before we met him and lived with him, he had been a certainty waiting us in our future. I still felt only barely convalescent from the actuality of him. I could have coped with him on my own—there are ways of "NO"-saying without a voice. But it was my mother's allegiance, my mother's alliance with him I couldn't cope with, not while retaining my pride in her. Quar had not mangled me—he had destroyed only other people, strangers, the people in his bed. Quar had not greatly tormented me, as I knew some girls are tormented by their mother's man. She allowed him to hurt her. That was the darkness.

We were cold in the ruin. But it was not so dark as the forest.

The ruin had loomed up over us in a most ruins-in-forest way. A chill struck out from it in all directions. During the day birds would be able to "bathe" and "splash" in the cool air of the ruin-area—it was for us almost like wading through chilly waters. The immense halves, always earless, of stone faces loomed. The light coldly lay in some place beyond aisles and columns. "It is like your maps—the chill and the pulse," Juzd reminded my mother.

"I have always distrusted them," my mother said. "What do they tell you about your own Atlan, Stranger with Gray Eyes?"

"They tell me, Cija, where the dikes are—even the old forgotten overgrown or built-over dikes. They tell me where the plug is."

"You're not going to pull the plug out of Atlan?" Cija said lightly.

What was put out, very suddenly indeed, was the light. Wasn't this meant to be a perpetual lamp? Had it not burned for a thousand years according to the fashion in perpetual lamps? It was a horrible moment of blackness.

"Stay calm," Juzd's voice said calmly. "Stay still. Now grope to your left. That was where we were in relation to each other."

"Seka. Stay still," my mother bade in a voice of "reassuring calm" near hysteria.

"I can't reach you, Cija," Juzd said, "and I think the best thing we can do is stay still. We are only steps away from each other, or should be. Our voices are not far from each other. Yet we cannot find each other."

". . . Is something preventing us?" Cija asked.

"It would seem so," said Juzd, and for the first time his voice seemed muffled. "Cija. Stay still. Seka. Still. We must wait."

We waited, I presumed, though I had no remotest idea where my mother was, nor what she did. We presumed Juzd was gathering his power together.

A strange hope came up in me, very tiny, like a seedling hope in blackness. These things were being done to us openly. This was in direct contradiction to the rest of our lives (and I know this by my mother's diarized records) in which if things were done to us, they were done as is usual to human beings in the form of pattern, of dovetailing cause and effect, often of a jigsaw or several-level jigsaw like mosaic visible only in retrospect and hinging mostly on one's own actions or states of hatred, need, caution, cowardice, foolhardiness, advance or recoil.

Now suddenly things were being conducted differently. It appeared we were directly under attack. And yet the last time we had been cut off, taken out of context, lifted out of perspective and dimension and possibly sequence, something incredible had happened—my voice had happened.

I felt in my sash for my precious coin. It was a wonder it was not embedded in my waist by now. I tossed it into the darkness, expecting to hear it ring and tell me whether it had fallen near or far, and on stone. But there was no sound.

An air was blowing. It was so much later, and I had not heard either my mother's or Juzd's voice for so long, that I made toward the air was as though bidden. It was after all the only *incident* around. I did not feel pushed, nor shoved, nor rebellious. My voice had come from one such strange suspension.

"Cija. Mother. Juzd." I called loudly once more, and was relieved to hear no reply. Now I was free to follow the blowing air.

It drew me to a series of blocks against which I did not stumble, pausing quite before I reached them, aware by some sense.

I put my hand on the blocks. They rose in a fair semblance of regularity.

I put my foot on one great step. I had to raise my knee high to place my other foot on the next great step. The raising after a while became a strain physically. The physical strain became in its turn a relaxation mentally— there was nothing to think about, rising alone in the dark, and this could have been a torment but for the helpful physical strain.

I discovered the steps each sloped. You couldn't rest on one, or you would fall and slide. Once started, you must keep climbing.

I do not know how long, I have no feeling of how long, neither physically nor mentally any idea of how long I climbed. It cannot, certainly, have been as long as it would "in reality" have taken to ascend that abysmal height when eventually I was to see with my "real" eyes where I had reached to. But it was "after" this unspecified length of "time" that I became aware of a slithering behind me, a following slither.

I looked behind—a hopeless thing to do. I could see nothing.

Still the air drew me upward, like a thread which

pulled. I had no sensation of horror at the *behind* of me—
at the depths into which I could at my own bidding lean a
little backward—but now I had a sensation that something
alien was behind. I suppose the knowledge of its alienity
was near true horror. Whatever was behind, ascending
after me, calculatingly (for when I slowed, it slowed) was
nothing to do with me. Yet it pursued. For that was the
horror. It was a pursuit—and yet I knew the thing behind
me was not a thing which I should ever, would ever,
could ever in the normal universe have met.

A slight glimmer now appeared above me. I could see
stars. They seemed very clear. Perhaps they seemed near.
Immediately I turned to look behind me. I saw a thing
indeed, pulling its length over the big steps behind me, a
snout, very large and heavy, turned up toward me. I never
saw eyes, though I presumed at the time that it was a face
of some type turned up to me, and in this respect the thing
I suppose resembled the mer-male on the floating island—
whose eyes also could not be seen, without his in the least
giving any impression of a blank face—on the contrary,
too much was going on there to be looked upon and
pinned down as being eyes.

The pursuit was now naked. Aware (I could feel the
"click," rather slow, with which it became aware it was
visible)—aware that I could now see it, aware it was no
longer a secret, which with its alien senses and its alien
grasp of my own perceptions it had perhaps believed itself
to be, it suddenly quickened its pace into a terrible eager
shambling slither of great power upwards. We were in
night. That was all we were in. I think there must have
been walls till now (certainly, when I had stretched my
arms to their full and tried to touch anything to either
side or ahead of me, there had been nothing; but my
armspread was very little) . . . but now we had emerged.
We were approaching a sort of plateau, or table or platform, which projected above us. I knew that this was in
my plane. It was a projection friendly to me. If I could
reach it, I would be on home ground. The thing would not
be; could not "land" on it. Here on the steps we were on
neutral territory: I hastened. The physical strain of lifting
my knees became a pain which ran through my body like
shocks, like torture, and *lifted* me—shocking me higher at
each terrible heart-thudding strainful physical lift, each
of which had to be effortfully made, and yet each of which
resulted in a floating higher so that I encompassed maybe
two or three of the gigantic steps, before I had to make

again the next terrible physical effort. The thing, on the
other hand, in spite of its speed and rattling chinkling
rapid eager shuffling competence could not equal my
levitations—for it was not in pain.

The platform, the plateau was ahead. It was just above
me. One step more, or one and a half steps more, and I
would have it. I glanced behind. The thing was failing. It
was falling farther and farther behind me in the race. My
pain had been too much for it, had vanquished it. It
was laboring. I could see how its "breath" or whatever
kept it fueled was coming shorter.

Beside me, a spring gushed from the last step, a huge
step stretched above my head—only by now that meant
nothing to me.

I thought at the time the spring was water. Only looking
back now, I am sure it was actually light. I was able to
judge how life-giving, how pure, how strong it was. I had
plenty of time to cup it in my hands and put my mouth
in it—I know now that what I drank, and indeed it was
delicious, was pure light. On an impulse, having won,
being clear and away, having become a self without
urgency and fear, unlike the self on the earlier (and less
gigantic) steps, I threw some water down on the thing. I
knew its toiling hot scales would be cooled. I knew that
though it could never now attain its desire, which was to
catch me, it could at least have its panting assuaged.
There is never anything wrong the thought shot through
me *in assuaging others' discomfort.*

In another, terrible, flash (terrible most of all because
with despair *shame* wallowed and oozed over me, yes, I
was in shame above my head) I found I had placed
myself by my own ridiculous cocksure *conceited* action
immediately back in the creature's power. It swallowed, it
reared, it grew in stature, it kept hold of the light—which
would not leave my fingers, which dragged me down to
the creature on which I had showered it—and I was
joined to the creature, stuck to it, linked to it by my own
sentimental action.

The creature had been enemy. What business had I
joining myself to it in a moment of self-satisfied "compassion"—which was not compassion, (since the thing was
evil and was besides nothing to do with me) but was
utterly disgusting sentimentality?

I flapped my hands. I would have bitten them off if I
could just have freed myself in the few instants left to

me of the link I had formed between myself and the voracious rearing approaching triumphant snout.

I remembered my voice, which I had never needed as I did now, and which I owned. With an effort that nearly burst my heart, I shouted: "Help me!"

The light that joined me to the creature, and which I had misused and misinterpreted when it was offered to me for my own honest efforts, broke from my fingers and the creature. The creature, upon me, its shadow and stink oppressing and enveloping me, tumbled and dropped. It fell as though obliterated, plummeted and there was no more of it.

I found that I had fallen to the flat of the penultimate great step and stretched prone on the sloping stone, so oppressive had been the weight of the creature's very presence.

I lay shaking against the stone. Presently the drops of light spattered me gently, amusedly, sprinkling me with heartfulness. I raised myself and looked around. I was not yet on the ultimate platform, but for the time being I did not wish to raise myself to it. I was very high above what had been.

As a giant sun rose, I saw that I sat above the world, the forest lay below like one of Scridol's charts. What a boon to a cartographer it would have been to be upon this Rod! For this was what I had seemingly mounted in the night, although in fact I could not possibly have done so —for one thing it would have taken me a year, alone, with my child's legs, to mount the thousands of steps within the Rod that rose above Atlan's Interior, and for another thing the Rod had been nowhere visible to the campment and forest of our hosts. I had started on steps in the ruin, and had an adventure on neutral territory, and had ended on steps at the top of the Rod.

My mother had told me I had seen the Rod when I was little in Atlan. It appeared to me now that even Ancient Atlan knew nothing of the Rod, nor of the power which was righting and returning the balance which Ancient Atlan had juggled by.

I watched the rosy rising of the morning. And thus, and thus, I shuddered with my escape to myself, thus it was in the world for Cija. Thus it was that she gave in to Quar, thinking it was of her bounty, of her largeness that she could afford to tolerate and shower him with her securer light, and thus she had been trapped. That thing in the night, whether it had been the evil of the culture Ancient Atlan had allowed into the ruined temple, or whether it had been a temptation of my own and my mother's soul, it had nearly seized me because I had not been true.

I had pretended I could afford to "give" when I could only afford to get away.

I heard the sounds of the reed-kites—there came into view far off in the sky of morning the figures of men flying with discs strapped on their backs, each giving off a melodious fluting which was the isolated and volatile gases (not to mention vivacious airs) emitted at such a rate as to propel both disc and man.

My friend, with the flowered plaits, had told me in the forest how each genuine Atlantean is born with his own tone, as it were his own "frequency" she had called it, and so when his lifting-disc comes to be made it incorporates this.

Atlanteans are still born with this knowledge of their own frequency, I am sure, scattered as they are around the world, but rapidly they will lose the knowledge: How can the scattered colonies maintain, in their now primitive and mundane surroundings, the re-creating of all that was their way?

I stood. I looked into the rose sky, and at the fleeting far-off figures of the fliers—taking, as Juzd had said, the viruses to the coast. I was not to stay here on this now-barren Rod, that was sure. There was nothing else for it to offer me. Or, I am sure, much else—maybe everything and anything else—but not now. Now it was sterile stone. I could fly without a disc. I lifted my shoulders and threw them into the bright morning. I could fly without a disc because I must fly and I had no disc.

I flew into the gold air.

I flew to the slopes of a mountain which as I flew rose nearer and nearer singing its great heart out. You could not hear the mountain. What you caught in the air fluctuating stirringly against you was the noble pulsing, the beating and majesty of the mountain's "frequency." There, yellow and ivory and exquisitely tiny, my mother was climbing the mountain's swelling long flank.

3

Dissolve

I DROPPED DOWN through the cadences of beating air. My mother looked up, her honey hair thick on the warm wind, and raised her arms to me. I fell against her, my own size, small and hug-size against her mother-size breasts, and she said: "Seka, Seka."

"We have lost Juzd," I said.

"He has spent his own night." Thus she said, *I know we each have spent our night.* "You looked like an opal-fly, Seka. You were iridescent and so strong flying in the sun."

"What is happening, Mother?"

"I don't know, Seka. Atlan is like this. Atlan is alive, and we find ourselves now in the Interior, where it is more so. This may all be simply Atlan. But I feel something more is afoot. An upheaving. A splitting apart and a thrusting through."

"What shall we do? Shall we be broken?"

"We can only do as Juzd advised us. Stay whole."

We traversed now a whole rippling of the mountains' grace-notes—high conical crystal rocks whose mats of moss and tiny lichen threw purple and silver shadows on to the glassy stillnesses within.

Abruptly a somber note entered the mountain's song. A harsh slope, dark tuft and tough weed, spread out before us in a low resonant cadenza.

We stumbled somewhat on this, and the mountain I believe noticed our discordancy and produced some of its own in answer: a wind ran from nowhere through the harsh dark grass, and the grasses whipped back on us, stinging. A rock-wall dropped sheer below us, on which the dark wind played sonorously, beginning arpeggios and leaving them off and starting quite somewhere else. We would have had to scramble down this as best we could (for even if I could still fly, I would not do so while my mother climbed) had several little bright green serpents who gambolled about our feet near the edge here not suddenly linked themselves into loops and knots. "They are linking themselves into foot-holds for us!" cried my mother, looking down over the edge. "Set your foot in one loop, Seka, we shall be safe, I swear." The snakes who had already served us wriggled down to join the end of the chain, so that we continued safely to the bottom. "It proves," said my mother, "that one must not pre-judge. This may even," she continued, "be a result of the sinking into me of the great serpent last night. I am now akin with serpents, and to advantage, horrible though that was at the time."

"Was that your dream in the temple, mother?" I asked, hoping I had misunderstood.

"Not a dream, a vision," said my mother. "There is no mistaking a vision ever. You can mistake a dream for a vision, but never a vision for a dream. Judz has said this. I was pursued, sucked up a funnel and still pursued—by a thing which in the end, although I struggled my fastest, leaned upon me *and disappeared inside me*."

She must have seen my look of horror, for she said gently, "It was terrible, terrible until it happened—and then when I gave in, because I had to, because you can't fight something already most sunk in you—" Oh, you can't? I thought "—it was not too terrible after all," my mother said. "And I found that because I had acquiesced, the alien quality of the thing fitted in me as though it had never been away. It had *returne*d into me."

We are each our own specter, our own vampire, I thought, for I had heard the camp-followers' legends of vampire, the suckers of others. Smahil had been Cija's—but she is her own too.

Here the mountain laid a gold flat hillside out for us and at stark intervals on it large flat pink rambler blooms.

The mountain, knowing of course how difficult a time its discords had been for us, now did its best to sing softly while we trod its warmer slope. But it erred on the side of *un*sentimentality, and was unable, quite rightly one supposes, to make things particularly comfy.

Interrupting the mountain's melody came a wild threnody, the trembling call of wolves.

Huge dark clouds gathered at times and then rolled onwards but never quite away now.

I saw a girl in a pretty gown coming toward us through the meadow. I saw the ribbons flutter from her hair. She held what I thought a conventional, quite delightful bouquet in her hands but when she came nearer my mother in a rigid silence pulled me aside from her and I saw how the bouquet threw the shadows upwards on her face and how it in fact was a candle. A light in the gathering storm, she passed onwards trailing as much amusement as the lightning which now shrivelled a tree for the sake of shrivelling behind us.

The wolves howled again.

The wolves were travelling at a fast rate, but we now saw the valley and a river which divided us from them.

From time to time flurries of rain fell. The rain made a tattling noise. Horizons in Atlan were vaster than on the mainland continent. Perspectives went on and on, it seemed. Tall trees were far, far taller—you needed to crane your neck to see the tops.

Wet was much *wetter*—the rain was almost like oil only without a slightest taint of grease—it reminded me of the lanolin in sheep-wool and the lovely hands of the shepherdess who herded by Mill.

I could see my mother was attending really to only one thing. She was noting only the wolves.

We could see the wolves clearly, though a valley and a river still separated us from them.

There were the gray strung-out trotting loping pack, their noses down or then up to apprise them of the wind, of us. They were gigantic wolves, their withers high like those of horses. At times, like a sharp jewel very distant, their eyes could be seen glinting pale under the rapid ragged storm-cloud.

We were still mainly in the sun, hot fluctuating sun blowing along the mountain's flank and down into the river-valley where it paused on the water in thick layers, piling up on itself, hesitating.

Figures ran with the pack, sometimes down on all fours, sometimes leaning into the wind on hind legs as a beetle may run. At other times they were, I would swear, actually upright—but were they human beings or akin? They looked too small beside the wolves for me to be sure. I noted again my mother's absolute intent thought bent with her gaze to them.

What did I know of wolves? Only what Ael and bandits had muttered—wolf was much in the bandit language and seemed to them to be a parallel with man as the bandit knew him. For thousands of years the bandits had been in direct competition with wolf for beef, veal, mutton—the wolf was their enemy and their equal and they used him in their imagery. I knew, thus, that only the dominant male and the dominant female can mate. If the others in the pack try to mate, the dominant pair stop them. The dominant pair, obviously, were consequently inter-bred. They were closely related to each other. You might even call them sister and brother.

Was this why my mother, whose own brother had been close to her, stared in the fluctuating sunlight and storm at the loping far-off pack? No, it was because there, there ran with them, hair blowing like a blizzard, naked under wolf-skins in which were caught peacock feathers, there occasionally upright ran my elder brother Nal, the child of my mother and her family-minded sibling.

As I saw Nal with the wolves, a great howl of greeting sobbed out over the peaks—Nal and the wolves lifted up their heads as they heard and attempted to test and recognize it. It had not, of course, come from my *throat* but was nevertheless echoing now from every hill. I don't think my mother could hear it.

I called *Nal* with all my brain at top-stretch, and instantly, almost before the thought-call had left me, so fast is thought, he had answered *Seka*. He knew us. He remembered me—this surprised me, though it did not surprise me that I remembered him. The figure in the wolf-skins now paused, shielding its tiny distant face with its hand and gazing into the sun, searching us out on our gold flat bronze hillside.

My mother murmured, with trembling lips, "Is it he, Seka?"

"We know it is he."

The earth started shaking.

There came showering down winding filaments of glass (well, of raw obsidian)—hot, clingling, somewhat sticky although they veered away from you twisting if they touched—but luminous.

The distant Nal started toward us, then leaped on the biggest wolf. It was a horrible thick-chested wolf with a red ruff running over its withers. As it loped at its great greedy pace toward us, Nal's wild face came into focus—the unmanageable face, a face of essentials, very cleft chin, too little jaw, cheekbones so high and prominent there were almost rings on them. A short delicate nose that could have been blown off him. Two long slanting eyes with heavy circles under them. Both slanting, both lazy and un-utterably bold, one much narrower than the other and slanting steeper, with a glance that made the other seem almost noble. The wolf galloped toward us over the wet grass. Nal leaped off it. He was on the brink of the river. He called something to us.

"What did he say?" my mother asked in agony. The sound had been tossed away from us on a new wind.

Nal plunged into the river. He was some way across when the river threw itself up into the air. Great water-spurts hurled up from whatever till now unsuspected cliffs, holes and fissures had lain underneath. Whirlpools began buzzing, malicious currents and, obviously, savage suctions.

A woman ran up out of the river. She turned to watch it boiling. She was quite near us. She was only myth. Her bare pubes were ears of corn, and what I would swear was corn sprouted from under her arms. As for her hair, the hair on her head, it fell rippling in a rush all lilies and leaves twined—till I glimpsed between their thickness the hair itself, which they mostly hid and sheathed, and I saw that her hair was one continuous cataract of glorious thick river-water, *springing* in dew from her forehead, where drops burned and bounced, and ending in mid-air as though it then disappeared quite swiftly into another dimension.

"Where is the Emperor?" Cija asked of her abruptly to disturb her reverie.

The myth continued to stare at her boiling home. But a creature now jogging toward us from some separated slab of plateau, a sort of man with its long lively sinuous tail erect behind it reaching almost the nape of its neck, checked and regarded us, its tail flicking round under and between its legs, to saw reflectively against its ringleted testicles for a moment or two. My mother, not much liking this creature, drew back from it as imperceptibly as she was able to as not to offend or provoke it.

"The Emperor?" it enunciated gracefully, although our language was possibly foreign to it. "The Emperor is now *beneath*."

This seemed only too like. Beneath the heaving river, which now thrust ribs of rock into view. Yet—in Atlan—"What *places* are *beneath*?" I asked the creature.

"We are allowed now only to think of above," it answered.

A channel had broken free of the river-bed proper and run uphill near us. A white rainbow arched below the stormdark over the farther channel—an albino rainbow.

Something was wading up the channel toward us, waving a torch, something on two legs striding well. It was Juzd, holding aloft a phosphorescent squid he must have seized from the river to light his way.

"What is happening, Juzd?" we cried as he came up to us and sank with us on to the distinctly warm ground, on which we might as well stay as not—there was nowhere else to go.

And indeed as large animals (and myths) fled, the small crept closer to their nests on the ground as it was warm and comforting.

"The viruses have been loosed by the crazy Ancient on its own soil to spite Zerd," Juzd, said.

"Zerd will never know,'" my mother said.

"Did you pull the plug, Juzd?"

Juzd had done the only thing there was to do—or so it appeared to him. And if it were allowed to appear so, to Juzd who is devoid of false notes, then indeed it was to be allowed.

"The dikes are dilated. These caused geysers, subterranean floods, quakes. The continent is dissolving, its structure broken."

"I have brought my land to ruin," Cija said in a low voice, "and by my love, as it was foretold of me. For Atlan has been my true place, and it is destroyed," she added not without a note almost of satisfaction, for at least she could now see how neatly everything was working.

"For your love provided Ancient Atlan with Nal and the crazy rising up in possessive frenzy to create the sick homunculus-cell, sick vampire-cell, the parasite-cell which will stay in the world."

"In spite of Atlan's destruction?"

"But not as terribly as if Atlan stayed to spread its sickness knowingly."

"But with Atlan gone, where in the world will there be such *alive* land?"

Juzd in stormy sunlight: "Atlan was too alive for this world. Most of the souls in this world are still children, they need bread and milk, not nectar. They are only just learning to touch with their hands and understand that. It would cripple them to force on them too early the touching with the essence."

Amused balls of lightning were playing games in the destruction.

The singing mountain, forgetful of the fact that it was geology, booming to the air such great chords, you could almost hear them.

The slope on which we reclined lifted of itself as the mountainside otherwise slid in debris, bore us up so that we faced snow and eagles. Glowing striped horses, far below, were galloping in tumult across floating plain shifting its contours, tilting, making sudden steeps. We saw, between dark intervening turbulent clouds, how the horses tossing manes and kicking up their heels were ecstatic. "But they will be swallowed by the rifts opening up!"

"Is it not the total stampede?" Juzd asked.

Explosions disturb a thickened part of the sky, and out from it dart a dozen premature angels, which had been gestating in there, and glare around with their swift arrows of lidless gaze, taking in the sight of a world they should not have seen—and at the same time seeing the last of this ancient most spiritual heart of it.

Of course, it was nearly winter, and the time when most angels must be born, for angels I suppose are generally born swift fiery zooming gold Sagittarians.

Lightning laughed in massed splinters.

Such turbulence. Like an average evening on the scarlet planet.

And with such turbulence, almost turning upside down the essential femininity of our world with all its passive receptive regular predictable moody tides, seasons, flat solid passive physical inert feminine masses. Here came the winds, storms, dust, volcanoes, viruses, thoughts, quantum physics, spirits, ideas, and the winds and gales struck into my nostrils and mouth with that same male unutterable taste of curuba and salt like Ael's sperm. It was now on my hands as it had been then. For a new season, a non-regular season, the femininity of the nature of our physical world was being turned inside out.

You see, these are words the world knows by now, Juzd tells me.

Atlan had broken up into energy and atoms, electricity and anarchy, and was blowing into the rest of the world.

"What's gone wrong? What's gone wrong?" cried an Atlantean from our campment of (two nights?) ago as he climbed up the moving mountain, clawing in horror up it, as Atlan's bitter act of keeping-out Zerd and his materialism and militarism turned into colored glory. "What's gone wrong," said Juzd, "is that you can't ever make things really go *all* wrong."

Chasms open—we can see into the rose throat of the earth.

"Zerd is simply an everyday conqueror pursuing his trade," my mother said blankly. "This fanatic noble nationalist panic at his matter-of-fact invasion is very understandable. I have been suffering it myself for some years. But Zerd—Zerd is fighting and winning another war quite somewhere else at the moment."

And I knew, finally, that Zerd must be genuinely called.

Without emotion at last, easily and effectively as soon as it was real Zerd-calling time, I called my father. My mind stretched out to call him because he must come now.

I suppose at that very moment, as though he had heard already the out-of-sequence echo of my call, his ships had beached on the inner harbor of Atlan.

As the Rod reared near us, if such a shape and height could be called near, rushing funnelling in the cataclysm, it appeared we had been pulled from our side of mountain and were arking out toward the sea masses.

Immense leviathans, half-ooze, half-alive, had been stirred up from the depths of the ocean by the tremors and now were visible between surging darknesses as they hung, their eyes pained by what to them was unbearable light, on the surfaces of swingeing waves.

Luminous vapors blew lightly. The great blossoming blowing glory of Atlan destroying herself, rather than submit (either to Zerd, *or* to Ancient Atlan)—this was ebbing, evaporating. All Atlan was destroyed to Atlan's utter amazement.

You could feel the amazement too, dwindling around us since those amazed were mainly with us no longer; feeling it for a space longer, blowing listlessly hither and thither, as you had been able to feel the amusement of the playing lightning.

"Has Nal lost his soul?" Cija asked.

"No. No *soul* is ever *lost*.". . . Juzd supported her on his arm and held his hand to me. We moved up the flank of the now stilling, steaming mountain, away from the corpses littering the rocks as the waters pulled back with a queasy silver froth.

"Why the Fall of Atlan?" my mother inquired as though she still could not quite believe the untroubled rainbow air now covered nothing much in the way of a broad continent.

"Atlan was polluted by self-interest," Juzd said gently, searching out a cave for our weariness. "It was putting the self before God. It had thought in frantic feverish magics any means to be justified so long as it survived —forgetting why it had been precious, that was because it had been nearer to the first plan of God."

Beings, I think they were beings, they were hard to see, formed huge series of funnel-like circles around the sun, each limned with savage light.

The continent did not immediately go under. It would cool, harden, steam, crack, fissure, explode and lie under darkness without daylight for years.

At the moment clear, burst waters were gushing over corpses. A red-cloaked man was striding between the waters like a wound.

My mother rose in the very-cave-mouth as Juzd discovered it for us, her exhausted shoulders straightening as she stood still. I stared, I saw (I do not know why this was clearest of all) the shorn cloak corner, and I raced down the slope shouting confusedly to him.

He looked at me with a face of disbelief as though he had seen me suddenly rise from the dead, and he caught me and turned me in his arm. "Child. Daughter? Where is she, she, where is she?"

I loved him, I suppose, at that moment.

"What has been happening in Atlan?" he asked, as I led him up the slope.

Here was one person I could not tell what had happened, nor that there was no more Atlan. "There has been an earthquake," I said and led him up to the cave.

Cija and Zerd, the red and the yellow fluttering around them, stared at each other as the vapors curled over the rainbow mud.

Their hands touched in a whirling fold of the red cloak, and it blew curling around them for an instant, enveloping them. Wrapped in the red cloak of his campaigns, in its smell of blood and smoke and long nights in the saddle, Zerd took Cija by both shoulders; staring into her mouth, into her eyes, into everything he was baffled by in her, he remained thus and slowly began touching her eyelids, her face with his fingers—touching her mouth, he was drawn on to it: he seemed to fall into it; the cloak swirled again about them, double-wrapping them.

The floor of the little cave perked and bubbled. Zerd bowed his head to Juzd, as Zerd entered. Zerd had not noticingly seen Juzd since he had had him imprisoned in Atlan, at the time or so I gather of my brother's birth.

"Did you set off this fireworks display?" Zerd asked at once. I don't know what suggested to him such seemingly vast suspicion.

"Yes, sir, I set it off," Juzd told him, "and so did you."

Zerd turned on the heel of his soft square boot. "And my little one," he said attending to business by order of priority, "how is it that she spoke to me?"

"I spoke to you," I answered him for myself, "and I have a voice."

The General kneeled on the cave floor beside me. "Shall you keep your voice?" he asked intently. And, when I told him I would, he said it had been a waste of time to teach me any letters, then.

"Are you surprised to see me?" he asked Cija accusingly.

She assured him very, in confusion which had in fact gone beyond surprise or even amusement.

"You beached with your fleet as the End began?" she asked him.

Zerd's dark mouth quirked. "This is a Beginning," he said gracefully. "I see no end. Yes, beached with some part of my fleet." The General told, as Juzd without many words of his own kindled a fire in our cave from the many fires still smoldering outside, how—"How you took Northstrong!" my mother said as though congratulating any soldier. "No," Zerd said, accepting the strange meat Juzd fried us. "I have no Northstrong."

There was a pause. Wild colors blew past us. "You had the city," my mother said presently. "You took it."

"I did not march in," Zerd said, as though everyone should understand quite easily this following move in the game. "My army stayed substantially outside. I have not declared myself in Northstrong. I spoke, of course, with Quantumex." He spoke of his meeting with his once-king without particular interest.

"You gave Northstrong to Quantumex?" Cija unbelievingly repeated.

"We fed the birds rum to hearten them before the possible onslaught of Quantumex re-gathered together," Zerd said, "and formally repudiated any claim to Northstrong and the North. We had won. That was enough."

I wondered if Zerd had even believed Northstrong to be at last in his hands. Had he stood there on that slope outside the famous Northwall, his eyes restless, seeking for another enemy, another ruse, another battle—anything but the ultimate boredom of victory? How could Zerd have faced the kingship (and all the sheer desk-work and admin.) of the civilization he had always been outside, always rejected by, always part of?

"I am a conqueror," Zerd said, gnawing at a bone in the red glow, his boot stretched out to the blaze as the Atlan mud caked. "Not a ruler."

"Is Quantumex now your regent, however, in Northstrong?"

"I would think he is your mother's regent," Zerd explained, pushing away his sword. "It was to your mother that I gave Northstrong."

Cija liked that very much indeed. After a moment of shock and sheer delight, she began to laugh in the desolate End. We did not see it, we did not watch it then, but we were to see the next morning as we gazed from our night's cave, that the continent by now had mostly sunk. Colored mud-flats and flowered seaweeds and land-shrubs of great lushness and glee were left, and great seasnakes twining among them, for decades slowlier sinking.

"And your wife?" Cija asked presently by the fire.

"Sedili too," Zerd said in a voice less possible to fathom than he had been using. "Sedili too was a present. I have presented her to Quantumex, to do with as he will."

Cija did not laugh. As Zerd had not wanted nor known what to do with Northstrong, so she did not want nor believe in this end to the woman in the splendid uniform, to whom a battle was always a good setting for her flair and horsewomanship and to whom (I had seen this myself) a battle was above all a meaty chance to demonstrate to the General how much her own men 'admired her and cheered with affection, and followed into bad places.

This had all been too intense for the General. He had yawned. He had turned away all this impractical clinging. What had Cija to offer him, she who was not at all practical?

"Your child, by the way," Zerd said to Cija, not taking his eyes off her, is with my brothers in the saltdales. So are your Diaries."

A lovely rose, like a very delicately sugared cake, suffused her face by the mud-fire. "Oh, not Diaries, simply jottings," she said and: "The tiny one is all right?"

And she asked questions about the well-being of apeling to which Juzd and I listened carefully and to which Zerd answered warmly. I did not yet know of course, as Juzd did, of the strange soldering of soul which was already at work joining the still-soulless apeling and the all-but-lost souled Nal.

"I have read the Diaries," Zerd said and she fell silent.

The weed-fire crackled.

This man could indeed do quite well for my mother, I thought. A man who has read a woman's diaries and still wishes for her is the man for her. It struck me only years later that in this case, of course, the man was semi-illiterate anyway.

Cija was very quiet. I don't think even her heart was allowed to thud. She was trying in moments to remember the adverbs and adjectives of years. Finally she said, "What did I say about you?"

"You said I did things," Zerd said in surprise.

"But how was the way I said it?" she asked in equal surprise.

"Very good," he said briskly.

He put his scaled hand on her arm. He looked as questioning and as intense as only Zerd could ever look. When this General looked what I call intense, it was not that he looked expressionful: it was only that he became so very much himself.

Juzd, I noticed, had withdrawn to the back of the cave: not so much discreet, possibly, as bored. He had seated himself cross-legged and was so relaxed that he was no longer outside himself with us, but inside himself with himself. So I thought: What can I do that is more fun than sitting here with these grown-ups? I walked off on to the glimmering mud. A flight of small blue birds, wheeling and darting, flew overheard chirruping small-ly, celebrating, frequently diving to the mud to come up with some luxury turned up by the End of things: huge indignant worms, fat angry beetles with coruscating carapaces. Flying with the blue birds, looping and darting with them, was a tiny scaled dragon, the first and last I have ever seen: no, it was not a pterodactyl, it was a little long-snouted leathern-winged crested scaled creature, flying and wheeling with its brothers and sisters the birds: as I caught its smoky unwinking red eye, I recognized my friend the egg; I had placed the crystal egg, with its embryo, in a nest among blue bird eggs, obviously, but no matter, when recently hatched the creatures had grown up together and obviously the dragon was convinced it was a blue bird.

Zerd came and found me. He picked me up in his arm and the red cloak. "Seka," he said, pleased I thought with my name and his confident use of it. I had once wondered if he would even remember it. Maybe he too had wondered this. A great snake reared up from the mud and came at us, its head on a level with ours, very huge and squelchy outside its inner coiled controlled power. Zerd had me in one arm leaving only one hand free and I relaxed ready to be tossed to the ground to give my father both hands. But he simply leaned his head rigidly forward past my own, and spat straight into the rearing snake's attacking yawning mouth. The flickering vermilion tongue paused, curled, withered, the mouth and its inner walls splotched pallidly: the snake drew back, obviously in pain. It no longer reared, it no longer attacked.

"Where shall we live?" I asked.

"Wherever I can find her," he said.

"You have her."

"I have her, but I have not found her," Zerd mused, pulling at his chin in a sideways direction.

I disapproved of this talk, for it gave me the shiver of premonition and, besides, of fervor, to which I am not partial. For of course now she has left us indeed, she has found her One, although he did not arrive before she and Zerd and I had lived together long enough for me to grow—and now I am old enough to decide to stay with Zerd, rather than to go with her and her true beautiful love whom we have found at last. If Cija had not gone with her one, as was right as soon as he arrived, he would have had to wander his life alone, as so will Zerd. Perhaps Zerd will not be entirely alone. I am glad now to be with Zerd as he searches for my mother. I am glad to be with Zerd as he told me to be that day: "Shall I learn by you, experience?" he asked me as he carried me back through the glorious pastel muds to our family cave.

"You are my experience." He was hugging me as we saw Cija come to the gap of the cave to watch for us and he began to wade more hurriedly in his soft square boots toward her.

"You were your mother's experience. She did whatever she did—you experienced it." He looked slyly at me again, his narrow eyes waiting, teasing me but waiting to see if the child recognized his statement. "You come to me now, you creature without pity or pangs, but with compassion and pride, come with me now. For," the General said, "it is possible that I have needed a soul."

While Juzd helped them make a bed of grasses warmed up and all their scents heightened by the volcanic exertions of the End, Zerd's men began arriving. A few bandits, who had been hunting, came walking up the slope with two big speckled bush-swine slung on twine, their sweat-glands already cut out so that the flesh should not make anyone think of bush-swine. They leaped on Zerd while he still held me, he and the bandits swung each other around: "Hye, hyeh," they were yipping. "Were we silly girls then, or have we discovered a good cooking-pot, a country where you don't even need to broil the meat, just lay it on the rock?"

One bandit tugged gently on my ear to show welcome at the finding of me. They turned to Cija and all bowed. They and the mud were our new country for a while.